Irish author **Abby Green** ended a very glamorous
career in film and TV—which really consisted of
a lot of standing in the rain outside actors' trailers—
to pursue her love of romance. After she'd bombarded
Mills & Boon with manuscripts they kindly accepted
one, and an author was born. She lives in Dublin,
Ireland, and loves any excuse for distraction. Visit
abby-green.com or email abbygreenauthor@gmail.com.

USA TODAY bestseller **Lucy Monroe** lives and writes
in the gorgeous Pacific Northwest. While she loves her
home, she delights in experiencing different cultures
and places on her travels, which she happily shares with
her readers through her books. A lifelong devotee of the
romance genre, Lucy can't imagine a more fulfilling
career than writing the stories in her head for her readers
to enjoy.

Discover more at millsandboon.co.uk.

BOUND BY HER SHOCKING SECRET

ABBY GREEN

HIS MAJESTY'S HIDDEN HEIR

LUCY MONROE

MILLS & BOON

First Published in Great Britain 2021
by Mills & Boon, an imprint of HarperCollins*Publishers* Ltd,
1 London Bridge Street, London, SE1 9GF

www.harpercollins.co.uk

HarperCollins*Publishers*
1st Floor, Watermarque Building,
Ringsend Road, Dublin 4, Ireland

Bound by Her Shocking Secret © 2021 Abby Green

His Majesty's Hidden Heir © 2021 Lucy Monroe

ISBN: 978-0-263-28266-5

10/21

MIX
Paper from
responsible sources
FSC™ C007454

This book is produced from independently certified FSC™ paper
to ensure responsible forest management.
For more information visit www.harpercollins.co.uk/green.

Printed and bound in Spain using 100% Renewable Electricity
at CPI Blackprint (Barcelona)

BOUND BY HER
SHOCKING SECRET

ABBY GREEN

MILLS & BOON

CHAPTER ONE

DANIEL DEVILLIERS SURVEYED the scene below him, where guests thronged the main *salon* floor. The iconic Devilliers jewellers, which had been standing at this location on Place Vendôme, one of Paris's most exclusive addresses, since the eighteenth century, had been totally updated and refurbished in the last six months and this evening was the grand reopening.

Since his father's death a few years ago, when Daniel had inherited one of the most enduring brands in the world, he'd slowly but surely been working with a very conservative and resistant board to haul Devilliers into the twenty-first century. And his efforts were finally paying off.

It was a triumph. The party of the month. The year. Invitations had been sought after by heads of state and royalty. But Daniel was eager to open up Devilliers to a more varied and vibrant demographic, and more than a few VIPs had been reduced to begging for admission.

Actors and actresses rubbed shoulders with politicians and titans of industry, and amongst them moved the most beautiful models in the world, male and female, showcasing the brand's latest and legacy designs, from a new cutting edge wristwatch design to a diamond tiara that had been made for Empress Josephine.

Diamonds, rubies, pearls, sapphires and emeralds, set amongst gold, platinum and silver, sparkled and vied for attention on the models, complemented by dresses specially chosen to display the jewellery to best advantage.

Vintage champagne flowed freely and guests were offered hors d'oeuvres that resembled small pieces of sculpture, yet still eminently edible and delicious.

Framed black and white photos adorned the walls, depicting the history of Devilliers. An oil painting of the wife of the man who had founded the company hung in pride of place on a central wall, her intricate tiara sparkling amongst the elaborate up-do of her thick dark brown hair. Distinctive grey eyes looked out from a haughtily beautiful face. The same eyes and aristocratic features that had made it down through the generations to Daniel.

Except in Daniel those aristocratic features were hewn into something far more masculine and uncompromising. High cheekbones and a surprisingly sensual mouth were countered by deep-set eyes and a hard jaw. Together with thick dark hair cut short, and his tall, powerfully lean build, the whole package of an Alpha male in his prime was a siren call to anyone with a pulse.

A movement caught Daniel's eye, and he saw his PR advisor motioning for him to come down. He knew he should join the party. But he'd taken a moment out to observe, to feel… He wasn't sure what he'd been hoping to feel. A sense of triumph that his vision was finally being realised? A sense of satisfaction? But he didn't feel either of those things. What he did feel was a certain kind of anticlimax. A flatness.

And then something else caught his eye. A strapless black satin dress. A flash of tawny-gold hair, piled high. The smooth slope of bare shoulders, lightly golden. His insides clenched in helpless reaction before he could control his response.

Whoever it was had disappeared behind a column. Out of sight. It had only been a flicker of recognition. It wouldn't have been her. She wouldn't have the nerve to appear on his turf again. *It couldn't have been her.* And yet Daniel's pulse was hammering under his skin at the very notion.

Memories, vivid and provocative, clawed at the edges of his mind, seeking purchase. A laughing face, bright white teeth. Lush mouth. Sparkling light green eyes. Wild tawny hair wrapped around his hand as he thrust deeper and deeper into an embrace so hot and tight he'd never wanted to stop.

And other memories, less carnal. A pale face, huge eyes red-rimmed from tears. Pain. A block of ice in his chest, freezing the blood in his veins.

'It's probably for the best. We both know this.'

'Get out, Daniel. I don't ever want to see you again.'

Daniel shook his head to dislodge the very unwelcome memories. The present returned. The chatter from the level beneath him. The music from the string quartet he'd had flown in from Vienna.

Angry with himself for indulging in this moment, Daniel pushed back from the railing that bordered the mezzanine area and moved to go downstairs. The past was the past and it had no place here. The future beckoned, and as Daniel came down the wide spiral staircase he pushed every lingering wisp of memories of *her* down so deep that they would be crushed for ever.

He caught the eye of one stunningly beautiful woman at the bottom of the stairs. She smiled and it was explicit. It didn't move him in the slightest. *Perfect.*

Mia Forde knew she couldn't hide in the toilet cubicle all night. She cursed herself. How on earth had she thought it would be a good idea to confront Daniel again at the re-launch party for the iconic Devilliers *salon*?

She knew why and she felt pathetic now. She'd thought that by being in a public setting it wouldn't be so daunting. And also, weakly, she'd thought that wearing the full armour of designer clothes and make-up would make it easier to stand in front of Daniel again.

Even though, when they'd been together, their relationship had never been about that. Their relationship had been the antithesis of this sleek, rarefied world. She'd never appeared in public with Daniel in an official capacity. Not like his other lovers. She hadn't wanted to. For lots of reasons that she didn't have time to dwell on now.

A security guard was waiting outside, tasked with guarding the stunning yellow topaz and diamond necklace and matching earrings she was wearing as she had managed to get herself hired as one of the models to showcase Devilliers jewels for the evening.

She took a breath and left the cubicle, went back into the main part of the bathroom which was mercifully empty. She caught a glimpse of her reflection and grimaced. Her eyes looked too big and scared. The lipstick that had been applied earlier was all but bitten off her mouth. Her cheeks were still pink after catching her first glimpse of Daniel, where he'd been standing on the upper level, those cool grey eyes surveying the scene.

She hadn't been able to breathe at that first sight of him, paralysed by the onslaught of so many things—memories, emotions, anger… But worst of all the return of a physical awareness so acute and visceral that it had been like a punch in the gut.

His eyeline had turned towards where she'd stood and somehow she'd managed to make her shocked limbs move, tucking out of sight before he could see her.

And now here she was, trembling like a leaf. Which was pathetic when she considered what she'd been through in the past two years. She'd become stronger than she'd ever been. Fierce, even. She could handle seeing Daniel Devilliers again. She was just here to impart a message and then she would leave, head held high.

The jewels glittered against her skin, set off beautifully thanks to the simplicity of the black satin dress. She looked at them dispassionately. Worth many thousands of euros. And yet they left her cold. Because she knew they were just pretty stones. Dead inside. Like her relationship had been with Daniel. Oh, there had been heat and fire. She felt weak at the thought of it. But no heart. No soul. No depth.

In fact, the man couldn't be more perfectly suited to his inherited profession. All fire and heat on the surface but cold inside.

And was that his fault? a voice asked.

Mia sighed. No, it wasn't his fault. He'd never made her any promises because she'd explicitly told him that their relationship was just about the physical and the transitory. She'd put up so many walls to guard her heart against him that when they'd crumbled it had all been too late. There had been no relationship to save.

At that moment Mia heard approaching voices and straightened her shoulders. She had to go and find him now. The door opened and a couple of women came in with a flurry of overpowering perfume. Mia avoided their eyes but couldn't fail to hear their conversation.

'Did you see him standing up there? Like some kind of god?'

'I've never seen anyone so sexy in my life...'

'He's divorced now...it was all over the papers. Single again...'

A sharp pain lanced Mia when she heard those words: *divorced...single again.* She forced the pain and sting of jealousy down. They had no place here.

She was almost at the door when her clutch bag vibrated. It could only be one person. She pulled out her phone and immediately her forehead creased in worry.

The other two women were in cubicles now, still continuing their indiscreet conversation.

Mia quickly made a call. 'What's wrong, Simone? Is everything okay?'

Her friend spoke on the other end and Mia's blood ran cold. She forgot everything and had one primal response. *She had to get home now.*

She said, 'Don't worry, I'll be right there.'

Terminating the call, she put her phone back in her clutch and left the bathroom, all thoughts of Daniel Devilliers eclipsed.

Daniel was doing the social rounds in the belly of the party. He could see a long line of people waiting to speak with him and swallowed a sigh of frustration. And then he berated himself. This evening was the first glittering milestone in achieving all he wanted to achieve with Devilliers. So why couldn't he just damn enjoy it?

But the frustration prickling under his skin wouldn't go away. Taunting him. A small voice in his head said: *If you're not satisfied with this then when will you ever feel satisfied?*

It irritated him intensely, because he'd never been under any illusions that his loyalty to his inheritance was born out of sentimental emotion. The opposite, in fact. He'd always viewed it with a very dispassionate discerning eye. Any loyalty he did feel came from a sense of responsibility to the hundreds of workers behind this legacy, some of whom had worked for Devilliers over generations, and his own personal ambition to see the brand evolve and become an even bigger success.

You're doing this for your sister too, a small voice reminded him.

A familiar tightness made Daniel absently touch his chest. Yes, if there was any sentiment attached it was for his sister, who had loved coming to the *salon* as a child, staring in awe at all the sparkling gems, asking reverently, 'Do we really own all of these?'

Daniel pushed the past aside. He found that his gaze was wandering, looking for a glimpse of tawny gold hair.

It hadn't been her. Let it go.

Angry with himself for dwelling on a ghost from his past, he reminded himself that there were plenty of beautiful, willing women in his immediate vicinity. Not ghosts. And he didn't need the reminder of how long it had been since he'd had a lover in his bed.

Not since her.

One was approaching him now. Blonde. Icy cool in a white dress. Blue eyes. Her throat, arms and ears literally dripped with diamonds. She was smiling with the kind of sexual confidence mixed with avarice that Daniel knew all too well. He told himself this was exactly what he was looking for, even as something inside him recoiled when she came closer.

But just before she could reach him someone else approached from the side. One of his security detail, who said, close to his ear, 'Sorry to bother you, sir, but there's been an incident.'

Daniel looked at him, the approaching woman forgotten. 'Incident?'

'A woman—one of the models—was trying to leave with her jewellery.'

Daniel raised a brow. 'If she's been apprehended why do I need to be involved?'

The man looked uncomfortable. 'She's saying she knows you and that you can vouch for her.'

A prickling sensation tickled the back of Daniel's neck. He asked, 'Where is she?'

'In the security office.'

Emitting a sound of irritation, Daniel strode towards the front of the *salon*. The security office was near the main entrance, its door camouflaged to look like a mirrored wall. Another security guard was waiting there for him, looking grim.

'Sorry to disturb you, sir. She's in here.'

The man opened the door into a large room with its walls covered in screens showing every inch of the *salon* and all the other rooms.

It took a second for Daniel's eyes to adjust to the dim bluish light so he didn't see her at first, standing in the centre of the room.

But then he did. And for a heart-stopping moment he thought he might be hallucinating. But then he forced oxygen to his lungs and brain. *She wasn't a ghost*. He hadn't imagined seeing her earlier.

Mia Forde. The last woman he'd ever expected to see again. The last woman he'd wanted to see ever again.

And yet even as he told himself that he couldn't stop or deny the helpless physical reaction heating his blood and making his body tight. Forcing him to exert control.

She looked as beautiful as he remembered. More so. After two years. She'd been twenty-one when they'd met. Now it was as if a layer had been removed to reveal the woman underneath. Her face seemed more…angular. Cheekbones more defined. That lush, wide mouth was as provocative as ever, even when pursed in a line of tension.

It was only then that Daniel noted the black satin gown. Strapless. Hugging her curves. The top of the dress couldn't hide the swells of her breasts. He could still see them in his mind's eye, full and high. Her tempting nipples—

Daniel slammed down on that incendiary memory. The knowledge that this woman still had the ability to short-circuit his rational brain was like pouring acid onto an old wound.

It made his voice curt. 'What the hell are you doing here, Mia?'

Mia had to lock her legs to stay upright, when every instinct was telling her to curl up, hide. *Run*.

The expressions crossing Daniel's face might have been

comical if Mia had felt remotely like laughing. There had been recognition, shock, disbelief, and now blistering anger.

Fatally, she couldn't take her eyes off his lean face, even as she said faintly to the security guard who had hauled her in here, 'See? I told you I knew him.'

Daniel folded his arms, which made his biceps bulge against the fabric of his tuxedo. 'What are you doing here? Is this some kind of sick joke?'

Mia recovered some of her wits. 'A joke? Do you really think I set out to be here this evening just for a few lols because I've nothing better to do on a Saturday night?'

The fact that her usual Saturday night routine was dinner, maybe a TV movie and then faceplanting into bed before ten p.m. was not something she was about to divulge in this hostile atmosphere.

His eye dropped to where the necklace and earrings she'd been wearing were laid out on the table beside where she stood. 'Were you really trying to steal the jewels?'

'Of course not. I just… I got a call. I panicked. I forgot I was wearing them. I'm not a thief.'

Daniel frowned. 'How did you even get in here?'

Hurt lanced Mia. 'I was hired to work here this evening. I know we share a…a complicated history, but I wasn't aware that I was on some persona non grata list.'

Now Daniel looked frustrated. He unfolded his arms and slashed a hand through the air. 'I don't mean like that. I just mean…' He stopped. And then, 'Why would you come here?'

'I needed to talk to you. When my agent arranged for me to be one of your models I figured it would be an easier way to…to get to you.'

A man as famous and wealthy as Daniel Devilliers was nigh on impossible to contact unless he wanted you to contact him. As Mia had found out to her cost when she'd discovered that the number she had for him was no longer in use.

But the panic that had galvanised her to leave in the first place, before she'd even spoken to him, surged up again. She said, 'Look, I really do have to go. It's an emergency. Can I leave, please?'

Much to Daniel's chagrin, his first reaction to Mia saying she wanted to leave wasn't abject relief. It was a tangled mess of many things, including a resurgence of desire that was as powerful as it was unwelcome.

'You said you needed to talk to me. What about?'

He noticed now that Mia looked pale beneath her natural all-American tan. 'I can't explain now. I just have to go.'

'You were caught in the act of leaving while wearing hundreds of thousands of euros worth of jewels. You owe me an explanation.'

Mia was wringing her hands in front of her. 'I know. Look, I wasn't thinking. I forgot I had them on. You *know* me. You know I'd never steal anything!'

A memory assailed Daniel before he could stop it. He'd opened a velvet box and Mia had looked down, her eyes widening with predictable awe, as she'd taken in the stunning pearl bracelet with a diamond-studded flower in the centre. She'd even touched it reverently, saying, 'It's beautiful.'

Daniel had said idly, 'One of our new designs.'

Then she'd looked at him with genuine confusion. 'What is this?'

'A gift.'

She'd shaken her head. 'But...this isn't that kind of relationship.'

Daniel could remember feeling a sense of frustration that she wasn't behaving as he expected. As he was used to. Even though, at every step of the way since he'd first asked her out, she'd behaved contrary to any other woman he'd ever known. At first she'd told him it would be one date. Then, when they'd slept together, that it would be one night. But one date and one night had bled into more dates, and more nights, because the chemistry had been just too strong to ignore.

Even then, she'd always made a point of making sure he knew that she didn't expect more. In many ways it should have been Daniel's dream scenario: a woman who set out boundaries before he even had to. Because he certainly didn't want more either. But some rogue part of him had been prompted at that moment to ask, 'What kind of relationship is this, Mia?'

'Not one where you give me...stuff.'

He'd felt bemused. 'Do you have any idea what this *stuff* is worth?'

She'd backed away then. 'I don't care, Daniel. It's lovely...truly. But I don't want it. I'd feel uncomfortable.'

It had been the first time a woman had refused a gift from him. Daniel might have cynically suspected it was some kind of ploy, in spite of Mia's protestations, but the following morning when he'd been leaving her apartment she'd handed him the box saying, 'Don't forget this.'

'You really don't want it?'

'Thank you, but no.'

The past faded. The present returned. Mia said with a desperate tone in her voice, 'Please, Daniel, I need to go.'

'If it was anyone else we'd be calling the police.'

Now she went so pale Daniel thought she might faint. He even reached out, but she backed away, her hip bumping awkwardly on the corner of the table.

'Mia, dammit... Why are you here?'

She bit her lip and Daniel had to curl his hand into a fist to stop himself from reaching out to tug that lower lip free.

It had been one of her habits before, which he'd suspected she'd played on because she knew it drove him crazy.

She spoke so fast he almost didn't hear her.

'It's my daughter. I have to get home to her. My friend is babysitting and Lexi has a high temperature and she's vomiting.'

Daniel went cold inside. 'You have a baby?'

It had been two years. Of course she could have had a baby by now. *Another baby*. With someone else. *Lexi. A girl.*

'Yes.'

Daniel shook his head, words coming out before he had time to rationalise why he needed to know. 'How? Who…?'

Mia looked at him. The moment stretched.

Daniel became aware of the silent presence of at least two guards, who had been watching this interplay. He said abruptly, without looking at them, 'Please leave us.'

The guards left.

Mia looked at him.

His sense of the ground beneath him shifting slightly was disconcerting. There was no need to think at all that this child could be—

Mia said, 'I really don't want to get into this now. I have to go to her.'

But something dark compelled Daniel to say, 'I'll let you go when you tell me who her father is. Are you still with him?'

Mia swallowed. Her heart was beating like a trapped bird in her chest. She'd hoped against hope that Daniel would have lost his appeal since she'd seen him last, that any desire had been incinerated by the words he'd said to her before he'd walked out.

'I think this is for the best.'

But no. Her body was still attuned to his as if it was an

instrument that sang only in proximity to him. And when she thought of the amazing things her body had done since she'd seen him last it was even more galling.

She'd had a baby. She'd experienced one of the most primal, beautiful things on earth. And yet right now all she could think of was the fact that Daniel looked even leaner and more powerful than the last time she'd seen him.

He'd never had any softness, but it was as if a layer had been removed to reveal the starkness of the man underneath. All edges and angles and hard muscles. Unforgiving.

'It's for the best.'

She tried to stay focused. Her main priority was getting out of here ASAP. 'No, I'm not with the father.'

'Who is he?'

Mia's heart stopped and then started again. She longed to be able to say, *You don't know him* or, *It's none of your business.* But she couldn't lie and she couldn't prevaricate.

This was why she had come here after all.

She took a deep breath but still felt breathless.

'Mia—'

'She's yours.'

They spoke at the same time. Daniel's mouth shut. His expression went blank. She wasn't sure if he'd heard.

Mia said, 'She's your daughter. Eighteen months.'

It wasn't often that a man like Daniel Devilliers was left lost for words—not that Mia could enjoy the novel experience right now.

'Look, I'm sorry… That's why I came this evening. I was hoping to get a chance to arrange a meeting with you. I didn't want to tell you like…this.'

In the security office of the Devilliers *salon*, with every important and famous person in France just feet away, having been accused of trying to steal Devilliers jewels.

Eventually Daniel spoke. 'But…how?'

Mia's phone started to vibrate inside her bag, which

was on the table. She reached for it, seeing her friend's name. She answered and listened for a second and then said, 'Okay, look… I'm leaving now. I'll be there as soon as I can.'

She terminated the phone call and looked at Daniel. 'I'm very sorry to have had to tell you like this, but I have to go *now*.'

She spied a pen and paper on the table and scribbled down her address and phone number. 'If you are going to insist on calling the police, or whatever, or when you're ready to talk, this is where I live now.'

She handed the piece of paper to Daniel, who took it, still looking shocked.

Mia took her bag and walked to the door. She opened it and went out, but a security guard held up his hand.

He looked over her shoulder, presumably at Daniel. 'Sir…?'

There was nothing from behind her, and Mia was close to shoving the security guard out of the way, but then she heard Daniel's deep voice.

'Let her go.'

Relief flooded her system. She vaguely heard Daniel say something else, but she was already at the entrance of the *salon*, where a bank of paparazzi were waiting. She saw them lift their cameras and then lower them again. She wasn't recognisable to them. She might have been a model, but she'd never attained supermodel status. And when she'd gone out with Daniel they'd managed to evade the glare of publicity.

But Mia couldn't care less about not being recognised. What was far worse was that she couldn't see any taxis waiting. Feeling panic rise, she was about to take out her phone to try and use a taxi app when her arm was taken by a big hand. A familiar touch.

Daniel.

She looked up. 'What…?'

He was grim. Not looking at her, tugging her back towards the *salon* before the photographers noticed. 'Come on, I'll take you home. My car is at the side entrance.'

Mia was so relieved that she would shortly be in a vehicle heading to her baby that she just followed Daniel along a corridor that led to another entrance.

A sleek black car was waiting in the street. The driver was standing by an open back door. Daniel handed the driver the piece of paper with Mia's address on it and helped her into the car before getting in on the other side.

Then they were moving. It was only as they left Place Vendôme behind that Mia realised what was happening. Daniel was coming with her. A different kind of panic gripped her. She wasn't ready for him to meet Lexi yet. To explain everything.

She looked at him in the gloom of the back of the car. His profile was stern. As she watched, he tugged at the bowtie at his throat, undoing it, flicking open a button on his shirt with long, dextrous fingers. His hands were masculine. She remembered being surprised that they weren't soft, as she might have expected of a businessman…of a billionaire who handled precious gems every day.

To Mia's disgust, flames of desire burst to life in her belly at that memory.

'You shouldn't have left the party. It's an important night,' she said.

He looked at her and her skin prickled with heat.

'Yes, it is. But the news that apparently I'm a father has managed to eclipse the importance of the evening.'

The driver put up the privacy partition. Mia knew Daniel. She had been subjected to his very persuasive and determined brand of seduction, so she knew it would be nigh on impossible to persuade him to change his course of action.

Nevertheless, she tried. 'It's really not appropriate to come with me now. Lexi might be—'

'Lexi. What kind of name is that?'

Mia bristled defensively. 'It's short for Alexandra.'

'You say it's not appropriate for me to come with you now? Yet you thought it was "appropriate" to come and disrupt one of the most important nights in the Devilliers calendar?'

Mia refused to feel as if she was in the wrong. 'If I had been able to contact you through regular channels then obviously I would have done that. And I did try. But the number I have for you is no longer in operation, and when I tried to contact you through your office they refused to pass on just my name. I had to give more detail, and I wasn't prepared to tell a stranger what I had to tell you. I would have come to the *salon*, but as it was being renovated, obviously you weren't in the office there.'

'We set up temporary headquarters nearby.'

'It would have been easier to try and arrange a meeting with the President of the United States.'

Daniel wasn't amused. 'If what you say is true and this... this baby is mine—which I can't understand is possible since I saw you after—'

Mia cut him off before he could say it. 'She's yours.'

Daniel's jaw clenched. 'If she is, then why didn't you come to me before now?'

A familiar ball of pain that Mia hated to acknowledge lodged in her gut, dousing the flames of desire. 'You were married.'

A muscle in Daniel's jaw ticked. 'Nevertheless, I deserved to know.'

'As soon as I read about your divorce I started trying to contact you.'

'What if I hadn't divorced?'

The ball of pain got heavier as she considered that. In

truth, Mia hadn't really contemplated the long-term plan, and that made her defensive. 'If you hadn't divorced, I would have told you at some stage.'

Daniel made a disbelieving sound.

Before Mia could lose her nerve, she said, 'I'm sorry, by the way. About the divorce. No matter what the circumstances of your marriage were, I can't imagine it was easy.'

'By "circumstances" you mean the fact that it was an arranged marriage?'

Mia and Daniel had been dating for almost two months when a headline had appeared in the newspapers, speculating about a long-standing arrangement for Daniel to marry an heiress from one of France's other great dynastic families. The news that he was promised to someone in marriage had blindsided her, reminding her painfully of a similar experience at the hands of her first boyfriend.

When she'd confronted Daniel about it, he'd been dismissive. 'It's not an *engagement*. It's an ancient agreement that was arranged by my grandfather when he had to borrow money from the Valois family. To be honest, I'd forgotten about it.'

Mia had replied angrily. 'Well, it seems your intended fiancée hasn't forgotten.'

She'd thrown the paper down on the floor between them in her apartment, leaving the luminously pretty face of his future wife, dark-eyed and dark-haired, staring up at them impassively.

And at that moment Mia had suddenly thought of something. 'No wonder you were so happy to go under the radar with our affair—because you knew this was imminent and you didn't want our relationship to appear in the press right now.'

He'd looked at her, his dark grey gaze narrowing. 'You were the one who dictated the terms of this affair. You specifically said you didn't expect any commitment, that you were happy to keep things casual, discreet.'

She had. And it had hit her in that moment that, in spite of her best efforts to protect herself from developing any feelings beyond the physical for this man, she'd failed woefully.

A prickling sense of shame and exposure had made her realise how badly she'd exposed herself. She'd vowed never to fall for a man like Daniel again—rich and privileged—and yet there she was, her heart feeling as if it had been sliced open.

Mia's attention came back to the present moment when she noticed the car was turning into her quiet street. Daniel had been right that day. She hadn't wanted anything more. But somewhere along the way she'd forgotten the lessons of her past and had humiliated herself spectacularly.

The car pulled to a stop outside the tall building where she had an apartment on the top floor. She looked at Daniel. 'I really would prefer if we could arrange another time to meet.'

He looked at her. 'Tough. I deserve answers, and I'm not going anywhere until I get them.'

CHAPTER TWO

AT MIA'S FRONT door she stopped and turned to face Daniel, who was behind her, taking up an inordinate amount of space in the small landing. 'Can you just give me a minute? I need to make sure Lexi is okay and if she sees you she might get upset... She's not used to men being in the apartment.'

Mia hated admitting that, but there were more important considerations right now.

She could see the struggle on Daniel's face. Eventually he said, 'Five minutes, Mia.'

Mia turned back and opened the door and slipped inside. Simone appeared in the doorway to the bedroom, holding a flushed-looking Lexi. Mia's heart clenched. She was a mini carbon copy of the man outside the door. Dark curly hair framed a cherubic face and huge grey eyes. But, as Mia was discovering lately, the cherubic exterior could change in a heartbeat to something far less angelic!

'Mama!' Lexi held out her arms and Mia scooped her into her chest, murmuring words of comfort while assessing her.

Her friend Simone said, 'I'm so sorry, Mia, I probably overreacted. But I've never seen a baby get sick before and it scared the life out of me.'

Mia sent her a wry smile. 'Honestly, it's way better to overreact than do nothing. This little one has given me quite a few scares along the way.'

Mia took Lexi into the bathroom and checked her temperature. A couple of minutes later she let out another sigh of relief. 'Normal.'

Her friend grinned and chucked Lexi under the chin, making her giggle. 'You little fiend—you had me all wound up!'

Aware that Daniel was undoubtedly pacing up and down outside her front door, Mia said, 'Look, thanks, Simone. You should try and make something of your evening while you can.'

Her friend looked at her. 'You could go back to the party if you want?'

There was a peremptory knock on the door. Her friend frowned. Mia shook her head. 'I don't need to go back.'

Mia walked to the door with her, Lexi a sleepy weight in her arms. Her friend gathered her bag and coat and looked at her with a mischievous expression. 'Did you bring the party home?'

Mia smiled weakly at the thought of Daniel's grim face. 'Not quite.'

She opened the door and could see Simone's eyes widen as she took in the vision of an impatient Daniel Devilliers being made to wait.

Ever the gentleman, though, he greeted her friend. 'Good evening.'

Mia remembered her manners. 'Simone, this is Daniel Devilliers. Simone is an old friend of mine. She was kind enough to babysit this evening.'

Her friend was uncharacteristically silent. When Mia looked at her she was staring at Daniel as if she'd never seen a man before, and then she looked at Lexi. And then at Mia, who said hurriedly, 'Thanks again for tonight.'

Simone left.

Alone again, Mia sucked in a breath and steeled herself to deal with Daniel—only to find him staring at Lexi with such an arrested expression on his face that she immediately felt concern.

'What is it?'

She looked down at Lexi to check her, but she seemed fine. Her colour had gone back to normal. She had her thumb in her mouth and she was just looking at Daniel.

Mia looked at him again and could see that he was pale. Did he see the marked resemblance?

A little nervously she asked, 'Are you okay? You look like you've seen a ghost.'

Daniel didn't even hear what Mia was saying. All he could see was his sister's face. Right in front of him. The same black curly hair. Huge eyes. Rosebud mouth. Plump cheeks. She'd used to reach out her pudgy arms and call him to lift her up. *'Danny... Danny.'* Even when she could say Daniel, she'd used to keep calling him Danny.

He could still hear the panicked shriek of his name as if it was yesterday, and then the splash of water...

'Daniel... *Daniel?*'

The past receded and he saw Mia was looking at him. He felt exposed.

She stepped back. 'Please, come in.'

Mia went into the small apartment and he followed her. High ceilings gave it a sense of space. It was uncluttered. Simple. Comfortable furniture demonstrated Mia's good eye for classic pieces. He remembered that from her old apartment. How he'd found it soothing.

Lexi's face appeared over Mia's shoulder as she twisted to look at Daniel. She took her thumb out of her mouth and declared, 'Man!'

Mia turned around to face Daniel. The sight of his ex-lover in a full-length evening gown holding a child—*his child*—was almost incomprehensible.

'What happened just then?' Mia asked.

Reluctantly Daniel said, 'She reminded me of someone.'

'Who?'

Even more reluctantly, Daniel said, 'My sister.'

Mia frowned. 'You never mentioned you had a sister.'

A solid weight lodged in Daniel's chest. 'She's dead.'

'Oh... I'm sorry.'

'It was a long time ago.'

'But Lexi reminds you of her?'

Daniel couldn't help nodding, looking at the child again. It was too huge to think of her as *his*. As his daughter. 'They could have been twins.'

Mia made a small sound and Daniel's gaze moved to her. She'd gone pale again.

Before he could wonder about her reaction she shifted the baby in her arms and said, 'I need to change her, give her a bottle and put her down—then we can talk. Help yourself to a drink, or there's a coffee machine in the kitchen.' She turned, but then stopped, looked back. 'That is if you still drink coffee like you used to...'

Another memory blasted Daniel. Mia shaking her head and saying, *'Honestly, you drink too much of that stuff—it's no wonder you can't sleep.'*

She'd taken the coffee cup out of his hand to come and straddle his lap, pushing aside his laptop on which he'd been looking at a document. He'd looked up at her, at the wild tumble of her tawny hair over her shoulders. She'd been wearing only his shirt, haphazardly buttoned, the luscious curve of her breasts clearly visible.

He'd put his hands on her waist. No underwear. His hands had explored the smooth roundness of her buttocks, finding the centre of her exposed body, making her squirm against him as his mouth had fastened on one taut nipple and—

'...back in a few minutes...'

Daniel blinked. Mia was disappearing into another room, presumably a bedroom. The door closed behind her. He took a deep breath and ran a hand through his hair, still reeling from the vividness of the memory and the fact that there was no doubt in his mind that the child she'd held in her arms just now was his. His daughter.

So all that left was the burning question of how on earth it could be possible.

Daniel spied the drinks trolley in a corner of the room and went over, finding an unopened bottle of whisky and a tumbler. He poured himself a generous shot and swallowed it in one gulp, the fire racing down his throat doing little to make him feel any calmer.

Mia looked down at a sleeping Lexi for a long minute, knowing it was futile to delay the inevitable any longer. Daniel had been waiting for half an hour now—she could only imagine how irritated he would be. He'd never been good at waiting for other people, having little tolerance of those who couldn't keep up with his demanding pace.

But babies adhered to their own schedule, and it had taken some time to put Lexi down after the distraction of Simone babysitting her and then the strange man. But Mia was certain that she was okay now, and that was the main thing.

Mia stepped away from the cot and realised she was still wearing the evening dress. It felt too constrictive now. Too revealing. She quickly pulled down the side zip and tugged the dress down and off, finding a pair of worn jeans and a long-sleeved shirt, doing up the buttons hurriedly.

She tugged at her hair, pulling it down from the elaborate up-do, knowing it would look unkempt and wild, but it made her feel more herself.

She took a breath and opened the door, and saw Daniel immediately. Impossible not to in the small space which seemed even smaller now. He was sitting on her two-seater couch, dwarfing it to Lilliputian proportions. He'd taken off his jacket and his bowtie was hanging loose. One arm was stretched carelessly across the back of the couch and one ankle rested on the knee of his other leg.

He looked relaxed, but Mia could feel the tension. He had a glass resting on his bent knee, the golden liquid at the bottom catching the light.

He lifted the glass towards her. 'I hope you don't mind? I had to open the bottle.'

She shook her head. 'No, of course not.'

Her throat felt dry. She went and sat on the edge of the armchair that faced the couch, feeling like a guest in her own apartment. Part of her longed for a drink too, to give her some sense of confidence, but she also needed her wits about her. Daniel Devilliers had an ability to make her forget...*everything*.

'So, are you going to explain to me how it's possible that I have a child—a daughter—when the last time I saw you was in hospital, after you'd miscarried the baby?'

Mia was clasping her hands so tight she wasn't aware of her knuckles showing white. The memory of Daniel standing at the foot of her bed, pale and grim, was still too vivid. And those words.

'It's probably for the best.'

She shook her head, as if that could rearrange her thoughts into some sort of coherency.

'Mia, you owe me an explanation.'

She looked at Daniel and realised that he must have thought she didn't intend telling him. She stood up, agitated. Too many memories were crowding out the present moment.

'I know. I just... Give me a second, okay?'

She went over to the window that looked out over the rooftops of the Parisian buildings nearby. Always one of her favourite views. She could see other people moving around their apartments. She could also feel Daniel's gaze, boring between her shoulderblades.

She turned around, arms folded. Before she could speak, though, she saw Daniel's gaze drop to her chest. Something flashed in his eyes. Something that was all too memorable and that precipitated an answering flash of heat in her solar plexus. She looked down to see that she'd done the buttons of her shirt up wrongly and there was a clear view of her ample cleavage through the gap above her folded arms.

She cursed and quickly uncrossed her arms, fingers fumbling to straighten the buttons. Embarrassment flooded her. She hoped he didn't think she'd done it on purpose.

When she looked up again, Daniel was sipping his drink, expressionless. More embarrassment flooded Mia—she must be imagining this *heat*. The man had been married, and he'd probably taken countless lovers since. She knew how voracious he was in bed. A man like that would crave stimulation.

Now he frowned. 'Mia…'

Right. The baby. *Lexi.*

She cursed herself. She couldn't blame the baby for baby brain when she was eighteen months old.

Suddenly an expression crossed Daniel's face. Something like shock. He put his glass down on the table and moved his leg, sitting forward. 'Did you lie about the miscarriage?'

It took a second for his question to register, and then Mia recoiled in horror. 'No, of course not. How could you think such a thing?'

Daniel stood up. He waved a hand in the direction of the bedroom. 'Well, how else can you explain the baby?'

The baby.

All of Mia's protective instincts snapped into place. 'Her name is Lexi. She's your daughter.'

Daniel's jaw clenched. 'A daughter I had no idea existed until about an hour ago.'

Mia deflated. He was right. She forced herself to meet

that penetrating grey gaze. 'I did have a miscarriage. I would never have lied about that.'

'Go on.'

In a rush, Mia explained. 'It was twins. But I didn't know that at the time. And they didn't pick it up in the hospital. I only discovered I was still pregnant about a month later, when I knew something wasn't right.'

'So why didn't you tell me then?'

Because she'd found out on the day of Daniel's dynastic wedding. The official engagement announcement had come about a week after Mia had miscarried. He'd wasted no time in moving on with his life. And even though the wedding had been a fairly modest affair, and conducted in the office of a *mairie*, it had still made headlines all over the world.

She avoided his eye, feeling as if he could see all the way through her to where her hurt still resided. 'I wasn't very well. I had an infection. I almost lost Lexi. To be perfectly honest, the reason I didn't tell you when I realised I was still pregnant was because I didn't know if everything would be okay.'

'Clearly it was.'

Mia nodded, forcing herself to look at him again. 'Yes, thankfully. As the pregnancy progressed I got healthier, and the birth was without complication.'

'And your reason for not telling me then was…?'

Mia looked at him, wondering how on earth she could start to try and explain a process that she didn't even fully understand herself, even though she'd been through it. How to explain how her world had contracted to only her baby and how every day had been a feat of survival and coping and learning how to navigate a new world. A terrifying one. Not to mention the bone-crippling exhaustion. The constant mental fog. She felt it would sound paltry. Weak.

She said, 'I did think of contacting you a few times, but

Paris seemed very far away and I was afraid of what the news would do to your marriage...your wife. The longer it went on the harder it got to make contact, and then when I did try I didn't get very far.'

He frowned. 'You haven't been in Paris all this time?'

She shook her head. 'No, I moved down to the south of France after we...after I lost the baby. A fresh start. A friend has a small modelling agency down there. I did some catalogue work. That's where I discovered I was still pregnant and had Lexi. I've only been back in Paris a few weeks.'

Daniel seemed to take a moment to absorb this. As the silence grew, so did Mia's sense of guilt. The full enormity of what she'd kept from the father of her child was hitting her now.

Defensively she said, 'Based on your reaction to finding out about the pregnancy the first time around, I knew you weren't likely to be more receptive the second time.'

Daniel wanted to say that that wasn't fair, but he knew he had little defence against her statement. Mia had turned up in his office about a month after they'd split up, pale and visibly nervous.

Much to his disgust—because usually women...lovers... didn't linger in his mind or memory when he was done with them—seeing Mia again had precipitated a surge of desire as strong as if they'd never parted. Much the same as when he'd seen her again this evening.

He'd just arranged to have a meeting with Sophie Valois to discuss the proposed marriage, and seeing Mia again in the flesh had made him realise that his decision to go ahead with the meeting with Sophie had had a lot to do with her. Because she'd got too close. She'd got under his skin in a way that no other lover had, prompting him to remember that he didn't *want* any emotional entanglements. And that perhaps an arranged marriage was the perfect solution to carving out a life free of such risks.

His parents had been unloving, cruel and dysfunctional, breeding in him a desire never to repeat their mistakes or visit their toxicity on another generation. The grief of losing his sister had almost destroyed him, and guilt for his part in her death had given him a lifelong sense, rightly or wrongly, that he didn't deserve the happiness that most people seemed to expect and take for granted as their due.

And yet the day that Mia had seen the article about his proposed engagement in the paper, when he'd seen the hurt in her eyes, he'd suddenly resented the guilt and the grief and the darkness that had dogged him all his life. The duty he'd taken on. The responsibilities. A tantalising vision of another kind of life had existed in his mind's eye for a moment, before he'd reminded himself that he was not that person. He was not the kind of man who could offer an uncomplicated life to Mia. Nor did he want to—no matter how much he'd enjoyed his time with her.

When Mia had robustly denied she'd been looking for anything *'more'*, he'd told himself he'd imagined the hurt in her eyes. She was the most independent woman he'd ever met. He'd walked away, vowing never to let another woman get that close again. It had made him yearn briefly for an existence that wasn't possible for him. It wasn't his due.

Daniel had spent the next month restoring his sense of control. Realising that while he'd been consumed with Mia he'd taken his eye off the business and that his attention was needed to get it back on track. He'd buried himself in spreadsheets and projections. Meeting new jewellery designers. But nothing had seemed to pierce the numbness.

Until she'd appeared in his office that fateful day. Hair pulled back. Wearing jeans and a soft long-sleeved top. Looking pale.

He'd had to battle a primal urge to haul her against him, to trace every contour of her body with his hands and mouth until she was breathless and pliant in his arms.

His helpless reaction had made him curt. 'What do you want, Mia?'

Because, ultimately, everyone wanted *something* from him, and in that moment he'd desperately wanted Mia to show him that she was just as avaricious as every other woman he'd ever met—that she couldn't be all that different.

And then she'd blurted out, 'I'm pregnant.'

Daniel's insides had turned to ice. *Pregnant. A baby.* The very scenario he'd vowed to avoid. In that moment all he'd been able to think about was the cavernous dark chateau where he'd grown up. His mother's twisted angry face. His father's endless cold dismissal. And, worst of all, his sister, floating face-down...

He'd said to Mia, 'How can you be pregnant? We used protection every time we were together.'

Mia had blushed and said, 'We did...but the last few times...maybe we weren't as careful as usual...'

And his conscience had stung, because she'd been right. As zealous as he usually was about protection, the heat between him and Mia had been growing, not diminishing, and there had been moments when passion had overcome the need to be cautious.

Daniel looked at Mia now, disentangling the past from the present. He knew he owed her an explanation for why he'd behaved so coldly that day—the day she'd come to tell him of the pregnancy, only to then, a short time later, double over with pain in his office, which had precipitated a dash to the hospital and the subsequent miscarriage.

He'd found out about the pregnancy and lost it within hours.

He'd tried to explain at the hospital that day, but it had

been too late. She hadn't wanted to hear and he hadn't blamed her.

'The reason I wasn't…receptive to the idea of a baby was because I'd never had any intention of having children. A family…' His voice felt rusty from the weight of past memories.

Mia unfolded her arms. She frowned. 'But what about the business? If you don't have children, what happens to Devilliers?'

'Things have changed. The brand name will exist whether it's in the family or not.'

'You would let the business go?'

'No, I would ensure that the brand lives on no matter what, whether that's through a bloodline or via a trust.'

'I wondered…you didn't have a child with your wife.'

Daniel folded his arms. '*Ex*-wife. And, no. We didn't. The marriage wasn't about that.'

He could see that that had sparked Mia's curiosity but he had no intention of going into detail about his marriage.

It was slowly sinking in, amidst the onslaught of too many memories and the resurgence of a very inconvenient desire, that he was a father. It was a fait accompli. A situation he'd never envisaged allowing to happen. Yet it had.

'Look,' Mia said, 'I just wanted to let you know… I'm sorry I didn't tell you before now. I should have made more of an effort. You'll probably want to do a DNA test—'

'Why?'

'To prove that she's yours…'

'I know she's a Devilliers.'

Now Mia folded her arms. 'Well, she's not a Devilliers. She's a Forde.'

Daniel felt something very alien take root inside him. A sense of possessiveness. Proprietorial.

'She's a Devilliers, Mia. Heiress to a vast fortune. Whether you like it or not.'

* * *

Mia felt a cold finger trace down her spine. She hadn't expected Daniel to accept so quickly that Lexi was his. She'd been prepared for horror, shock, and then denial. She'd assumed that he would want to distance himself as quickly as possible.

She realised now she'd totally underestimated him and his reaction. And that she'd hoped that once she'd told him she would feel she had done her duty and could get on with her life.

She should have known better. She'd been ridiculously naive. Which was galling, because she'd lost any sense of naivety a long time ago.

'I don't expect anything from you, Daniel. I can support Lexi on my own. I just wanted you to know. And of course I would have told you eventually. I grew up not knowing my father. I wouldn't have wanted that for Lexi.'

'Yet she's been without a father for eighteen months already.'

Mia's face grew hot, and she felt panicky. She didn't like the look on Daniel's face. 'You just said you've never wanted a family. Children. That day in the hospital you told me that the miscarriage was probably for the best.'

Daniel's jaw clenched and unclenched. 'Because after the childhood I experienced I never wanted to risk inflicting the same on another innocent child.'

Mia's panic drained away. 'You never spoke of your childhood or your family. It was that bad?'

Daniel was grim. 'It was worse.'

Mia had always had an impression of him standing apart from everyone else. She'd used to tease him that it was because he thought he was better than everyone else around him, and for the most part he was certainly superior—intellectually, physically. But now she saw something else. That perhaps his past had kept him apart from others.

There was something there she wanted to tease out, but not while she was under that grey gaze. The evening was catching up with her.

She said, 'It's late. Lexi might wake again. I need to watch her and make sure she's okay. You should go back to your party.'

Daniel didn't move. Mia was afraid he was going to refuse to leave. But then he glanced at his watch. And then back at her. 'This discussion isn't over, Mia. I'll contact you tomorrow.'

'But—'

He stopped in the act of pulling on his jacket. 'But what?'

Mia knew it was futile to argue. 'Okay.'

Once Daniel had left, Mia couldn't relax. The awareness in her body lingered like an overload of electricity that had nowhere to go. She went over and stood at the window, just in time to see Daniel's tall, broad figure emerging from her building and then disappearing again into the back of his sleek car.

She'd always wondered what he'd seen in her. She was nothing like the women from his world. She was somewhat of a free spirit. Independent. She wasn't polished. Intellectual. Socially savvy.

But from the moment they'd met a powerful force had surged between them. She'd been one of about ten models who'd been hired to go to a shoot for Devilliers. She'd been surprised to be cast, as she knew their advertising campaigns and they were very slick. Effortlessly glamorous. Sophisticated.

Mia had known she didn't really fit the brief, with her Californian aesthetic and her hair that refused to be tamed no matter how much product was used. In fact, she would have considered herself the very antithesis of a Devilliers model.

Yet there she was. Amongst lots of taller and far more

angular models from Russia, the UK, France and Ukraine. She'd felt like the odd one out, with her more athletic shape and breasts that were probably three cup sizes bigger than everyone else's put together. She wasn't considered a plus-size model, but sample sizes were not her friend.

The stylist had kept passing her over for the shots and so, growing a little bored, Mia had found her way to the table where all the Devilliers jewels were laid out, guarded by at least two security guys.

Even though she had no love for jewellery, after a toxic experience a couple of years previously, there was one necklace that had stood out—an oversize ruby in a simple setting. A markedly different style the other ornate designs. More modern.

Mia had picked it up and fastened it around her neck and then looked in a mirror, lifting her hair and twisting it so that she could see how it looked. She'd grinned at herself, because of course it looked a bit ridiculous against her plain white T-shirt, and then she'd almost had a heart attack when a deep voice near her had said, 'It suits you.'

Mia had dropped her hands and whirled around to see the tallest, most breathtakingly handsome man she'd ever laid eyes on. He'd been wearing a three-piece suit in steel-grey, and that was when she'd noticed his eyes. They'd reminded her of the slate-grey clouds that rolled in from the Pacific Ocean during storms.

Her heart had stopped for a long moment before palpitating back to life at double its regular rate. Mia had thought that after her experiences she was immune to a ridiculously handsome face, but evidently there was no accounting for taste. She'd assumed that he was one of the executives overseeing the shoot. She'd smiled sheepishly and reached behind her for the catch to take off the necklace, but he'd stepped forward.

'Let me.'

She'd turned around again and he'd stepped up behind her, his scent reaching her nostrils, subtly potent and unashamedly masculine. She'd felt a flutter deep in her belly.

He'd said, 'Lift your hair.'

She'd pulled it up and his fingers had brushed the back of her neck, turning the flutter into a tsunami of sensation.

He'd expertly undone the necklace and taken it off. Their eyes had met in the mirror, where she'd noticed he towered several inches over her. A tall woman herself, it wasn't every day she met a man taller than her. But he had to be at least six foot four.

She'd only noticed then that the security guards had melted away discreetly. But before she'd been able to wonder about that, and who this man was, he'd said, 'Come over to the set. I want to try something.'

Mia had turned to face him. She'd gestured to her clothes—jeans and the white T-shirt. 'The stylist hasn't dressed me yet.' And she'd suspected had no intention of it. But she kept that to herself.

'You're perfect as you are.'

His accent was unmistakably French, but he spoke English fluently. He'd led her over to where there was a black backdrop and suddenly, as if a silent message had been issued, Mia had been surrounded by a flurry of activity. She'd been perched on a stool and over the next hour photographed with her hair up, down, and in various combinations of jewels. Necklaces—the one she'd tried on first, and then others—earrings, bracelets and rings.

And all the time the enigmatic man in the suit had watched her. It had been deeply unsettling, but also exciting. As if there was a line of tension tugging between only them, drawing her eyes back to him over and over again, to find he was looking at her with that impenetrable slate-grey gaze.

When the shoot had wrapped Mia had still been none

the wiser as to who the man was, or why he'd instructed her to be photographed in the most inappropriate clothing to showcase the famous Devilliers jewels.

She'd gathered up her things and tried not to feel self-conscious about the fact that she was the only model who hadn't been dressed in designer dresses, feeling fairly certain she wouldn't be seeing any of the pictures they'd taken of her on a billboard any time soon.

And then, just when she'd hated herself for wondering where the man had disappeared to, she'd turned around to leave and had run straight into a steel wall. A very broad steel wall.

His hands had gone to her arms, to steady her and she'd looked up. He had been smiling and she'd almost lost her life. His mouth was perfect. Surprisingly sensual for a man, yet not remotely *pretty*. Sexy.

He'd taken his hands down and said, 'I never introduced myself. I'm Daniel Devilliers, and I would very much like you to join me for dinner this evening.'

CHAPTER THREE

MIA HADN'T JOINED Daniel for dinner that first evening. She'd been in too much shock to find out that he was *Mr Devilliers*. Not just some suited executive. That he was the scion of one of the oldest and most established jewellery brands in the world. A billionaire. An entitled and privileged man. Practically aristocracy.

That alone had raised about a million red flags for Mia. She wasn't in his league. Never would be. Never wanted to be. She'd been burnt badly before, by someone who had come from a rarefied privileged world, when for a moment she'd believed that she could be part of it too. She'd never forgiven herself for that weakness.

Daniel couldn't know that part of her reluctance was not only because he came with the baggage he did—wealth, entitlement, et cetera—but also because she'd slept with precisely one man in her life. And that man had decimated her by winning her trust and then betraying her when she was at her most vulnerable.

But she hadn't counted on Daniel's single-minded determination to seduce her, and in spite of all those red flags he'd finally, fatally, worn her down.

He'd sent her flowers with a note.

Mia
I want you, on your terms.
I don't play games.
Call me.
Daniel

There had been something unexpectedly humbling about the fact that he was willing to let her dictate how the affair would play out, and when she'd told him that she didn't want any part of his world he hadn't balked.

Yet she'd dreaded the moment Daniel would realise how inexperienced she was—and, worse, that she really didn't find sex all that exciting. She'd even told him, hoping it would put him off. But he'd only grown more determined. As if she'd laid down a challenge to prove to her that her inexperience didn't matter and that she was a sexual, sensual woman.

Even now Mia's blood grew hot just at the thought of that first night they'd slept together. The experience had altered her in a very fundamental way. He'd returned something to her that she hadn't even been aware she'd missed. The knowledge that there was nothing wrong with her. That her previous bad experience had had nothing to do with her and everything to do with her first, very ungenerous lover.

Daniel had shown her how intoxicating it was to be with a man who didn't let his ego get in the way. How it felt to be put first, before a man's own pleasure...

They'd conducted their affair without attracting any attention. Under the radar. Low-key. And Mia had got the impression that Daniel found it somewhat...refreshing. Hanging out in her apartment... Eating in modest restaurants... She'd always refused any invitation to go beyond their little bubble, knowing that at all costs her self-preservation depended on not getting seduced into Daniel's world.

But in the end keeping strict boundaries had done nothing to stop her from falling—

'We're here, Miss Forde.'

Mia blinked. The sleek car had come to a stop outside the Devilliers *salon* on Place Vendôme. It was quiet this evening. No glittering guests or flashes of light from the paparazzi. The party was well and truly over.

Mia sucked in a breath as the driver got out and came around to her door. Daniel had sent her a curt text earlier.

My driver will pick you up at seven and bring you to my apartment.

She'd been tempted to text back that she couldn't come, but of course that would have been immature, and she did need to discuss Lexi with Daniel. After all, she'd set this chain of events into motion. And she should have probably done it a lot sooner.

All day, Daniel's revelations about his family had buzzed in her head, making her want to know more.

The driver opened her door, cutting off her thoughts. She got out. The autumn air was chilly enough to herald the winter season just around the corner.

She'd dressed carefully, wanting to feel somewhat put-together in Daniel's presence. She wore a rust-coloured soft jersey dress with a wide leather belt. High-heeled boots. Her leather jacket on top. She'd pulled her hair back into a rough bun, eschewed any jewellery.

Daniel had always found it highly amusing that Mia had zero interest in jewellery. And she'd never told him why. Never told him that her ex-boyfriend had given her a gift of a diamond necklace which she'd interpreted naively as evidence that he really loved her.

Until she'd discovered it was just cubic zirconia and that it had meant nothing at all. It had been an empty, cynical gesture and she'd fallen for it.

To the left of the *salon* there was a set of discreet doors. They opened now and a uniformed butler stepped out. 'Ms Forde?'

Mia went over to him.

He said in perfect English, 'Please allow me to show you up to the apartment.'

She followed him into a black-and-white-tiled reception hall. A massive crystal chandelier dominated the almost cathedral-like space, and the biggest vase she'd ever seen sat on a polished round table, filled with exotic blooms that sent out a subtle and very expensive-smelling scent.

A grand marble staircase led upstairs, but the butler walked over to an elevator. The doors were open. Mia got in.

The lift ascended and Mia's insides dropped like a stone. The thought of coming face to face with Daniel again was daunting, and she cursed herself. She should be more prepared. A man like Daniel Devilliers didn't take prisoners.

The lift stopped and the doors opened onto another reception space. Light colours and a parquet floor gave it a classically elegant feel. The butler took her coat and Mia became aware that the soft jersey material of her dress suddenly felt very clingy. Especially around her breasts, belly, hips and bum.

But it was too late. A door was opening and Daniel appeared on the threshold, dressed in a three-piece suit.

He addressed the butler. 'Thank you, Paul.' And then Mia, eyes narrowed. 'You didn't bring Lexi.'

Mia shook her head. 'No. It's not a good idea to disrupt her routine. She goes down for the night around now.'

'Who is taking care of her?'

After eighteen months of being solely responsible for her child, Mia chafed at the proprietorial tone in Daniel's voice. 'My friend Simone is babysitting again.'

'The one who rang you in a panic when there was no need to panic?'

Mia smiled sweetly. 'Yes, that's the one.'

Daniel stood back. 'Please, come in.'

She felt ridiculously nervous. Very aware of Daniel's physicality and scent in an almost animalistic way. She held herself tensely as she walked past him into the apartment.

* * *

Daniel watched as Mia looked around the formal reception room, taking in the big abstract paintings on the walls—the only modernity in the otherwise classically designed space, which was dotted with antiques. It suddenly felt a little overdone with her here. As if she was highlighting its fussiness with her far more relaxed aesthetic.

He could smell her unique scent. Light and fresh. Citrussy but with a hint of musk and roses. And her body...tall and strong...curvier than was fashionable. It was probably the reason she'd never made it into the upper echelons of modelling—because she didn't have the androgynous aesthetic that was required by most fashion houses.

The material of her dress clung to every dip and curve, reminding Daniel all too easily of how those curves had felt under his hands. *Under his mouth.* He cursed himself silently and diverted his mind from dangerous territory.

Mia had always been happy to achieve a certain level of success without hungering for more. Something that had fascinated Daniel who, ever since he was born, had felt a constant pressure to attain ever higher levels of success and wealth.

The couple of months he'd spent with Mia was the first time he could remember in his life when he'd taken his foot off the accelerator. It had been a revelation. And, perversely, once he hadn't been working with such tunnel vision, he'd been able to see areas where the business could do with improvement.

'Would you like a drink?'

He remembered his manners at the last moment. This woman had always had the ability to distract him.

'A small glass of white wine would be nice, thank you.'

Daniel poured her drink and went over to hand it to her. A rogue devil inside him made sure their fingers touched.

Zing. Wide, startled green eyes met his. Lust bit into Daniel's gut. She still felt it too.

Mia snatched the glass and stepped back. Cheeks deep pink. Avoiding his eye.

Daniel went back to the drinks table and poured himself something stronger than wine. He gestured to a couch. 'Please, make yourself comfortable.'

Mia looked at the furniture warily, as if it might be some kind of trap. But then she sat down, her movements effortlessly graceful. He remembered that she'd wanted to be a dancer, but a teenage knee injury had put a stop to those dreams.

He took a seat on the other side of a low coffee table. Before he could speak, she said, 'I'm sorry for disrupting your party last night.'

'Are you?'

An expression of guilt crossed her face. She'd never been good at hiding her feelings. That reminder caught at Daniel's gut.

She said, 'I know it was a big night for you and Devilliers, but it genuinely seemed my best opportunity to get to you.'

'What if I hadn't got divorced? How long would you have made me wait to learn that I have a daughter?'

Something jagged entered Mia's belly. If he hadn't got divorced he would have been there with his wife last night. Petite and dark. As refined as him. Not that she'd looked them up. *Much.* Shame filled her at her weakness, her need to torture herself by looking them up on the internet.

She had to admit the truth. 'I probably wouldn't have come last night but, as I said, I would have tried to contact you somehow. I knew you had to know about Lexi, married or not.'

'I should have known about her as soon as you knew you were still pregnant.'

Mia clutched the glass in her hands. 'I found out the day of your wedding.' She shut her mouth, aghast that she'd let that slip out. She stood up, feeling agitated now. 'I told you—I wasn't even sure I wouldn't lose Lexi. What would have been the point of telling you and disrupting your marriage only for something to go wrong again? I felt I had good reason to say nothing. And then, when she was born…it was seriously overwhelming. Holding down a job, becoming a mother…just getting through each day was a challenge.'

Daniel frowned. 'You can't blame me for not being there to help when you deliberately excluded me.'

Anger mixed with guilt surged inside Mia. 'And you can't blame *me* for feeling reluctant to tell you after what you said about losing the baby.'

Daniel's face turned stony. 'I told you… I had good reason not to want to create a family.'

Mia moved behind the seat, as if that might provide some protection from this conversation. When he didn't elaborate, she said, 'I think I deserve to know what you're talking about. We have a child together.'

Daniel ran a hand through his hair, jaw clenching. He stood up too, and moved over to the window. The suit emphasised his broad back and slim waist. The long legs.

His reluctance to speak was palpable, but as if he knew she was right, he said eventually, 'I grew up with privilege—extreme privilege. I would never deny that. But my parents were of the view that once we had that inherited privilege nothing else was required. Like love. Or caring. Or nurturing. We were just left…left to our own devices.'

'You and your sister?'

Daniel turned around to face her. He nodded. His face

was in shadow. She couldn't read his expression. It was disconcerting.

Mia asked, 'How old was your sister when she died?'

Daniel's voice was clipped. 'Six. I was nine.'

Mia's heart twisted. 'She was so young—how did she—?'

But Daniel cut her off. 'It was a long time ago. The point is that we might not have been beaten, or abused in any tangible way, but what we—*I* witnessed was something unbelievably cruel and cold. Neglect is its own form of torture. I don't have the tools to create a happy family, but I will not shirk my responsibility to Lexi.'

That assertion sent a prickle of foreboding down Mia's spine, but the tone in Daniel's voice was so bleak it caught in her chest.

She bit her lip before asking a little hesitantly, 'Is that why your marriage broke up? Because your wife wanted children?'

He stepped out of the shadows and into the light. She was surprised to see a flicker of something at the edge of his mouth. 'No, that's not why we broke up. My ex-wife may well decide to have children in the future, but it wasn't ever going to be part of our arrangement.'

Mia shook her head. 'So why bother getting married in the first place, if it was going to end so soon?'

'It was a business arrangement. We agreed to the length of our marriage from the very start.'

'Oh.' That didn't mean that he hadn't wanted his wife, that they hadn't still enjoyed—

'I can hear your thoughts from here, Mia.' Daniel's tone was dry.

She hated it that he still had that ability—it made her want to scowl.

He said, 'Not that it's any of your business, but my wife and I didn't consummate the marriage.'

Mia hated the burst of relief in her solar plexus. 'What do you mean?'

He arched a brow. 'Do you really need an explanation?'

She blushed. 'No, but…why?'

Daniel said, 'Because she's gay, and her family are ultra-conservative. She never would have received her inheritance if they'd found out. The marriage was purely to fulfil the agreement and throw up a smokescreen to distract her family. That's why she leaked it to the papers. She was afraid that I would renege on the agreement. When we met, she explained her situation, and I agreed to marry her and then divorce her once she was sure she'd receive her inheritance.'

So he'd married her as a favour? Mia absorbed that. It was huge.

And they hadn't slept together.

Mia hadn't slept with anyone since Daniel—unsurprisingly. But she didn't doubt that, in spite of his chaste marriage, he'd notched up several conquests, so her relief was a little misplaced. She'd be incredibly naive if she believed he'd been celibate all this time.

Not that any of his affairs had appeared in the media. He was too sophisticated for that, and the Devilliers brand certainly wouldn't have stood for it.

'So you are still modelling, then?'

Mia welcomed the distraction from imagining Daniel in bed with other women. 'Yes, I'm back with my agent here in Paris. I did some pregnancy modelling in the South of France, until I became too big. After Lexi was born I worked part-time in a café, until I was in some kind of shape to try modelling again.'

Daniel's eyes dipped to her body, and Mia cursed her choice of words. She felt self-conscious under that far too assessing gaze. After all, this was a man who was an expert at spotting imperfections in his jewels. Mia knew she was far from perfect, and that whatever had attracted him to her in the first place had burnt out long ago. She was very different now.

His gaze lifted again. 'I should have been supporting you.'

She felt another dart of guilt. 'We were okay. I had savings. We didn't need much to live on. We had a nice apartment near the seafront.'

And yet the whole time she hadn't been able to relax fully, conscious of Daniel in Paris, unaware that he was a father.

Mia took a sip of wine, hoping it might make her feel she was on more of an even keel. Daniel had always made her feel too aware of herself.

She said, 'Look, I truly don't expect anything from you, Daniel. I just wanted you to know…about Lexi. We can support ourselves.'

Mia chose not to think about what Daniel had said last night about Lexi being a Devilliers. She hoped he wouldn't mention it again.

'So…what? That's it? I'll just get to see my daughter growing up from a distance while you work to make ends meet?' He shook his head, before answering himself. 'That is not how this will go, Mia.'

Panic fluttered in Mia's breast. 'We really don't need anything.'

Daniel emitted a harsh-sounding laugh. 'If I didn't already know you, I would think this is all an act. A ruse to extract as much as you can by feigning otherwise. But because I know you, and know how independent you are—to a fault—I know this isn't a ruse.'

Daniel took a step closer to where Mia stood, an intense expression she'd never seen before on his face.

'She's my daughter.'

A daughter you never wanted.

It trembled on Mia's tongue, but she stopped the words from falling out. That wasn't fair either.

Feeling nervous, she said, 'So what are you saying…? You want to be involved with Lexi? We can draw up some kind of custody arrangement, Daniel. I wouldn't stop you trying to see your daughter or being involved in her life. That's why I'm here.'

Daniel shook his head. 'Not good enough, Mia. You've kept her from me since her birth. I know I said I never wanted a family, but that was before Lexi existed. She's my daughter and she's a Devilliers.'

Icicles pierced Mia's heart. 'So what are you saying?'

'I'm telling you now that I won't expect anything less than full access to my daughter, and the most expedient and practical way for that to happen is for us to marry.'

Daniel was surprised at how easily those words had tripped off his tongue. He hadn't even consciously decided *what* the best solution was, but something about Mia's proximity and the tangled emotions she was evoking, not to mention the memories, had prompted him to say what he had.

And now he found that he couldn't even drum up much regret or even shock at his words. But he could see shock on Mia's face. And fear. And—

Suddenly her face blanked. It was as if she was aware she was giving too much away and had learnt to hide behind a bland mask. It irritated Daniel intensely.

She was pale. She shook her head. 'No way.'

Daniel was not used to being refused much—in fact this woman was the only one who had ever made him work for anything. He had a flashback to his feeling of triumph when she'd finally capitulated and agreed to go on a date with him. Not to mention the first time he'd slept with her. And every subsequent time. He'd never experienced chemistry like it. Before or since. He'd been desperate. Unable to get her out of his head. Consumed by wanting her. Insatiable.

With an effort, he pushed the rogue memories down deep. That was the past. They were dealing with the present and the future, and Daniel was sure that the madness that had existed between them before would be well burnt out by now. It couldn't still exist.

Yet your blood hums even now. And you can't take your eyes off her.

He scowled.

Mia was taking a step back, shaking her head. 'I am not marrying you, Daniel. It's a ridiculous suggestion. I shouldn't be surprised, though—the last thing the Devilliers brand will want is a child and an ex-lover hanging about on the margins. Much neater to marry and incorporate us into your world.'

'And what about Lexi? Doesn't she deserve to be part of her inheritance?'

Mia was agitated now, with colour in her cheeks. 'I wouldn't dream of denying her her inheritance. She can even have your name if she decides that she'd like that when she's old enough. We don't love each other, Daniel, and I know how you feel about having a family. So I won't go along with a charade just to help keep your world neat and tidy. Lexi deserves more and I deserve more.'

Daniel snorted. 'Since when did you turn into a romantic who wanted a perfect picket fence existence?'

Mia's cheeks went pinker. 'Maybe since I had a baby and my priorities changed. I'm under no illusions about what to expect from relationships, Daniel—believe me. But I want more for my daughter than to be a single parent with an absent father. At least she will know who you are and have some kind of relationship with you.'

She put down her glass and turned as if she was going to leave. With two steps Daniel put his hand on her arm, stopping her. He took his hand away, seriously afraid that he might haul her against his body and stop her speaking such nonsense by putting his mouth on hers.

'So you're telling me you'd marry someone else, but not the father of your child?'

'In order to have a happy life and home environment for Lexi? Maybe.'

Mia's head was spinning. *Marriage*. She wasn't sure what she'd expected, but it hadn't been that. To her eternal shame, her initial reaction when Daniel had said the word 'marry' had been a flutter of something very illicit deep inside. That part of herself that she'd packed in ice after his cruel words in the hospital that day. When he'd told her that losing their baby had been 'for the best'.

It wasn't much of a salve to know the reason why he'd believed that now. It only made her heart ache to learn about his less than idyllic childhood and losing his sister. Which was an indication that after only twenty-four hours in Daniel's company she was seriously in danger of losing her footing all over again.

She needed space from Daniel. He was seeing too much. Saying too many ridiculous things.

She blurted out the first thing she could think of to put space between them. 'I need to use the bathroom.'

Daniel pointed to a door at the other end of the vast room. 'There's a guest bathroom through that door.'

Mia walked towards the door, asking herself why she wasn't just leaving.

Because you created this situation and you need to deal with it. For Lexi's sake.

She found a plushly carpeted corridor on the other side of the door, and another door leading into an opulent bathroom. She shut herself inside, sucking in deep breaths to counteract the shock of Daniel's suggestion of marriage.

Although 'suggestion' was far too gentle a word. It had been an assertion. An expectation that she would just agree.

She forced the panic down and told herself that Daniel couldn't force her to marry him. She'd never entertained any romantic notions of marriage after being brought up by a single parent, but her first boyfriend had exposed a weakness she'd denied to herself. A secret dream for a lifelong connection. Love. A family with two parents who loved and respected each other. She'd discovered she wanted more for her own children than a one-parent family, and that dream being unearthed had felt like a betrayal of her mother.

And then that dream had shattered at her feet anyway, when her ex-boyfriend had sneered at her, *'Of course this was never going to go anywhere, Mia, you're trailer trash.'*

Any notion of marriage she had now was far more pragmatic, and she'd vowed that if it ever happened it would be with someone who she respected and trusted and who wouldn't hurt her. Not intentionally, at least.

Daniel Devilliers was literally the last man she would marry. While of course Mia wanted Lexi to know her father, and have a relationship with him, she wasn't going to allow it to happen in a sham marriage.

Mia had made a huge error of judgement once in her life, and had come close to another lapse with Daniel the last time. It wouldn't happen again.

CHAPTER FOUR

'HAVE YOU EATEN?'

Of all the things Mia might have expected Daniel to say to her on her return from the bathroom, feeling marginally more composed, it hadn't been that.

He said, 'I've been in back-to-back meetings all day and the chef has made me something—would you join me?'

Much to her chagrin, Mia felt her stomach respond to that question with a slight hollow ache. She remembered her appetite had never failed to amaze Daniel but, as much as she longed to say no, she hadn't eaten much herself that day.

She put her light-headedness down to that, and not the man standing a few feet away who had just upended her world with one word.

Marriage.

As much as she wanted to leave right now, she knew they had to talk about this and get it sorted.

'Okay,' she said reluctantly, 'if it's not putting your staff to too much trouble.'

Daniel held out a hand, indicating that Mia should precede him out of the room. 'Not at all,' he replied smoothly.

When they walked into an elegant dining room, Mia noted that he'd taken off his jacket and tie. But he was still wearing a waistcoat which drew attention to his slim waist and lean torso. He managed to look both debauched and yet elegant.

Maybe it was down to the fact that she'd slept with him, so she knew just how debauched he could be…

Not where she wanted her mind to go now. Not when she was feeling so exposed.

There was a long table and two places set at one end. Daniel held out a chair for her and she sat down, trying not to inhale his scent, which was far too evocative.

A middle-aged woman appeared with starters. Mia's mouth watered when she saw a pear and watercress salad with walnuts.

When the woman had left, Mia said, 'I wasn't expecting anything fancy.'

'It's not. Eat up.'

Mia took a bite of salad, the sweetness of the pear contrasting nicely with the peppery watercress and walnut. She had to bite back a groan of appreciation. She'd got used to throwing together any old thing to eat, after feeding Lexi, and it had been a long time since she'd had anything remotely sophisticated.

Daniel poured more wine into Mia's glass and poured some for himself. 'You never did tell me where your interest in food came from,' he said.

Mia was suspicious of this innocuous direction in conversation, but she went with it. She'd made lots of meals for Daniel in her little apartment. She'd never seen food as sensual, or a precursor to passion, until she'd met him.

'My mother. She was a great cook. An amateur, though. She taught me to appreciate it. I think she would have loved to train to be a chef, but we didn't have the money.'

'It must have been tough for her…being a single parent.'

Mia nodded. 'She had to work hard to make ends meet.'

Daniel sat back. 'And yet in spite of that you're willing to let our daughter go through the same experience?'

Mia glared at Daniel. She'd walked into that one. She should have known he wasn't making idle conversation because he was genuinely interested. This was all part of his strategy.

'It won't be similar at all. Because Lexi will know you and I earn a lot more than my mother did, so I can support us comfortably.'

'Until you can't.'

'What's that supposed to mean?'

More staff appeared, to clear away the starter plates, and Mia forced a smile. When they were gone, she looked at Daniel.

'What happens when you don't want to model any more?' he asked. 'What will you do then?'

His question struck a nerve, because in all honesty Mia had been wondering the same thing herself. But he didn't know that she was feeling ambivalent about going back into modelling.

She lifted her chin. 'I can worry about that when the time comes. I might go back to school…get a degree.' She'd always been interested in the arts, but the death of her mother and the need to survive had put paid to going to college.

'And who would take care of Lexi?'

'As you'll be in her life, I'm sure we can come to some arrangement.'

Although, try as she might, Mia couldn't quite visualise Daniel standing at the school gates, waiting to pick up his daughter. It was more likely to be an assistant in a chauffered car.

Mia felt a pang at that. She wanted more for her daughter.

Their main courses arrived: tender fillet steaks with fresh vegetables and baby potatoes. Except Mia's legendary appetite was fading fast. After a few mouthfuls of the exquisitely cooked food, she put down her knife and fork.

Daniel looked at her. 'Not to your liking?'

Mia shook her head. 'No—I mean, *yes*. It's delicious. But…can we just talk about Lexi and come to some agreement? I don't want to be gone too long.'

Daniel put down his own knife and fork and picked up his wine. 'You really think it's that simple?'

No.

'I don't think we need to make it complicated.'

Daniel's jaw clenched. 'You made it complicated when you didn't tell me you were still pregnant.'

Mia fought down the guilt. 'I can't change the past. Can we please move on and discuss where we go from here?'

Daniel stood up and went over to the window. Darkness had fallen over the square outside. He turned around and said, 'I've already told you what will happen.'

Marriage.

Mia's insides knotted even tighter. She put her napkin on the table and stood up. 'If you're not going to make any attempt to be rational then I'm leaving.'

And not just because of what he was saying, but because the longer she spent in proximity to Daniel, the more she found herself remembering what it had been like to be with him. The more she found herself yearning for his touch again. Yearning to be consumed by passion. Which was the last thing she should be thinking about or wanting. That was what had led to here. This moment.

The realisation hit her that, no matter what, her life was entwined with Daniel's for ever. Entwined with a man who didn't want her any more but who felt a responsibility to a child he'd never wanted.

Mia returned to the drawing room and looked around for her bag. She couldn't see it.

'Where are you going?' asked Daniel.

She was feeling panicky. 'Where's my bag?'

Daniel walked over to the other side of the room and picked something up from a table near the door. 'Here it is.'

Mia walked over and moved to take her bag, but Daniel held it out of reach. 'You're really refusing to continue discussing this?'

She glared at him. 'There's nothing to discuss. We are not getting married.'

A muscle ticked in his jaw. 'So how do you see this panning out, then? Some loose arrangement where I get to be on the periphery of my daughter's life and see her intermittently?'

Mia dropped her hand. Daniel put her bag back down on the table. He folded his arms. *Why* did she have to be so aware of him? It was so inappropriate—and not conducive to clear-headed thinking.

Mia moved back into the room in order to try and put some distance between them. She even put a chair between them again. Not that Daniel looked as if he was about to bat it aside to get to her.

'Are you saying your feelings have changed and that you now want a family?' she asked.

'I now *have* a family.'

Mia blanched.

He had a family whether he liked it or not, and clearly he didn't like it, but he wasn't going to shirk his responsibility.

She shook her head. 'I will not marry just for the sake of it. But I'm perfectly happy to sit down and come to a mutual decision about visitation and access to your daughter.'

Daniel's face became stony. 'I won't agree to anything that's not legally binding. If we take this to court, Mia, it'll cost a lot of money.'

Mia stepped out from behind the chair. 'If it goes to court that'll be down to one person—*you*. And I don't think Devilliers will look too favourably on their CEO's personal life being splashed all over the press. It works both ways.'

Daniel felt frustration rise at the same time as admiration. Mia had always stood up to him. One of the few people who ever had. And she was right. If they went to court it would be messy, and the board were still letting it be known that they were less than happy with his short-lived marriage.

Daniel wanted to usher a modern era into the Devilliers brand but announcing a secret child, an ex-lover and a potential legal battle for custody, while certainly very modern, was not going in the right direction.

As if sensing that she'd got through to him, Mia said, 'I'm fully prepared to go through mediation so we can both be satisfied. I'll sign anything you want once it's reasonable. I want what's best for Lexi.'

Daniel's body tightened at the word *satisfied*. It reminded him that he'd never felt as satisfied as he had with this woman. Every time. She'd been like a sorceress. And it hadn't even been down to experience. She was probably the most inexperienced lover he'd ever slept with. Not a virgin, but not far off. And, inexplicably for such a beautiful sexy woman, seriously lacking in confidence.

The first time they'd slept together she'd been so nervous, and when he'd made her come... The look on her face had been one of wonder, gratitude, relief, and a very carnal awakening. It had blasted apart any notion he might have had that conducting an affair with Mia Forde was going to be like every other relationship he'd had. Short and satisfying but ultimately fleeting.

He still woke sometimes in the middle of the night amongst sweat-soaked sheets, his body pulsing with desire for that moment all over again. It definitely hadn't been fleeting and forgettable...

Daniel focused on the other word she'd mentioned: *mediation*. The thought of sitting around a table with a bunch of men and women in suits made something curdle in his gut. He might not have ever set out to have a family, but seeing Lexi had awoken something long dormant inside him: the desire to protect. And seeing Mia again had revived something far more potent and adult: a desire to *have* her again.

Everything Mia was suggesting was eminently reasonable, but Daniel knew that *reasonable* was not good enough. Not by a long shot. Last time they'd been together Mia had resolutely refused to enter his world, but now things were very different and she really didn't have a choice. He wouldn't accept anything less.

Mia didn't like the look on Daniel's face. His gaze was narrowed on her and it was far too calculating. She should have known this wouldn't be easy.

'Daniel, look—'

He cut her off. 'It's getting late. You should probably return to Lexi. We can continue this discussion another time. After all, there's no rush, is there? Unless you're planning on leaving Paris again?'

Mia shook her head, immediately suspicious at Daniel's volte face. 'No, that's why I came back. To tell you about Lexi. To be here so that we could make an arrangement that works for all of us.'

Daniel picked up her bag again and held it out. 'I'm sure we can do that. I'll have my driver take you home.'

Mia walked forward and took her bag, a little winded at the speed with which Daniel was despatching her. Her little finger touched Daniel's hand and a crackle of electricity sparked up her arm. She looked at him, but he seemed oblivious.

He must have sent a telepathic message to his butler because the man appeared in the doorway with Mia's jacket.

Daniel took it and held it up. 'Here, let me.'

Mia turned around and let Daniel help her put the jacket on. Did his fingers linger at the back of her neck? Or maybe she was craving his touch so much that she was just imagining it. It sent a shiver of awareness down her spine anyway.

She turned around again quickly, mortified that she

couldn't control her reactions around him. He walked her to the door and opened it.

She said, 'When will—?'

'I'll call you. We'll make a plan.'

He sounded positively benign, which Mia didn't trust for a second. This was the man who had managed to pick away at all of her very strong defences to seduce her, and then, even when she'd given in on her terms—or so she'd believed—had still managed to prove that any defence she'd thought she had left was an illusion, by making her fall for him.

It was only when she was almost at her apartment that she had a thought and went cold inside. Perhaps Daniel had been so eager to get rid of her not because he had some nefarious plan, but because of something much more prosaic. He had a date.

It was all too easy for Mia to imagine some sleek blonde or sultry brunette being welcomed into his apartment. Daniel smiling, helping her to take off a coat, revealing a clinging silky dress. Smiling at her the way he'd used to smile at her. Full of wicked sensual promise.

Maybe he'd be considering the fact that even though he hadn't ever wanted a family, he now had the best of both words; the freedom to pursue his pleasures and an heir to pass on the Devilliers legacy to—which had to be a seductive prospect, no matter what he'd told Mia about the brand enduring with or without a bloodline.

It should be of some comfort to Mia that he seemed to be giving up his fight to convince her to marry him. Clearly he'd decided it was a mistake. But, much to her irritation, relief wasn't her predominant emotion. It was something far more ambiguous and harder to decipher.

About an hour later, Mia was changed and in soft comfy pyjamas. Lexi had woken, crying, and Mia had given her some milk, and now she was falling asleep again on Mia's shoulder.

The solid and surprisingly heavy form of her daughter was curled so trustingly into Mia that it almost broke her heart, thinking of her own mother and grieving her loss all over again.

She allowed herself to feel some measure of relief that Daniel knew now. Lexi deserved to know who her father was. To have some kind of relationship with him, hopefully. And Mia hadn't wanted history to repeat itself.

She'd never had the option of knowing her father. It had been the one subject that had been guaranteed to wind her normally mild-mannered mother up—any mention of who Mia's father was and she'd say, *'You don't need to know. It's better that you don't.'*

Mia sighed and moved from the window, taking Lexi into the bedroom and placing her back into her cot, before crawling into her own bed.

The fact that Daniel appeared to want to engage in getting to know Lexi was more than Mia had hoped for, based on how he'd reacted when she'd lost Lexi's twin. She'd never forget the stony look on his face. The way he'd been so cold.

Maybe when the dust settled and they came to an agreement about visitation et cetera, Mia could finally break out of this limbo she'd been in for two years and get on with her life. While Daniel Devilliers got on with his too. Surely over time she would be able to interact with him without feeling as if he could see right under her skin to where her blood hummed whenever he came close. To where her blood was humming even now, when he wasn't even close.

Mia cursed silently as she thumped her pillow and tried to get to sleep. But sleep was elusive, and when it did finally come it was full of dreams filled with carnal images that left her gritty-eyed and filled with a sense of aching frustration as dawn broke the next morning.

It had taken Mia a while to get going that morning. She was tired, and still unsettled after the last encounter with Daniel, and Lexi was fractious, so neither of them was on the best of form by the time Mia had buckled Lexi into her buggy and was heading out for a walk to the park and the playground.

But she was totally unprepared for the barrage of flashing lights and shouted questions as soon as she opened the door of her building. They were caught on the threshold, with half of Lexi's buggy on the other side of the door.

Mia was so shocked and stunned she couldn't move. Questions bombarded the air around her.

'Is Daniel Devilliers the father of your baby, Mia?'

'Where is Daniel? Did he know about the baby when he got married?'

'Are you back together?'

'Are you looking for a settlement?'

The only thing that broke Mia out of her stasis was the sight of one of the photographers pointing his lens directly at Lexi. Mia reacted with the fierce instinct of a mama bear. She pushed down the buggy's hood and rain cover and moved back inside the building.

As she did, she heard a sort of commotion at the back of the crowd. She saw a couple of photographers being bodily moved out of the way and then a figure appeared, tall and dark. And grim. Very grim.

Daniel.

He came to the doorway, his dark grey gaze moving over Mia and down to the pram. 'Are you okay?'

Mia nodded. 'I… I think so. We were just going out. Who…? What?'

How did they know?

Daniel said, 'I'll explain in a minute. Go back up to the apartment. I'll follow you.'

Before she could respond he turned around to face the mob, effectively shielding Mia and Lexi from sight, blocking the doorway. He spoke in rapid French to the paparazzi, and all Mia could make out was some reference to sending out a statement. Or an announcement.

She went to the lift and pressed the button. Daniel was still talking to the crowd in a clipped, authoritative voice.

When Mia was back in the apartment she put Lexi down with a bunch of toys to amuse herself. She went over to the window and sucked in a gasp. There was now what seemed to be hundreds of paparazzi outside. Cars trying to drive by were beeping. People were stopping, looking. One of the photographers had moved back and was now pointing his camera up at the building. He shouted something and pointed directly at Mia.

She pulled back, closing the shutters.

Lexi looked up. 'Mama?'

Mia bent down and lifted her up, a sick feeling pooling in her belly. 'Shh...it's okay, sweetheart.'

There was a sharp rap on the door and Mia went and opened it. Daniel came in, immediately and effortlessly dominating the space. He was wearing dark jeans and a dark top under a battered leather jacket. His jaw was stubbled. A sly voice whispered that perhaps he hadn't had time to shave after a night in bed with his date...

At that moment Lexi clapped her hands and said, 'Man!'

Mia pushed aside her rogue thoughts. 'What on earth was that all about...? Why were they asking those questions? And how did you know to come?'

Daniel took his phone out of his pocket and did something to the screen before handing it to Mia. She put Lexi down and Lexi immediately toddled back over to her toys, seemingly oblivious to the tension.

Mia looked at the phone and the blood in her face and head drained south. She saw grainy pictures of her arriving in Place Vendôme yesterday evening, being admitted to Daniel's apartment.

And one blazing headline: *Qui est Mia Forde?*
Who is Mia Forde?

She looked at Daniel. 'How do they know my name? How do they know I even have a baby?'

Daniel was grim. 'I suspect one of the security guards who overheard our initial conversation at the party. Whoever it was must have sensed a story, leaked your name and the paparazzi dug up the rest. I'm making sure I get to the bottom of it. The press have been watching me more since the divorce, so that's why you were caught arriving last night. It's my fault.'

She looked at him, a suspicion forming. '*You* made sure they saw me arriving.'

She cursed her naivety. A man like Daniel never gave up until he got what he wanted. She should know. Lexi was proof of that.

He shook his head, his jaw clenching. 'Not intentionally, no. I wouldn't do that. I hate those vultures.'

Mia stopped. She had to grudgingly admit that it wasn't his style. He was ultra-discreet.

'I'm going to release a statement,' he said.

Mia's insides froze. 'Saying what?'

He looked at her. 'That we are happy to announce that we have a child together from a previous brief relationship and that we would appreciate privacy at this time.'

Mia was suspicious. 'That's all?'

Daniel nodded. 'There's no point trying to deny it. They'll only go digging and find out the truth anyway— and any other dirt they can find.'

Mia shivered to think of the invasive media picking apart her early life. It wouldn't be pretty. She'd grown up in a trailer park. Perfectly respectable, of course, but coupled with her association with Daniel Devilliers it would undoubtedly be portrayed in the worst light possible, to maximise damage to Devilliers.

Mia had never told Daniel anything about her past beyond very superficial stuff. Maybe now was the time to—

'My security team will get rid of the paparazzi, but now they know where you live, and that we have a child together, I can't see them leaving you alone for long, Mia.'

Mia promptly forgot about filling Daniel in about her past. 'We'll be under siege.'

'Yes, I'm afraid so.'

She sat down on the arm of her couch.

Lexi had been amusing herself, but walked over to Daniel now, and held out a unicorn. 'Man play?'

Mia held her breath, watching as Daniel went down on his haunches.

He took the unicorn from Lexi. 'What's her name?'

'Hossy!'

'Do you want to show me where she lives?'

Lexi nodded her head vigorously and grabbed Daniel's hand. She started pulling him over towards her play area.

Mia stood up. 'Lex—'

But Daniel quelled her with a look, telling her that he didn't mind, and for the second time in as many days Mia had to contend with the fact of having brought Daniel into their lives, and with the realisation that no matter how much or how little he engaged with them, there was now a new paradigm.

And she didn't like how watching him interact with Lexi was making her feel. Seriously vulnerable.

Okay, so he obviously wasn't used to kids—he was talking to Lexi as if she was a very small adult—but for a man who'd professed to having no interest in having children he was making an effort, and he wasn't looking too uncomfortable.

In fact, Mia could imagine all too well that with a bit of time Daniel might actually prove to be quite natural with his daughter. And that was something she would never have expected in a million years.

A ringing noise made Daniel pluck his phone from his pocket.

Lexi said imperiously, 'Me say hello.'

Daniel shook his head. 'Not this time, *chérie*.'

Mia went and picked Lexi up and Daniel stood too, answering his phone and speaking in rapid-fire French, too fast for her to grasp everything. He was frowning when he terminated the conversation. Mia had understood enough to know it affected her and Lexi.

'What is it?' she asked.

'The media interest is getting more intense.'

He went to the window and opened the shutters and looked out. Mia followed and gasped. The crowd of photographers had doubled.

'And this is before we've put a statement out.' Daniel sounded grim.

Mia felt panicky. 'It's going to get worse?'

Daniel nodded.

'What will we do? I can't stay in here all day every day. Lexi needs to get out and run around.'

'There's only one solution.'

Mia was sure she wasn't going to like this. 'What solution?'

'You and Lexi will have to move in with me until things die down a bit. I can protect you both better there.'

CHAPTER FIVE

MIA HAD PUT up a fight, but it had been weak and short-lived. She'd had no defence. Not with that baying mob outside. She couldn't subject her daughter to all that attention and potential danger.

Within hours Daniel had assembled a team of people who had come and helped Mia to pack what they needed. He'd also told her to write a list of things they required for Lexi and given it to another assistant.

They'd gone out through a side entrance and slipped into Daniel's car before any photographers had noticed.

And now they were in the hushed and exclusive confines of Daniel's apartment at Place Vendôme. The place was even more intimidating in the daylight. It looked vast. And also, more worryingly, very child-unfriendly. Especially for a toddler who had a mind of her own and could disappear faster than snow on a hot stone.

'What is it?' Daniel asked. He must have seen something on her face.

Mia looked around with Lexi in her arms. She was tired after all the unexpected activity over the past few hours and her head rested on Mia's shoulder, her thumb in her mouth.

'It's just...not really designed for a small person.'

Daniel frowned. Then his eyes drifted to Lexi and understanding dawned. 'Of course. Tell me what we need to do.'

Mia's chest tightened at the use of the word *we*. All her life the only *we* had been her and her mom, and her and Lexi. But now it was different. A feeling of vulnerability swept over her again. She didn't like it. She felt exposed. Out of control.

'Short of redesigning the whole apartment?' she said, half joking. 'For a start it needs to be made child-proof. Sharp edges are out—she's low to the ground and prone to falling over a lot. And we need a play area. She can sleep in my room. But first she needs to eat.'

The butler appeared and Daniel said, 'Go with Paul to the kitchen and talk to the chef. He can make whatever you need.'

Her head still spinning at the speed with which their lives had been turned upside down, Mia dutifully followed Paul to the kitchen—a vast, gleaming space full of state-of-the-art equipment with an elegant dining area. There was no highchair yet, but the friendly chef made something simple for Lexi and she sat on Mia's lap while she fed her.

After that Mia sensed Lexi was approaching being over-tired and would come perilously close to having a small meltdown if she didn't get some rest. But no way was she going to go down while everything around them was so different. The little girl was torn between exhaustion and wanting to explore.

Mia found Daniel in his study, a bright room full of bookshelves and a massive desk with three computers. He stood up when she came in and her arms tightened reflex-ively around Lexi.

'I need to take her out for a walk. She'll sleep in her stroller. I could do with some fresh air too.'

'I'd go with you, but I can't at the moment. I've got some people coming shortly, to have a look at the apartment and see what they can do to make it as safe as possible.'

The power of unlimited funds. It made Mia think of the small trailer where she'd grown up with her hard-work-ing mother. She'd been constantly bruised from hitting the edges of tables and doors.

'Okay, thank you.'

Daniel followed her out of his study. 'You won't be alone, though. I've got security standing by in case you wanted to go out.'

Mia looked at Daniel. 'That's a bit over the top, isn't it?'

'You're not going without Security and that's non-negotiable.'

Once again she knew it was futile to argue.

Mia bundled Lexi up in her coat and they went downstairs, where the stroller was waiting with a burly man called Pierre. He said, 'Don't worry about where I am. You just go where you want.'

They went out through a back entrance which led into an enchanting landscaped private garden, and then another entrance out to a side street. Mia sucked in the cool autumn air gratefully. They walked out to Rue de Rivoli and across it to the Jardins des Tuileries, another of the city's most famous and beautiful parks.

Mia let Lexi out in one of the playgrounds and couldn't stop a smile at her daughter's carefree joy. Another pang of guilt gripped her, knowing she'd kept this from Daniel.

He could have easily thrown her to the lions today and left her to fend for herself with the press. There were plenty of men who would deny paternity until proved and try to wriggle out of responsibility. But he had stepped up without question. And he'd accepted Lexi on sight—which made her wonder about his sister and what she'd been like.

When Lexi got bored with the swings and slide, Mia took her back to the apartment. There were already a couple of trucks parked outside and delivery men carrying boxes inside.

When she got up to the apartment she saw nothing much changed at first, but then she noticed that the sharp edges of the tables were covered in thick pieces of foam. Also, some smaller tables and *objets d'art* had been removed.

Paul appeared in the doorway and said, 'Let me show you to your suite of rooms, Ms Forde.'

Mia checked Lexi quickly. She had fallen asleep in the stroller, so she put a blanket over her and left her, having learnt from previous experience to make the most of these snatched moments.

She followed Paul, saying, 'Please, call me Mia. I don't stand on ceremony.'

He inclined his head and then led her further into the apartment, down a thickly carpeted hall to a door at the end. When Mia went inside it was hard not to let her jaw drop. There was a massive bedroom with a four-poster bed. An en suite bathroom led to a dressing room. And then, back in the bedroom, Paul opened a door that was cleverly designed to match the wallpaper into a smaller anteroom.

'Mr Devilliers is suggesting that this could be a good room for the nursery?'

A fluttery bird of panic beat at Mia's chest. 'Thank you, but Lexi's cot can go in the bedroom. We won't be here for too long, so there's no point going to all the trouble of setting up a nursery.'

'As you wish. The cot should be set up within the hour.'

Back in the main part of the apartment Lexi hadn't moved, still deeply asleep. Mia placed another light blanket over the hood of the stroller, creating a kind of cocoon.

She went over to the window and looked out. Her thoughts flew to the future when, once access arrangements had been made, Lexi would inevitably have a room and a life here of her own, without Mia. It made her feel hollow inside. Because now more than ever she had to come to terms with the fact that those very deeply secret dreams she'd once had of having a happy family would never come true.

She'd allowed herself to fantasise about it with her first boyfriend. He'd told her he respected her. He'd told her he loved her. And she'd been so grief-stricken after her mother's death, and desperate for connection, that she'd believed in him and his words and she'd projected her fantasy onto a relationship that had been a cruel lie.

It was only after he'd humiliated her and exposed her dreams for the fantasy they were that she'd realised how desperate she'd been to believe in a fairy tale. And that she'd never really loved him.

But she hadn't realised that bit until she'd met Daniel and—

'Where's Lexi?'

Mia whirled around. Her jaw felt tight from thinking of the past. She relaxed it.

She pointed towards the stroller in the corner. 'She's asleep…worn out after all the activity.'

'And you? Are you okay?'

There was a flutter near Mia's heart. She crushed it. Never more than right now did she need to remember the past and the lessons she'd learnt.

'I'm fine. I didn't say thank you for taking us in. I don't know what we would have done if—'

Daniel waved a hand. 'It's nothing. I was hardly going to leave you defenceless. Lexi is my daughter.' Then he said, 'There's something you should know.'

'What?'

'I've put out a statement to quell the media interest, but I've added a piece at the end.'

Mia looked at Daniel. 'What, specifically?'

He walked over and handed her his phone. She took it and looked at the screen, where there was a press release. It said:

Daniel Devilliers and Mia Forde are very pleased to announce that they have a child from a previous brief relationship and that they are happily reunited. They ask for privacy at this time. Thank you.

Mia's jaw went slack. She almost dropped the phone. She looked up as Daniel took it out of her hand. She tried to make her mouth work, but nothing came out.

She tried again. 'Happily reunited?'

A dull roaring was building in her head. Daniel had manoeuvred her and Lexi with such skill and ease...

Words spilled out. 'I actually gave you the benefit of the doubt when you said you hadn't tipped off the press.'

'I didn't.'

Daniel kept his voice low, mindful of the sleeping child.

Mia started to pace in front of him, and that drew his eye to her tall body. She was wearing a long button-down dress. Dark red with golden flowers. A belt around her slim waist. The buttons were open low enough that he could see the tantalising vee of her cleavage. She wore that battered leather jacket she seemed to love so much.

Soft, flat ankle boots gave the whole look an effortlessly chic and bohemian élan. He remembered that she'd always been self-conscious about her sense of style, or what she saw as her lack of style. But she had style in spades.

Her hair was down. She wore practically no make-up. It reminded him of the first time he'd seen her at that photoshoot. She'd reminded him of a lioness, with her green eyes and wild hair. She resembled a caged lioness right now.

She didn't seem to have heard him. 'I can't believe I trusted you enough to let you do this to us—'

'Mia.'

She stopped. Looked at him.

He said, 'I didn't tip off the press and I added the piece about being reunited at the last minute because it will be the most expeditious way of getting the press off our backs.'

She put her hands on her hips. 'How, exactly?'

Daniel curbed the urge to cover her mouth with his until all that spikiness was turned into passion.

'Because,' he said, 'if the press thinks we're back together they'll be interested for a while but they'll soon grow bored. But if you're here and we're not a couple they'll hound us until they find out more.'

Mia looked suspicious. 'Lexi and I could stay somewhere else.'

'It'll be exactly the same as it was at your apartment. I can provide better protection here.'

Mia started to pace again. Eventually she stopped. Bit her lip. And then said grudgingly, 'I guess I can see some logic in that.'

She folded her arms, and Daniel had to grit his jaw against the urge to drop his gaze to where he could already imagine the swells of her lush breasts. *Dieu.* He was no better than a schoolboy.

'But how long exactly does this charade have to go on before they lose interest? A week? Two?'

Daniel saw the trepidation on her face. The sense of things being out of her control. And he almost felt sorry for her. Until he remembered that she'd kept his child from him for eighteen months. Lexi was a rapidly forming little human being, with spades of personality, and up until now she'd had no father figure.

That reminder firmed his resolve. 'For as long as it takes for this story to no longer be a liability.'

'But…that could take weeks.'

Daniel shrugged, trying not to let Mia's huge green eyes affect him. Eyes big enough to drown in. Eyes that had captured him from the moment he'd seen her.

'I doubt it,' he said. 'There's bound to be another story that takes precedence. They'll move on.'

'But right now they think that we're a couple.'

'Yes. And to that end I propose we take the heat out of the story by appearing in public together as soon as possible.'

She was suspicious again. 'What do you mean *as soon as possible*?'

'This evening.'

The colour faded from Mia's face. 'This evening?' Her voice was a squeak. He remembered how reluctant she'd been to appear with him in public before—in his world— and how he'd found it refreshing after being with women who had maximised their relationship with him to improve their own social profile.

But Mia had never wanted that kind of exposure. In spite of the fact that she would have got a lot out of it profession- ally to be seen on his arm. At the time he hadn't looked too deeply into her reasons for why that might be, but now... Now he cursed his lack of foresight.

It hadn't mattered before, because they'd broken up and no one had been much the wiser, but this was very different.

'We should talk before we appear together,' he said.

'About what?'

'About why you were always so averse to being seen with me in public. If you have any skeletons in your closet you need to tell me now, Mia, because they *will* find them.'

'If you have any skeletons...'

Mia felt claustrophobic. She needed air. She instinctively moved towards the windows and opened them, stepping out onto the small balcony outside.

Within seconds she heard shouting from the square below and looked down to see people—mostly men, as far as she could make out—with cameras in their hands, tilting them up towards where she stood.

She hadn't even fully grasped who they were or what they were doing until two big hands went to her waist, pulling her back inside. Daniel closed the window again and faced her. Mia felt a little shaky, but she feared it was more from the imprint of his hands on her than the photographers.

'Those were—'

'The same paparazzi. They've followed you here.'

Mia felt hot. Constricted. Daniel held out a hand. 'Here, give me your jacket. I'll get you some water.'

Mia shrugged off her jacket and handed it over. Daniel went to the drinks cabinet and Mia checked on Lexi, trying to gather her wits as she did so. Lexi was still out for the count. It wouldn't make for a pretty night later, but right now Mia was willing to bend the rules.

It was all hitting home—just how much their lives had changed and were going to change further. On some level she'd known this, but she'd been blocking it out. Like a coward. She had never expected Daniel to say that they were a couple again, though.

And yet she couldn't deny that the logic behind it did make sense. She'd seen how some other more high-profile models had been sucked into the maelstrom of various scandals, and she'd always thanked her lucky stars she wasn't at that level of fame.

But now she *was* the one in the headlines, and Daniel was obviously realising that she was a potential liability.

'Mia—'

'I wasn't—'

They spoke at the same time. Mia accepted the glass of water Daniel offered, took a breath and said, 'I wasn't averse to being seen with you because I was afraid of press attention. I have nothing to hide...not really. Beyond growing up with a single parent in a trailer park in the shabbier end of Monterey, California.'

'You never spoke of your father. Is he around?'

They hadn't spoken of him because Mia had been deliberately keeping Daniel at arm's length last time. But now she knew she had no choice. And if she had a skeleton this was it. Mia put the glass down on a nearby table.

'The truth is that I don't know who he is.'

Daniel frowned. 'How is that possible?'

'I know that might be hard to understand, when you come from a world where you can date your ancestors back to the dawn of time.' Mia's voice was tinged with bitterness.

Daniel's eyes flashed pewter and his jaw clenched.

Before he could say anything Mia held up a hand. 'I'm sorry, that wasn't fair.' She lowered her hand. 'The truth is that my mother always clammed up whenever I asked her about him. She never gave me a name. Didn't want to talk about him. Ever. It was only after she died that an old friend of hers told me that my mom went to a party after high school graduation. She was drugged and woke up the next morning dishevelled. Not feeling well. Sore. She fell pregnant as a consequence of that night. Her friend told her she should go to the police, tell them that something had happened to her, but my mom was so ashamed that she wouldn't. Her parents were strict, religious. They would have thrown her out. She moved to California and had me, and brought me up by herself.'

Mia looked at Daniel, expecting to see disgust or horror. But there was an expression she couldn't read on his face. He said, 'I'm sorry. That can't have been easy. For her or for you.'

Mia shrugged. 'I didn't know anything else, and she was a good mother. She made up for the lack of a father.'

Until she'd died, and Mia had felt so unmoored that she'd blindly sought out the first port in a grief-stricken storm.

'Is there a chance your father knows about you?'

'I guess...whoever he is...he might have heard something... But, given the circumstances, I don't think he'll be coming forward, do you?'

The bitterness in Mia's voice was hard to hide. She wasn't responsible for her parents' actions, but she'd always felt a little tainted by what her father had done. How he had violated her mother.

'That still doesn't explain why you were always so reluctant to step into my world with me. What was that about, if not fear of the press?'

Mia went cold.

No way was she going to tell Daniel about her ultimate humiliation.

She avoided his eye and shrugged minutely. 'You were—*are*—rich and powerful. I just had no interest in that world. It was that simple.'

Daniel made a snorting sound. 'Things are rarely that simple. It was more than mere lack of interest, Mia.'

Damn him. She glared at him. 'It's really none of your business and it has no bearing on anything now.'

Daniel leaned against the back of a couch and crossed one ankle over the other. 'Now I'm really intrigued.'

Mia wanted to stamp her foot. She recognised the obstinate expression on Daniel's face all too well. He would push and probe until she gave up all her secrets.

'Fine. If you must know, it was my first boyfriend. He was rich. Very rich. He came from a family that could date itself back to the *Mayflower*. I worked as a waitress in the local country club and he saw me there…and seduced me. Then he dumped me. It turned out the only reason he'd spoken to me was to get me into bed. He never intended on having a relationship with me because I was, in his words, *"trailer trash"*. He led me to believe that he wanted me in his world, that he was prepared to introduce me to his family, while at the same time he was getting ready to announce his engagement to a far more suitable woman. The worst thing was that I fell for it. It wasn't long after my mom had died and he offered a sense of connection. I thought I wanted to be accepted by him and his world.'

'Are you saying I reminded you of him?' Daniel's voice was like steel.

Mia swallowed. She couldn't in all honesty say that, because at no point had Daniel ever reminded her of *him*. But he had stirred up enough powerful emotions and sensations to make her scared enough to keep him at arm's length.

'No, you're nothing like him. He was a coward. I'm ashamed to admit I allowed him to—'

Daniel stood up and shook his head, cutting her off. 'No, don't say it. He took advantage of you, Mia. He saw a beautiful young woman, and maybe a chink of vulnerability, and exploited it.'

Mia hated the emotion that climbed up her chest at Daniel's perspicacity.

'Is he also the reason why you don't like gifts of jewellery?'

She nodded. 'He gave me what he told me was a diamond necklace, but it was just cubic zirconia. All part of the act to make me think he wanted more than sex.'

Daniel said a rude word in French. To Mia's surprise, she didn't feel exposed or newly humiliated after telling Daniel—she felt vindicated. Lighter. But then she'd never told anyone else what had happened to her, and to realise that it was Daniel she'd just confided in... *Now* she felt exposed.

Suddenly eager to move on from the past, Mia asked, 'This evening...where are we going?'

'It's the Paris Ballet's gala night at the Palais Garnier.'

Mia was immediately intimidated at the thought of the stunning Paris *opéra* building. It was one of the most iconic landmarks of Paris and she'd never been inside.

'But I couldn't possibly go—what about Lexi?'

'Paul's daughter works as a nanny but she's between jobs at the moment. She can babysit.'

'That's convenient.' In Daniel's world, everything fell into place. Mia shouldn't have forgotten that. She said, 'I'm not going anywhere until I meet her and feel that I can trust her with Lexi.'

'Of course. I've arranged for her to come in an hour—that should give you plenty of time to see how you feel about her and see how she interacts with Lexi.' Daniel looked at his watch. 'I have to take some calls in my study. You'll find a range of dresses for this evening in your dressing room. It's a black-tie event.'

He was turning to go and, feeling claustrophobic again, Mia said, 'That's *if* I go.'

The tiniest of smiles played around the corner of Daniel's mouth, making Mia remember how it had felt to be kissed by him. All-consuming. Drugging. Addictive. She'd never forgotten.

She half expected him to say something smart, arrogant, but all he did say was, 'Of course. Only if you feel comfortable enough to leave Lexi for a few hours.'

He turned and left and Mia felt curiously deflated.

There was a sound and movement from the stroller in the corner. Lexi was waking up. Mia welcomed the distraction—anything to avoid thinking about their new situation and the very real possibility that she would be appearing in public in a few hours on Daniel Devilliers' arm.

'She's adorable.'

Mia smiled at the woman, who was just a year or two younger than her. They were sitting cross-legged on the floor of Lexi's new playroom, watching the toddler wreak happy havoc around her. 'She likes you.'

Lexi was besotted with her 'new friend' Odile, Paul's daughter. The young woman was clearly experienced, and had already managed a mini meltdown with an equanimity that had given Lexi no alternative but to calm down.

Much to Mia's chagrin, it wasn't looking as if she'd have an excuse to duck out of accompanying Daniel to this event. Nevertheless, she said a little hopefully, 'Are you sure it's not putting you out to babysit at such short notice?'

Odile smiled. 'Not at all. To be honest, I'm saving to go travelling next year, so every extra euro helps.'

Mia knew what that was like. She'd scrimped and saved to fly to Europe to further her modelling career and see something of the world. The fact that she'd got no further than France was a twist she hadn't expected, but when she looked at Lexi now her heart swelled with so much love she couldn't regret anything.

A shadow darkened the doorway and Mia looked up to see Daniel.

Lexi toddled over. 'Hi, Man! Play!'

Daniel smiled and Mia's heart hitched.

'Not right now, *mignonne*. I need to speak to your Mama.'

Odile expertly distracted Lexi and led her over to look at some toys. Mia stood up and went out of the room, closing the door behind her.

Daniel lifted a brow. 'Well?'

Mia sighed. 'She's perfect. Lexi loves her.'

'Okay, then, we leave in an hour.'

Mia wished she could avoid this, but she couldn't. He was Lexi's father, and if she wanted some kind of order restored in their lives she would have to go along with his plan. For now.

The strapless dress was ice-blue. It was low-cut enough to make Mia want to tug the fabric over her breasts, but the other dresses hadn't been much more discreet. The material hugged her torso just under her breasts, and then fell in soft swathes of material to the floor. It was elegant and romantic. She'd managed to tame her hair back into a rough chignon, and she'd applied a little more make-up than she'd normally wear, using it like a tool that might give her some sort of illusion that she was working and not playing herself.

The thought of appearing in front of the world's press on Daniel's arm was intimidating, but it also touched on a very secret part of her where she'd once allowed herself to dream that possibly her relationship with Daniel *was* different from the experience she'd had before, and that perhaps she could allow herself to let him bring her into his world gradually, until she built up her trust again.

But then she'd seen the article in the paper about his 'arrangement, not engagement'. Just in time—before she'd made a complete fool of herself. Again.

Her reaction to the article had exposed her enough. This time she was prepared. Under no illusions. Daniel could not hurt her again.

Mia shut down her circling thoughts. Slipping her feet into high-heeled silver sandals and doing them up, she gave herself a last once-over and picked up the clutch and matching cape.

Daniel was finding it hard to keep himself from mentally undressing Mia. There was a discreet slit in her dress and a tantalising length of toned golden thigh, tempting him to place his hand there and move it higher, to the apex between her legs where he would feel the throbbing heat at the centre of her body.

He shifted in the back seat of the car, his own body throbbing in response. She'd taken his breath away when she'd walked into the reception room a short while before. He'd seen her transformed before, from her more casual aesthetic into something far more sleek when she was working—but he'd never seen her transformed for *him*. For a date.

Other women had. But not Mia. Because everything about being with her had been different. Challenging. She'd made him work to be with her. But it had been worth it—and not just on a carnal level. That had been the most surprising thing.

Mia turned to look at him now and her scent tickled his nostrils, light and fresh but with a musky base. Not unlike her. His first impression of her had been that she was sunny and carefree, but as he'd got to know her she'd shown more complex layers.

She said, 'I'm not wearing any jewellery. Will that be an issue?'

When Daniel had first seen her in the dress he'd automatically known that diamonds would show it, and her, off to their best advantage. And he'd known exactly which ones.

He looked at her. 'You wouldn't mind wearing it?'

She avoided his eye and he felt a physical surge of anger again at the thought of what her so-called boyfriend had done to her. *Trailer trash.*

'It wasn't the jewellery I had an issue with, it was the gift. I didn't want to be made a fool of again.'

Unable to help himself, Daniel reached out and touched Mia's jaw, making her turn her face towards him. 'He was the fool, Mia. Never you.'

He saw her throat work as she swallowed. Saw the flare of emotion in her eyes making them brighter green.

'You don't need to say that.'

The urge to kiss her in that moment was huge. Daniel almost shook with the effort it took not to tug her close. But they were pulling up outside the majestic Palais Garnier now, so Daniel reluctantly took his hand down and said, 'We're here.'

CHAPTER SIX

MIA'S FINGERS TIGHTENED around Daniel's hand as they stood at the bottom of the steps leading up to the majestic entrance. He shot her a look. She gave an imperceptible nod to say she was ready, when she was anything but.

They walked up the steps that were overlaid with a red carpet. Mia was very aware of Daniel's physicality next to her, oozing Alpha male energy. His bespoke classic black tuxedo fitted like a second skin, enhancing his lean strength. She'd been blisteringly aware of him in the back of the car beside her, and she was still breathless from the way he'd touched her and looked at her. From what he'd said.

'He was the fool.'

It hadn't meant anything. Not really. She had to get her desire and her rampant imagination under control. If he suspected she still wanted him she would literally have no dignity left.

People were turning to look at them. Eyes widened when they recognised who Daniel was. Then slid to her. Instinctively Mia lifted her chin. And then the paparazzi spotted them. But this time she was prepared, and she felt herself automatically slipping into work mode, so she could pretend this was just a photo shoot and counteract the intimidation she felt.

When they reached the entrance Daniel stopped. Mia looked up at him, hoping that he couldn't see the effect he was having on her. And then, before she could say or do anything, he was sliding an arm around her waist and pulling her into him.

It all happened too quickly for her to put up her guard, especially when she still felt a little raw after his words and the way he'd looked at her in the car. She couldn't fight the helpless temptation to go with the flow of her blood—which was towards Daniel. To get closer. With his free hand, he tipped up her chin. All she could see were those grey eyes.

The emotions he aroused were fading into the background to be replaced with pure physicality. She craved to have his mouth on hers with a hunger that blotted everything else out. All concerns. Without even being aware of it, her hand found and curled around the lapel of his jacket, as if to stop him pulling away.

It had been like this between them from that first day they'd met. Instant heat. An urgency.

And then Daniel's mouth was on hers and a deep sigh moved through Mia. The past fell away. There was only this moment and the familiar firm contours of his mouth, enticing her to open up to him, to take the kiss deeper. She did it without thinking, acting instinctively. It was as if they'd kissed only yesterday, and also as if it had been a thousand years ago. Both achingly familiar and new again. His tongue touching hers lit a fuse that connected directly to the pulse of heat between her legs.

But then Daniel was pulling back, taking his mouth off hers. Mia heard the sound of people around her, the outside world slowly breaking through the heat haze in her brain. And with the sounds came the crash of reality.

Her eyes snapped open. Daniel was looking down at her with no discernible expression on his face.

The full impact of what she'd just allowed to happen—enthusiastically participated in—hit her like a body-blow.

Daniel's arm was still around her waist. She pushed against his chest, when a moment ago she'd been pulling him closer.

'What was that in aid of?' *Bit late for outrage now*, jeered a voice in Mia's head.

'We're meant to be reunited, remember? The object of this evening is to convince people that there's really no story.'

Mia was aware of pops of light coming from the direction of the photographers. Self-consciousness crawled up her spine. Daniel had known what he was doing. He'd executed a perfectly clinical kiss for the cameras. And it was too late for her to act blasé.

She pulled away and Daniel's arm slackened enough to let her step back. 'Next time,' she said, 'do me the courtesy of asking first.'

She turned and stalked ahead of him into the building. Not even the sight of the grand marble staircase and the lavish Baroque-inspired interior could distract her from the fact that even if he'd asked her permission she still would have said yes.

Mia had been to plenty of glittering events before, but usually for work. Never like this, on someone's arm. And not just someone. A man everyone recognised on sight.

Daniel took her arm and gently guided her up to another level where there was a private drinks reception before the performance started. After someone had taken her cape Daniel handed her a glass of champagne.

Mia was more interested in the hors d'oeuvres. She hadn't had time to eat much while making sure that Lexi and Odile were going to be okay together. She tried to eat a concoction of caviar on the smallest piece of toast she'd ever seen, with as much grace as she could, but a steady stream of people were approaching Daniel, and he snaked an arm around her waist, pulling her into his side, effectively ruining her appetite for the evening.

One older, very well-preserved woman spoke to Daniel

while barely glancing at Mia. She said, 'She's an American? You have a child with her? I hope this won't damage the brand, Mr Devilliers.'

Shocked at what she was hearing, and incensed that Lexi might be subjected to any kind of judgement, Mia cut in, 'Yes, I am American—and, yes we have a child. And I can assure you the Devilliers brand is quite safe.'

The woman looked at Mia as if she had two heads, and then she stalked off.

Mia looked at Daniel. 'Sorry, I couldn't help myself. Who was she?'

To Mia's surprise, Daniel's mouth quirked. 'One of the longest-serving members of the board.'

'Oh.'

'Your French is impeccable, by the way.'

Mia shrugged, self-conscious. 'I've had plenty of time to practise it over the last two years.'

Then she added tentatively, 'She looked angry...will this cause problems for you?'

Daniel took a sip of champagne, and even that relatively innocent movement made a skewer of desire arrow right to Mia's lower body.

'No. It's dinosaurs like her I'm trying to ease off the board. She and a few others are the only ones clinging onto the past. We have to move forward.'

At that point a melodic bell sounded to indicate that they needed to move into the theatre. Daniel took Mia's hand and led her out of the function room and along a corridor and into a private box.

Mia gasped when the full majesty of the auditorium was laid out before her. Tiers of seats rose up around the stage in a circle. The furnishings were lavish and totally over the top. Baroque. Dramatic. The ceiling was adorned with lush frescoes.

The crowd—most of whom had taken their seats—were

as glittering as their surroundings. The men handsome in their tuxedoes.

'This is amazing,' she breathed as she sat down, momentarily distracted from everything else.

For a while, when she'd been younger, she'd had dreams of becoming a dancer. A teacher had even helped her apply for a grant to get into advanced classes, and Mia had had visions of going to Juilliard in New York. But one day she'd damaged her knee, and her dreams of becoming a dancer had turned to dust. And then, as if conspiring against her, her body had started to develop, giving her curves that would never have been acceptable in a ballet dancer.

So being here now was making her feel nostalgic and wistful. She had a sudden vision of an older Lexi, being brought here with her father to see a ballet performance, and emotion gripped her before she could stop it, stinging her eyes.

She cursed herself and kept her head averted from Daniel. Ever since she'd given birth to Lexi her emotions had sat just under her skin, and the most innocent and benign of incidents or things could set her off. Not to mention the tumult of being back in Daniel's orbit.

The lights went down and a hush fell over the crowd. Mia sat forward, her skin prickling with anticipation. Well, she told herself it was anticipation, and not because Daniel's tall, powerful body, his long legs stretched out before him, was close enough to touch. Smell.

She let the performance distract her from the man beside her, knowing it would be an all too brief respite...

A week after the ballet performance Mia spotted the floppy ear of Lexi's favourite bunny peeking out from under a couch and grabbed it. She looked around and saw the other detritus belonging to a small person. A cardigan shoved down between some cushions. A small shoe discarded by the door. And a sticky handprint on a glass coffee table.

She sighed. Already Lexi was treating this place like a small queen in her new domain, and even Mia had settled into the luxurious space far too easily. But she had to keep reminding herself that it was only temporary. And surely these transgressions into Daniel's pristine space would make him realise that having them here wasn't conducive to his newly acquired bachelor lifestyle?

That was if he was here to see them—which he wasn't. After the night at the ballet, which had left Mia feeling very emotional, Daniel had told her the following morning that he had to go to New York for a few days.

She'd schooled her expression while inwardly relishing the thought of a reprieve, to take stock of everything that had happened without Daniel's disturbing presence.

'Don't look so pleased,' he'd said dryly.

'What's in New York?' she'd asked.

'Our North American head office. We're having some discussions about a new campaign.'

'When will you be back?' Mia had asked nonchalantly.

'Before the weekend.'

But it was Friday night now, and he was not back. He was still in Manhattan on business. Not that Mia had any jurisdiction over him, so she shouldn't even be wondering about it, or feeling a disturbing pang of disappointment.

He'd called a couple of times during the week, mainly to ask about Lexi. He'd asked that Mia send him videos of Lexi every day and she had, feeling a very disturbing glow of warmth in her chest at his interest in his daughter.

During their conversation on Wednesday night he'd commented, 'You were working today?'

Mia had immediately felt defensive. 'Yes, it was a small job, booked in before…all this. Odile came with me and brought Lexi.'

'It wasn't a criticism, Mia. I know you work.'

She'd relaxed marginally and said dryly, 'Actually, my agent told me today that she's never had so many calls asking about my availability. It would appear my stock has risen all of a sudden.'

'You know you're not under pressure to work, Mia,' Daniel had responded. 'You don't have to worry about money.'

She'd tensed. 'I support myself, Daniel. I always have and I always will. We don't need—'

'You're the mother of my child,' Daniel had cut in, and then muttered something under his breath about her being stubborn. 'Lexi is now my responsibility too. You can work and save all you want, but you're not her sole provider any more.'

Mia had bitten her lip. Of course she wouldn't deprive her child of support from her father, but after that call she'd wondered how it would work—Lexi living a life of luxury with her *papa* and then coming back to a much more modest existence with her mother.

Now, feeling the onset of a headache, Mia was picking up Lexi's discarded items when she heard her mobile phone ringing and plucked it out of the back pocket of her jeans.

Daniel.

She answered, her voice sounding unaccountably husky. 'Hi.'

'Hi,' Daniel replied.

He sounded a little tired, and Mia had a mental image of him loosening his tie. Sitting back in a big chair. The skyline of Manhattan behind him. Because surely he must be in one of those sky-skimming buildings with a jaw-dropping view?

Mia perched on the edge of a couch. The apartment was dimly lit. It somehow felt more intimate to have Daniel's voice in her ear through the phone than if he was here himself.

He said, 'I'm sorry I didn't make it back before the weekend.'

Something fluttered in Mia's chest. She crushed it. 'That's okay. You don't have to explain your movements, Daniel.'

There was a dry tone in his voice. 'You're not my roommate, Mia. You're the mother of my daughter.'

Mia scowled into the phone.

Then Daniel said, 'Actually, my plans have changed.'

'Oh?'

'Are your and Lexi's passports up to date?'

As it happened, Mia had had to renew her passport recently, so she'd ordered Lexi's first passport too.

'Yes…' she answered cautiously, with no idea where this was going.

'Good. I have to fly to Costa Rica tomorrow for a week, to oversee a shoot. I'd like you and Lexi to join me. You'll fly out tomorrow on a private plane. Odile is free to travel with you, to help take care of Lexi. I've already spoken to her to check.'

Mia's mouth dropped open in shock, but before she could say anything or object Daniel spoke again.

'To save us all some time, I'll explain why it's a good idea. With all of us being absent from Paris for a while, it'll speed up the process of the press losing interest. By the time we return they'll have moved on. We'll be old news.'

Mia's mouth closed. Then opened it again. 'So by the time we return Lexi and I can return to our apartment?'

For a moment Daniel said nothing, and then, 'It'll certainly make it much more likely.'

She knew he was right. If they weren't here, there was no story. She'd noticed paparazzi in the park these last few days, even though the security presence had kept them back. But she didn't like exposing Lexi to their lenses. So any method of minimising that had to be a good thing.

She said, 'Okay, then.'

Daniel was brisk. 'Good. I'll have my assistant come and help you pack in the morning. She'll arrange transport to the airport, and anything else you might require for Lexi. Odile will meet you at the plane. See you in Costa Rica, Mia.'

Mia was tempted to change her mind at the last minute, but Daniel had terminated the connection.

Too late.

She wondered if she was completely delusional for thinking for a second that it was a good idea to go to a tropical paradise with the most disturbing man she'd ever met.

The following day, after a twelve-hour flight and then a shorter hop from San José to Santa Teresa on the Nicoya Peninsula, Mia and Lexi and Odile were in…paradise. That was the only way to describe it.

The air was warm, inviting Mia to melt and relax and forget all her worries and concerns. Like a siren call. The sun was setting over the Pacific Ocean in a glorious cascade of pinks and oranges and reds.

In front of where she stood, stupefied with awe, Mia could see people on a beach in the near distance, strolling, surfing… Dogs running alongside owners. Children playing. All against the backdrop of majestic surf. Behind them lay the lushest forest she'd ever seen. And in between these two things was this villa.

It was modern, but it sat in the tropical forest seamlessly. On several levels, it flowed down through the forest to a path which led to the beach, and it was truly breathtaking. Each level held a range of rooms, and at the top was a lounging/dining area, with an infinity pool that looked out over a canopy of trees to the ocean and the vast sky.

The lower levels held bedrooms and a gym and media centre. Also a room that looked like an office. From all these rooms the ocean was visible through a lush tangle of forest. And from this lowest level there was a private path to the beach.

But even in spite of all these distractions the back of her neck prickled just before she heard Daniel say from behind them, 'Sorry I wasn't here when you arrived. The preparation meeting for the shoot ran over.'

Mia braced herself before turning around. Lexi was sleepy in her arms. She hadn't slept much on the plane and now she was exhausted. But even bracing herself couldn't prepare Mia for the sight of a far more relaxed Daniel.

He was wearing a dark blue short-sleeved polo-shirt and linen trousers. His skin looked darker already. Shades covered his eyes. He looked cool and unbelievably suave. And masculine. The musculature of his chest was all too evident under the thin material of his top.

Mia immediately felt creased and gritty, in her long broderie anglaise dress and cream blazer.

Odile greeted Daniel and reached for Lexi, saying to Mia, 'I'll take Lexi up to the house and get her fed and ready to put down.'

Mia wanted to object, but Lexi was perfectly happy to be transferred to her new best friend Odile, and Mia knew she needed to go down before she tipped over into extreme over-tiredness.

She handed Lexi over as Daniel said thank you to Odile, and then, as Odile and Lexi made their way back up to the main part of the house, he pushed his shades onto his head and said to her, 'You met Gabriela?'

Mia nodded. 'She greeted us when we arrived and showed us around. She seems very nice.'

Daniel came and stood beside her. Mia tried not to feel

self-conscious under that cool grey gaze. 'She is. She lives locally and her son maintains the property for me.'

Mia looked at him. 'You own this? It's not a rental?'

Daniel nodded. 'It's part of my portfolio, yes.'

Along with the family chateau outside Paris, and the apartment in New York, another in London, and undoubtedly more properties dotted around the world...

'How was Lexi on the journey?' Daniel asked.

Mia made a face. 'Okay...not great. Fractious. Her ears were sore.'

Daniel frowned. 'I never considered that.'

'People don't until they have children. That's why there are so many screeching babies on planes.'

'Will she be okay?'

Mia nodded. 'She'll be fine once she's been fed and put down. I'll go and make sure she's okay. Odile is exhausted too. She should have the rest of the evening and tomorrow off.'

'Of course. I have some calls to make, but I'll be eating in about an hour if you want to join me?'

The warm breeze caressed Mia's body. The sky was turning lavender now, and the smell of sea and sand and exotic blooms made the air fragrant. Night birds started their calls. And there was this man, as elemental as his surroundings in spite of the trappings of civilisation.

She could feel the pull to move closer, to have him envelop her in all that heat and steel. Transport her to an even more seductive paradise. It was dangerously romantic.

Mia stepped back before she made a fool of herself. She shook her head. 'I'm quite tired myself, actually, I'll just grab something and then go to sleep with Lexi.'

Daniel watched Mia go, her flowing dress doing little to hide her long bare legs. She moved gracefully, her tawny hair trailing down her back and over her shoulders. For someone who'd just got off a transatlantic flight with a small child, she looked pretty perfect. In fact, she fitted into this wild landscape very well, with her naturally sun-kissed skin.

Daniel felt something ease inside him at the knowledge that they were here. It was a subtle shift. A sense that he could relax.

That thought registered and he scowled at himself—at the notion that Mia and Lexi's proximity was somehow beneficial for him.

Having Mia and Lexi here, far away from the French media and his conservative board—*that* was beneficial. As was the fact that he now had time to convince her of what he'd spent the last week realising was the only solution for them. The only solution he was prepared to accept.

Full commitment from Mia.

This wasn't what he had ever planned for his life, but the reality of having a daughter had aroused emotions and protective instincts he'd buried a long time ago with his sister. He wanted more for Lexi. He wanted to be able to nurture her and protect her. He'd failed his sister and he vowed now that he would not fail his daughter.

And, more selfishly, he wanted Mia back in his bed. For good.

The following day, after Mia had woken and fed Lexi and dressed her, she explored a little. There was no sign of Daniel, which brought her a mixture of relief and something else she refused to call disappointment. Gabriela told her he had gone to work—to wherever they were setting up the shoot.

Odile had gone into the pretty little town of Santa Teresa to explore. While passing through it yesterday Mia had thought it looked charming, and rustic. Full of cafés and artisan shops. Very bohemian. But she was happy to stay around the house and take Lexi to the beach to paddle in the surf, which delighted her. It was a long time, if ever, since they'd been able to relax like this.

In the afternoon, when Lexi didn't seem remotely inclined to go down for a nap, Mia dressed them both in swimwear and liberally applied a high-factor sunscreen.

To her surprise, when she'd explored more yesterday evening, she'd found the dressing room adjoining her very luxurious bedroom suite to be fully stocked with clothes. All in her size. When she'd mentioned it to Gabriela that morning the woman had told her that Daniel had instructed her to get a local boutique to deliver clothes for both her and Odile, and baby clothes for Lexi, in case they needed anything.

The fact that the clothes weren't a permanent fixture made Mia feel somewhat off-centre. She wondered if Daniel had ever kitted the dressing room out for anyone else. Surely he'd come here with lovers? It would almost be a crime not to—the place was so romantic and full of earthy sensuality.

But Mia quickly diverted her mind from that line of thinking. She didn't care if Daniel had been here with lovers. He could do what he liked with his properties.

She checked her reflection before they went out. She was wearing a one-piece swimsuit which had looked very conservative on the hanger, but it felt a lot more revealing now. One-shouldered, it had a cut-out above her hip, high-cut legs, and a top cut a little too low across her breasts for her liking.

But Lexi was grizzling now, and Daniel wasn't even here, so Mia told herself she was being ridiculous, plonked hats on their heads and went to the pool.

When Daniel rounded the corner of the building to walk onto the decked area by the pool he stopped in his tracks and his blood ran cold.

All he saw was Lexi in the pool.

He couldn't move. It was as if cement had been poured into his legs.

Helpless. Any minute now she was going to tip face-forward and—

'Hi, we weren't expecting to see you until later...'

Daniel's stricken gaze finally took in more detail. They were in the shallow end of the pool, and Mia had Lexi securely under the arms, holding her as she pulled her forward and back through the water. Lexi was splashing and babbling in baby language.

Not about to drown.

Not like his sister.

Mia must have seen something on his face. She stopped moving and said, 'Are you okay?'

Somehow Daniel managed to move forward, nearer the edge of the pool, but still at a distance. He hadn't considered this scenario.

He didn't answer Mia's question directly. He wished they would come out of the water. 'Shouldn't she have armbands?'

Mia smiled. 'She's a water baby. She's fine. I'm a qualified lifeguard, in any case.'

'Still, it's not safe. I should put something around the pool.'

Mia's eyes opened wide. 'It's fine, honestly. She won't ever be here unsupervised.'

She could be, though.

This was one of the reasons why he'd sworn never to have children. To avoid this crippling fear. That pool was a lethal accident waiting to happen—something Daniel never would have noticed before now, because to him it was merely an ornamental feature.

Mia said, 'It's probably time we came out now anyway. Lexi needs a wash and her dinner.'

She came up the steps out of the water with Lexi in her arms, and for the first time since he'd seen them in the pool the dread inside Daniel eased a little. The distraction of Mia in a swimsuit that clung like a second skin, leaving little to the imagination, helped too. Her hair was piled up on her head in a rough knot, showing off her spectacular bone structure and long neck. He seized on her beauty as something to cling to—something that brought him back from those awful tendrils of fear.

She came over to a lounger and wrapped Lexi in a voluminous towel, rubbing her briskly and making her laugh.

The sound finally broke Daniel out of his stasis.

He went and sat on the other lounger and Lexi stretched out her arms towards him.

'Hi!'

Mia held on to her. 'She's all wet. She'll ruin your—'

Something swelled in Daniel's chest. Emotion and an instinct he couldn't ignore, part possessive and part fear. He plucked Lexi out of Mia's hands. 'It's fine.'

He'd held Lexi before, but he was surprised again at how solid she was. And trusting.

She immediately placed her hands on his face and declared, 'Hair face!'

Daniel smiled. He nuzzled his face against her cheek, making her squirm and giggle. When he looked at Mia he was surprised to see an arrested look on her face. Their eyes met and the expression disappeared as if he'd imagined it. An electric spark zinged between them. Her cheeks went pink.

She reached for Lexi again and he let her take her—but not before their fingers touched.

The colour in her cheeks deepened and Mia said, 'I should wash her off and prepare her dinner.'

She stood up, all long limbs and tantalising curves.

'Join me for dinner this evening,' Daniel said.

He could see her mouth open, could anticipate the refusal. But then she surprised him by saying, 'Okay. I'll join you once Lexi is down for the night.'

Mia looked at herself in the mirror. Her hair was curling wildly in the evening heat after her shower. Not much she could do about that. Anyway, it wasn't as if this was a date. She was having dinner with the father of her child, and they would stick to topics concerning only their daughter.

She'd chosen to wear a long kaftan-like dress which couldn't be remotely construed as sexy. But then, out of nowhere, an image popped into her head of Daniel with Lexi earlier, tickling her with his stubble, and suddenly Mia felt breathless.

She hated the tender part of her that it had affected. Seeing Lexi being held in his big hands. Protected. Safe. Already Lexi had experienced a more meaningful father-daughter relationship than Mia ever had.

Mia could also recall all too easily how Daniel's gaze had lingered on her body, making her blisteringly aware of the clinging wet swimsuit.

But she'd imagined the heat in Daniel's eyes. Must have. Projected her own desire on to him.

He didn't want her any more.

She'd never forget the way he'd looked at her that day when she'd told him she was pregnant. The shock. Horror. And then panic. And then later in the hospital, in the aftermath of her miscarriage, with a cold remoteness that had scared her.

After checking Lexi, and the baby monitor to make sure it was on, Mia went up to the next level, where they would eat.

When she saw where Gabriela had set the table she cursed silently. It was out on the terrace. The sky was dusky and gently flickering candles illuminated the space and the table. The scent of exotic blooms filled the air. It was all too seductive.

Daniel was standing at the rail that curved around the terrace. He had his back to her and he was wearing a white shirt, sleeves rolled up, and dark trousers.

He turned around and the first thing Mia spotted was that his hair was damp and his jaw was clean-shaven. Need pierced her so acutely that she had to suck in a gasp.

Her hand tightened around the baby monitor.

He was holding a drink. 'What can I get you?'

Mia knew alcohol was the last thing she needed, but she needed the edges of her desire for Daniel blurred a little. 'A white wine, please.'

Daniel came back and handed her a cold glass.

Mia took a sip and relished the dry aromatic wine.

He lifted his glass, '*Santé*, Mia.'

She touched hers to his, avoiding his eyes like a coward. 'Cheers.'

She moved over to where he'd been standing. The lights of fishermen's boats were already visible, bobbing up and down in the sea. Presumably they were out because it was a calm evening.

She sensed Daniel coming to stand beside her. The little hairs stood up on her arms. 'It's so beautiful here,' she said.

'Yes, it is.'

'You must use it a lot. I would. I don't think I'd ever leave.'

'Actually… I don't use it as much as I'd like. I haven't been here now for a couple of years.'

Mia glanced at him. He'd put his back to the view and was leaning against the rail. Her mouth was open as she absorbed that nugget of information but she rapidly closed it.

Daniel's mouth quirked. 'I can practically hear your brain whirring. What are you thinking?'

A very timely discreet cough sounded from behind

them, and Mia was relieved not to have to try and hide how much she wanted to know if he'd ever brought lovers here.

Gabriela had served up their starter—a deliciously light crab salad. Mia sat down and eyed the food with appreciation. But any hope that Daniel might not pursue the line of conversation turned to dust when he said, after a few minutes, 'You were going to say something, about me not coming here?'

Mia cursed him. She wiped at her mouth with a napkin and took a sip of wine. Then she forced herself to look him in the eye. 'It's so beautiful here—and private. I just thought that if you and your wife weren't…weren't sleeping together, it would be the perfect place to bring lovers.'

'Are you asking me if I took lovers during my marriage, Mia?'

Damn him, he was enjoying this.

She smiled sweetly. 'Never mind. It's none of my business.'

CHAPTER SEVEN

DANIEL WAS ENJOYING THIS. Watching Mia squirm.

'You're right, it's not your business. But, to sate your curiosity, no, I didn't. Nor did she. Sophie was conscious of the serious repercussions if she was found to be having an affair with a woman, and I... I respected her too much to risk it.'

Not to mention the fact that his libido at that time had flatlined.

He shifted in his chair as his now fully refunctioning libido made itself felt. Mia's hair was tumbling over her shoulders in wild abandon. She'd already acquired a golden glow to her skin, and freckles across her nose from the sun. The kaftan effectively covered her from neck to toe, but it was diaphanous enough to show tantalising glimpses of her perfect body.

Acting on an impulse, he found himself divulging, 'For what it's worth, I haven't ever brought a lover here.'

'Oh...'

Clearly she hadn't expected that.

Gabriela appeared then, to take the starter plates away and deliver the main course. A traditional Costa Rican beef and bean stew, light and tasty.

Daniel watched with interest as Mia tucked in. She'd never been shy about eating. He remembered staring at her the first time they'd gone for dinner, and she'd put down her fork.

'What? Is there something on my face?' she'd asked.

He'd commented dryly, 'I don't think I've ever seen a woman eat with so much relish.'

She'd blushed, and said a little tartly, 'It's a crime to waste good food.'

'I agree,' Daniel had said, beyond amused, and enthralled by her appetite and her defensiveness.

As if playing a cruel trick on him now, she looked up at him and swallowed her food before saying, 'What is it? Have I got something on my face?'

Daniel shook his head, not liking the swell of something in his chest. Something close to what he'd felt earlier when he'd played with Lexi.

Yet in spite of that unnamed emotion he found himself admitting, 'Actually, I haven't taken a lover since you.'

Mia's eyes went wide. Colour poured into her cheeks. She looked at him suspiciously. 'Did you just say—?'

He nodded, looking at her carefully. 'I haven't had a lover since you.'

She took a gulp of water.

'Have you?' he asked, suddenly feeling exposed.

He'd assumed she hadn't, because of Lexi, but maybe that had been naive. After her initial reticence Mia had been a voracious lover, and there was no reason for her not to have taken lovers in the interim.

The prospect sat like lead in his gut. But then she said, 'I…no. No, I haven't.'

A sense of satisfaction rushed through Daniel. He told himself it was satisfaction and not relief. She was avoiding his eye now. Her cheeks still flushed. Desire twisted in his gut.

Gabriela came out and took away the dinner plates, appearing oblivious to the crackling tension in the air. Mia suddenly appeared to be fidgety. She picked up the baby monitor and turned it on and off again, as if checking to make sure it was working.

Daniel said quietly, 'I haven't wanted another woman since you, Mia.'

Those huge green eyes met his. He saw her throat work. 'I… I can't say it's been the same for me.'

Daniel could see the pulse beating near the base of her throat. 'Liar.'

She sat up straight. Indignant. But no words came out. She left the baby monitor on the table and stood up and went over to the railing. Daniel followed her.

She said, 'I've moved on, Daniel. I've had a baby. I have more important priorities now.'

'You had *my* baby—which you kept a secret from me,' he pointed out. And then, 'And you might have different priorities, but you're still a desirable woman. Not just a mother. In case I haven't made myself completely clear, I still want you, Mia.'

Mia was reeling. *Daniel did want her.* She hadn't been imagining the heat between them. She hadn't been projecting her desire on to him.

As much as this made her feel somehow vindicated, it also terrified her. Because believing that Daniel didn't want her had enabled her to stay somewhat sane. Protected.

But now…if he knew how much she still wanted him… there would be nothing between them. Literally. No walls. No barriers. Nowhere to hide.

The fact that he hadn't slept with anyone since her was almost too much to try and comprehend. It stripped away her defences even more, leaving her dangerously exposed. Not helped by the all too seductive surroundings.

She turned to face him, feeling desperate, willing herself to say whatever it took to push him back. 'Look, Daniel, whatever was between us died the day our—'

He cut her off, his face taut. 'Do not say it.'

Mia swallowed her words, shocked at the stark tone in Daniel's voice. Shocked that she'd been willing to go so far as to remind them both of that awful day in the hospital.

He said now, 'I am sorry for how I reacted that day, but I can't go back and change it.'

Mia felt chastened. 'I know. I'm sorry too.' Especially now she knew why he'd reacted the way he had.

He said, 'Just because the relationship ended, it doesn't mean that our desire did. And if you're maintaining that it did then you're fooling no one but yourself.'

Still feeling desperate, she said, 'I don't want you any more.'

Daniel's eyes flashed.

Wrong thing to say.

She knew it as soon as his gaze narrowed on her mouth. 'You really expect me to believe that?'

Mia thought of the incendiary kiss that night at the ballet in Paris. Her cheeks burned, but she forced a shrug. 'Believe what you like, Daniel. I don't really care.'

He moved closer. Mia forced herself to stand firm, even though she could see the darkness of Daniel's chest under his shirt and smell his scent. Woodsy and musky and, oh, so masculine.

'Want to put it to the test, Mia?'

Mia quivered inwardly at that challenge. But she knew the only way to persuade Daniel that she didn't want him was to show him. He was a proud man. If he truly believed she didn't want him then he wouldn't push it.

She'd gone through a twenty-four-hour labour and given birth naturally—she could do this. Resist Daniel. Pretend that he didn't affect her.

She shrugged nonchalantly. 'Sure, knock yourself out.'

Mia fixed her gaze on a neutral spot just over Daniel's shoulder. But then he said, 'Close your eyes.'

Rolling her eyes a little first, Mia did as he asked, steeling herself not to react.

For a long moment Daniel did nothing. Mia cursed him. She desperately wanted to open her eyes, but didn't want to give him the satisfaction. But then the air shifted around her and she felt her hair being pulled over one shoulder.

He was behind her.

Every nerve-ending pulsed with awareness. She felt his breath feather against her skin before his fingers pulled her kaftan away slightly, and then his mouth touched the spot between her neck and her shoulder.

He knew that was a sensitive spot for her. The fact that he'd even remembered—

The low-down, dirty...

Mia sucked in a breath when she felt Daniel's tongue touch her skin. Hot. Her hands gripped the railing. She refused to let him see an ounce of the battle she was fighting.

His hands—where were his hands? So far it was only his mouth on her skin, the tip of his tongue. Then it was gone.

Mia opened her eyes. She'd done it. She'd managed to withstand him.

She turned to go—but came face to face with Daniel's chest.

He tipped up her chin. Smiled. It was wicked. 'You didn't think you'd get away so easily, did you?'

Before Mia could formulate a response, and still just holding her chin with the lightest of touches, Daniel bent his head and covered her mouth with his, leaving her nowhere to hide.

It was an open-mouthed, explicit kiss. She opened her mouth to object, but somewhere in the moment of breathing in Daniel's essence and feeling his tongue touch hers in a bold move, she forgot why she wanted to.

Being surrounded by Daniel's heat and all that steely strength was an aphrodisiac that fatally scrambled every brain cell, until all she was aware of was that it wasn't enough. She wanted more. Needed total immersion.

She twined her arms around Daniel's neck, coming up on her tiptoes. Her breasts pressed against his hard chest.

He shaped her waist, her upper back, hauling her closer. And then his hand was in her hair, fingers funneling deep, angling her head to take the kiss deeper, and his other hand found the curve of her bottom, caressing it through the thin material of the kaftan.

He pulled up her kaftan, baring her leg to the warm breeze. She felt his arousal press against her and moved instinctively against him. Like a needy little kitten. But still he didn't take his mouth off hers. His hand was on her bare bottom now, caressing. Fingers were sliding under the silk and lace of her underwear, coming close to where heat radiated out from the centre of her body.

Mia broke the kiss, pulled back. Vision blurry. She was breathing heavily. A few things sank in simultaneously—chief of which was that she'd withstood nothing. Proved nothing. Except that he was right.

Hot recrimination and something far more disturbing—sexual frustration—rose up inside her, giving her the strength to push back. Her kaftan fell down around her legs again.

Daniel was watching her with a neutral expression. She couldn't have borne it if he'd been smug.

At that moment a sound came from the baby monitor. *Lexi.* It jolted Mia back to reality.

She said to Daniel, even though she was aware that her dignity was in tatters, 'I didn't come here to be seduced by you.'

She walked back to the table on unsteady legs and picked up the baby monitor.

Daniel said from behind her, 'You can't deny this just happened and hide behind Lexi for ever.'

Mia fled.

Mia didn't sleep that night, and it had nothing to do with the heat and everything to do with that kiss, and Daniel's revelations, and the fact that he still wanted her. All together it was a powerful combination, and it left her feeling raw and gritty-eyed.

To her relief, the following morning Odile was more than happy to entertain Lexi, packing her up in the buggy and taking her for a stroll into the small town.

But then, instead of capitalising on her time off, Mia was restless. She walked down to the beach, but the surf looked too big to swim in, so she walked along the beach for a bit, and then back, trying not to consider what might happen between her and Daniel now.

If he properly set out to seduce her, as he had before, she didn't have a hope.

She saw a movement in her peripheral vision and looked to the tree line, where a path led back up to Daniel's house. Someone was waving at her. *Daniel.* Mia's heart skipped a beat. She was wearing a bikini top and shorts and felt too bare.

Daniel didn't come onto the beach. He waited till she was almost at the trees. He was wearing faded jeans and a white T-shirt, and he looked so ridiculously sexy that when he said to her, 'I need you,' she stumbled.

He reached out and caught her. And Mia thought to herself that if he kissed her right there, right now, she wouldn't be able to say no. She was almost trembling with the need rising in her body, and she knew she didn't have the strength to hide how he made her feel.

'Look, Daniel,' she said. 'What happened last night doesn't mean anything. I'm not interested in another affair—'

Daniel was shaking his head. 'I'm not talking about that.'

Now she felt foolish and exposed. But then she thought of something and went cold, her hands tightening on his arms. 'What is it? Is it Lexi?'

Daniel shook his head and tugged her further into the

trees, away from the beach. 'Lexi is fine. Odile is giving her lunch right now.'

'Oh, okay…' Mia became aware of Daniel's very hard biceps under her hands. She took them down. 'What's up?'

Had she imagined him saying he needed her? She was losing it…

'We have a problem with the shoot. With the model, specifically.'

'Oh?'

'She developed pains in her abdomen last night and she's been taken to hospital. It looks like it could be appendicitis. She's being flown to San José today to get checked out. And that,' he continued, 'means we're now minus a model for the shoot.'

'I need you.'

Mia's eyes widened. 'You can't mean me. I don't have a high enough profile for one of your campaigns.'

'You'd be perfect. Trust me.'

Mia shook her head and started walking back up the path towards the house. 'We both know I'm not a Devilliers model. I don't even know why I was cast for that first photoshoot.'

'Because I requested you.'

Shock made Mia stop and turn back to look at Daniel. Her heart thumped. 'You asked for me…specially? But you didn't even know me.'

'I saw you on a billboard. The picture where you're blowing a bubblegum bubble.'

Mia saw the image in her mind's eye. It had been an ad for a teen clothing line. Youthful and playful. Hence the bubblegum.

She shook her head. 'But that couldn't be further from the elegance and sophistication of Devilliers. What were you thinking?'

Daniel's eyes stayed hidden behind his shades. 'It was an

instinctive thing. Your image resonated with a freshness I wanted to bring into Devilliers. Something less…reverent.'

She'd been less reverent, all right. They hadn't even styled her that day, and the photos that Daniel had asked her to pose for hadn't been used in the final campaign.

But, the knowledge he'd specifically asked for her made her feel even more vulnerable now. She said, 'It wouldn't take long for you to get another model here,' she said.

Daniel shook his head. 'This shoot is off the radar. It's something I want to present to the board as a fait accompli. I'm trying to move them in a more modern direction, and they're resistant to change, to say the least.'

Daniel had spoken of this before—his desire to haul the company into the new century before it became known as just a legacy brand.

He said, 'If I have to book a new model now, the chances are they'll hear about it. They think I'm here on a personal holiday. With you and the baby.'

Mia felt silly for not realising he had an agenda. 'So it wasn't just to get us out of Paris and away from the media?'

Daniel shrugged. 'When you said you'd come, I made the best use of the situation to deflect their attention.'

Mia didn't know why she hadn't expected that. A man like Daniel was all about strategy. He took advantage of every angle.

'I…' She trailed off, realising she didn't have an excuse to say no.

'Please?' Daniel said.

Mia's mouth quirked. 'Now I *know* you're desperate.'

Daniel put a hand to his chest. 'You have such a low opinion of me.'

A delicate moment hung between them, reminiscent of the past and the very easy banter they used to have. Mia didn't have a low opinion of Daniel at all. In fact, from the moment they'd met he'd blasted through all her prejudices and confounded her expectations. He'd proved himself to be surprisingly humble for a titan of industry. He was arrogant, but never rude. More intelligent than anyone else she'd ever met. But he'd never used that intelligence to make someone—*her*—feel stupid, even if he had used to tease her for being a typical American with no appreciation for culture.

He'd hurt her, yes. Badly. But it was her fault. She'd let him in too deep. And there was no way she was going to let that happen again.

Mia folded her arms. 'I don't know if you can afford me.'

Daniel listed the fee they'd been paying the other model. Mia nearly fell backwards. This was another league.

She unfolded her arms. 'That sounds…reasonable.'

'You'll do it, then?'

Mia looked for a smirk or a hint of triumph on Daniel's face, but it was impassive. 'Okay. I don't see why not.'

In truth, Mia had never been good at relaxing. She preferred to be busy. So the thought of having something to do other than ruminate on memories or think about that kiss last night was all too welcome.

Except Daniel hadn't alluded at all to that kiss. In fact, he'd behaved as if nothing had happened. Maybe he was already regretting it and realising that pursuing Mia again wasn't worth it.

Which would be a *good* thing, she told herself now, as she followed Daniel back up to the house and tried to keep her gaze off his very taut backside.

A few hours later, Daniel was regretting his impetuous decision to ask Mia to fill in for the model. Not because she wasn't suitable for the job—the minute he'd seen her ready for the cameras he'd known that, actually, she was better than the original model—but because right now it was taking all his control and strength not to haul her away from the small crew, tear that skimpy swimsuit off her body and ease the throbbing ache that emanated from his groin to every part of his body.

Uncannily, he'd also realised at this moment that *she* had been the genesis for this very shoot—seeing her play around with the jewellery dressed in her jeans and T-shirt that first time he'd seen her had sparked something inside Daniel that was coming to fruition right here.

The whole concept was sexy decadence, which was a world apart from the refined elegance of most Devilliers campaigns, and that was why Daniel wanted to keep it top secret until he knew it would work.

The original model had certainly oozed a certain type of glamorous sexiness, but now Mia was elevating it to a level of sensuality that he knew the whole crew could feel. There was a buzz in the air that hadn't been there before.

The photographer—a woman—came up to Daniel during a change of set-up and held out her arm. She pointed to it, saying, 'Look, I've got goosebumps. Who *is* she? How come I've never seen her before? She's amazing, Daniel.'

'Yes, she is.'

He watched now as Mia stood up from where she'd been posing on her knees. An armed security guard came over and the stylist took off the jewellery Mia had been wearing for the last photos and placed it into a box he held. Another security guard watched over the rest of the jewellery on a nearby table. Together the collective value of jewels for this campaign was worth the debt of a small country.

Mia's deep-green-coloured swimsuit was a one-piece and perfectly modest; on anyone else. But not on her. The high-cut design made her legs look even longer, and the low-cut top edge drew the eye to her high, firm breasts.

Her skin glowed a darker shade of gold, thanks to a liberal application of false tan, and her hair was slicked back.

The make-up was cutting edge. Red lips dominated her flawless face. Her eyes were huge.

The whole effect was a little lurid to the naked eye, but it was showing up on camera exactly the way Daniel and the team had envisaged—a very rich, colour-saturated, high-glamour decadent feel.

This was the backdrop for the stunning jewels that Mia was modelling. Bold, simple designs featuring big gemstones set in different metals. Silver, rose-gold, gold, platinum. It was luxe and very modern, framed perfectly by the lush green forest they were shooting in.

An assistant handed a wrap to Mia, who pulled it on. She slipped on flip-flops and came over to Daniel. 'Can I borrow your phone to call Odile and check on Lexi?'

Daniel pulled his phone out of his pocket, dialled a number. 'Here.'

Mia walked away with the phone held out. It was a video call, and he heard Lexi's excited, 'Mama!' followed by some unintelligible babble.

And then he heard Mia say, 'Really? Wow!'

He couldn't help but compare Mia's obvious love and care for her daughter with his own mother's distinct lack of care—and his father's. He could never recall his mother talking to him with that loving tone of voice. It had always been cold. Or dismissive. Or irritated. And then angry, accusing...

It's your fault, Daniel...'

Mia was coming back now, holding the phone out, just as the stylist came over.

'Mia, we need to get you into the next swimsuit.'

Daniel took the phone and said, 'You're doing really well.'

She looked embarrassed. 'I'm so not prepared for this, and I'm not sure what you're looking for. I hope it's okay.'

Daniel took her by the hand and said over her head to the stylist, 'Two minutes, please?'

He led Mia over to the laptops where they were looking at the images, and the crew faded discreetly away to let Daniel show Mia what they'd done.

Eventually, she said, 'Wow, that doesn't even look like me.'

'It *is* you.' Her humility struck Daniel again. Her lack of ego.

She said, 'The jewellery isn't like anything you've done before. Is it a new line?'

Daniel nodded. 'It's a capsule collection, called Delphine. It'll test the market to see if there's an appetite for a more modern design along with the legacy and classic designs we do.'

'I like it. It feels fresh and new.'

Daniel watched as the stylist took Mia into a makeshift tent to change. *Fresh and new.* Like their relationship. Because after that incendiary kiss last night Daniel was even more determined to convince Mia that they could start afresh.

By day two of the shoot Mia was feeling a little more comfortable and confident—helped by the fact that the photographer was female, which was still not that usual on shoots like this. It reminded her that Daniel had always appreciated talent and skill over gender. A trait she'd found surprising in someone who came from a background steeped in history and legacy.

Day one had been a baptism of fire. It was a long time since she'd done a high-fashion, high-glamour shoot, and she'd got used to the world of catalogue modelling, which was all about trying to pack in as many different outfits in one day. Whereas this was much slower and more intense, but more creatively satisfying.

Now that she knew what to expect, though, it left more room for her to be aware of Daniel. Yesterday, she'd barely noticed him, she'd been so intent on not messing up. And when he'd driven her home last night she'd been so tired it had taken all her energy just to spend some time with Lexi before putting her down for the night and following her into bed.

But now all she could feel was his eyes on her, and her skin hummed with awareness even as she listened to the photographer's instructions, contorting her body into various shapes that felt anatomically ridiculous, but which she knew would look amazing in the photos.

When they broke for lunch, which was provided al fresco by a local catering company, the stylist gave Mia a wrap to cover up and she went over to put some food on a plate. Daniel was talking to one of the crew members, and Mia took the opportunity to go and sit on a fallen branch that was near the shoreline. They were shooting in a lush area of forest a little further down the coast from where Daniel's house was.

Mia was enjoying the peace, but then the back of her neck prickled, reminding her that she was still finely attuned to Daniel's proximity in a way that was seriously irritating. He came and stood beside where she sat, hands in the pockets of a pair of board shorts. In a short-sleeved polo T-shirt, he still managed to ooze a certain kind of elegance while also looking sexy enough to make Mia's insides twist with need.

'You're doing an amazing job, Mia.'

Mia shrugged, feeling self-conscious. 'Adele makes it easy to be in front of the camera.'

Daniel shook his head. 'The two of you are creating something very special.'

'Well...thank you.'

She risked another glance at Daniel. His sunglasses were on his head and he was looking at her, his mouth quirking. 'Was that hard to say?' he asked.

She scowled. She'd never been good at accepting compliments. He knew too much about her. And she'd revealed even more since she'd seen him again.

'Lexi and Odile—'

'Are fine,' he said. 'I just called them. They're having ice-cream in town.'

Mia felt a pang, missing her baby. As if hearing her thoughts Daniel said, 'They can come to the set one of these days, if you like.'

'That'd be lovely, thank you. I haven't spent much time away from her before. She's getting so independent.' Mia shot him a warning look. '*Don't* say *like mother, like daughter.*'

But Daniel looked serious. 'You're a good mother, Mia.' He shook his head, looking away. 'My mother was *not* a good role model. She was cold and angry. All the time. Unhappy with my father, mainly. She viewed us children as irritations. Once she'd done her duty by giving birth, her job was over.'

Renewed guilt lanced Mia. She hadn't been fair to him. She opened her mouth to say something, but just then Adele's assistant said from behind them, 'Mia? We're ready to go again.'

She closed her mouth and stood up. Daniel took her plate out of her hands. The stylist and hair and make-up team were approaching, to make her ready for the camera again.

When Mia started posing, she tried her best to block out what Daniel had just told her and the emotions it had aroused. But that only made her focus on his physicality, and her awareness of him was even more heightened. He stood behind where the laptops were set up, arms folded, distracting Mia with the bunched muscles of his arms. Distracting her from the thought of his cold and uncaring mother.

Much to her embarrassment, she couldn't control her

body's reaction when his eyes rested on her. It was as if a layer of skin had been stripped back, removing any armour she might have had. Her nipples peaked into hard points under the thin, stretchy material of the latest swimsuit she was wearing, and even though Adele called out for numerous minute adjustments to Mia's poses, she couldn't help her mind going to extreme places.

She remembered the feel of Daniel's hands on her body, urgent, strong. His mouth moving over her skin, leaving a trail of fire before closing over the tip of her breast, sucking the peak deep into his mouth, making her bite her lip so hard she tasted blood...

'Mia?'

Feeling dazed, Mia blinked at Adele.

The woman said, 'One more change and then I think we've got it for today. You've been a trooper.'

Mia studiously avoided Daniel's eye as she got up and stretched her limbs, diving into the cover-up kaftan and wishing she could dive into the sea, to wash away this burning ache in the pit of her belly. And another ache nearer her heart.

Damn Daniel Devilliers.

CHAPTER EIGHT

'WHERE'S MIA?' DANIEL asked one of the assistants.

They were packing up the equipment ready for the next location and the last day of the shoot, which would take place after the weekend. They would have worked through, but Adele had to fly back to New York for a previously booked job, so everyone else would have two days off in paradise.

The young man was sheepish. 'Sorry, boss, I forgot to tell you. She's gone for a swim in the sea.'

Immediately Daniel's insides tensed. He grabbed a towel, making his way to the beach. There was no sign of Mia, and he looked to the sea, which appeared unbelievably rough to him. Big waves crashed along the shore, sending up sprays of sea water.

People meandered along the shoreline, dogs at their heels. Children frolicked in the evening heat. Sunset was spreading across the horizon, bathing everything in a pink and red hue.

This really was the simple life—the *pura vida* that Costa Rica was famous for—and it was why Daniel had bought his house here on a whim. Because it had appealed to the part of him that wanted to cultivate a freer, less constricted life than the one he had had growing up. It wasn't something he'd analysed in great depth, but it had definitely been his most spontaneous purchase.

But now he wasn't thinking about any of that. He scanned the sea, growing more and more tense. No sign of her.

Just when he was starting to feel panic he saw her, waist-deep in the water, wading out. For a moment his heart stopped. He thought she was naked. But then he realised she was wearing a skin-coloured swimsuit. One of those they'd photographed her in earlier. Evidently they'd let her use it for her swim.

She came out of the water, body glistening, bringing her long hair over one shoulder and squeezing it. She looked like a goddess. Aphrodite. More than one person almost stumbled as they passed by.

Daniel forced oxygen to his brain. She was okay.

She looked up at that moment, as if she could hear his thoughts, and he saw how she tensed. She started walking towards him and he could see that she was self-conscious. It amazed him how she could be so beautiful and not take advantage of it, like every other beautiful woman he knew. But her lack of arrogance added to her allure. It was what had captivated him from the moment he'd seen her in real life.

She came closer. 'Sorry, am I holding you up?'

Daniel handed over the towel even as he lamented the fact that she would cover her body up. She took it and wound it around herself, tying it under her arms.

'No, not at all.'

She made a motion with her head towards the water. 'You should have a swim—it's glorious.' Then she frowned. 'Actually, I've never seen you use the pool at the house... don't you like swimming?'

A solid weight lodged in Daniel's gut. He knew he could say something flippant, but some force was compelling him to admit, 'I know how to swim, but I don't. Ever.'

Mia stopped. Eyes widening. 'Why not?' And then she said, almost to herself, 'You were weird that day...when you came back and saw me with Lexi in the pool... You said something about putting up a protective rail. Did something happen to you?'

Daniel regretted whatever force had compelled him to tell Mia something he'd never told anyone else in his life. But it was too late now.

'I told you my sister died…'

'Yes.'

'She drowned in the pool at our chateau.'

The pool that had subsequently been filled in and covered over.

Mia put a hand to her mouth. 'Oh, Daniel… I'm so sorry. She was only six?'

He nodded. 'We'd been playing. I ran back into the chateau to get something, and while I was gone I heard her scream, and then a splash. It seemed to take me for ever to run back to the pool…and when I got there she was floating face-down in the deep end. She'd only just started learning how to swim. She had no armbands on. I jumped in. I knew how to swim but I was panicking, and it was so deep. I tried to push her, to turn her over, but she was heavy. And then I couldn't breathe…she was on top of me… I blacked out—'

'You obviously nearly drowned too.' Mia's horrified statement cut through the painful memory.

'I suppose I did. I never saw it like that.'

'Where were your parents?'

Daniel's mouth thinned. 'Probably fighting. The gardener was the one who pulled us out…it was too late for Delphine, though.'

'Delphine… The new jewellery collection is named after her?'

Daniel nodded. How could he explain that everything he did was infused with the loss of his sister? She was one of the reasons he'd accepted his inheritance—because she'd always loved the jewels so much. At every step along the way he was aware of how old she would be now. How beautiful. Living her life. And it was *his* fault. He hadn't been able to protect her.

Mia was shaking her head. 'You blame yourself, don't you?'

Yes. But he didn't admit that to Mia. 'My mother blamed me for Delphine's death. They were pretty much the last words she said to me before she left the chateau for good. For years I thought I was the reason she'd left… But then I found out that she'd been having an affair.'

Mia looked angry. 'She was projecting her own guilt onto you.'

'Perhaps. But the fact remains that I was there. I should've been watching Delphine. I *knew* we couldn't count on our parents for care because they'd never given it.'

Mia said, 'I trained as a lifeguard as a strong, athletic teenager, and I know how difficult it is to save someone panicking or unconscious in the water. It's almost impossible unless you're strong and trained. You were nine.'

When she put it like that, Daniel could appreciate it was perhaps irrational to blame himself, but Mia's words weren't any comfort. They just rubbed along all the jagged edges he'd held deep inside him for years.

'It's in the past,' he said.

'But it's not, is it? Because it's still affecting you. You don't swim as a result.'

'I don't need to swim.'

'You might… What if—God forbid—something happened to Lexi? If I wasn't around…'

Daniel's blood ran cold at the thought of history repeating itself. 'I would never put Lexi in danger. I'm going to arrange to get a protective fence around the pool.'

'You can put up all the fences you want, but accidents will still happen, Daniel. It was a tragic accident.'

* * *

Much later that night Daniel was in his study, staring into a glass of golden liquid. Golden liquid that couldn't burn away the seam of pain that had been exposed earlier. He still couldn't believe he'd told Mia about his sister and his mother. Even though he could see that she had a right to know.

Nevertheless, he resented the ease with which she seemed able to burrow under his skin before he knew it was happening.

He'd only come to his senses the first time around when he'd seen the hurt in Mia's eyes at the speculation in the paper about his possible engagement to Sophie Valois. It had been like a bucket of cold water in his face, clearing the sensual haze in his mind.

But now that sensual haze was back.

Daniel cursed softly and tossed back the rest of his drink. If it was just about him and Mia, and the desire that had clearly not fizzled out, then Daniel would have no qualms about seducing her again and slaking his lust until whatever it was that bound him to her was well and truly burnt out. Then he could ignore those huge green eyes tempting him to spill his guts and get on with his life.

But it wasn't just about him and Mia. It was about Lexi too. And, like it or not, she called to every protective instinct he had.

He'd failed Delphine. But when he'd told Mia that today, instead of looking at him with horror, or judgement, she'd looked at him with pity. Compassion.

'It was a tragic accident.'

She didn't understand. She thought she could absolve him. But he knew nothing could. Except maybe a commitment to protect his daughter. And he would do whatever it took to—

Daniel's circling brooding thoughts came to a standstill

when he heard a noise. He looked up and his pulse tripled, blood pumping in an instantaneous reaction to the sight before him.

Mia was standing in the open doorway, dressed in a T-shirt and, as far as he could see, nothing else. Her legs were endless and bare. Her hair was tangled and wild, tumbling around her shoulders. He could see the thrust of her breasts against the material of her shirt. Full and round. He'd spent the last couple of days in agony, looking at those perfect breasts, barely contained by the thinnest of swimsuits, each sexier than the last.

She looked as shocked as he felt. Eyes wide. Those same eyes that had looked at him earlier with such—

He blinked.

He told himself he was conjuring her up, like some form of mental torture. But, no, she was still there. Not a figment of his imagination. And now he saw that she was holding a water bottle in one hand and the baby monitor in the other.

He sat up. 'Mia?'

Mia swallowed. She shouldn't have come to explore why the light was spilling out of Daniel's office.

Unable to sleep, she'd gone to the kitchen to get some water and had seen the light.

Only to find Daniel staring into the bottom of a glass as if it held all the answers, long legs stretched out before him, in jeans and a T-shirt. Bare feet.

She hadn't been able to sleep because she'd been thinking of what he'd told her about his sister earlier…

Tension crackled in the air. 'I… I couldn't sleep… I didn't mean to disturb…'

Great—now she couldn't string a sentence together.

She started to turn around. 'Sorry, I'll—'

'Wait.'

She stopped, still facing away. But she could see Daniel

reflected in the glass, behind her. He was standing. He'd put the glass down. She could see how his gaze dropped and moved over her legs, and suddenly it was hard to breathe.

'Don't go, Mia.'

Her heart was thumping so hard she felt light-headed. She watched as he came up behind her.

'Turn around.'

She knew that if she took a step, and then another, back towards her bedroom, Daniel would let her go. But the thought of *not* turning around was impossible.

She didn't know if it was the culmination of everything that had happened, or this magical place, or what he'd told her earlier, but she was no more capable of denying this pull any more than she was of stopping breathing.

She turned around.

Daniel was just inches away.

He took the water and the baby monitor out of her hands and put them down on a table.

At that moment Lexi gabbled something unintelligible, breaking the silence, and Mia froze.

Daniel asked, 'Is she awake?'

Mia waited a second and then shook her head. 'No. She talks in her sleep. It scared the life out of me the first time she did it. Now I sleep through it.'

An expression crossed Daniel's face. Something nakedly emotional. 'Delphine used to do that too.'

Mia's heart clenched. 'Daniel... I'm so—'

But he put a finger to her mouth. His eyes roved her face. His hand moved to the back of her neck, where it was hot and damp under the heavy fall of her hair.

'I want you, Mia.'

Right here, right now.

He didn't have to say it. She could feel it pulsing between them.

'I...' She hesitated for a moment. As if she had a choice.

As if she could just walk away from this man and the fact that he was the one who had truly awoken her. As if she could walk away from the need that had been building ever since she'd seen him again. The need to sate the deepest craving she'd ever felt.

He was Lexi's father.

That knowledge sent something primal through her. Possessive. Her man.

'I want you too.' Her voice was rough with need, and she realised that she was giving herself permission to do this. Pushing aside the consequences.

He tugged her closer, until they were almost touching, and then he brought his other hand up, caught her chin, angled her face towards him and covered her mouth with his.

Mia combusted on contact. The kiss turned deep in seconds, tongues twining. Mia relished Daniel's taste, sucking him deep. She groaned. Or he groaned.

His hands moved down to her T-shirt, pulling it up. She lifted her arms. They broke the kiss and Daniel pulled the garment off. Mia's breasts felt heavy under his appreciative gaze, which devoured her. He'd always made her feel so…beautiful.

He cupped one breast and rubbed a thumb back and forth over one hard nipple. Mia bit her lip.

'Si belle…' So beautiful.

It was too much. Mia could feel emotion threatening to rise.

She said, 'You… I want to see you too.'

Daniel looked at her before taking his hand off her and pulling his T-shirt off, behind his head and over. Now they were both bare from the waist up.

Mia sucked in a breath at the expanse of wide, muscled chest covered with dark hair. She put her hands on him, feeling the heat and the strength. Exploring the ridges of muscle and the flat discs of his nipples. Her nail caught on one and he sucked in a breath, took her hand.

He took her out to the deck outside the office, where there were two loungers. He said, 'Lie down.'

Mia did, before her legs could give out. She lay back and watched as Daniel's hands went to his jeans and snapped them open. Pulled down the zip. And then he yanked them down and off, kicking them aside. His underwear was despatched with equal efficiency, and Mia's eyes widened on that part of his anatomy—long, thick and hard. For her.

The fact that he hadn't slept with anyone else—and neither had she—was too much to absorb right now.

He came down on his knees and put his hands under her hips, tugging her down the lounger towards him. He pulled her underwear off and down her legs, throwing the wisp of material aside.

They were both naked, but Mia had never felt less self-conscious.

'Open your legs,' Daniel instructed.

Mia did, and heat washed up from her core when she saw how Daniel looked at her. He put his hands on her thighs and pushed them wider, and then he hooked her legs over his shoulders before coming down and placing his mouth... *right there.* At the centre of her body.

His hands were under her buttocks, holding her. She had nowhere to hide as Daniel laid her bare and feasted on her sensitive flesh, exploring her with his tongue, stabbing deep, licking, sucking. It didn't take Mia long to tip over the edge, pleasure rocketing through her body before she could try and hold it back. It had been so long, and she'd never expected that it would be this good again...

Daniel lifted his head and she saw him smirk. She didn't even have the energy to make a face. Her blood was pumping too hard and her heart was beating too loudly.

'Still so responsive.'

Daniel came up on his knees between Mia's spreadea-gled legs. He reached for something in his jeans pocket, and then she heard foil rip and watched as he pulled a pro-tective sheath over his straining erection.

Good, she thought, even as she lamented the lack of skin-on-skin sensation. They didn't need to create any more drama. Just pleasure.

He surveyed her body, laid out before him, and it didn't even bother her. It sent fresh spirals of need through her, making her desperate.

'Please, Daniel…'

Answering her plea, he came down over her body and with one smooth, cataclysmic thrust seated himself deeply inside her. To her horror, she felt tears prick her eyes—not because of the earth-shattering sensation of Daniel's big body penetrating hers, but because of the emotion it evoked.

She lifted her hips, urging him silently to move, and with a muttered curse he did. Slowly. Pulling back out, almost all the way before thrusting back in again. Over and over again. Until the emotion was driven away by pure physical sensation and their bodies were covered with a fine sheen of perspiration.

Mia couldn't take her eyes off Daniel as he caught one of her legs and pulled it up, hooking it over his waist, deepen-ing his penetration. Mia almost cried out but held it back, aware of the hushed night around them.

Daniel's movements grew less smooth, faster, harder, and Mia wrapped her other leg around his waist. The ten-sion in her body was starting to tighten and spiral as the crescendo rose between them, all the way, inexorably, until Daniel said in a rough voice, 'Let go, Mia, fly.'

But in spite of her desperation something stubborn in-side her made her shake her head. 'You first…'

Daniel's eyes went wide. She felt the tremor moving through his body as he fought for control, and then he uttered just one rough, indecipherable word as he thrust deep enough to touch her heart, and his whole body tensed as his climax ripped through it.

And that was the moment when Mia couldn't hold back any longer, with pleasure exploding at her core and crashing through her body in wave after endless wave, her intimate muscles contracting around Daniel's body until she was limp with exhaustion.

After long moments of their breath returning to normal, and with Daniel's body a heavy but delicious weight on hers, he lifted his head and said, 'You'll pay for that.'

Mia lifted a hand and touched Daniel's stubbled jaw. 'I was right behind you.'

She only noticed her hand was trembling when Daniel caught it and pressed a kiss to the middle of her palm. *Damn.* That emotion stirred again. Forcing him to lose control first hadn't made her feel any more in control herself.

Mia said, 'I should go…check Lexi…'

Daniel disengaged his body from hers and Mia winced when over-sensitive muscles protested. She couldn't quite believe what had just happened, even though she knew well that she'd been with him every step of the way.

She didn't want to think too closely about what it meant. But she was already very afraid that tasting Daniel again had sparked a renewed hunger that would be hard to satisfy.

She sat up with effort, just as Daniel reappeared with his jeans on, unbuttoned, holding out her T-shirt. She slipped it over her head, avoiding his eyes. He put out his hand and she looked up. His face was unreadable, and that comforted her somehow.

She put her hand in his and let him pull her up. He kept hold of her hand and led her back up to her bedroom suite. They stopped outside. She tried to take her hand back, but he held it until she looked at him.

'No regrets, Mia.'

She swallowed the regret already forming and pushed it back down. She'd chosen this.

She shook her head. 'No regrets.'

When Mia woke up she was disorientated, and her body felt achy but in a pleasant way. She shot up as soon as the events of last night came back to her in glorious Technicolor, a mixture of cold horror and heat rushing through her.

The sun was already high outside, and Lexi wasn't in her cot, which only compounded Mia's sense of disorientation. And then she heard it: the sound of Lexi's mostly unintelligible babble. Maybe Odile had come in and got her? Although Mia didn't think the young woman would feel that familiar yet...

Which left only one other possibility...one that Mia couldn't quite imagine.

She got up and washed her face, tried not to notice the faint stubble burn along her jaw. She threw on underwear and a pair of cut-off jeans, and a sleeveless shirt that tied at her waist.

When she arrived on the kitchen/dining level, nothing could have prepared her for the sight before her. Daniel was sitting at the table and Lexi was in a highchair. She wore a pretty floral romper suit and her hair was held back with a clip.

'Baba!' Lexi declared loudly, while banging a plastic spoon up and down on the table of the highchair.

Mia could see a spray of various foodstuffs in an almost perfect arc around the chair. They hadn't seen her yet as she was hidden by a wooden pillar.

Daniel shook his head. 'No, that's you.' He pointed to himself. *'Papa—c'est moi.'*

Lexi pursed her lips, as if she was trying very hard, and then said, 'Abba!'

Daniel shook his head again. '*Non, cherie,* that's a Swedish pop group. It's *Papa.*'

Mia felt a rush of conflicting emotions. Relief. Pride. Concern. Protectiveness. *Vulnerability.*

Still too raw after last night. She'd almost thought it might have been a lurid dream, but the aches in her body were too real—especially the ache between her legs. And she felt emotional to see the two dark heads so close together. Lexi was her father's daughter. Of that there could be no doubt.

Then Lexi spotted her. 'Mama!'

Daniel looked around. Mia's heart skipped a beat. She moved forward, trying to appear blasé. Nonchalant. As if what had happened last night and what was happening right now wasn't as earth-shattering or significant as it was.

'She'll say it when you're least expecting it. That's how she likes to roll. She takes her own time.'

Mia picked Lexi up out of the highchair, kissing her and making her giggle. She finally looked at Daniel and took in the fact that he was wearing jeans again, and a grey T-shirt that made his eyes look steely. She felt breathless when she recalled all too easily how he'd taken off his jeans with such efficiency last night...

'You should have woken me,' she said. She couldn't believe she'd slept through Daniel taking Lexi this morning.

He sat back. His jaw was clean-shaven. He looked as if he'd had twelve hours' uninterrupted sleep when she felt far too crumpled and raw.

'Actually, Odile heard Lexi chattering to herself. She asked me if she should go in and get her, so you could sleep, and I told her I'd do it.'

So Odile had noticed that Mia had been all but rendered unconscious by this man this morning. Brilliant.

'I will admit that Odile changed her nappy, so I can't claim that.'

Once again Mia felt it strange to acknowledge that she was no longer on her own with Lexi. 'That was sweet of her.'

'I told her she could take the day off because we'd be going out.'

'We are?'

Daniel nodded. 'If you like. There's a waterfall not too far from here. Gabriela is happy to make up a picnic.'

Mia felt unaccountably resistant to the idea, while at the same time knowing she was being ridiculous. If Daniel wanted to spend time with Lexi, that was a good thing. But after sleeping with him she felt as if the whole situation was morphing out of her control faster than she could try to control it.

At a total loss as to know what alternative she had, and feeling as if she was stepping off a ledge into very unknown territory, all she could do was nod and say, 'I'll change Lexi into something more suitable.'

'I insist,' Odile said. 'I've had the whole day off and I'd be more than happy to babysit Lexi. That's why I'm here, after all. And I'm going to put her cot in my room so you can get a decent night's sleep.'

Mia glared at Daniel above Odile's head. This was *his* sneaky doing. Arranging to take her out for dinner and conspiring with Odile. And she hated the betraying little frisson of anticipation that sizzled in her blood at the thought of going on a 'date'.

Where was her resolve from earlier?

Mia feared it had been fatally eroded due to spending the entire day with Daniel and watching him bond with his daughter. Not to mention the fact that she'd been in a weakened and susceptible state since last night.

She threw up her hands. 'Okay, fine. I'll get changed.'

She swore that if Daniel so much as smirked she'd

change her mind, but he seemed to have the presence of mind not to push it.

She grumbled at herself as she took a quick shower and changed into a very plain sundress that she'd found in the dressing room. Dark green, thin straps. A little scallop detail around the edges, buttons down the front. Sandals.

She put her hair up in a rough bun and didn't bother with make-up. She didn't want Daniel to think she was making an effort, as if this was a real date. But her belly flip-flopped to think of exactly where they stood now. After last night. After today.

The day had passed far too easily and pleasantly in a national park. Lexi had loved the exotic colourful birds flying over their heads, and Daniel had carried her in a papoose against his chest, making Mia feel positively, shamefully, weak-kneed.

They'd conversed easily. It had reminded her painfully of how it had been between them before. How it had always taken her by surprise that she felt so comfortable with a man like him. It had reminded her of how close she'd come to hoping for more from Daniel.

But she'd excised those feelings from her heart. No matter how much he tugged on her emotions now she would not be so foolish again. She couldn't let him continue this seduction, because she knew that, no matter what their physical connection said, emotionally Daniel was not available.

He'd never wanted a baby, or a family, and he was only making this effort now because he felt a sense of responsibility.

By the time Mia and Daniel arrived at a charming two-level restaurant in the pretty little town of Santa Teresa she was almost rigid with the effort it was taking not to respond to

Daniel—casually sexy in linen trousers and a white shirt that stretched almost indecently across his broad chest.

The same chest where he'd cradled their daughter for most of the day. An image that Mia could not get out of her head.

When he put his hand on her back to guide her into the restaurant she tensed even more, earning a frowning glance. But the maître d' approached before Daniel could say anything, fawning over them and taking them up to the top outdoor level and leading them over to a secluded table set out on a small balcony, overlooking the town and the sea beyond.

A full moon hung low in the lavender-hued sky. Candles flickered in the gentle breeze. It was simple and rustic and elegant all at once. There were small posies of local flowers in the middle of the table. Soft music played, and Mia recognised a world-famous Cuban band.

When the maître d' had left, Mia said, 'You really didn't have to go to this trouble.'

Daniel sat back. 'I like to eat, and we know you like to eat—it's no trouble.'

She would have scowled at him, but a waitress approached to give them water and tell them the specials.

When she was gone, Daniel sat forward. 'You look beautiful tonight.'

Mia looked at him suspiciously. Her dress really wasn't special. She'd made no great effort. She wondered if Daniel was making a point. She looked around and saw women in sleek tunic dresses, limbs glowing with their Costa Rican tan. Men in suits. Gold jewellery catching the light. Perfume scenting the air.

She felt churlish now. Guilty. 'I probably should have made more of an effort.'

Daniel shook his head, mouth quirking. 'You really don't know how beautiful you are.'

Now she blushed. 'You don't have to say that.'

'It's true. When the Delphine campaign is launched, your life is going to change. You'll be in serious demand.'

Mia rolled her eyes. 'I doubt that. I've never been in high demand and that's okay with me.' Before he could say anything else to seriously unsettle her, Mia said, 'This is all very nice, but you need to know that I'm not here to be seduced, Daniel. Last night was…a mistake.'

A mind-blowing mistake.

She shook her head. 'It can't happen again.'

The waitress came back with a bottle of white wine and poured it. Daniel lifted his glass and held it out. *'Salud.'*

It was as if she'd said nothing.

Mia clinked her glass on his and said, 'I mean it, Daniel.'

She'd braced herself for any number of things Daniel might say, so when he said, 'You're probably right,' she felt a shameful rush of disappointment. She hadn't expected him to agree with her.

He took a sip of wine and then looked at her. 'But if you think you're strong enough to resist what's between us then you're stronger than I am.'

Mia felt panicky. She should have known he wasn't giving in. 'But it's just…chemistry. It'll burn out.'

'It hasn't burnt out in two years.'

Mia's insides quivered. No, it hadn't. And Daniel hadn't slept with anyone else in two years. That reminder made all sorts of illicit emotions spiral inside Mia.

Their starters arrived and for once Mia was barely aware of the food—a deliciously light seafood chowder.

Somehow they managed to keep to neutral topics while eating, as if there wasn't a thick undercurrent of tension running between them, but when they'd finished eating he said, 'I only realised after you told me about your first boyfriend what a betrayal it must have been to learn of the agreement between me and Sophie Valois. No wonder it upset you.'

Mia's insides went into freefall. She hadn't expected Daniel to think of that. She shrugged minutely, as if that moment hadn't destroyed her as much as she hated to admit it had.

'It was coincidental,' she said.

'Still... I'm sorry.'

She looked at him, her precious defences wobbling. 'How were you to know?'

His mouth quirked. 'You did a very good job of not revealing anything much about yourself or your life.'

All designed to keep him out and keep herself safe. Which had not worked.

She felt defensive. 'You weren't exactly an open book either.'

'I met my match in you. I was used to women seeking to unearth as much personal detail as possible. You were... refreshingly uninterested. But then I found myself resenting your lack of interest slightly.'

They were interrupted by the waitress with coffee before Mia could fully absorb that and figure out what it might mean. She sipped the rich, dark drink, hoping that it would dispel some of the intensity she felt in these far too romantic surroundings.

When a local came over to greet Daniel, Mia welcomed the distraction, and the diversion from her urge to point out that, contrary to what Daniel had believed, she'd been far *too* interested in him. And that holding him at arm's length had been the hardest thing she'd ever done. And ultimately futile.

CHAPTER NINE

WHEN THEY ARRIVED back at the house a short time later, Mia felt ultra-aware of Daniel. In spite of her best intentions and instinct for self-preservation, she feared that today and then this evening had fatefully worn down her will to resist the temptation Daniel offered. It hummed between them…the invitation.

He turned around to face her. The house was silent. Mia felt a mixture of panic and illicit excitement.

Ridiculously nervous, she said, 'I should check on Lexi.'

'She's in Odile's room.'

'Oh, yes,' she said weakly.

Daniel wasn't fooled for a second. He moved closer and Mia refused to let him see how conflicted she felt. She knew she should walk away…but she couldn't. She felt bound to him in a way that she hadn't felt before.

He brought his hand up, trailing a knuckle lightly along her jaw, which was almost as incendiary as if he'd kissed her.

'Mia, you know I want you. But, like I said, if you're strong enough to resist this then I won't push you.'

Mia's heart thumped so loud she was sure it must be audible. She swallowed. 'Last night…today… I don't know what's happening…where we are. How to…navigate this…'

'What's happening is inevitable when the chemistry is this strong. Maybe instead of fighting it, trust that it's taking us in the right direction. As a family. We're a family now, Mia, no matter what.'

It was that word that seemed to dissolve the last of the barriers that Mia had been so intent on throwing up. The chatter in her head stopped. She wanted Daniel. She'd never stopped wanting him. She'd used to look at men and wonder why they left her cold. Would any other man ever turn her on again?

The answer was standing right in front of her, and suddenly it seemed so simple.

'Trust that it's taking us in the right direction.'

All Mia knew right now was that there was only one direction she could go.

Towards the fire.

She stepped forward and reached up, wrapping her arms around Daniel's neck. Eyes fixed on his mouth. Firm and sensual. Anticipation mounted.

'Take me to bed, Daniel.'

He bent down slightly and suddenly Mia was being lifted into his arms. He carried her through the stunning house perched on a hill between the sea and the tropical forest and laid her down on his bed as if she was made of china.

He stripped himself bare and then, oh, so slowly, undid the buttons on her dress, one by one, kissing each piece of flesh as it was revealed, lavishing long moments on her breasts, until Mia was begging and writhing and panting.

Only then did he remove the rest of her clothes and, after donning protection, join his body to hers with such a powerful thrust that she was helpless against the spontaneous waves of pleasure that exploded from her core, wrenching any sense of control out of her grasp, making a mockery of her attempt to feel as if she'd been the one in control last night.

When Mia woke up, the first thing she noticed was the lingering sense of Daniel's arms around her, even though she knew she was alone in his bed. She stretched luxuriously, her limbs deliciously heavy and a sense of deep satisfaction flowing through her blood.

She couldn't even begin to analyse what had happened last night; she just knew that on some level she'd trusted Daniel enough to capitulate.

Trust. She'd thought she'd never trust anyone ever again after her first boyfriend. But she did trust Daniel. With Lexi, at least. His growing bond with her was genuine. Mia was sure of it.

As for herself, physically what they had was more than tangible. It was explosive. Last night had proved that. But emotionally... Mia knew she'd be very naive if she thought for a second that sharing confidences meant that things had changed.

She heard Lexi's babble and got up, not wanting to think too much about what Daniel had meant by moving forward as a family. She blushed when she picked up her dress and pulled it on, recalling Daniel undoing each button so slowly.

'Morning.'

She looked up from doing up enough buttons to be decent to go back to her room and take a shower. No underwear underneath. Daniel was wearing shorts and a T-shirt, no shoes, and he looked rested and...smug. Too smug for Mia's liking.

Her hair felt like a rat's nest, tumbled around her shoulders. She must look a sight. She'd been so weak...

As if reading her mind, he said, 'Don't be hard on yourself. I'm quite irresistible, you know.' He handed her a cup of coffee and Mia's heart lurched at this side of him she hadn't seen since they'd been lovers the first time. Flirtatious. Playful. Funny.

She took the coffee and resisted the urge to throw it over his head.

He said, 'I've told Odile to take the rest of the day off. Lexi has had breakfast and I'm going to take her down to the beach. Join us when you're ready.'

Once again, the ease with which Daniel was becoming a

part of their lives was disorientating. Feeling prickly and exposed, Mia said, 'Make sure she's got sunscreen on, and a hat.'

Daniel's smugness increased. 'Of course. And Odile has packed a bag with essentials.'

He disappeared, and Mia stood staring stupidly at the empty space he'd left behind for a long moment before she finally moved.

A little later, feeling somewhat refreshed after a shower and some breakfast, and dressed in cut-off jeans and a T-shirt, Mia made her way down to the beach. She spotted Daniel and Lexi and walked towards them. They were building a sandcastle and there were various items strewn around them. Toys, buckets, shovels.

Daniel looked up, shades covering his eyes. He should have looked ridiculous, cavorting with a toddler, but he didn't. Damn him.

Lexi stood up and came and grabbed Mia's hand. 'Mama, play.'

Mia dutifully let her daughter drag her down to the sand. Lexi handed her a bucket and said something incomprehensible.

Daniel said, 'I find it's best to pretend you know what she's saying.'

Mia's heart clenched at this further evidence of Daniel and Lexi bonding, even as every self-preserving instinct she had urged her to grab her daughter and run, far away. Which obviously was not an option.

Growing tired of bossing them around, Lexi wandered off a little way to fill her bucket with sand.

Daniel caught Mia's arm when she moved to follow. 'Wait a second. I want to say something.'

Mia looked at him warily. 'What?'

He pushed his shades onto his head. 'I know I mentioned marriage before—'

Mia stood up in one fluid motion, panic galvanising her movements. He was too close. Things were moving too fast for her to be able to assimilate how she felt. 'No way. I'm not talking about this again.'

Daniel stood up too. 'Just hear me out. You don't have to say anything now.'

Mia folded her arms, but she didn't walk away and she didn't say anything else.

'When I mentioned it before it was a reflex. I admit that. I saw it as a solution to a problem. But now…now I really mean it, Mia. I want us to marry and be a family. Because we *are* a family, whether you like to admit it or not. I don't want Lexi growing up on the other side of the city, only to see her once a week or less. I want her to be with me every day.'

A ridiculous dart of envy made Mia say tartly, 'And me? Do I fit into this neat equation?'

Daniel took a step towards Mia and snaked a hand around the back of her neck. His gaze roved over her face and she saw the lick of heat in his eyes. An answering heat bloomed in her belly.

'Of course you do. I want you, Mia. You know that. I haven't stopped wanting you, and the more I have of you, the more I want. We have amazing chemistry. We like each other. We respect each other. And we have Lexi.'

But I don't love you. That was what he omitted to mention.

'You never wanted this, remember?' Mia couldn't quite keep the bitterness out of her voice.

'I know. But that was before Lexi existed. I don't regret Lexi, Mia—not for a second. Neither of us had the family experience we wanted. She deserves more.'

Damn him. She'd told him too much.

They stared at each other for a long moment. And then, from a few feet away, came, 'Papa!'

Mia saw the shock on Daniel's face. He dropped his hand and looked at Lexi. 'What did you say, *mignonne*?'

He went over and bent down. She said, very clearly, 'Papa make castle.'

Papa. Mia put a hand to her mouth, emotion rising before she could stop it. Tears pricked her eyes. Daniel looked up at her and she couldn't hide the emotion.

He said, 'I'm just asking you to think about it, okay?'

Mia swallowed the lump in her throat. She owed him that much at least. She nodded.

That night Mia lay wide awake in bed, Lexi was on her back, legs and arms akimbo, in the cot nearby. She'd come to bed early, using Lexi as a pretext, afraid that Daniel would look at her and scramble her brain cells again—or, worse, touch her and make her agree to something she really wasn't sure she was ready for.

Marriage.

She'd always thought she was against the idea after her upbringing, until her first boyfriend had exposed her weakness for the dream. She'd learnt a harsh lesson. And then, with Daniel, she might not have dreamt of marriage, but she'd certainly come close to letting her defences down, to trusting him.

And she'd been humiliated again with the news of his arranged marriage. Reminded of her unpalatability. The fact that Daniel had acknowledged that last night only made her feel more vulnerable now.

And yet Mia knew that hundreds of thousands of marriages started with a lot less and lasted for a long time. Chemistry, respect…a child. Those were all solid foundations on which to build a lasting partnership. She'd convinced herself she would be happy with such a union, built on respect and mutual trust.

But she knew she wanted more. She wanted Daniel to

love her as she still loved him. It was pointless trying to keep denying how she felt. She'd fallen for him two years ago and she hadn't stopped loving him, no matter what she might have told herself. Now she was fathoms deep, with no hope of escape. And the fact that he was growing to love Lexi and building such a good relationship with her only made her love him more.

Mia turned over and thumped the pillow, trying to plump it up. What it really came down to was this: was she selfless enough to sacrifice her own happiness for her daughter's?

In her heart of hearts, she knew there was only one answer to that.

The following day was the last day of the ad campaign shoot. They were down at the edge of the sea this time. So far Daniel had kept his distance from Mia, which she'd been simultaneously grateful for and irritated by.

Odile had brought Lexi to visit the set today, and Daniel was behind the table of laptops, monitoring proceedings with Lexi in his arms.

Everyone had *oohed* and *aahed* over Lexi—who had, of course, lapped up the attention.

It was seriously distracting. But Mia focused as best she could and eventually the assistant called out, 'That's a wrap on Delphine, everyone! Great job!'

Mia felt wrung out, but also exhilarated, if she was honest. She'd never worked with this calibre of crew and it had been a whole new experience, demanding things of her she hadn't been sure she could deliver. But she had.

Adele came over and hugged her impulsively. 'You were fantastic, Mia. Seriously, you need to prepare yourself for global attention once people see these pictures.'

Mia hugged her back. 'Well, I hope so, for your sake, but I really don't mind.'

Adele slid an expressive glance to where Daniel was handing Lexi back to Odile. She said with a wry smile, 'I guess I can't blame you. You have a beautiful family, Mia. I wish you all the luck in the world.'

Family. It would be up to her if they were actually to become a family.

Trying to block out the sense of impending pressure, Mia went with the stylist to the tent, to change out of the last outfit and back into her jeans and a shirt. She wiped off as much of the make-up as she could.

When she emerged nearly everyone was gone. She saw Odile walking back up the beach with Lexi, towards the house. Daniel was standing looking out to sea. A safe distance from the incoming tide. That detail made Mia's silly heart clench.

She knew this was it. He'd be expecting an answer.

She went and stood beside him, her body humming with awareness just to be near him.

He said, without looking at her, 'We'll fly to New York tomorrow for a couple of days, before returning to Paris.'

Mia barely heard him. Her answer was rising up inside her, and she was afraid if she didn't get it out she might change her mind.

'Okay,' she blurted out.

Daniel turned to look at her. 'Okay...to New York?'

Mia looked at him. 'No, I mean, yes...whatever. I mean, okay, I'll marry you.'

He went still. 'Are you sure?'

No!

But she nodded. 'Yes, it's the best thing...for Lexi.'

'What about you?'

'Like you said, we have chemistry, respect...'

'Is that enough for you?'

No.

Mia searched Daniel's expression to see if she could see

even a smidgeon of something…but he just looked genuinely concerned. Which was even worse.

Without answering him directly, she said, 'You're right. I want more for Lexi too, and she deserves two loving parents, together.'

But just not in love with each other, hissed a little voice. She pushed down her misgivings.

Daniel closed the distance between them and cupped her face in his hands, tipping it up to his. He smiled, and for a moment Mia could almost pretend that maybe—

'You won't regret this, Mia. I'll do my best to make you and Lexi happy. I promise.'

He covered her mouth with his and Mia stretched up, wrapping her arms around his neck, bringing her body as close to his as possible. The familiar fire raced along her veins, heating her blood. She could feel his body responding to hers and she felt that if she could just have this effect on him…and if he could just never stop kissing her, making love to her…then maybe she could pretend that it would be enough to sustain her.

'You want us to get married in New York?'

Mia's voice was a hissed whisper across the aisle of the private plane that was taking them from San José to New York.

Daniel didn't like the look of sheer panic mixed with horror on her face. He shrugged. 'Why not?'

Her mouth opened and closed a few times.

She looked…amazing. She was wearing a light green silk shirt dress. Casual but sexy. Her skin was even more golden after their time in Costa Rica, and more freckles were liberally dotted across her nose. Her hair, too, had turned lighter, and she'd plaited it today. It hung over one shoulder, enticing Daniel to wrap his hand around it and pull her over to him so he could take that look off her face by kissing her.

He needed her.

She'd been packing last night, and by the time he'd wrapped up his own work she'd been in bed, with Lexi asleep too. He dragged his gaze back to her face. She was still looking stunned.

Finally she said, 'I thought we might have a period of engagement. To get used to the idea.'

Something curdled in Daniel's gut at that suggestion. The need to make Mia his wife ASAP was a compulsion he didn't want to analyse too deeply.

He reached across and took her hand. 'I want us to be a family, Mia. Why wait?'

Her eyes were huge. She bit her lip. 'Can it even happen that quickly?'

Daniel nodded. 'Once we obtain a licence, we can marry in twenty-four hours.'

She glanced behind, to where Odile was occupying Lexi with a game, the little girl chattering happily. Daniel saw Mia's expression soften and felt a spike of jealousy—at his own daughter! But then Mia looked back, and Daniel knew he didn't want that softness to go out of her expression.

He said, 'I want everyone to know you're my wife and that we're a family.'

Mia looked a little pale. 'I guess there's no reason why we should wait. Things aren't going to change, are they?'

There was a quality to her voice he couldn't quite decipher, but the rush of triumph drowned out the need to analyse it.

He took her hand and pressed a kiss to the palm, her scent filling his nostrils and heating his blood. 'I'll let my office know to obtain the licence.'

At that moment Lexi's voice rang out. 'Mama!'

Mia took her hand from his and made her way to their daughter.

It was the strangest sensation, but even though Mia had just agreed to marry him within the next few days, and Daniel had exactly what he wanted, he felt inexplicably as if something was slipping out of his grasp.

Later that afternoon, after they'd arrived at JFK and then taken a helicopter ride into Manhattan, during which Lexi had stayed wide-eyed and silent, they'd landed on a tall building which turned out to be owned by Daniel. It housed the North American offices of Devilliers, plus his private apartment and a shop on the ground level.

They were greeted by staff and taken down to the apartment—a vast, elegant, luxurious space with a terrace overlooking Fifth Avenue and the greenery of Central Park visible just a few blocks away.

Mia was looking around the fully stocked nursery which was across the hall from the master bedroom suite. She felt Daniel's presence behind her, and all the little hairs on her body stood up.

She didn't turn around, afraid he'd see something of the emotion she'd been feeling since earlier, when he'd told her he wanted to marry her as soon as possible.

'You really didn't have to kit out an entire closet full of clothes,' she said. 'She'll have outgrown most of them within a couple of weeks, she's growing so fast.'

'I'll ensure anything that isn't used is donated to charity.'

'That'd be good.'

'Mia.'

She turned around, careful to shield her expression. She felt too raw at that moment, as the enormity of their impending nuptials sank in.

Daniel was leaning against the doorframe, impossibly tall and broad. He said, 'My staff have obtained the marriage licence, and someone will come up with the paperwork you need to fill out shortly. They'll also have a pre-nuptial agreement for you to look at. All going well, we'll be getting married tomorrow afternoon.'

So it really was happening.

Mia's heart-rate sped up. This time tomorrow she would be Mrs Devilliers. Lexi would have two parents who loved her. She would be part of a family.

In spite of everything, Mia felt a tiny flame of hope flicker to life. Maybe by *becoming* a family they could truly be one. Daniel could grow to love her.

And then Daniel said, 'But first I need to give you something.'

Mia frowned. 'Wha…?'

Her voice faded when she saw Daniel take a box out of his pocket—a small velvet box—and she tensed. He opened the box and she sucked in a breath. It was a circular cut emerald ring, with two small diamonds on either side, in a platinum setting. It was simple and…perfect.

Daniel said carefully, 'This isn't like what happened to you before, Mia. This is the real deal. I would be proud and honoured for you to become my wife.'

She hated the emotion that clutched at her chest.

As if he'd been waiting for her tacit permission, he took the ring out of the box and picked up Mia's hand, sliding the ring onto her finger. It fitted.

Mia *knew* this marriage was really little more than a marriage of convenience, and yet right now it was hard not to hope that perhaps it could become something else.

She looked up at Daniel, but his expression was unreadable. Very quickly she doused the rogue emotions. She was losing it. She had to keep it together.

'Is it okay?' he asked.

Mia pulled her hand back. 'Yes, it's lovely.'

'You won't mind wearing it?'

Mia felt exposed again. 'I'm sure I'll get used to it.'

Daniel took a step back. He became brisk. 'I've arranged for a stylist and a hair and make-up team to come to the apartment. The stylist will bring a range of choices for you to choose a wedding outfit from. They'll also have clothes for Odile, who will be our witness, and Lexi. I have to go down to the offices, and I'll probably be working late, so you guys go ahead and eat dinner.'

Mia's head was spinning with all the information by the time he walked away. She found Odile feeding Lexi a late lunch in the kitchen. The young woman was beaming.

'I can't believe you're getting married tomorrow,' she said. 'It's so romantic.'

Mia smiled weakly. It couldn't be less romantic. 'You don't mind being a witness?'

Odile's eyes looked suspiciously shiny. 'I'd be honoured. You and Daniel and Lexi…you guys are amazing, and I've already seen so much of the world because of you.'

Mia gave her a quick, impulsive hug. She'd become very fond of the girl, and was glad of a grounding force when everything suddenly seemed to be spinning out of her control.

Within hours the apartment had become a hive of activity, with assistants from Daniel's office bringing paperwork to sign, and then the stylist and her team coming to help Mia prepare for the following day.

Mia signed the pre-nuptial agreement, which to her eyes would be ridiculously generous if she should ever divorce Daniel. The outlined custody arrangements in case of a divorce were also fair, and skewed in Mia's favour. She really had nothing to complain about.

By the time she and Odile and Lexi had eaten that evening she was wrung out, and more than happy to crawl into bed not long after Lexi had gone down to sleep.

It was only when she woke a few hours later, instantly aware that Daniel was in the bed beside her, that she realised that of course the master suite was his room too. And, as his fiancée, of course she'd be sharing his room.

She didn't open her eyes and she held her breath, even so her body came alive, knowing Daniel was just inches away. But, as much as she was tempted to drown out all her concerns and doubts and fears by losing herself in the physical, she felt it was important in that moment to hold back. As if by not giving in to Daniel's silent but potent pull, she could exert some last vestige of control.

Somehow—miraculously—she managed to fall asleep, and she didn't wake when Daniel curled his body around hers and wrapped an arm around her waist, holding her to him.

When Mia woke the next morning she almost wondered if she'd dreamt that Daniel had been in the bed beside her last night. There was no sign of him now.

She heard Lexi babbling in her room and got up to tend to her, seeing a note on the pillow beside hers.

She picked it up.

Morning. I didn't want to wake you.

Mia's heart thumped. So she hadn't imagined him beside her.

The note went on.

*I have to do some work at the office, but I'll be back at one p.m. to take you to the venue for the wedding.
D*

Mia sighed. Not even an X. Her flicker of hope yesterday mocked her.

She got up and went to Lexi, her heart swelling at the sight of her beautiful baby girl. Picking her up and hugging her close, she told herself she was doing the right thing. Lexi would grow up secure and loved. By two parents. She would make this work.

A few hours later, Mia surveyed herself critically in the mirror. She'd chosen a very simple white Stella McCartney wide-legged trouser-suit, with a sheer lace body underneath. She'd matched it with white high heels, the pointy toes just peeping out from under the trousers. The only jewellery she wore was her engagement ring.

Her hair had been washed and blow-dried into big loose waves. Her make-up was minimal. She wanted to feel like herself as much as possible, and at all costs avoid anything floaty and romantic. This wedding was not about romance.

A hush went around the dressing room, where she'd been getting ready, and she looked up to see Daniel standing in the doorway in a steel grey three-piece suit. Jaw cleanshaven. He looked breathtakingly handsome.

And in his arms was Lexi, who was wearing a white dress, with a flower clip in her hair.

She put out her arms towards Mia. 'Mama…'

Mia could see that she was feeling a little overwhelmed with all the activity and cuddled her close. Lexi put her finger in her mouth.

Everyone who had been getting her ready melted away discreetly.

Daniel said, 'You look…stunning, Mia.'

She felt shy. 'Thank you, so do you.'

Odile appeared behind Daniel. She looked very pretty in a deep red maxi dress, her hair up. 'The car is downstairs when you're ready to go.'

Mia's heart pumped.

Daniel led the way to the elevator and down. The lobby of the building was empty except for some security men and the concierge, who said, 'Best wishes, Mr Devilliers and Miss Forde!'

Mia smiled. Lexi waved, perking up again.

Then they were in the car and heading to a hotel, where a room had been booked for them to have a private ceremony.

Once inside the beautiful Art Deco hotel—one of Manhattan's most exclusive—they were whisked up to a private suite by the manager. Apart from Odile there was a staff member from Daniel's office, acting as the other witness, and a handful of guests, some of whom she recognised as his legal team.

The ceremonial part of it was a bit of a blur to Mia, who still couldn't quite believe that it was happening. Daniel slid a plain gold band on the finger where her engagement ring had been—she'd put it on her other hand for the ceremony—and Odile handed her a slightly thicker ring for him, which she slid onto his finger, feeling something very possessive wash over her. Primal.

When Daniel kissed her at the invitation of the officiant Mia found herself tensing, aware of everyone watching them. She felt like a fraud and pulled back. Daniel frowned slightly, but then just took her hand and led her out of the room to the sound of everyone clapping.

'Do you mind that we didn't have a bigger reception?'

Mia looked at Daniel where he stood on the apartment terrace beside her. They were both holding champagne glasses. They'd returned a short while before and the staff had met them with a little fanfare and champagne. It had seemed churlish to refuse.

Daniel had taken off his jacket and his tie was gone, top shirt button open. She'd taken off her jacket too. And her shoes. Odile had just taken a very overtired Lexi off for a bath and then bed.

Mia shook her head. 'No, it was perfect. It's not as if it was a real wedding.'

'It *was* a real wedding. You're officially Mrs Devilliers now.'

A flutter came from deep inside Mia's belly. She stamped it out. 'You know what I mean. Anyway,' she said, 'I'm not really one for big glittering functions.'

Daniel leaned on the terrace wall and surveyed her. 'I hate to break it to you, but there'll be a few for you to go to as my wife.'

Mia immediately felt daunted, but forced a smile. 'I'm sure I'll cope.'

'I have no doubt you will. You're formidable, Mia.'

She shook her head, hating how his words made her feel, made that hope flicker. 'I'm really not—and you don't have to say those things. It's not as if you need to woo me, Daniel. We're married now.'

An expression crossed his face, but it was too fast for her to decipher. He said, 'Yes, we are married.'

Daniel moved closer and took Mia's champagne glass out of her hand, putting it down with his on a nearby table. He drew Mia into his arms and the thin material of her lace body and the silk trousers was no barrier to the heat and steely strength of Daniel's body, not to mention his arousal.

Instant heat flooded Mia, and unlike the previous night, when she'd felt the need to keep a bit of herself back, right now she desperately craved the exquisite oblivion Daniel could offer her. She needed to be reminded of what was binding them together apart from Lexi.

She stretched up, winding her arms around Daniel's neck. When he lowered his head, though, to cover her mouth with his, she moved instinctively, pressing a kiss to his hard jaw, avoiding that intimacy without really understanding why, knowing only that it was necessary in that moment.

'Take me to bed, Daniel.'

'Your wish, Mrs Devilliers, is my command.'

CHAPTER TEN

WHEN MIA WOKE in the morning she could hear the faint hum of Manhattan traffic far below. She'd always loved New York—it had been the first place she'd come to start her modelling career and she'd never forget that first view of Manhattan, coming across the bridge from the airport.

And now here she was, in one of those tall buildings. Married. A mother.

She lifted her hand and looked at the rings, nestled side by side. She hated to admit it, but she liked them. Liked the feeling that they marked her as Daniel's wife.

She sat up in bed, holding a sheet up to her chest, and winced when she saw the torn lace of the body she'd worn under her wedding suit. Unable to find the opening, Daniel had ripped it, making Mia gasp, but then he'd put his mouth to the heated flesh between her legs, hands cupping her buttocks, making her squirm and writhe under his wicked mouth, torn clothes forgotten.

There had been something almost desperate between them…insatiable…as Daniel had taken her over and over again. They had only fallen asleep as the dawn had risen outside.

The apartment felt silent and empty. Mia got up and had a quick shower, and dressed in a pair of casual trousers and a matching long-sleeved rust-coloured top, pulling her hair back into a loose ponytail.

The housekeeper, a genial older man, was in the kitchen. 'Good afternoon, Mrs Devilliers.'

Mia gasped and checked the time. It was after midday.

She blushed profusely. 'I'm so sorry. I had no idea it was so late.'

'Don't be silly—you just got married. Can I fix you some brunch?'

'Um…where is everyone?'

'Odile has taken Lexi to the park, I believe, and Mr Devilliers is down in his office. He said you weren't to be disturbed.'

It was a long time since anyone had cared for her welfare. It was a strange feeling. Seductive.

'I'd love something small-—maybe just an egg and toast? If that's not too much trouble?'

The housekeeper gave Mia a slightly funny look, before smiling and saying, 'That's no problem at all. And, please, call me Tom.'

'Thank you, Tom.'

After she'd eaten an exquisite brunch of scrambled eggs and smoked salmon, on delicate pieces of toast, Mia debated calling Odile and catching up with them, or going down to see Daniel.

She found herself acting on impulse, taking the elevator down to the main offices. She would find Odile and Lexi afterwards.

At the main reception area everyone was very friendly, and they showed her to where Daniel's corner office was. An older lady in the anteroom stood up and introduced herself as Martha. She said, *sotto voce*, 'He's on a call but I'm sure he'll be pleased to see you if you want to go in and wait. Congratulations on your marriage, by the way.'

'Thank you.'

Mia pushed at the heavy door, which was ajar, and went in, thick carpet muffling her footsteps. The first thing she noticed was the astounding views of Manhattan on both sides.

Daniel had his back to her. He was standing at the window and had his phone up to his ear and his other hand in his pocket. His back was broad under a white shirt, and her eye travelled down to those slim hips and taut buttocks.

And then he spoke, his voice low but distinct in the silence. 'Yes, we're married. It's the perfect solution. It takes the heat out of any potential news story and it'll defuse any interest in my daughter. We're a family unit now.'

The person on the other end was obviously speaking, and as what Daniel had said sank in, and Mia interpreted the businesslike tone of his voice, a cold chill crept through her.

Daniel sounded exasperated. 'Look, Nikki, it's done. She's the mother of my child, and if we hadn't married I couldn't have guaranteed that this wouldn't have ended up in the courts. She's no pushover and money doesn't sway her. This *is* the best solution to a potential PR nightmare. Returning to France unwed, with a child in tow, would have left us wide open to scrutiny and completely overshadowed the launch of Delphine, which is going to be challenging as it is—'

He suddenly stopped talking and turned around.

Mia wasn't sure why she was feeling so winded all of a sudden. Daniel hadn't said one thing she didn't already know. But to hear him lay it out like that, so cold and stark, had sliced right into her heart.

Daniel terminated the call and looked at her. 'Mia—'

She cut him off. 'That's why you brought us to Costa Rica, isn't it? Because you wanted to use that time to seduce me again and persuade me to go along with your plans.'

Daniel was nothing if not honest. 'Getting you away from the press *was* a concern. But I knew that I wanted us to be a family, yes. And I knew I wanted you. As for the marriage... I hoped that you'd agree. Because I do feel that this is the best outcome for all of us.'

She'd fallen into his plans within the week, like a ripe peach. She realised that even up to this moment she'd been harbouring a tiny illicit flame of hope for *more*. But what she'd just heard had killed that flame for good.

She forced breath into her lungs, dazed—and annoyed with herself for feeling blindsided. She couldn't even say that Daniel had manipulated her. She'd wanted him too. And she had agreed to the marriage of her own volition, for all the right reasons.

'Mia—'

She put up a hand, not wanting him to hammer home the message. It was loud and clear. Her emerald ring sparkled in her peripheral vision, mocking her. This one might be real, but it meant no more than the cubic zirconia necklace had.

'It's fine. I'm sorry I disturbed you. I just… I was actually on my way out to catch up with Odile and Lexi. They've gone for a walk.'

'I know. Security are with them.'

Mia turned around, but Daniel said, 'Wait.'

She turned around reluctantly. She just wanted to go— get away from that far too incisive grey gaze.

'Are you sure you're okay?'

She pinned a smile on her face. 'Absolutely fine. Will we see you later for dinner?'

'Actually, we're going to take an overnight flight back to Paris tonight, so you should probably prepare for that.'

'We'll be ready.'

Mia left the office and avoided catching anyone's eye. It was only when she was out on the street that she let her mask fall and put sunglasses over her eyes to hide the sting of tears, hating herself for the weakness.

Paris was grey under leaden skies when they returned from New York early the following morning. Odile had gone home, and Mia and Lexi were in bed, sleeping off the flight. Daniel was restless, and had come down to his office above the *salon*. But he was alone. It was too early for any staff to have arrived yet.

He wasn't remotely superstitious, but the slate-dark skies felt like some kind of omen and he scowled at himself.

He didn't like how the image of Mia standing in his Manhattan office the previous morning kept coming back into his head. Her face had been pale, with the same stricken expression he'd only seen twice before. When she'd seen the leak in the newspaper about his proposed engagement to Sophie Valois, and when she'd come to tell him she was pregnant.

He recalled the conversation she'd overheard, his conscience pricking again.

He'd felt under pressure. His chief PR advisor had been freaking out at the news that Daniel and Mia were married, without any prior warning. Daniel had felt exposed. He knew marrying Mia in haste had been an impulse to make her his as soon as possible, out of a primal need that didn't have much to do with logic. And it was as if his PR advisor had intuited that.

But he'd reassured himself that everything he'd said to Nikki had made total sense. And it was everything Mia had agreed to. To make a marriage based on respect and mutual chemistry for the sake of their daughter.

Marrying Mia and ensuring Lexi's security and future was the right thing to do. He couldn't offer Mia empty platitudes and promises, much as he knew it might make things more palatable for her. But they were his family now, and he was going to do everything in his power to ensure that the toxicity of his past did not infect the future. He would do things differently from his parents, and already he and Mia had a foundation stronger than anything he'd ever seen between them.

It was enough. It would have to be.

So why was he feeling guilty?

That sensation of something precious slipping out of his grasp was haunting him again, mocking him. He pushed it down deep and told himself he was being ridiculous.

'I feel like you're avoiding me.'

Mia looked at Daniel across the dinner table at the end of the first week since they'd returned to Paris. 'What gives you that impression?'

Daniel arched a brow. 'The fact that this is the first meal we've shared since we got back to Paris, and the fact that you're not sleeping in my bed.'

A pang of sexual need gripped Mia. In spite of the deep vulnerability she felt around Daniel now, she couldn't dent the aching need at her core. Every night she had lurid X-rated dreams and woke up aching and frustrated in the morning.

'Lexi has been unsettled at night since we returned. I don't want to disturb you.'

'Where is Odile? I offered her a full-time job.'

'I told her she didn't need to start straight away.'

'The launch of the Delphine line of jewellery is next week. We'll have press junkets and the launch party to attend.'

An assistant of Daniel's had informed her of the schedule, and it alternately terrified her and excited her.

She looked at Daniel now. 'I've never been involved with anything this high-profile before.'

'I'll be right by your side.'

That thought should have comforted Mia, and it would have at any other time. But every minute she spent in close proximity to Daniel now left her terrified that she'd reveal her feelings, or he'd see something. And if he knew how she felt she wouldn't be able to continue pretending she was okay with a marriage in name only.

That was why she'd been avoiding him. Because she

didn't know if she could truly do this. And she felt like a failure because she should be stronger for her daughter's sake.

People lived through marriages of convenience all the time—what was so special about her that she thought she deserved more? But Mia knew that she did. And so did Lexi. Living with Daniel and knowing that his feelings only ran to *like* and *respect* would wear away at her soul until she was a husk.

And that couldn't be good for Lexi.

Hearing Daniel during that phone call had brought home just how clinical he was about this marriage. And yet when he touched her he made her think that there was a chance of *more*.

But that was just sex.

That was why she couldn't let him touch her again.

And yet even as she thought that her body ached. The thought of not making love to Daniel ever again... That was obviously not something he would tolerate. Did she really want to drive him into the arms of a lover? The mere notion of that made Mia feel violent.

Daniel's gaze was narrowed on her face. 'Want to share your thoughts? You look like you want to commit murder.'

Desperation mounted inside Mia. Something had to give or she'd lose it completely. Clearly avoiding Daniel and depriving them both of release was not working, and it would only invite scrutiny and, yes, possibly murder.

Could she do this and hide her feelings, not confuse passion for emotion? She had to. Or she might as well get up and leave now.

Baldly, before she lost her nerve or changed her mind, she said, 'I want you.'

His eyes flared at that. 'Right here? Now?'

She blushed. She felt gauche, like the first time she'd gone out with him. But he took pity on her, standing up and taking her hand, pulling her up from the chair and leading her out of the dining room and down to the bedrooms.

After Mia had checked on Lexi quickly, just across the hall, she stepped into Daniel's bedroom. His shirt was already off and the top button of his trousers was undone. He closed the door behind her and caged her in with his arms, hands either side of her head.

'Now, where do we start to make up for lost time? This week has felt like a month, Mia.'

She reached up, pressing kisses to his jaw, her hands exploring his chest, revelling in the feel of taut muscle under hot silky skin. She pressed kisses there, trailing her mouth down, her hand finding the zip of his trousers and pulling at it, then urging his trousers off his hips along with his underwear, until they fell to the floor.

He stepped out of them, kicked them aside. Still wearing all her own clothes—a pair of trousers and a silk top—Mia dropped to her knees and heard Daniel suck in a breath. *This* she could handle, she thought, as she wrapped her hand around Daniel's erection, which was straining towards her.

She took him into her mouth and his hands went into her hair. 'Mia…you don't have to…' But then his breath hissed out. *'Dieu, tu me tué.' You're killing me.*

Mia was ruthless, wringing every ounce of pleasure out of Daniel, and when she was done he lifted her up and stripped her bare, eyes feverish with pleasure and fresh desire. Like this, there was no time or room for words or tenderness. And that was how Mia would get through this and stay sane.

A few days later Daniel woke at dawn, as he habitually did, his body naked and feeling so heavily pleasured that he wasn't sure if he would be able to move. Every night he and Mia made love and fell asleep in an exhausted tangle of limbs. But when he woke she was gone.

Sometimes, like this morning, when the rush of last night's images came back into his head, he wondered if he was losing it. If he was hallucinating these torrid nights with his wife, when she disappeared like a ghost before dawn.

He couldn't put his finger on it, but something had changed. Making love to Mia had always been an incendiary thing, from the very first time, and it had only got hotter. But since they'd returned to Paris, there was an edge that Daniel hadn't noticed before.

It was as if she was deliberately doing her best to send him into orbit, with a pleasure so intense and all-consuming that his days were populated by fevered daydreams. As soon as he returned to the apartment they didn't even bother with the niceties of sharing dinner before tearing their clothes off. Dinner had become a midnight kitchen interlude.

Daniel cursed his introspection. Was he seriously analysing and scrutinising the fact that sex with his new wife was off-the-charts hot?

He got up and had a shower, before he lost it completely.

When he was on his way out of the apartment to go to work that morning, he paused at Lexi's bedroom door. It was open a crack and he pushed it open all the way. Lexi was on her back in the cot. Mia was in the bed on the other side of the room, also on her back, asleep, hair spread around her head in a wild tangle.

The bed that was for the nanny. Not his wife.

Immediately Daniel wanted to scoop her up and place her back into *their* bed. And then he wanted to bend down, wrap her hair around his hand, wake her with a deep, drugging kiss and have her beg and moan for mercy, in punishment for leaving him feeling weak after so much pleasure.

A little stunned at the intensity of his thoughts, Daniel stepped back. Mia moved minutely on the bed and he noticed slight shadows under her eyes. A faint tension around her mouth. Something wasn't quite right, but he couldn't put his finger on it. And Daniel instinctively shied away from looking too closely, telling himself again that he was being paranoid. They were in the honeymoon phase that every couple went through, and their marriage wasn't about regular intimacies like waking up together.

Everything was fine. What more did he want?

'So, Mia, can you tell us how you met Daniel Devilliers?'

Mia was totally out of her comfort zone, talking to the radio host, but she was doing her best to sound confident.

This was the last PR interview before the launch party for the new jewellery line this evening. She'd already seen the huge billboards featuring eye-catching images from the Costa Rica campaign, but the images were so hyper-stylised they didn't even really look like her.

Instead of marvelling over them, all she could think of was of the time she'd spent there with Daniel. Watching him bond with Lexi. Making love again for the first time. Discovering his fear of water, what he'd told her of his sister. All those moments that had felt tender, but which she knew now had been contrived to get her where he wanted her.

In his bed and shackled to his side.

'When did you know you were in love with your husband?'

Mia blinked and came back to the present moment. Maybe she'd misheard? 'I'm sorry, can you repeat the question?'

'Of course. We would love to know when you fell in love with your husband?'

Mia longed to say something blasé, but the memories of Costa Rica were still vivid in her mind's eye. She knew Daniel was outside the small radio studio, listening, and the words that she was terrified of speaking now tumbled out of her mouth, as if she knew she had a licence to say them without fear of censure. After all, it was what everyone expected. They didn't want to hear that there was no love in their marriage. They wanted the fairy tale.

The problem was, so did she—in spite of everything.

She said, 'I think I always loved him…from the first moment I saw him. But we went our separate ways, and it wasn't until we met again that I knew I'd never stopped loving him. And then, when I saw him with Lexi, our daughter…that's when I knew I would love him for ever.'

The radio presenter sighed theatrically. *'Ah, l'amour… c'est fantastique, non?'*

They wrapped up the interview after that and Mia emerged, feeling a little dazed. Daniel led her to his car, and when they were in the back, speeding away, he tugged at his tie.

'You did well,' he said, and then, 'What is it with this obsession with romance and love? Everyone wants there to be some fairy tale story.'

He looked at her, and her skin prickled with awareness. He said, 'You answered well. I almost believed you myself.'

Daniel's careless remark broke the last remaining barrier around Mia's heart. She'd spent the week trying to pretend that she could endure a purely physical relationship if she felt as if she was in control. But any sense of control was rapidly fraying at the edges. Maybe if he hadn't said the words *fairy tale* with such derision she wouldn't feel so reckless right now.

She wanted to dent that arrogant cynicism.

She turned to Daniel, an unstoppable force rising inside her. 'Actually, I answered it well because I wasn't making it up.'

Daniel's hand stilled on his loose tie. He looked at her. 'What?'

'You heard me.'

Mia's heart was thumping. Daniel said something to the driver, who put up the privacy partition, cocooning them in the back.

Then he shook his head. 'You're going to have to say that again.'

'What I said to that interviewer… I meant it. I didn't have to lie or make it up. I love you, Daniel. And, believe me, I wish I didn't. Because things would be so much easier. But I do. And I have done ever since we met. Even though I thought I hated you for a while…after the baby… I didn't really.'

Daniel looked shocked—stricken. 'But you agreed to this marriage on the basis of mutual desire…respect…you knew I wasn't offering more.'

Mia suddenly felt deflated. 'I know… And I thought I could do it, for Lexi's sake. But when we got married I couldn't help hoping that perhaps things might change. I was wrong.'

Daniel was shaking his head. 'My background broke me, Mia. I can't promise you—'

'More. Yes, I know.' Mia cut him off, not wanting to hear him spell it out.

She knew she'd crossed a line now, in articulating her feelings. But she couldn't continue to be physically intimate and yet have no emotional connection. Daniel believed he was broken. She couldn't fix him if he wasn't willing to be fixed.

She shook her head. 'I can't do this, Daniel. I'm sorry. I thought I could, but it'll destroy me to continue a charade… and I don't think that's good for Lexi either. You know what it was like to have unhappy parents. I won't do that to her, and I don't think you want to either. She'll still have two parents who love her, because I know you love her.'

'What are you saying, Mia?'

They were pulling up outside the *salon*. Mia put her hand on the door handle. 'I think it's best if we divorce. I'll obviously wait until you and Devilliers deem it a good time. But I want a divorce, Daniel. I want to have a chance at finding happiness, even if you don't. As you said yourself, I'm no pushover and I'm not swayed by money. So I'm not going to change my mind.'

Daniel watched Mia get out of the car and walk into the apartment. He couldn't move. He felt numb. He couldn't believe what she'd just said. She didn't mean it. She couldn't.

Love.

Having that responsibility for someone else's happiness made Daniel feel a blackness descending over him. The only person he'd ever loved had died. And that grief and toxicity had spread outwards, infecting everything. Love only brought pain, grief, abandonment.

They didn't need love. And after the launch tonight he would show Mia—convince her that what they had was enough.

A few hours later Mia was ready for the launch party. She hadn't even been aware of being got ready. She'd stood still as the team had worked around her, allowing her to feel hollowed out, which suited her fine. She didn't want to talk to anyone. She'd done enough talking today.

She was made up to resemble the way she looked in the campaign. Her hair was smoothed and slicked back, caught in a low ponytail. Her dress was strapless and black, down to her knee, with a slit up one thigh. So far, so simple—except that it was leather.

When Mia saw herself in it, her eyes almost fell out of her head. 'I can't wear this,' she whispered in shock. It clung to her body like an indecent second skin. It was pure...*sex*.

'*Madame*, it is...sublime.'

Mia shivered in spite of herself as a purely feminine thrill went through her.

The woman in charge of the jewellery brought over the necklace Mia was to wear tonight—a very stark and bold piece. A huge ruby set into a gold neckpiece that coiled around her neck and trailed down to sit just above her cleavage. It was eye-catching.

Mia took off her other jewellery: her engagement ring and wedding ring. She felt a pang, because she'd worn them for such a short time, and probably wouldn't be wearing them for much longer.

At that moment Daniel appeared in the doorway, in a black tuxedo. Every inch the sexy, suave billionaire. The shocked expression from earlier was gone. Now he looked impassive.

Her silly heart clenched. Had what she'd said made any impact or had her words almost literally rolled off his back?

The moment Daniel looked at Mia in that dress, the numbness encasing him since she'd stepped out of the car earlier was obliterated by pure electricity.

She looked like a sultry siren from a *film noir*. All sleek golden limbs, with her body shrink-wrapped into a dress that was pure sin. He wanted to tell the stylist to change the dress immediately—in this she would cause accidents, heart attacks. But they didn't have time. And he had approved the dress after all. Except in the picture on the mannequin it had looked positively benign.

He looked at Mia's face. She was watching him warily. What she'd said earlier had been so outrageous that he still wasn't entirely sure that she'd actually said it.

Paul the butler appeared. 'The car is ready downstairs.'

Daniel forced himself to focus. What Mia had said earlier was nonsense. They just needed to talk about it.

He led her out of the apartment. Her scent was fresh and

light—at odds with the outfit— reminding him of who she really was. Of her contradictions.

Odile and Lexi were waiting to say goodbye in the foyer and Odile said, 'Wow, Mia...you look amazing.'

Lexi copied Odile. 'Wow... Mama...'mazing.'

Mia laughed and hugged Odile and Lexi. Then Lexi put her arms out towards Daniel. He lifted her up, inhaling her sweet scent. She planted a kiss on his cheek.

His chest felt tight. *'Merci, mignonne.'*

He handed her back to Odile, and they left.

There was silence in the car as it wound its way from Place Vendôme to the venue. Daniel could see the toned length of Mia's thigh. She was looking away, out of the window. He wanted to turn her face to him, make her look at him. Cover her mouth with his.

It suddenly occurred to him, then, that in the past week, in spite of the intensity of their lovemaking, she hadn't kissed him on the mouth once. Everywhere but the mouth. As if she was denying him something that some considered more intimate than actual intercourse. In fact she hadn't even kissed him on the mouth on their wedding night.

No. Not possible. He was losing it. Imagining it.

What she'd said earlier...it was scrambling his brain.

An ache built in his chest, but he ignored it. They pulled up outside the venue and Daniel got out and went around to help Mia out of the car. He had to clench his jaw to keep his body under control as she uncoiled her tall body in that dress.

As soon as they saw her, the paparazzi went wild.

Now they knew her name.

'Mia, Mia! Over here! Mia!'

Daniel stood to the side, for once out of the limelight and not minding it one bit. Mia posed with professional ease, but he could see that she was trembling lightly.

He went over and took her hand, saying to the photographers, *'Ça suffit.'* Enough.

He led her to the entrance. Her hand was tight around his.

He looked down at her. 'Okay?'

She looked up and nodded. 'I'm just not used to this level of attention.'

Daniel put his thumb and forefinger to her chin and tipped it up. He bent down to press his mouth against hers, but at the last second she turned her head, denying him her lips.

Something dark spiralled in Daniel's gut as his kiss landed on her cheek.

He hadn't been imagining it.

As soon as they walked into the venue a hush fell over the crowd. Daniel felt a surge of protectiveness. He kept hold of Mia's hand, but after a while her death grip loosened and she let go. And at one point she turned to him and said, 'I'm okay now. You can do whatever you have to do.'

Daniel saw that she was with Adele, the photographer. He said, 'I have to make a speech, but we can go after that.'

Mia nodded and her gaze slid away from his.

They got separated by the crowd.

He kept looking for her over the heads of everyone else, but only caught glimpses here and there. This was a pinnacle moment for him and the business, and yet he couldn't focus on it.

Someone touched his arm and he almost snarled at them to leave him alone. It was his chief assistant.

'Okay, boss?'

Daniel forced himself to relax. 'Fine.'

'It's time for your speech.'

His speech. Damn. It was the last thing he felt like doing now.

He said to Pascal, 'Can you find Mia and stay with her? Make sure she's okay?'

'Of course.'

Daniel made his way to the dais and was introduced by one of France's best-loved actresses, who had been a brand ambassador for Devilliers for a long time. She graciously mentioned that Mia was part of a new generation of ambassadors and wished her well.

Daniel still couldn't see Mia in the crowd, but finally caught sight of her. She was standing with Pascal and Adele. Relief flooded his belly. He launched into his speech, not having to check his notes because he'd been preparing for this a long time.

He mentioned Mia too, and thanked her for elevating the campaign beyond the ordinary and into something extraordinary. He could see her blush from where he stood, as everyone clapped and congratulated her.

That ache resurfaced, and absently he put a hand to his chest as he made his closing remarks. When he looked to where Mia had been standing just moments ago, though, she was no longer there. He kept speaking on autopilot as he searched for her. And then he saw her, slipping out of an exit, shoulders bare.

He stumbled over his words. Had to stop, look at his notes.

Where was she going?

Eventually he finished his speech and there was deafening applause, but all Daniel cared about was finding Mia. He kept getting stopped by people. And she was nowhere to be seen. The pictures from the campaign were on the walls all around the room, like a gallery exhibit, and everywhere he looked, Mia's face stared back seductively. Mockingly.

'I want a divorce, Daniel. I want to have a chance at finding happiness...'

Finally, *finally*, he got to the exit and saw his driver. He went over. 'Have you seen Mia?'

'I just dropped her home, sir, and came back to wait for you.'

Daniel looked behind him and saw the glittering crowd. He knew he had to go back. *Should* go back.

But he got into the car instead.

CHAPTER ELEVEN

Mia winced as she contorted herself again in front of the mirror in the dressing room. It was no good. She needed help to get out of the dress but she'd sent Odile home when she'd arrived back a short time before, and she wasn't about to scandalise Paul, so she would have to wait.

She'd done her best to comb the gel out of her hair, but washing it would have to wait too. At least it didn't feel as if it was shrink-wrapped to her head any more.

She felt bad about leaving the party early, but—

She heard a noise and looked up. Daniel stood in the doorway, looking a little wild-eyed. 'You're here,' he said.

Mia felt guilty. 'Sorry. I just… It all got a bit overwhelming. I went out to get some air and saw the driver. I asked him to bring me home. I sent you a text.'

Daniel pulled out his phone as if he'd never seen it before.

Mia said, 'You should go back. I'm sorry for pulling you away.'

Daniel put his phone back and shook his head as he tugged his bowtie loose. 'The speech is done. No one will notice I'm gone at this stage.'

Mia doubted that very much. 'You should go back,' she repeated. 'It's a big night.'

He said, 'I'll go back if you come with me.'

Mia pointed to her undone hair. And then her bare feet. 'Like this? I don't think your board would approve of the *"before"* version of the model in their campaign.'

Daniel walked towards Mia. 'I think the "before" version is better.'

She swallowed. 'Daniel, I'm serious. You should be there.'

He stopped just inches away. Mia had to look up.

He said, 'I'm perfectly happy here.'

There was a volatile energy coming off Daniel that Mia had never noticed before. He was always so in control. Even when he lost control. But this connected with something equally volatile in her. The desperation that had led her to say what she had earlier. And she still didn't know what Daniel thought about it.

'Daniel, we should talk…about what I said…'

But his gaze was dropping down over her body in the leather dress. Lingering on her breasts, belly, hips. Legs. Back up. Eyes glittering.

'I don't think I can talk while you're wearing that dress.'

Mia turned around, presenting him with her back. 'Then can you help me get out of it, please? So we can talk. I can't undo it myself.'

She pulled her hair over one shoulder. She hated herself for it, but when Daniel moved close behind her she wasn't thinking much about talking either.

Familiar tension coiled in her gut as she waited to feel his fingers on the zip. But instead his hands came to her shoulders. Breath feathered over her and she felt his mouth touch her skin, pressing kisses along her upper back.

'Daniel…' she said weakly, her legs turning to rubber.

'Do you want me to stop?'

Yes, Mia said inwardly, because she knew that after what she'd said today she had no defences left. But the temptation was too much. She needed this. Needed it like a lifeforce. And after this she might never experience it again.

She turned around, eyes locking on Daniel's mouth. She'd denied herself that mouth on hers in some misguided idea that it would be easier to *have sex* than *make love*. It hadn't worked.

'No, damn you,' she said now. 'I don't want you to stop.'

She reached up and wrapped her arms around his neck and kissed him, almost sobbing with relief when, after a moment's hesitation, he kissed her back. Mouths open. Tongues tangling. Why had she denied herself this?

Because it's going to shatter your heart into a million pieces when you leave...

Mia shoved the voice down deep. Not now.

Daniel hauled her up against his body and carried her over to a wide chair in the dressing room, sitting down and taking her with him.

'Put your legs either side of mine.'

Mia looked down at the unforgiving dress. 'I don't think I—'

There was a sound of material ripping and Mia saw that Daniel had ripped the slit in the dress so that it reached her hip. She looked at him, and he looked like the devil incarnate. Her skin went on fire.

He said, 'Now try.'

She put her thighs either side of his, and he reached around her back to pull the zip down. She shivered as the dress loosened around her breasts and Daniel pulled at the bodice, freeing her breasts. He cupped them, thumbs finding her nipples and stroking them to hard points.

Mia couldn't think straight. Her hands were on the back of the chair behind Daniel's head, and then her own head fell back when Daniel leant forward and put his mouth on one breast and then the other, suckling her flesh until she was panting and moving against him, seeking a deeper connection.

He put his hands on her hips. 'Come up for me, *chérie*.'

Mia came up on her knees. Heard Daniel undo his belt and trousers. Heard the ripping of a foil packet. And then his hands were on her hips again and he was bringing her down slowly onto his shaft.

It was exquisite torture as he slowly urged her up and down, lubricating his body with her own, her muscles massaging his length until they were both half crazed. Daniel held her still so that he could dictate the pace, and he surged up into her body over and over again, putting his mouth on her breast and sucking her nipple so hard that she had nowhere to go except hurtling over the edge.

For long moments they stayed in that embrace. Daniel's head on Mia's breast, her head buried in his neck, her thighs trembling in the aftermath.

The following morning when Daniel woke he noticed the utter stillness. He felt cold. He'd had dreams…awful dreams. Dreams of being in a large venue, seeing glimpses of Mia, but then she'd disappear again. Round and round he went, searching for her endlessly…

Last night…

The frantic sex came back to him in snatches. Ripping Mia's dress to her hip. Her breasts falling free of the restrictive leather. The desperation that had fuelled them to that explosive climax.

Eventually she'd extricated herself and gone. Daniel had presumed to change, freshen up. He'd waited for her. But she hadn't come back. The door to the nursery had been closed and, aware of Lexi, he hadn't wanted to disturb her.

He'd taken a shower and come into his bedroom, half expecting—*hoping*—that she might be in his bed. But it had been empty.

He remembered the way she'd looked when she'd said, *'No, damn you, I don't want you to stop.'* As if she'd wanted him but resented it.

Daniel went even colder now. She'd whispered something into his neck before she'd left him sitting on that chair in a stupor. He'd heard it at the time, but he'd ignored it. Now it came back.

She'd said, very clearly, 'This doesn't change anything.'

Daniel jack-knifed up to sit in the bed. The stillness in the apartment seemed to permeate his bones.

She was gone.

He got up, pulling on sweats. Lexi's bedroom door was open. The bed was made. Lexi's cot empty. No unintelligible chatter signalled her presence.

Paul wasn't even here. No one was here.

Daniel had a flashback to walking around the chateau where he'd grown up. He'd woken up one day to find the chateau empty. Totally empty. It had been shortly after Delphine's death. Finally, that evening, his father had returned from Paris to find Daniel curled up in the corner of his bedroom, practically catatonic with fear and bewilderment.

He'd believed he'd been abandoned because he'd been responsible for Delphine's death.

'What's wrong with you, boy?'

Daniel had looked up and known he should be feeling relief that his father was there, but all he'd felt was cold.

'Where did everyone go?' he'd asked.

His father had cursed. 'You were left here today?'

Daniel had nodded.

'Your mother was supposed to take you with her to the South of France,' his father had spat out. 'The staff were given the day off to go to a fête in the village.'

There had been no apology or acknowledgement of the fact that he'd been abandoned. He'd just spent the rest of that week going into the *salon* with his irritated father. And when his mother had returned from the South of France she hadn't said a thing.

Daniel thought of Lexi and subjecting her to a similar experience. It made him feel physically ill and gave him a wholly new perspective on the cruelty of his parents.

He rubbed at his chest.

He knew one thing above everything else. Mia couldn't leave him. And he had to tell her that.

He forced himself to be rational. She couldn't be far. She wouldn't have just left so suddenly. He needed to talk to her. To try and explain something he couldn't even explain to himself.

Mia watched Lexi throw morsels of bread to the ducks. She felt numb. She'd made herself feel numb to stop images from last night running in her head. Last night had just proved that she wasn't strong enough to love Daniel and stay with him.

Lexi started toddling towards the playground. Mia took her hand.

'Mia!'

She stopped, turned around. Daniel was behind her, looking very dishevelled. A loose shirt over jeans. Shoes with no socks. No coat. She'd never seen him like this.

'Daniel?'

'I need to talk to you.'

Mia saw Odile, not far behind Daniel. 'What's Odile doing here? Has something happened? You're scaring me.'

He shook his head. 'No, nothing is wrong. I just need Odile to watch Lexi so we can talk.'

Bemused, Mia greeted Odile and handed over Lexi's bag and stroller. Odile was discreet enough to say, 'Don't worry. I'll stay with her until I hear from you.'

Lexi trotted off happily with Odile to the playground. Mia turned to Daniel. Even now she was aware of the looks he drew. Mainly because he looked as if he'd literally just tumbled out of bed. She wanted to snarl at all the women that he was *hers*. But he wasn't. Not really.

'What is it, Daniel?'

He indicated a bench. 'Sit with me for a minute?'

They sat down.

Daniel turned to Mia and she tried to channel every bit of inner strength she had to withstand his proximity and his effect on her.

'I don't want you to leave, Mia.'

'Look, Daniel, I really, really wanted to make this work—especially for Lexi's sake. And maybe it would if I didn't feel the way I do... But it'll kill me in the end, knowing you don't feel the same way.'

'But that's it... I do... I mean, I think I do. Or that I can.'

Mia felt sick. 'I think I'd prefer it if you pretended you were in love with me, Daniel. But you don't even know...'

Mia stood up and started walking. This was humiliating. Daniel was so desperate for her to stay that he was clearly doing his best to conjure up some sort of emotion to persuade her.

'Mia, wait.'

She stopped. Daniel came alongside her.

'I'm not making sense, I know. I need to show you something that might help you understand...will you come with me?'

Mia wanted to say no, but she was more intrigued than she liked to admit, so she said a grudging, 'Fine.'

When they got to Place Vendôme there was a car she hadn't seen before out front—a low-slung sports car. Daniel opened the passenger door.

She hesitated. 'Where are we going?'

'For a drive. It's about an hour—is that okay?'

Mia shrugged. 'Do I have a choice?'

'Of course you do, but I'd like you to give me this chance.'

Dammit, that flicker of hope was back.

Mia got into the car. It was a luxurious cocoon. Daniel put on some music. They were soon out of the city and speeding along the motorway before turning off and taking country roads.

Mia tried not to think about what Daniel had up his sleeve to convince her to stay. She was determined not to be swayed. He didn't even know how he felt about her. It was insulting!

At about the hour mark they passed through a postcard-pretty village, and on the other side followed a high stone wall for about ten minutes, before Daniel turned into an opening where there were huge gates. She saw his hands tense on the wheel as he waited for a security guard to open the gates and let them in.

Daniel's tension was palpable now. His jaw was tight. Mia felt uneasy. 'Where are we?'

'The Devilliers chateau.'

Where Delphine had died. Where he'd grown up.

His words came back to her: *'My background broke me'*.

Mia said nothing as they made their winding way up a seemingly endless drive. And then suddenly the chateau appeared around a bend. Mia sucked in a breath. This was not your quintessential pretty French chateau. This was something out of a gothic nightmare. Forbidding grey stone. Spiky ramparts. Small windows. It looked cold and oppressive.

Daniel parked in the front courtyard and got out, opening Mia's door and helping her out too. She didn't want to let go of his hand but had to. She was here to break with him, not cling to him.

He went up the steps and the door opened as he approached. A dour-looking man said, 'Welcome, Mr Devilliers, we weren't expecting you.'

'No,' he said, sounding grim. 'It's fine, we won't be here long.'

Mia smiled at the older man, but he stared at her as if

she was a ghost. She really didn't like this place. It was as cold and forbidding inside as out.

The man walked away, and Daniel waited till he was gone. Then he looked at Mia. 'I really would prefer if you hadn't had to see this place, but it's the only way I know how to show you...'

Show me what? she wanted to ask.

But instead she just let him lead her from room to room. He pointed out Delphine's room, untouched from the day she'd died. Mia's heart broke to see the toys and books.

Daniel told Mia about the day he'd found himself alone, with no idea where everyone was. Ice crept into her blood at the thought of him as a small boy, grief-struck, alone in this inhospitable place.

And eventually he took her outside to the back, where the manicured gardens looked frozen in time. The sun was shining but she still felt cold.

Daniel led her around the side of the chateau, to an area of ground that looked slightly different from the rest. She recognised the shape.

'This was the pool, wasn't it?'

Daniel nodded.

'You had it filled in?'

'My mother did.'

'Oh, Daniel...' Mia couldn't stop the emotion.

He didn't look at her as he said, 'I know rationally that it wasn't my fault she died. As you pointed out, I was only nine. But it's embedded on my soul in a way I can't seem to erase. I loved Delphine so much...she was the only joy in my life, and me in hers. I probably would have survived this place quite well if she had lived. Our parents' neglect made us even closer. But when she died, I felt that somehow I'd caused it by needing her too much. That I didn't deserve to have her in my life. Then my mother's reaction...my father's lack of emotion...compounded my guilt.'

He turned to her then. He looked so tortured that Mia's heart broke all over again.

'But I know that I have to let it go, or I'll never be free to trust that something good can come of needing you and Lexi in my life. To trust that needing you won't somehow… destroy you. I didn't want to bring you here to tell you all of this,' he continued, 'but I had to. Because it's the only way I know to show you what's in here…' he put a hand over his heart '…and to try and tell you how you make me feel.'

Mia took Daniel's hands, her heart speeding up a little. 'How *do* I make you feel?'

'When I saw you walk out of the party yesterday evening I couldn't concentrate. I had to find you. The thought of you and Lexi…going…of not seeing you every day…of not having you in my bed, in my life…it makes my chest physically hurt. I feel like I can't breathe.'

He said, 'I know now that's love, Mia. I love you and Lexi. I loved you from the minute I saw you, but I had no capacity to recognise it. When you said you were pregnant… I felt sheer terror. The thought of bringing a child into the world, when all I knew was abandonment and the pain of grief… I didn't see how I wouldn't pass that on. That's why I said what I said that day.'

Mia kept silent. Letting him find his words.

'But then you came back…with Lexi…and I couldn't hide from the demons. I had to let you in. I thought I could do that and somehow stay removed from how you made me feel. The reason I wanted to marry you so quickly was because I knew that if you had time to think about it you'd realise it was too much of a sacrifice. Not because I cared about what people thought. But I'm terrified that loving you will somehow harm you and Lexi.'

He took his hands out of hers. Mia's heart broke in two. The tone in Daniel's voice was the opposite of self-pity. He really believed what he'd said. She could see how damaging this place had been.

Mia said, 'I'm glad you brought me here.'

'You are?'

She nodded. 'You're right. I wouldn't have understood. But now I do. And there's one thing I know.'

'What?'

Mia shuddered lightly. 'Lexi is never coming here.'

Daniel's mouth thinned. 'No way.'

Mia took his hands again. 'And neither are we, coming back here—ever. Because we're going to sell it.'

A wary look came over his face. 'We?'

She nodded. Saw something very fragile make his eyes bright.

'But it's been in the family for centuries...'

Mia shrugged. 'So what?'

The ghost of a smile touched Daniel's mouth. 'Typical American. No appreciation of culture.'

Mia shook her head, joy bubbling up from deep inside her. 'Nope. We'll buy another chateau. A pink one.'

Daniel looked horrified. 'Pink?'

Mia cocked her head on one side. 'Yes. Pink. I've always thought they're so pretty.'

Daniel's expression became serious. Wary again. 'Mia, are you saying you'll stay?'

She moved closer and stretched up, pressing a kiss against Daniel's mouth. A sweet kiss. A benediction.

'If you'll have me. And Lexi.'

She felt the shudder of emotion that ran through Daniel. He gathered her close.

'If I have any chance in this world, it's with you and Lexi. And even though the thought of loving you and causing any harm to come to you and Lexi terrifies me, the thought of letting you go terrifies me more. Is that selfish?'

Mia kissed him again. 'No, my love, it's supremely

human. But loving us can't possibly harm us. I can't guarantee that nothing bad will happen, but I can guarantee that no matter what we'll be together, and together we can face anything.'

Daniel cupped her face and said fervently, 'Don't ever stop kissing me, Mia.'

'Never, my love.'

EPILOGUE

Costa Rica

MIA WALKED DOWN through the trees to the beach and sat down on the seat that Daniel had had made, set in the shade. She sat there and adjusted the baby, so that she could feed him under the strategically placed muslin cloth. Not that there was anyone to see her breastfeed. It was off-season, and the beach was practically empty.

They'd exchanged their vows again here, about three years ago, in a beautiful dawn ceremony, with Lexi bearing the ring that Mia now wore on her right hand. A simple band of gold on one side, and inlaid with diamonds on the other. An eternity ring.

She was slowly but surely accruing more jewellery—which was only befitting the wife of one of the world's most renowned jewellers.

She smiled as she took in the scene before her. Daniel was standing in the sea, with five-year-old Lexi in his arms. She was squealing with delight every time he dunked her under the water and lifted her up again.

'Again, Papa, *again*!'

He obliged. Indefatigable when it came to his beloved daughter, catering to her every whim without ever spoiling her. They were as thick as thieves, and it gave Mia such bittersweet joy to see their bond, because now she had an even truer sense of what she'd missed out on.

And now their little family was growing, with Dominic—Dom for short. They'd waited a while to have another baby, giving Lexi time to get used to Daniel, and time for them all to get used to being in a family. A *real* family.

The baby suckled contentedly at Mia's breast. The birth had been incredibly emotional, because seeing Daniel's joy had compounded her guilt that he'd missed Lexi's birth. But that night after the birth, as he'd held Dom and sat by Mia's bed, Daniel had taken her hand and kissed it, and then he had shaken his head, intuiting her distress.

'Stop it, *mon amour*. I'm as responsible as you for what happened and how it happened. More so. We have so much to be grateful for. I love you, and you've made me the happiest man in the world. I can't wait to spend the rest of my life with you and our children. No going back—only forward. I love you.'

Mia had cried, exhausted and emotional and full of love, and Daniel had kissed her tears away, healing the past, anointing the future.

As if sensing her presence, Daniel looked over and saw her. He pointed over to them and Lexi squealed.

'Mama and Dommy!'

Daniel strode out of the water, Lexi held high in his arms, her dark hair slicked back with water, exposing her pretty face.

In the past few years Daniel had not only overcome his demons about his sister's death and his fear of the water, he had gone a step further by learning how to scuba dive. Now he was never out of the water, and it made Mia stupidly emotional every time she saw it or swam with him. Although admittedly, if they were in the water together, inevitably not much swimming happened...

'Thinking lusty thoughts again?' he asked when they came close, with a familiar gleam in his eye.

'What's lusty, Papa?' Lexi piped up as she scrambled down from Daniel's arms to go and sit beside Mia and check up on her beloved baby brother.

Mia's cheeks burned betrayingly and she scowled at Daniel, who of course knew exactly what she was thinking. He sat down on the bench beside her, moving Lexi to his lap.

Lexi asked, 'Can I hold Dommy, Mama?'

Dom was already pulling away from her breast, hearing his sister's voice. Mia gave up for now. Plenty of time to feed later. She adjusted her clothes, winded Dom briefly, and then handed him carefully to Lexi, who took him into her arms with a deeply furrowed brow, handling him as if he was a fragile piece of glass.

'That's it, *cherie*, very good,' Daniel said encouragingly, careful to support Lexi in holding the baby without making it too obvious.

At that moment an older couple who had been walking down the beach passed by, hand in hand. They looked at Daniel and Mia and their family and smiled indulgently, saying, *'Pura vida.'* The Costa Rican saying that encapsulated everything from *Hello!* To *Life is good!* To its most simple translation *Pure life!* or *Simple life!*

Good life.

Mia smiled and looked at Daniel. Understanding passed between them.

What they had was so much more than a pure or simple life. They had the perfect life. And a family full of love. And a deep and intense understanding that love was always deserved. For ever.

And, yes, they'd sold the dark and scary chateau and bought a pink one…covered in ivy and filled it full of happiness and love.

* * * * *

HIS MAJESTY'S
HIDDEN HEIR

LUCY MONROE

MILLS & BOON

For my new editor Carly Byrne.

This is the first book we worked on together
and I enjoyed it immensely.

I'm looking forward to your insights on many more.

CHAPTER ONE

EMMA WALKED INTO her bank in downtown Santa Fe, her son's hand clasped tightly in her own.

There had been a tech glitch with the automatic deposits on payroll this month and the company had been forced to cut paper checks for all their employees. She hoped it was an anomaly.

Errands like this with an active four-nearly-five-year-old were not her favorite thing. Besides, since she was now working full-time as a bookkeeper, Emma preferred her time with Mickey to be focused on things that her son enjoyed.

He'd gotten used to having her around as she'd worked as a childminder to put herself through college, taking online courses part-time. She'd kept him with her since birth. The past year had been an adjustment for both of them since she'd finally gotten her degree and landed a job with decent pay and benefits.

Waiting in line at the bank, where he had to be quiet and stay still, was not her son's idea of fun. He liked to be moving, not still and quiet.

"Mom, how long?" he demanded, the spitting image of his father, his tone and manner only adding to the similarity.

Sometimes, Emma found it jarring how alike Mickey was to his biological father, though her son had never met the man. Anyone who knew the Prince would see His Royal Highness in his son within seconds of meeting Mickey.

Emma smiled down at her son. "Just a little while longer. See? There are only three people ahead of us."

"Then we can go for shaved ice?" Her son loved his

shaved ice, but always managed to cover himself in sticky syrup by the time he'd finished even a small cup.

Inwardly sighing at the mess to come, Emma nodded nevertheless.

"Yes!"

She laughed. "Indoor voice, all right?"

"Okay, Mom." Could her son's tone be any more long-suffering?

A disturbance near the back of the bank drew her attention and Emma looked up. A group of businessmen in polished suits were exiting into the large lobby of the downtown branch, the aura of power around them a palpable thing.

One of the security guards that discreetly accompanied the group seemed familiar to Emma. He turned his head and she recognized him only a second before her eyes collided with the decadent chocolate brown gaze of the man she'd been sure she would never see again.

Prince Konstantin of Mirrus.

Second son to the small country's former King and the man who had not only broken her heart, but abandoned their son.

His eyes widened in instant recognition.

Memories of the last time they saw each other assaulted Emma like a bad movie she couldn't look away from.

They'd both been at university when they first met. He'd been twenty-three, in his last year of getting his MBA. She'd been nineteen, in her first year of business school. They'd run into each other in the quad.

It had been such a cliché. She'd dropped some books; he'd picked them up.

Their eyes had met and she'd felt like she'd been hit by a train. She hadn't known he was a prince, or that the men standing at a discreet distance were not other students, but his security detail.

He'd smiled, white teeth flashing below gorgeous brown eyes. Nearly six and a half feet tall, he'd towered over Emma's respectable five feet seven inches. Muscular and handsome, he'd taken her breath away. And her ability to speak.

He hadn't been put off by Emma's inability to voice her thanks. Rather, he'd seemed charmed by it.

"I believe these are yours." He'd held out her books.

She'd taken them with a silent nod.

"New to campus?"

They were nearing the end of the first semester of the year, but she'd nodded anyway.

"Would you like to go out with me?"

She'd managed a word then. "Yes."

While that memory was bittersweet, it was the ones that came later that caused so much pain in Emma's chest.

They'd dated for nearly a year, moving in together against her parents' wishes the summer after her freshman year. Despite his having told her at the start that he'd signed some kind of medieval contract to eventually marry the niece of another country's king, Kon had acted like he couldn't live without her.

He'd been attentive and caring, always charming, and incredibly passionate.

Emma had built dreams of the future around his behavior, rather than his words.

Then the ax had fallen.

"What did you just say?" Emma couldn't take in the words.

Kon *couldn't* mean them.

"My father wants me to honor the contract now. We have to break up. You're going to need to find somewhere else to live."

"No. You don't mean that."

Kon looked pained. "Emma, you knew this was coming."

"No." She shook her head, screaming inside from the

pain. "No. You want to make love every day. You want to talk to me all the time when you're gone. You don't want to marry someone else."

He couldn't.

She'd thought, when he'd asked her to move in with him, that the contract was a nonissue. He'd never brought it up again. Emma had simply forced herself to ignore its existence, choosing to focus on the here and now. She loved Kon, and while he'd never used those words with her, his actions made her believe she was just as necessary to him as he was to her.

"It is not a matter of wanting to marry her. I made a promise. I must keep it."

"What? No, you signed that contract five years ago. You were just a kid."

"I hope not. You were the same age when we started dating."

She was twenty now, but not a lot wiser apparently. And he was twenty-four, also not a lot wiser if he was going to marry a woman he did not love for the sake of his family's consequence and business.

The argument had devolved from there. Emma had cried, and she wasn't proud remembering she'd begged him to reconsider. But Kon? He'd taken on his Prince Konstantin mantle, remaining aloof and cold, refusing to engage.

He'd offered her a year living in the apartment rent-free as a transition.

It had felt like a payoff and it was in that moment she'd known they were truly over.

Emma's heart had disintegrated in an explosion of pain. She'd moved out that night, going home to her parents with her tail tucked between her legs.

That hadn't worked out either, but those memories weren't going to take hold now.

She wouldn't let them.

Emma forced herself to stop playing the memory reel in her head and to focus on the present. The feel of her son's hand in hers. The sounds of the other bank customers and tellers speaking. Paper shuffling. Pens scratching as people signed things.

Knowing what was coming next, Emma should look away first. For her pride's sake. No way would His Royal Highness want to acknowledge he knew her.

She never considered he might not recognize her.

Even her ex-lover wasn't that oblivious.

She couldn't make herself look away though. Even after more than five years, her heart beat a mad rhythm at the sight of him and her eyes soaked him in like water to a thirsty plant.

But she was not thirsty. Not for him.

She had gotten over Konstantin. Had learned to hate him, in fact. And then learned to let that hatred go. Emma had had no choice. She wasn't living her life with the thorns of bitterness piercing her soul on a daily basis.

She did yoga. She meditated. She did not hate.

But right that minute? Seeing him so confident and unconcerned with his business cohorts, Emma was really having difficulty remembering patience, compassion and tolerance.

"Mom."

Her son's voice did what her own willpower had been unable to accomplish and broke her focus on the royal rat. Okay, tolerance wasn't going to be her strong suit today.

Emma looked down and found a strained smile for the little boy. "Yes, pumpkin?"

"I'm not a pumpkin." Her son's face, so like his father's, creased in a cranky frown. "I'm a boy."

Mickey was going through a phase of not liking endearments. He was not a pumpkin. Not sweet. Not darling. He barely tolerated the nickname Mickey over Mikhail, the name she'd had him christened. As he kept reminding her, he was a big boy. Almost five.

Heaven help her when he hit his teens.

"Yes, you are a wonderful little boy."

"I'm almost five!" he said loudly, clearly offended again. Being referred to as little was also on the banned list.

But she only grinned, despite the nervous tension thrumming through her at that sighting of his sperm donor. "You are four...*and three-quarters*," she tacked on to appease. "And while you may be big for your age, you are still *my* little boy."

"And mine too, I think." Konstantin had crossed the vast lobby of the bank very quickly.

But why he had done so when *he* had taken out the restraining order that prevented her from getting within fifty feet of him, she had no idea. And then his words registered, and Emma wanted to hit him.

With her fist. Not her palm.

The unutterable rat!

Compassion was definitely out the window too.

Of course Mickey was his. She'd tried to tell Konstantin, but he'd kept her at a distance and his efforts to do so had made life for her and their son so much harder than it had to be.

She glared up at him. "Go away, Konstantin." Her mouth clamped shut. Calling him by name felt way too personal now.

But she didn't think referring to him as Prince Rat was going to go over well.

"I am going nowhere." He pointed down to Mickey, who was watching them both in rapt fascination, the recognition in his eyes impossible to miss. "That is my son and you have withheld him from me, for years."

Heat and cold washed over Emma in waves. She knew only one thing.

She was finally going to get her say, but she didn't want to have it here. Not with a bevy of rich executives and bank customers looking on.

"It's my daddy. That man is my daddy." Mickey tugged urgently at Emma's hand, his voice carrying in the cavernous lobby.

Gasps could be heard and whispers, but Emma ignored them all, including the man staring at her as if the ceiling had just fallen on his head, to look down at her son. "Does he look like the pictures?"

Mickey slid eyes the same chocolate brown as his father's to the Prince and then back to meet his mother's gaze. "He doesn't look so mad in the pictures." His voice wobbled just a little, his usual confidence clearly shaken by Konstantin's attitude. "Doesn't he like me?"

"Of course I like you. You are my son." Konstantin's tone was nothing like filled with its usual arrogance. In fact, he sounded sick. "You've shown him pictures of me?" he asked her.

She didn't know if he was angry, relieved or entirely unimpacted by that fact.

Emma gave a short nod of agreement.

"But you did not tell me about him."

"Do we have to do this here?" she asked him, wishing they did not have to do *this* at all. She'd come to terms with the truth that her son would never meet his father until Mickey was of an age to contact the royal family of Mirrus on his own, DNA test results in hand.

This scene, right now, was out of some kind of horror novel. Her worst nightmare.

"We will go back to my hotel."

She shook her head. "No." She wasn't stupid. She knew this man had diplomatic status. She wasn't sure if that made his hotel room his own little fiefdom while he was in Santa

Fe, but she wasn't taking any chances. "You can come to our home. In an hour. I need to finish running errands."

"You and my son are not leaving my sight."

"Then I guess you can follow us around as I finish the things I need to do," she said sarcastically.

"Do not be ridiculous. We need to talk."

"I need to deposit my check and then *I* need to buy groceries."

"My staff can take care of both."

"You think I'd trust your staff with *my* paycheck?" She would never let him hurt her, or more important, their son, again.

He jerked as if she'd hit him like she'd wanted to only moments before. "Why not?"

Emma did her best to give her son a natural smile. "Mickey, can you be a big boy and hold my place in line. I'm going to be right there." She pointed to a spot about ten feet away where she planned to set Konstantin straight out of her son's hearing.

"You'll both be right there?" her son asked.

Emma nodded.

"Okay, Mom. I'll stand right here." Mickey drew himself up importantly.

Emma said nothing to Konstantin before stepping away to the spot she'd indicated, her attention never leaving her son.

"Because I don't trust you at all," she whispered to Konstantin fiercely while smiling reassuringly at her son. "I don't trust you not to have the check tossed just to cause me further pain and embarrassment. I don't trust you not to use the information on it to find my employer and have me sacked. I don't—"

"I get the picture. You think I am some kind of monster."

"No, just a royal rat who has hurt me before in ways I

never would have expected and I'll never make the mistake of not *expecting* it ever again."

He turned and strode back to the group of men who had been with him, saying something to one of the men in the business suits. Suddenly, she was collecting Mickey and they were being led to a teller and getting her check deposited with all due haste.

"If you give a list to Sergei, he will see that your groceries are purchased."

One of the security men stepped forward with a nod.

She sighed. "Fine, but I've only budgeted seventy-five dollars and if he goes over buying the more expensive brands, I'm not paying for it. And all fresh veg, meat and dairy have to be organic." She frowned up at Sergei. "You can get those things most economically at—" Emma named one of the three stores she had to shop at to get the healthiest food for her son on the tightest budget.

"I will take care of it," Sergei promised.

"Give me your number and I'll send you my grocery list." She kept it in an app on her phone.

That taken care of, she led the way out of the bank and into the Santa Fe sunshine. "What are you doing in New Mexico?"

She had never once anticipated quite literally running into a prince in the place she'd chosen to start over for its lower cost of living and family-friendly environment.

"A mining deal." He said it like that should have been obvious.

"But—"

"You are aware that minerals are a strong natural resource in this state." It was a statement, not a question.

"I am now." She'd come to Santa Fe looking for a fresh start.

The only major industries that registered with her were ones she might work in. She'd settled in Santa Fe, rather than somewhere else in New Mexico, because of the numerous art galleries and thriving artist community.

She'd been supplementing her income with small commissions from one of them since a year after her move from Seattle. For a place to live and her main income, she'd watched children for a wealthy couple who had a real estate business. When Emma had gone job hunting, none of the places she'd applied to had been mining companies.

It had taken her nearly four years to build her life back to something decent, where she and her son did not have to live a hand-to-mouth existence and she wasn't going to let Konstantin mess it up now.

She'd gotten her degree, only an associate's and not the bachelor's she'd planned for, but it was a degree. But in order to get away from the stigma of the restraining order he'd taken out against her, Emma had had to change her name.

It had hurt to give up her adoptive parents' name. She'd been a Sloan since only a few months after birth.

However, they'd washed their hands of her, so she'd done it, changing both her and her son's last name to the one she'd been born with, Carmichael. The only thing she had of biological parents she would never know.

There was drama at the car, Mickey not wanting his father to leave and follow in another car, his screams and tears not unusual for his age, but having a more profound impact on Emma because of the situation. Moisture burned in the back of her own eyes as she tried to explain that Konstantin would meet them at their small house.

"I will ride with you," he said as he walked around the car to the passenger side.

She stared at him and then down at her ten-year-old domestic compact and tried to compute that statement. Him ride with her and Mickey?

Konstantin's security argued, but he ignored them, opening the back door for Mickey and helping her incredibly independent son, who had stopped allowing her to help him more than a year ago, into his safety seat.

Hands shaking with nerves, Emma spoke to Konstantin across the roof of the car. "You can ride with your security. Mickey will settle."

Her son was no longer crying because he believed Konstantin would be riding with them, but was now busy doing up the buckles on his five-point harness.

She acknowledged ruefully that he was no longer the one in danger of having a meltdown.

Konstantin closed Mickey's door, tapped the hood and came around the car to speak to her.

"You kept my son from me." The accusation in his voice would have hurt.

If the words had been true.

They were not.

A parking lot was better than a bank, but the car was not exactly soundproof. She lowered her voice, but let her tone drip with accusation. "You ejected me from your life so you could marry another woman."

"And so out of spite, you did this thing!" The Prince was making no effort to keep his voice down.

"Spite? Are you delusional?" she demanded, her voice still low. "I tried to call you. You refused my calls. I tried to see you, and you had a restraining order taken out against me, remember that? I'd done nothing to warrant one, but men like you, they get what they want."

"I am not the delusional one. I took out no restraining order. More to the point, I did not *want* to be a nonentity in my child's life," he said in a driven tone.

"You couldn't tell from how you treated me." He had made it clear he wanted to be a nonentity in *her* life and his dedication to that endeavor had dictated his not finding out about their son.

"You should have tried harder."

How typical to expect her to have had options he would have taken for granted, but that he'd removed from her. He lived in such a rarified world, he probably really believed the garbage he was spouting.

"What do you mean, harder? I called and texted, but you blocked my number. You moved out of our apartment and I couldn't get a forwarding address." She'd tried, but the building super and doormen had held firm against charm, pleading and even threats. "I wrote and you never answered, I didn't even know if you got my letters. I sent emails through the contact form on the Mirrus Global website, but never got a reply."

It had been hellish. And once she *had* finally gotten in touch with someone in his family? That hell had only gotten worse, not better.

Something like guilt briefly showed in his expression and then it was gone.

Konstantin looked down at their son through the window, realized the small boy was watching them avidly even if he couldn't hear everything said and grimaced. "We will have this discussion later."

"Good call." She made no effort to temper her sarcasm. But neither did she reopen the conversation.

Emma tried to protest his riding with them again when he walked around to the passenger door, but he shook his head. "I told him I would, so I will." Then the Prince climbed into her car and pulled his seat belt into place, like he rode in such humble transportation all the time.

Mickey kept up a running dialogue with his father as Emma drove, stopping every few sentences, to get her confirmation. "Right, Mom?" was one of his favorite phrases when he was feeling nervous.

The number of times he used that phrase in the short

drive to their house on the outskirts of town indicated just how nervous he was feeling, despite the confident demeanor he put forth.

So much like his father, she ached. As she often did at that reminder.

When they arrived at the fixer-upper house she'd managed to buy only a month previously, Konstantin did not look impressed. She tried to see the one-level old adobe house through his eyes and failed utterly. She could see only what had drawn her to it first.

The coral-stained adobe contrasted happily with the wood trim painted turquoise. The landscaping needed work as odd scrub grew between and around the natural rock that acted as tile in the tiny front courtyard. She did her best to keep up on the weeds, but she had only so many off-hours.

"Is this your home?" Konstantin asked.

Emma didn't know if he was talking to her or to their son, but Mickey answered. "We just got it. I have my own room now and Mom is gonna put in a play structure in back when we get enough money."

Konstantin made a sound like he was choking, but he smiled at Mickey. "I would like to see your room."

"Okay. That's okay, right, Mom?" Mickey asked again.

"Of course." She turned off the car. "Let's go inside."

Konstantin stopped once they were in the living room and just stared around him. "This is where you and *my* son live?" he asked with what sounded like disdain to her sensitive ears.

Emma gritted her teeth, gave their son a significant look and then replied, "Yes. This is the home *our* son loves and is very proud to be able to call his own. Think before you speak, Konstantin. I mean, Your Highness."

He frowned. "You used to call me Kon."

"We used to be friends." They'd been lovers too, but she wasn't saying that in front of her son.

"We are going to be much more than that soon. Call me Konstantin if you must, but don't use my title. We are way beyond that." With that pronouncement he headed down the hallway with Mickey.

The next two hours were a revelation. Konstantin should not have been so good with Mickey. He had no experience with children. He was a tycoon prince, not a dad.

But he was patient with the little boy, showing no frustration when Mickey grew fractious.

"It's time for lunch, I think." Emma smiled down at her son. "Are you hungry, Mickey?"

"My name is Mikhail!" her son shouted.

Emma winced at the volume, but her reaction was nothing compared with how still Konstantin became. "You named him after me? But why?"

She stepped back, though he'd made no move to come closer to her. She'd been very careful to keep her distance and their son between them. She had no answer she was willing to say in front of Mickey for why she'd given her son his father's middle name.

It hadn't been because she wanted to honor Konstantin, but she'd thought her son deserved something of his father's and that was all Emma had ever been able to give him.

She just shook her head. "Lunch."

"Because you're my dad," Mickey replied with none of his mother's reticence. "Mom says I'm just like you."

"Does she?" Konstantin stared at her and then at Mickey.

Mickey nodded. "Mostly when I'm being stubborn."

"Like about eating lunch?"

"I don't want you to go away."

Oh, man. Emma had never doubted that Mickey needed his dad, but she'd had no way to give him access. Now Prince Konstantin Mikhail of the House of Merikov was here in the flesh and Mickey didn't want to lose him.

Resolve firmed inside Emma. Whatever Konstantin had

planned, he was going to play a significant part in his son's life from this point forward. Even if Emma had to go to the media and shame him into it.

Tiana, the former Queen of Mirrus and his sister-in-law, not to mention the woman who had threatened to take her baby away, was dead now. It was time for Emma to stop acting out of fear of Konstantin's family.

"I am going nowhere," Konstantin promised.

Emma only hoped he meant it.

"Would you like to eat lunch with us?" she invited.

See her remembering manners taught by her parents and patience taught by her yogi.

"Yes, thank you." Konstantin looked surprised by the offer. "What would you like? I will send Sergei out for it."

Sergei had been careful to stay close, but always shifting to a different room than the one she, Mickey and Konstantin were in. The rest of the detail were outside watching her front and back door for threats, but probably just as much for paparazzi sniffing around.

"Thank you for the offer, but Mickey needs to eat now, or he's going to get *hangry* and none of us wants to deal with that."

"Hangry? I am not familiar with this term."

"Hungry and angry together. *Hangry*."

Konstantin smiled. "I too can become *hangry*," he admitted to Mickey. "We should both eat lunch."

"We'll all eat together at the table, like a family. That's okay, right, Mom?" Mickey's nerves were showing again.

"Yes. We'll all eat together. Do you want to help me make sandwiches?"

"Will Dad…" He looked at Konstantin as if asking if that was okay.

The Prince nodded at his son, swallowing like he was having trouble containing emotion.

"Will *Dad* help us make them too?" Mickey asked, stressing his father's title like he was savoring it.

Tears burned at the back of Emma's eyes and she hated Konstantin more in that moment than she ever had before. For all he'd stolen from Mickey, for the fear of loss her son couldn't hide.

Konstantin met her gaze and something must have shown on her face because he flinched backward as if she'd struck him.

Emma forced her anger deep inside, repeating the mantra she'd used to let go of her hatred in the first place and gave her son the reassuring smile he needed. "I'm not sure Konstantin has ever made a sandwich before. You can show him how to spread the mayo."

Emma insisted on making sandwiches for the security detail as well as the three of them, which she knew meant she'd have to dip into the rainy day fund to buy more groceries, but needs must. Konstantin tried to argue with her that his people didn't need to be fed by her, but she ignored him.

What did *he* know about what the average person needed? He lived in his rarified world and had no clue what it meant to be just a regular guy.

Cooking with her ex-lover in her tiny kitchen turned into a test of Emma's strength.

He kept brushing up against her and sending her senses into orbit. And the worst part? She didn't think he even realized he was doing it.

There just wasn't enough space *not* to bump into each other with three of them working at the counter, putting the food together. She pulled a container of gazpacho she'd made the day before out and dished it up to go with the sandwiches for everyone.

The day was warm and chilled soup would be refreshing. Never mind it was supposed to be her and Mickey's dinner two nights next week.

"You're gonna like this, Dad," Mickey assured Konstantin. "Mom's the best cook!"

"I remember a time when she struggled to boil water." He smiled at her, inviting her to share the joke.

Emma's mother had been old-fashioned in so many ways, but her kitchen was her private domain and she never allowed anyone in it. Not even her daughter. Emma had had no clue how to cook when she'd gone to college.

"I learned." When she'd been pregnant and alone.

Konstantin frowned, like her thoughts were broadcast for him to see. Maybe they were. Emma had never had much of a poker face. Her dad used to tease her that he knew if she liked her presents, not by what she said when she opened them, but by what her face told him.

Some days, she missed her parents so much, it hurt.

But like Konstantin, they'd opted to eject Emma from their lives when she wasn't what they wanted her to be.

"You look sad. What is wrong?"

He was asking her that? Like he couldn't guess, if not the particulars, then certainly the gist. And what gave him the right to ask any personal questions of her at all anyway?

She inhaled and exhaled repeating *patience*, *compassion* and *tolerance* under her breath.

"Mom gets like that," Mickey said practically. "She says memories aren't always warm and happy, but they're still ours. It's okay if I cry sometimes when I remember Snoopy dying."

"Who is Snoopy?"

"He was the family dog for the people I worked for."

"Worked?" he asked, probing.

But she ignored him and started handing out plates.

"You are not their servant. They can come get their food if you insist on feeding them."

"Don't you think they deserve to eat?" she asked with bite.

He frowned at her, seemingly shocked. "You know me better than that. They could have gotten takeout. I would have paid for it."

"Instead, I chose to feed them."

"I don't remember you being this stubborn."

"Life changes us all."

Lunch was a surprisingly convivial meal, but by the end of it, Mickey was practically drooping off his chair. "Nap time for you."

"I will be here when you wake," Konstantin promised, staving off what might have been another meltdown.

Her son was tired. He was stressed. And he was terrified he'd never again see this person he'd just gotten to call *Dad*.

Mickey insisted on holding Konstantin's hand on the way to his bedroom.

"Bathroom first," Emma insisted from behind them.

Mickey didn't argue, just veered into the brightly tiled, if small room. She'd taken pains to get the grout clean, but she didn't have the knowhow to fix the chips in the mosaic tiles put in when the house had been built more than forty years ago, or the money to hire someone to do it.

Emma tucked her son in, but he extracted no fewer than three more promises from Konstantin that he would be there when Mickey woke up.

She just hoped the Prince realized how important it was that he keep that promise.

CHAPTER TWO

Typically, though they were in her home, Konstantin led the way as they left Mickey's room.

He went unerringly into the living room. Granted the house was small, so it wasn't likely he'd get lost looking for the main rooms.

Konstantin sat on the yellow sofa and she settled into the chair covered in a complementary print of Aztec shapes. The Prince looked around the room, his intelligent gaze taking in every detail.

It wasn't high-end decor, but it wasn't shabby. Emma had decorated with Southwestern designs and bright colors, throwing rugs over the wooden floors that needed refinishing.

She was proud of what she'd managed to accomplish for her and her son. "Not what you're used to?"

"I can see you here. Your love of color and interesting shapes. It's everywhere. You've really bought into the whole Southwestern motif, haven't you?"

Was he referring to the house, or the way she was dressed in a striped poncho-style shirt, denim capris and sandals with conches on the top? Probably both.

"This is my home now." She'd found a sense of belonging and acceptance in *The City Different*.

"So, you have gone native?" he teased.

She shrugged. "I think we have more important things to talk about than my sense of style."

He sighed, and then nodded, looking pained. "I gave instructions."

"Instructions?"

"Before. After we broke up."

"What sort of instructions?" As if she didn't know, but he could spell it out.

"I told my PAA to block all attempts at contact."

Well, that explained the lack of response to her emails, messages left on his work voice mail and letters sent to his office. It did not explain his ignoring the letters she'd sent to the palace in Mirrus or her attempts to contact him via his role as Prince.

Then again, she wouldn't have been on the approved contacts list and in that case it was unlikely he'd even had to *give instructions* to palace staff.

"I wonder if I had written about the pregnancy instead of leaving numerous messages asking you to call me, if your PAA would have ignored those instructions."

"I told her not to read anything from you, that there was *nothing* you had to say that I wanted to hear." And clearly he did not like admitting this.

Every strained line of his gorgeous face and his super-tense posture testified to that fact.

"So, whose fault exactly is it that Mickey has gone nearly five years without meeting his father?" she asked, insisting Konstantin admit his culpability.

He had broken up with her and broken her heart. Fine. But he'd also abandoned their son and that would *never* be fine with her.

And maybe she wouldn't need him to admit his guilt if he hadn't kept harping on how *she* should have tried harder.

"You should have tried harder."

Was he kidding? Fury began to bubble up inside Emma and her best attempts at releasing it were not working. This man!

"I really can't believe you! You are such a product of your privilege," she indicted with exasperation. "Are you telling me you would have welcomed a media storm, naming you the father of my illegitimate child, *Your Highness*? Because that was the only option left open to me."

His expression left no doubt how little he liked that idea. "You could have gone to someone in my family and told them."

"You think I had the resources to fly to Mirrus and try to get an audience with royalty?" This man was not for real.

"You could have sold some jewelry."

"Trust me, I've sold every stinking, meaningless present you ever gave me so I could do my best by my son. But what about the way things went down over five years ago would have given me any belief that wasting precious financial resources trying to talk to *your family* would have made any difference?"

"I realize now that I should have left you an opening to contact me, but if you had just contacted the palace, insisted of speaking to one of my family... They would have listened and gotten a message to me."

Could he even hear himself? "You think if *I* called the palace and *insisted* on speaking to one of the royal family, I'd just be put through? What planet do you live on? Anyway, that just goes to show how much you know. I *did* email your sister-in-law."

Queen Tiana had been the only one Emma could find contact information for.

Of course, it had been an email associated with her position at a children's charity, so the initial email had been circumspect. And talking to that selfish whack job had been a huge mistake that only made Emma's precarious situation feel even more so.

"You put news of your pregnancy in an email to Tiana?" he demanded, sounding shocked and upset.

"Now you're showing your true colors," Emma derided. "You would have been furious if I'd gone to the press five and a half years ago. And no, I told her I needed to speak privately to her. I begged her to call me."

"But she did not."

"Worse." So much worse. "She did. And I told her I was pregnant."

"No."

"Yes."

"Then she did not believe the child was mine. My sister-in-law would have contacted me otherwise. We were friends."

"You were friends with that vicious harpy?"

"What the hell are you talking about?" Konstantin sounded so shocked, it would have been amusing if Emma wasn't so angry. "Tiana was neither vicious, nor a harpy."

Emma knew better. "Ever get into an argument with her?"

"She argued with you about the child being mine? I find that hard to believe. She knew we'd dated. She was the only person in my family that did."

"You chose *her* as your confidante?" Emma asked, appalled.

"I do not know why you are talking about her like this. She died and we all grieved her loss."

"Funny, but if she *weren't* dead, I would have a run a mile when I saw you in the bank. So, think on that."

"What did she say to you to cause such antipathy?"

"Besides her offer to *buy* my baby and my silence? Besides threaten me if I refused? Besides inform me with a very menacing demeanor that she was a queen and I was a nobody and she would get her way? Oh, really, nothing much."

"That's ridiculous. Tiana would never have done those things."

"She told me you would never believe the child was yours. That her way was the best way to make sure my baby was raised in the royal environment it deserved, only

I thought he deserved a mother who loved him." Emotion choked Emma and she did her best to push it away.

She couldn't afford to let her own pain, remembered fear or even present anger take over during this conversation. Too much was at stake.

And while she wasn't a naive twenty-year-old any longer, she still didn't have the resources to fight a monarchy if he chose to go as crazy as his dead sister-in-law had.

"Surely you knew you had the trump card. You carried my DNA within your body."

"And I had the resources to force you to take a DNA test? Never mind how you could have paid someone off to give false results."

"I would never have done something so underhand." There he went sounding shocked again.

"Says the man who made it nearly impossible for me to get a decent job for the entire three years that restraining order based on *false* testimony was in place."

"I told you before, I took out no restraining order."

Something inside Emma just cracked open and all the anger she had been tamping down came surging up. She jumped up from her chair and pointed wrathfully at him. "You just stay there. I will be right back."

"No restraining order," she muttered to herself as she stomped down the hall. "He thinks he's going to gaslight me? Make me forget the hell he put me through? I've got the restraining order. I've got evidence. I'm not the crazy one here."

She spun the lock on the safe she kept copies of important papers in. Most had corresponding originals in her safe-deposit box at the bank. Call her paranoid, but after her trust had been betrayed by him, by her parents, by his crazy if dead sister-in-law, Emma was prepared for every eventuality she could be.

She stomped back into the living room and threw the

court papers at him. "No restraining order? Then what is that? A bedtime story?"

"You're going to wake Mikhail if you keep shouting like that."

"Then he can see for himself what a rat he has for a father." Emma stomped to her chair and plopped into it, glaring at Konstantin as he read the document he held.

Her fury did not abate as horror came over his features. It did not diminish as he looked up from the papers, his face waxen and pale, his expression on the verge of being ill.

She didn't know what all that shock and horror was about.

"Didn't you think I'd keep a copy? It will read well in any attempt you make to get custody of Mickey. I can prove the accusations of stalking made in there are false. I won't be the one sporting the criminal record this time!"

"A restraining order is not a criminal record." The words came out low and shocked.

Emma made a dismissive gesture with her hand. Semantics! "Tell that to the employers that ran routine background checks on me and it popped up. Do you know how impossible it made trying to provide for myself and later for Mickey?"

Konstantin went from pale to sickly green. "I did not do this. I did not take out that order of restraint. I never would have."

"And yet, you did."

"I did not. Look at the papers."

"Oh, I know… The palace lawyers did it. Some guy named Albert Popov, but it was on your behalf. And it was issued on the weight of your testimony." No further proof required.

But then he was a prince. And she was a nobody.

He'd claimed she'd *stalked* him, said she'd had delusions of a relationship that never existed, had told the court that she had threatened him that if she could not have him, no one could. Only his fabrications hadn't been well researched. He'd had to put dates and times with the claims, and Emma had proof she was with other people, in class and one time even at a doctor's appointment when she was supposed to have accosted him.

She had signed affidavits to that effect in her safety deposit too.

At one time, she'd considered forcing the issue, but she'd realized that doing so had to be a last resort. Because even with the proof the TRO had been gotten under false pretenses, she was still one person and he represented a monarchy.

She felt stronger now, more centered and capable of fighting than she had at age twenty.

"No. I never said any of those things," he said now, sounding so darn sincere.

She wanted to smack him and that thought made her feel guilty. Patience, compassion and tolerance, she reminded herself.

Without a lot of effect.

"Rewriting history now, *Your Highness*?" she sneered.

Allowing her anger to come out felt cleansing, good. Like a weight that wasn't hers to carry was being released. But she didn't feel any better about the past for voicing her pain to the man who had never cared that he'd hurt her in the first place.

"My son is nearly five and I have met him for the first time today. And it is my fault. That is what you are saying."

"Yes." She had no give in her for this man anymore. He'd done too much to hurt her, but even more damning, by his own actions he had also done a lot to make her son's life harder.

"You have grown very hard."

"I just opened my eyes to who you are."

"And it is not anyone good in your estimation."

She shrugged. "I wouldn't be open to your having a relationship with my son if I did not think there was any good in you." She just now knew how ruthless he could be. Knew that *she* could not trust him, even if Mickey might be able to.

She would never forget that truth again.

"He is my son too."

"Not so you would notice."

Konstantin winced. "What have you told him about me?"

"He only asked about his father when he started pre-school. Other children had daddies, but he did not."

"And?"

"And I showed him pictures, told him that he would meet you someday when he was older."

"You told him this? So, you had some faith in me, then?"

"Not so much, no. But he's your spitting image and I didn't think once you met him, even a coldhearted bastard like you could deny his existence." Though the quickness with which Konstantin had latched onto Mickey being his was a small point in the rat's favor.

It had clearly never occurred to him that she might have jumped from his bed into that of another man.

"How was this meeting supposed to happen?" Konstantin asked, still subdued.

"Not the way it did, that's for sure."

"But you planned to try again. To tell me about him?"

"He deserved for me to."

"But I did not."

"Frankly, your feelings did not come into it for me."

"You have changed."

"So you've said."

"Five and a half years ago, you lived for me."

"Five and a half years ago, if I hadn't been pregnant, I might well have died for you."

"Do not make melodramatic statements like that, even if you are merely trying to make a point." But he sounded shaken rather than condemning.

Which is why she maintained an even tone when she asked, "Melodrama?" She shook her head and that's when she told him about the mugging. It had happened the same night her parents had kicked her out.

She'd been mugged for the twenty-nine dollars she carried in her wallet. Emma hadn't had credit cards then. Her parents didn't believe in them. She'd just been taking a walk to clear her head, but the motel she'd landed in wasn't in the best part of the city.

"When I woke up in pain unlike any I'd ever known and remembered I literally had no place to go, no one to call to come help me, I had a moment when I just wanted to go back to sleep and never wake up. The doctor came in and told me that it would be touch-and-go for a while. For both of us. But that my baby was still alive inside me and I clung to that. I have never felt anything like my determination to give Mickey life. It *was* touch-and-go for almost a week, for both of us. But every time I surfaced to consciousness, I thought of my baby and determined to live."

Konstantin was gray. "Where were your parents?"

"Like you, they had decided that I was no longer suitable for the role I had in their life."

"They disowned you?" he asked in shock.

"Yes."

"And you probably blame me for this as well."

"No."

"Why not?"

"They adopted me, believing they could raise me to be a good, religious daughter. They tried their best, but I had sex with you outside the bounds of marriage and that was not acceptable. According to them, bad blood outed."

"Because you were pregnant and that was my fault."

"No, the choice to share my body with you? That was mine to make. And I made it. I took responsibility for it then and have done ever since."

"I seduced a virgin into my bed and kept her there as my mistress," he said with blatant self-condemnation.

But she'd never let anyone else take the blame for her choices. It wasn't in Emma to pass the buck like that. "I wanted to be seduced. The mistress part I could have done without, but if I wanted to share even a part of your life, I knew I had to be available to you when you had time for me and that meant allowing you to support me. Again, a decision I made."

A decision her parents had hated. Her coming up pregnant after moving home when he'd dumped her had been the final straw as far as Ansel and Belinda Sloan were concerned.

If Emma had been willing to give Mickey up, things might have been different, but she hadn't been. Not then. Not now.

Her son was her life and Prince Konstantin of Mirrus had better realize that.

"You did not decide to get pregnant."

"No. Even now I cannot credit that my IUD fell out without me being aware." What were the chances?

According to her OB, very slim, but not nonexistent. Obviously. Emma had just been unlucky. Though it was impossible to think of Mickey as anything but a gift in her life. The unplanned nature of her pregnancy was something else.

Emma shook off her thoughts. "My OB said it happens, not often, but it happens. I was just so happy the pain had stopped, I didn't question the whys."

"You never told me the IUD hurt."

"What part of the repressed, raised-to-ultraconservative-values me would have talked to you back then about something so private and embarrassing?"

"Sex is private and we talked about that."

She rolled her eyes. "Saying I want you is not the same thing as saying the lower half of my body feels like someone kicked it because of my IUD."

"It was that bad?"

"Yes."

"No wonder you did not want sex sometimes."

"No wonder."

"I thought you were losing interest in me."

"I guess that made you feel better about knowing you were going to dump me so you could marry another woman."

His expression said it all. Konstantin's belief she was losing interest *had* alleviated his guilt over making plans to marry Lady Nataliya.

That the woman had ended up married to his brother and *not* Konstantin was entirely beside the point.

"Five and a half years ago, that would have surprised me. I thought you were this amazing guy."

"But now you know differently." His tone was strange.

"You turned your ruthlessness on me when you excised me from your life. I've lived with the consequences of your selfishness every day since."

"You consider our son a consequence."

"I consider how hard it has been to provide for him with that stupid restraining order on my record a consequence. I consider how he has gone without any extended family since birth a consequence. I consider how he cried when he came home from school after they made gifts for their fathers a week after the ones done for Mother's Day, keeping it even, you see. Only for a little boy without a dad just the first of many times he would be faced with the knowledge he did not have a father."

"There are many single-parent households out there."

"Yes, and children with two parents of the same sex.

Schools should be more sensitive, but his was not and my son cried because he lacked."

"And that was my fault."

"Yes."

"You don't think much of me."

"No."

"I am surprised you are open to me seeing Mikhail."

"Whatever is best for my son, if I can give it to him, I will."

"You could have married and given him a stepfather."

"Because being raised by parents who had not given birth to me worked out so well." She'd thought her adopted parents loved her. Emma had learned differently, and she wasn't letting anyone do that to her son.

"A parent can be neglectful or abusive, or anything in between and have the strongest of blood ties with their child."

"Yes, but I wasn't going to risk bringing someone into Mickey's life that might not love him like I do."

"You are risking that with me."

"As much as it is not fair, and I cannot guarantee you will always be good for my son, you have had a place in his life since the day I conceived. You are his biological father and if you want to be his dad, for his sake, I have to let you try."

"You do not believe I will disappear from his life again, or you would not risk it regardless." He sounded very certain of that.

And he was right. "No, I don't."

"Even if I have more children at some later date?"

"Even then." Though something deep inside her recoiled at the thought of him having children with another woman.

"So, you at least have some faith in me."

Faith in him? Not likely. But he'd dumped her to do his duty by his family and despite how it all went down, even she could see at the time that doing so had cost Konstantin. Not enough to maintain their relationship, but walking away hadn't been easy.

At least she'd thought it hadn't. How efficiently he'd cut her out of her life and left no loophole for getting back in, even just to have a conversation so she could tell him she was pregnant?

That might tell a different story.

Regardless, she did know one thing about him. "If I learned one thing about you, it is how committed you are to your family, Konstantin. While I have *no* faith in you, I do have faith in that. Now you've acknowledged Mickey is yours, you won't try to shuttle him out of your life."

He opened his mouth to say something, but she forestalled him with a raised hand. "Even if you tried, I wouldn't let you. I will never let you hurt my son again."

"*Our* son and I have no intention of hurting him. Or you."

"Leave me out of it."

"You are his mother—you are in the center of *it*."

Emma stood. "I paint during Mickey's nap time. If you'll excuse me." She wasn't hanging out with Konstantin chatting about old times.

Emma had had her say.

In her opinion, the Prince needed time to digest the home truths she'd served up.

Not that he took it.

She could hear Konstantin on the phone and then instructing someone to bring him his laptop. Working. Typical.

He'd just found out he had a son, but Mirrus Global still came first.

It would do Emma well to remember the Prince's priorities.

She took some time to center herself and get her feelings back under control before she picked up her paints and went to work on her latest commission.

CHAPTER THREE

"So, you are a painter?" Konstantin asked Emma when he tracked her down to a glassed-in porch that overlooked the back courtyard, which she'd clearly turned into her studio. She'd always wanted to pursue her art. "Good for you."

She had a paint-splattered apron over her clothes, her shoes were kicked in a corner and the image she presented reminded him so much of old times, he sucked in a breath as emotions he did not *do* assailed him.

Emma looked up, her expression unfocused and a little startled, like she'd forgotten she had a visitor. A far cry from the days when she hung on his every word. He missed the way she used to look at him because he was pretty sure he still looked at her like she was the most desirable woman walking the planet.

"Painting small commissions is a way I supplement my regular income."

Her parents had refused her an education at a fine arts college, insisting she get a more practical degree. When they'd been together, she'd been working on a BA in business.

He looked at the canvas on the easel. It was a painting of downtown Santa Fe. "That is very nice, but not the art I remember you doing."

Five years ago her art had been splashy, vibrant colors filled with emotion.

She shrugged. "It pays the bills and I still get to put my stamp on the artwork."

"I see art still has the same effect on your attitude. You seem much calmer."

"Art and meditation. I spent the first ten minutes in here meditating." She said it with no apology. No embarrassment.

This woman no longer struggled with marching to her own drum. When they'd been together, she'd hated disappointing her parents, or being singled out as different.

"You meditate?" he asked. Fascinated.

"At least twice a day, more if Mickey is even more active than usual. I do yoga too. Trust me, single parenting takes every ounce of patience and calm I have and then some. So, I augment."

"In pretty unique ways."

"Not around here. Santa Fe is very proud of its *be different* vibe."

"Mirrus isn't exactly backward, but I don't know if we even have a yoga studio."

"You probably do, but since you don't use it, you wouldn't know."

"You're saying I'm oblivious."

She shrugged. "You will take my words the way you want."

"You sound very Zen."

"Mickey is going to wake soon. He'll be glad you kept your promise."

"Did you think I wouldn't?"

"I didn't think about it. Worrying wouldn't change your actions, only my anxiety levels." And she smiled.

Art and meditation. A winning combination for Emma's peace of mind. He would remember that, make it easy for her to do both whenever she felt the need.

And that smile? Went straight to his groin. Not the reaction she was looking for with her sound bites of wisdom, he was sure.

"I've been looking for you for the past several months." He'd been on the verge of hiring a private investigator, or swallowing his pride and asking his new sister-in-law for help.

"Why?"

"I'm sure you know Lady Nataliya is now the Princess of Mirrus. I think my brother is going to make her Queen on their anniversary." Which wasn't the real answer to Emma's question.

That was way more complicated.

Over five years ago, he'd been committed to following through with the marriage contract, but breaking up with Emma had been much harder than he'd expected. He'd needed time to grieve the loss of their relationship, even though he hadn't acknowledged that was what he was doing.

He'd dreamed about her nightly and then less frequently as time went on, but the dreams never stopped completely. He'd never stopped seeing Emma in other women only to realize it wasn't her.

She had *haunted* him.

And so Konstantin had put off marrying a woman he'd been pretty sure had a thing for his brother. As much as he'd wanted to please his father, he'd been unable to take those final steps to court Nataliya and announce a formal engagement.

Then Tiana had died, and the family had gone into formal mourning. The question of Konstantin getting married anytime soon became a moot point, not to be raised by anyone, but certainly not him, for another five years.

It shouldn't have surprised him, considering the role she'd played in him putting off his marriage to Nataliya to begin with, that once his commitment to Nataliya was out of the way, Konstantin hadn't been able to stop wondering about Emma.

What was she doing? Was she still single?

"You say Mirrus isn't backward, but seriously?" Emma was asking now. "Your brother has to *make* his wife queen, or he can keep her as a princess for their whole marriage? Talk about being under the thumb of the patriarchy."

"It's a political role, not just a title. You cannot blame my brother for being cautious." Why were they talking about Nikolai and Nataliya?

That's your fault, genius, his inner voice reminded him.

"The fact the law is written the way it is feeds the power of patriarchy."

"You've become very political."

"You think having an opinion about equal rights and opportunities for women makes me political?" she asked.

Put that way? Maybe not. "But the issues *are* politicized."

"Issues become politicized when you have one group trying to suppress another. That doesn't inherently make the issues themselves political."

"That's an interesting take."

"Isn't it?"

"Dad, you're still here!"

Konstantin spun around at the sound of his son's voice. Mikhail was still rubbing sleep from his eyes, his little-boy features so familiar it stalled Konstantin's breath for a second. He managed a nod.

Mikhail looked at his mother. "He's still here, Mom."

"Yes, he is, Mickey."

"When is he going away again?" Mickey asked.

Before she could answer, Konstantin found his voice. "I am not going away. Now that I have found you and your mom, I will never lose you again."

"You lost us?"

Konstantin looked to Emma. He didn't want to contradict anything she had told their son.

Emma's eyes glistened, but her features showed that newfound serenity she'd managed to achieve since coming in here. "He did."

"You didn't know he was looking for us?" Mikhail asked his mother.

She shook her head. "No. I thought he did not have a place in his life for us."

"Oh. But he does?"

"I do," Konstantin affirmed.

"Mom said you are a prince, but you know… Princes are only in fairy tales." Mikhail cast a sidelong glance at his mother, but he didn't seem worried she'd be upset he was checking on her veracity.

"Do you like fairy tales?" Konstantin asked him.

"Not really. I like…" Mikhail named a popular children's series about an animal family. "There's a mom and dad and grandparents and everything."

"You have a grandfather, two uncles and aunt who will be delighted to meet you. One of your uncles *is* a king, but we aren't a fairy tale."

"Really? Am I a prince?"

"No, but you are an earl." Though not officially. Not yet. But Konstantin would make sure Mikhail had his rightful place in the family as his eldest child.

"What's an earl?"

"It is a title of nobility. It means you are a member of the Royal Family of Mirrus."

Mikhail's nose and forehead scrunched in thought. "But my mom is not a princess."

"No." Not yet.

"That's good."

"It is?"

"Yeah. She gets real messy with her paints sometimes and when she gardens. And when she did the floors in my room? She got sweaty, like whoa."

Konstantin couldn't hold back a smile at his son's reply and phrasing. He looked at Emma, sharing the joke. "Like whoa?"

"He picked it up at his preschool day care."

"My teacher says it," Mikhail informed them, his tone revealing the boy's admiration for the teacher.

Emma's smile for their son was loving and a little amused. "Yes, he does."

"You don't think princesses get messy or sweaty?" Konstantin asked Mikhail.

"Do they?" Mikhail asked rather than answered, his face alight with little-boy curiosity.

"They do."

Mikhail gave Emma a dubious look. "I guess you can be a princess, Mom."

Emma laughed, the sound filled with genuine amusement. "That's all right, sweetie. I'll stick with plain old Emma Carmichael."

Not if Konstantin had anything to say about it.

Konstantin paced his hotel room while he spoke in rapid Russian to his brother King Nikolai of Mirrus.

"Yes, she had a copy of the restraining order," he said to his brother Nikolai now.

"But why would Sir Popov take it on himself to take out a TRO on your behalf? Did you say it is based on testimony given by you?" Nikolai demanded, sounding as judgmental as only an older brother who was also a king and had never done anything stupid like break up with the mother of his child could.

Needing to understand where the TRO had come from, Konstantin had called the senior palace lawyer, Sir Albert Popov, Esquire, before reaching out to Nikolai.

The phone call had been as confusing as it had been illuminating.

Konstantin was trying to figure out *why* Tiana had done what she had, even while he talked to his brother.

Popov had confirmed that the former Queen had been the one who had instructed him to take out the restraining order, based on trumped-up testimony supposedly supplied by *him*. After extracting further disturbing details from the palace lawyer, Konstantin had instructed the man to arrange an immediate flight to New Mexico.

Konstantin felt betrayed and furious and a lot of other negative emotions he was doing his best to keep a lid on. He had to keep his head for both this discussion with his brother and to figure out where to go from here with Emma.

"Supposed testimony," Konstantin reminded his brother. "I would never lie about Emma that way." His brother should know that about him.

"Are you sure?"

"What the hell? Nikolai, I know you and I don't agree on everything but you know me better than that."

A sigh came over the phone. "You are right. I do. Sometimes..." His brother let his words trail off in very uncharacteristic fashion.

"What?"

"Sometimes, I get jealous and it makes me look at you differently."

"Jealous of what?"

"You were practically engaged to Nataliya."

Was his brother serious right now? "Are you kidding me? She's only ever had eyes for you, and I knew it. Why do you think I dragged my feet so hard on going through with the marriage?"

Who wanted to be married to a woman who would probably fantasize he was his brother on their wedding night?

"You weren't ready to get married."

"When we first signed that contract, she was eighteen, I was only a year older. Of course I wasn't ready to marry her then. But five and a half years ago, I broke things off with Emma so I could marry Nataliya." His father had been putting the pressure on and Konstantin had realized that things with Emma were getting too deep.

"And then Tiana died."

"Da." And Konstantin had grieved the loss of his sister-in-law and friend, or so he had believed her to be, but part of him had been relieved.

Because the formal period of mourning meant their father would stop harping on the marriage contract for at least a year.

"Listen, whatever you think of me, believe me when I tell you that the thought of marrying a woman who had a thing for my brother was *never* something I wanted. I was prepared to do my duty, but that's it."

"And that duty had you abandoning the mother of your child," his brother said on a sigh.

"I did not know she was pregnant."

"Of course you didn't. You would never have let her disappear otherwise."

At least his brother trusted him that much. "She did disappear. I think she changed her name because of the restraining order, but I don't know how she managed to hide so well."

"Did she say she was hiding?"

"No, but Emma said she spoke to Tiana." He told his brother what Emma claimed Tiana had said. "It's still hard for me to believe she threatened Emma like that."

Even knowing Tiana had been behind the TRO, Konstantin had believed she was his friend.

"Is that what you said to Emma?" Nikolai asked in a tone that implied a yes answer was the wrong one.

Konstantin experienced a sinking feeling deep in his gut. Because while he *hadn't* said that to Emma. Exactly. He had sort of implied she'd exaggerated Tiana's desire to take their baby away.

"I hadn't spoken to the lawyer yet, Nikolai. Look, I know

you and Tiana didn't always agree on the lifestyle of a royal, but she was approachable."

"Where I was not?" Nikolai asked stiffly.

"Hell, Nikolai. You took on the mantle of King at twenty-seven. You became my sovereign and the brother relationship didn't feel as real after that."

"I am sorry. It was a hard transition, but it was not my intention to make you think you couldn't come to me. I'm still your big brother."

"And I believed Tiana was my friend."

"I am sorry you had to find out differently. Tiana really did not want to get pregnant. She must have seen Emma's pregnancy as a way out of having to go through one of her own."

"That's like a plot out of a novel."

"You know what they say…"

"Real life is stranger than fiction." Konstantin certainly could affirm that cliché.

"It certainly is, but Konstantin, you have something more important to think about than the melodrama of five years ago. You have gravely insulted the mother of your child on behalf of a dead woman who was not who she pretended to be."

"Gravely insulted?" What was his brother talking about?

"You doubted Emma's word about what Tiana said to her. If I know you, that wasn't the only thing you said that Emma could take offense to."

"I'm not a bad man." Though he hadn't been feeling like a good one since meeting his son for the first time. "She calls him Mickey."

"Mickey is a fine nickname. At least she named him after you."

Konstantin nodded, though his brother couldn't see it. "Giving him my second name was more than I deserved."

"Listen, brother, you are *not* a bad man, but you are a man with *a lot* to make up for."

"You're so sure."

"Since you were a small boy, when you feel guilty, you attack. Even if you did not do that, you broke up with your pregnant girlfriend to marry another woman."

"But it was my duty! And I didn't know she was pregnant." He could wish he had until the end of time, but that would not change the past.

"Which makes you a guy she can trust. It's just going to take her a while to see it."

"I've got a plan for that." He was going to ask her to marry him. What could be a more certain and binding commitment than that?

"Good. Just, be prepared to work for it."

"You don't think I know how to work for something?"

"In business? You'll go without sleep for days and sacrifice your personal time for the good of the company, but you've never worked for a relationship."

"And you have?"

"You know Nataliya. Can you doubt it?"

Konstantin had to smile at that. "No."

"I think this is my fault, even if I didn't have anything to do with the restraining order," Konstantin blurted out as his thoughts finally coalesced on a possible motive for Tiana's actions.

"What do you mean?" Nikolai asked, his voice lacking the condemnation Konstantin expected.

"I told Tiana I didn't know if I was strong enough to walk away from Emma and stay away." He hadn't been.

Konstantin had gone looking for Emma, needing her comfort after Tiana's death.

And he hadn't been able to find his ex-lover. He'd thought about hiring a private investigator then, but that marriage contract had still been hanging over his head.

Konstantin had believed it would be unfair to Emma to start something up again only to have to end it again somewhere down the line.

His every good intention had been turned back against him.

Even his recent search for the woman he'd never been able to forget had come up empty. Running into her in the bank had been some kind of miracle.

Which maybe meant not all of his luck was bad when it came to her.

"That does not make Tiana's actions your responsibility. A less ruthless, less manipulative person would have supported you without fabricating evidence for a restraining order you knew nothing about."

Konstantin knew his brother spoke the truth, but he still felt incredibly guilty.

He'd lost out on sharing Emma's pregnancy and almost five years of his son's life because he'd made too many bad decisions, not least of which was confiding in the wrong person.

Emma walked into the restaurant where she had agreed to meet Konstantin and wasn't surprised to find him and an older gentleman at a table already.

The tables on either side were taken up with his security detail, both for protection and privacy, she would imagine.

The Prince hadn't been thrilled when she'd once again refused to come to his hotel. Emma had stood firm though and Konstantin had eventually given in. Asking where she wanted to meet.

She'd named the restaurant because though Emma didn't often dine out, a friend worked here and Emma knew it would be nearly empty midmorning.

Which it was. Only one other table was occupied across the dining room from Konstantin and his entourage.

The Prince rose when Emma was a few feet from the table and pulled a chair out for her. The table was set for two, the older man sitting in front of a blank spot. A carafe of coffee sat in the center of the table as well as a plate of small sandwiches.

She didn't think this restaurant had sandwiches on the menu. They probably didn't, but the request had been made by royalty. Little chance of it being ignored.

She nodded her thanks to Konstantin and sat down, casting a curious glance at the other man sharing their table.

"Good morning, Emma. Mikhail is well I trust." Konstantin returned to his seat, his attention fully on her.

Even after all these years, it was a heady feeling. One she did her best to ignore.

"Mickey's great." Wanting to see his *dad* again, but Emma and the Prince had some things to work out first. "He's at his preschool day care."

"What does that mean, *preschool day care*?" Konstantin frowned. He didn't like not knowing everything.

There had been a time when she'd seen that as an endearing quality. She had to fight against doing so now.

But nothing about this man could be endearing to her.

"It's exactly what it sounds like," she told him. "A preschool that also offers day care. Mickey has four hours of preschool daily and the rest of the time there he's in the day care portion of the facility."

"How much time does he spend there every day? Does he like it?"

They were legitimate questions. Not really intrusive at all, but Emma had to force herself to answer them. For Mickey's entire life, there had never been anyone else to question, to offer input on her choices.

Now, suddenly Konstantin was here and making noises like he meant to stay in Mickey's life. Which was what

Emma wanted, but it was going to be an adjustment for her, on so many levels.

"I work full-time, though I've arranged to work my last two hours each day from home after Mickey is in bed. I also take thirty-minute lunches, rather than the hour the company offers. So, he's in day care about six to six and a half hours, depending on my commute time."

"Your world is arranged around our son," Konstantin observed as he offered her coffee.

She declined with a wave of her hand. "I don't drink caffeine."

She'd cut out all caffeine when she was pregnant and then been encouraged to keep doing so by her first yoga instructor. Since she slept better at night, she had to agree it had been a good, if difficult choice.

"It is. And yes, he likes his day care and preschool," she said, answering Konstantin's questions. "Though I'd already taught him a lot of what he is now learning, while I was still working as a nanny and had him with me all the time."

Mickey complained sometimes of being bored in his school, but for the most part he enjoyed it and he adored his teacher.

Hence picking up the man's phrases and using them.

"You worked as a nanny?" Even as he asked, Konstantin was texting something on his phone.

"Yes." She saw no harm in telling Konstantin what she'd done in the past. It had no connection to her position as a bookkeeper now. "It allowed me to be with Mickey while giving me the time to take a couple online college courses every term."

"You got your degree?"

"An associate's rather than a bachelor's degree like I'd meant to, but sometimes plans have to be adjusted to work in the life we live."

"That's a very wise attitude to take."

"A necessary one, in my life anyway." She was happy she'd found calm acceptance. At first, she'd resented all the losses in her life, and spent a lot of fruitless time despising the man in front of her.

"You are proud you've taken the upheavals with equanimity," he realized out loud. "As you should be."

"I'm proud of a lot of things, but that's not what we're here to talk about." She cast another glance at the older man who had sat quietly while she and Konstantin talked.

"No. It is not." Konstantin indicated the man. "Emma, this is Albert Popov. He has been on the palace's legal team since he passed the bar."

The lawyer who had drawn up the TRO. He had silver in his hair and the lines around his eyes indicated he was probably in his fifties. So, a long time, then.

"I won't say it's a pleasure to meet you, because I don't know if it will be," Emma said. "But I will wish you a good morning." She didn't know why the lawyer was there, but she suspected Konstantin wanted to hammer out a legal agreement for parental rights and visitation.

"I will try to make our meeting as pleasant as possible." The lawyer gave Konstantin a nervous glance.

Emma didn't trust either man, but she knew she had to hear them out. "Okay."

Konstantin's earlier text made sense as a server approached with assorted herbal tea sachets in a basket and another carafe, this one no doubt filled with hot water. He and Mr. Popov waited while she chose a tea and set it steeping in her cup.

Only then did Konstantin pour himself a cup of coffee, the scent nearly making Emma moan. She missed coffee.

"Albert is the lawyer who filed the restraining order." Konstantin looked at Emma expectantly.

CHAPTER FOUR

EMMA DIDN'T SAY ANYTHING.

He could have chosen a different lawyer to bring to this meeting, but the Prince had never been what she would term *sensitive*.

Konstantin continued to look at Emma like he thought she might start asking questions, or something.

Emma just waited.

"He did not do it on my behest," Konstantin said as the silence stretched.

Oh. So, they were going to discuss the TRO first. Emma did a calming count in her mind. "So you claimed yesterday, but he did do it on your *behalf.*"

"At my former sister-in-law's command, *not mine,*" Konstantin stressed. "He did not consult me before filing the paperwork, nor did he consult me after."

Mr. Popov cleared his throat. "I believed Prince Konstantin wanted the temporary restraining order taken out against you. What I believed to be his testimony about your stalkerish behavior was very compelling."

"Was it?" Emma asked noncommittally. She'd thought the allegations sounded dramatic and over the top.

But then she'd known them to be the lies they were.

"I know now that Her Highness had fabricated the document, but at the time I believed the accusations to be genuine."

"And you never even spoke once about this to Konstantin, I mean His Royal Highness?" Emma had no trouble believing the crazy Queen had instigated the TRO, though she had no clue why. But Emma found it difficult to accept that the lawyer hadn't ever once mentioned it to Konstantin.

"You are the mother of my son." Konstantin reached out

and placed his hand over hers on the table. "You always have leave to call me by my first name."

Emma tugged her hand away, tucking it with her other one safely in her lap. Touching from this man was not in the safety zone for her peace of mine. "I'm pretty sure that's *not* how it works."

Konstantin frowned at her withdrawal.

But it was the lawyer who spoke next. "I realize now that it was a grave error on my part, but no, I did not confirm details or intentions with His Highness."

Emma made no effort to hide her skepticism. "I find that incredibly hard to believe."

"I am finding it difficult to credit I was so easily led myself, Ms. Sloane."

"Carmichael," Emma corrected him. "I had to change my name to get a job."

The lawyer gulped. Konstantin's jaw went rigid at the reminder.

"I apologize most sincerely for that, Ms. Carmichael." Mr. Popov loosened his tie at his neck, looking uncomfortable. "His Highness has informed me that at no time did you stalk him and he would never have approved the restraining order."

The man's manner was stiff and the words sounded rehearsed.

Could he be believed?

"And yet you were able to get it in his name," Emma pointed out reasonably.

Mr. Popov gave Konstantin another nervous glance. "Our legal team holds power of attorney to do a great deal on behalf of the royal family. This is to protect them and their time, you understand."

"My brother and I have now agreed that all POAs held by our legal team will be reviewed and rewritten so that nothing of this sort could ever happen again." Konstantin didn't look nervous. He looked angry.

Really angry. And disgusted.

The lawyer winced.

She didn't imagine the rest of the legal team was going to be happy to have their purview limited, but Emma thought the move was long overdue. No one should be allowed that much leeway with another person's life, no matter how convenient it might be.

"How do I know you are telling me the truth?" Emma asked, genuinely wishing one of the men could have an answer for her. "What possible motive could Queen Tiana have had to instruct you to do such a thing, even going to the effort of making up supposed testimony for Konstantin?"

"As to that, I couldn't speak to our deceased Queen's motives." And the lawyer's tone implied Emma shouldn't even be speculating.

Like just because Tiana had been a queen, that made her above having her actions questioned.

Emma wasn't impressed. "Isn't it more likely that Konstantin has convinced you to lie for him so I don't think he's such a rat?" she mused aloud.

Konstantin had to know that the less she trusted him, the stricter the restrictions around his visits with Mickey would have to be.

"Rat?" Mr. Popov asked faintly, his eyes wide.

"I would never stoop to instructing a retainer to lie for me." Offense rang in every syllable of Konstantin's denial.

"Wouldn't you?"

"I have never lied to you, Emma, even when it would have been easier on us both if I had." Konstantin took a breath, clearly collecting himself. "Do you have any further questions for Mr. Popov?"

"No."

"You are sure?" Konstantin asked, like he expected her to change her mind.

"I thought he was here to negotiate the visitation schedule," she admitted. "He's not?" she asked, just to make sure.

"That is something you and I will work out between ourselves." Konstantin's tone left no room for argument.

Emma didn't actually want to discuss her private life with lawyers, but she had the urge to argue just because he was so sure of his own mind *and* hers.

"I have counseled against such a haphazard approach," Mr. Popov said, obliquely reproving the Prince, but not coming right out and doing so.

Emma gave him a wry look. "If what you told me is true, I'm not sure Konstantin should be taking any kind of legal advice from you."

The lawyer looked offended, but before he could say anything else, Konstantin dismissed the older man with a wave of his hand. "Emma is right. You made a grave error in judgment five and a half years ago and every day since by not telling me what you had done. Whether you should remain in our employ is still up for discussion."

The lawyer looked like he wanted to argue, but Konstantin's forbidding expression kept him silent. "Keep your phone on in case Emma changes her mind and wants clarification of anything."

Mr. Popov nodded and stood. "Of course, Your Highness." He bowed toward Emma. "It was a pleasure to meet you, Ms. Carmichael."

As the man walked away, Emma rolled her eyes at Konstantin. "Now, I *know* he lies."

"He is a lawyer, of course he lies, but he's not lying about the TRO."

"I'm sure there are lots of honest lawyers," Emma said rather than revisit the restraining order issue.

Konstantin looked more abashed than she expected from

her comment. "I am sure you are right. I spoke out of turn in my frustration."

"And because you are feeling guilty."

"Yes." He frowned. "I am surprised you realized that."

"There was a time I knew you very well, Konstantin." And not just his body. While he'd seen her as a convenient sexual partner, he had been the love of Emma's life.

And she'd paid attention to his every mood. His every reaction. Emma had naively believed they had so much in common.

They'd diverged in one crucial way that really said how very little any of the other aspects of their relationship mattered.

Emma would never have dumped him for the sake of duty.

"I never lied to you, Emma. I told you our liaison was to be temporary. I told you about the contract when I'd never told another person."

"That's not true. Tiana knew."

"As did the rest of our royal family and our legal advisors, but I never told other friends or women I dated."

"Slept with, you mean. You weren't a big dater."

"I dated you."

He had. Not at first, but she wouldn't move into his apartment if he wasn't willing to have at least a semblance of a normal relationship, which meant dating.

Konstantin had insisted they couldn't meet each other's friends and families, but she'd understood his reasoning. He didn't want to be at the center of a media storm when people found out he had a live-in lover.

"You dated me like a married man does his mistress. You were very discreet."

"And you said you understood the need for that discretion."

"I was a naive nineteen-year-old when we met. I fell

for you like a ton of bricks and you were from this world I couldn't even fathom." Emma gestured to the restaurant. "Even this isn't really my world. My world is a fixer-upper house that I love, a job that will allow for a trip to Disney World with Mickey once, maybe twice in his childhood."

"But that world, it is no longer yours either."

She sighed. "I know. I'm smart enough to realize some things will change now you've decided to acknowledge your son."

"It was not a matter of deciding but of knowing about him."

"You keep saying that."

"And you do not believe me." He took a sip of his coffee and stared at her over the rim of his cup, his expression unfathomable.

"What is there in our past relationship or even the present one for me to trust, Konstantin?"

"I broke up with you for the sake of my family and a promise I had made. Doesn't that tell you that at the very least, I keep my promises?"

She wasn't as impressed as he clearly expected her to be. In fact, she barely refrained from rolling her eyes. "You signed a contract, Konstantin. I never doubted how important business was to you." She just hadn't realized that marriage fell under that umbrella for him.

Even after he'd told her about the contract, part of Emma simply hadn't believed he ever planned to follow through on it. Not with the way he treated her. Not with the fact he'd signed it several years before they'd met and had never even dated the woman named in it, Lady Nataliya Shevchenko.

"Which was a commitment I made on behalf of my family and myself."

"It was a draconian agreement," Emma condemned.

Konstantin laughed, though there was little humor in the sound. "That is what Jenna says."

Tension stiffened Emma's spine. "Who is Jenna?"

"Nataliya's best friend."

"Is she your girlfriend?"

"No, of course not. I do not do girlfriends." He pinned her with a dark brown gaze. "You were the single exception."

That might have meant something if he hadn't dumped her. "Latest sex partner, then."

"No. I think my youngest brother would gut me if I made a play for Jenna. Not that I see her giving him the time of day, but that is not the point." Konstantin smiled, inviting her to share the joke.

Emma was all out of humor at the moment. Finding out he had a son might be every bit as easy for Konstantin as he was making it out to be, but Emma's entire life was changing.

Again.

Because of this man. Again.

The truth was, they'd veered completely off topic and it was her fault. "I believe the point you were *trying* to make is that since you keep promises to your family, I should trust you to keep any promises you make to me."

"Yes."

"I'm not sure if it has escaped your notice, but first, that was a business contract, even if family was involved. And two, I am not your family and you betrayed *me* pretty spectacularly in the past."

"How did I betray you?" he asked, like he really didn't know.

"You dumped me, but that wasn't enough for you. You evicted me completely from your life so I could not even reach you. You allowed your crazy-pants sister-in-law to have a TRO taken out on your behalf that made my life that was already imploding even worse. You let her threaten me and my role in my unborn child's life."

"I did not know about any of those things!"

"But if you had not cut me from your life with such precision, you would have. Now you want me to believe that *if* you had known, you would never have let any of that happen. It's a reach, Konstantin."

"I had no choice."

"Did you even try? Did you go to your father or your brother and say, hey, can we renegotiate that medieval contract so I can stay with this woman I fancy?" Emma didn't use the word *love* because he never had.

"You know I did not. You make it sound easy, but it would not have been. Nikolai took over his responsibilities as king decades before he should have had to. I could do no less than what was required of me for the sake of our country and my family."

"Which meant what? You had to marry a woman you did not love?"

"Love did not come into it."

"No, it didn't. Not for you anyway." He had never even come close to loving her. She saw that now, but she'd loved him. So much, she'd grieved his loss even after she thought he'd taken the TRO out against her.

"I did not love you," he acknowledged. "But I was obsessed by you. When I said I had no choice, I wasn't just talking about the contract."

She hoped he didn't think she was flattered to have been his *obsession*. An obsession was an object, not the target of genuine emotions.

"If not the contract, then what?" she asked.

"I knew that if I did not cut you completely from my life, I might not be able to stick with the breakup."

"You underestimated yourself. You broke up with me without looking back."

She'd been devastated, her heart shattered by the realization that all the emotion she had been feeling had been entirely one-sided.

No, he'd never lied to her, but his actions, his intense passion, it had all convinced her younger, more naive self that his emotions were growing just like hers had been.

Emma had been devastatingly wrong.

"That's the problem. I did look back. Too many times. And Tiana knew it. Although, I knew nothing about the restraining order, I think I know why she took it out."

"Why?"

"She was protecting me from myself."

"Because you told *her* that I was your obsession."

"Yes."

"And, good *friend* that she was, the crazy Queen lied and connived to take out a TRO on your behalf." Unfortunately, from her limited exposure to Queen Tiana, Emma had no trouble believing that.

Though she didn't think the woman had been protecting Konstantin. "She would have had her own reasons for taking out the TRO. I doubt very sincerely that woman ever did anything altruistically."

"Why do you call her crazy? You have so much antipathy for her."

"She threatened to steal my child." Did he not get how serious that was? How awful and terrifying that threat had been to a twenty-year-old who hadn't had the resources to fight a custody battle with a normal person, much less a monarch? "Sure she wrapped it up in legalese, but the end result would have been her taking my child to raise as her own."

"That is a side of Tiana I never saw, but I believe you."

"Do you really?" That would be a volte-face from the day before.

"Yes." Nothing but sincerity rang in his tone.

"Well, that's something."

"Perhaps you could extend a little belief to me as well."

Emma searched her own heart. Did she believe he hadn't known about the temporary restraining order? The answer was more complicated than simple belief or denial. "I spent more than five years believing you were cruel and callous enough to take out the TRO."

Changing her viewpoint of him wasn't going to happen in a single conversation.

"And that shames me because you are right. Ultimately, it was my fault."

Emma could not disagree. "I am willing to entertain the idea that you did not have anything directly to do with that. I'd rather believe that to tell the truth. I hated the idea that Mickey had a giant rat for a father."

"Maybe just a small rat?" Konstantin tried teasing.

She shrugged, not kidding herself.

Even without him being the source of the TRO, Konstantin had treated Emma badly and it had taken her a while to realize that it was his fault and not hers. She hadn't brought the pain down on herself. Innocence wasn't stupidity. And being trusting was not a defect in her nature, but a strength. One that might cause her pain in the future as it had done in the past, but she would rather have pain than spend her life thinking everyone was a liar, or worse.

"You made unspoken promises to me with your actions," she told him now, revealing an understanding that had come with a lot of soul searching and reading some very wise self-help books. "You implied a level of intimacy and even commitment that we did not have with how much you seemed to need me. Do you understand that?"

"But I told you our relationship was temporary."

"That first week we met, when you told me about a contract that was already years old, but you never mentioned it again. Not when you insisted we live together, not when you made sure we spent as much time together as possible.

You called me when we were apart. You treated me like I mattered. Until I didn't." Just like her parents had.

Although they had been strict, they had been loving and kind. Until she disappointed them and they decided they didn't want her as their daughter anymore.

"The contract was always there, hanging over my head. I never forgot about it."

Even when he'd been calling her in the middle of the night just to hear her voice when he'd been out of town on business, or duties with the palace. She believed him because right now, the anguish in his tone, it was genuine.

He'd felt conflicted. Just not conflicted enough to remind *her* he didn't plan for them to stay together, she told herself.

They could not change the past, but she had learned from it. Perhaps he had as well.

"What now?" she asked Konstantin. "Mickey isn't going to be happy seeing you only a few days a year, but I don't imagine you come to New Mexico often."

She really had no idea what Konstantin had meant the day before when he said he was staying in Mickey's life. As a secret father who saw their son sporadically? As a public dad who made an effort to see Mickey once a week?

The options and what they would mean to her own life had kept Emma up the night before.

"I come to Santa Fe, once or twice a year," he said dismissively. "Surely what comes next is obvious. Naturally, we will get married."

It took Emma's brain several seconds to parse what Konstantin had said because it was so out of the realm of what she had been expecting. "Married? You and me?" She grabbed one of the goblets of water from the table, not even sure it was hers, and gulped it down. "You don't mean that."

"If I had known about Mikhail before he was born, we would be married already."

"Now, I know that is a lie." And she'd just started to buy

the whole "I will never lie to you" shtick. At least in words. "There was still the contract."

"And it would have held no weight when compared to my impending fatherhood." He sounded like he truly believed that.

Emma wasn't as convinced, but neither of them would ever know because she had not been allowed to tell him the truth about her pregnancy and then she'd been well and truly scared off by a queen's threat to take away Emma's baby.

"You haven't asked for a DNA test." Which was a point in his favor. "You thought he was yours from first sight."

"He announced his age quite loudly. There was no chance in my mind that little boy could belong to anyone but me. Besides, he looks just like me." Konstantin sounded really proud of that fact. "As for a DNA test, *I* do not need one. I'm sure at some point the palace legal team will require DNA proof before my brother names Mikhail as part of his succession line."

"Mickey? In the succession to the throne. No. That can't be right. We weren't married when he was born."

"We will be married and he will be legitimized through all proper channels."

"I never agreed to marry you." And honestly? Right now, she could not fathom it.

Emma had no intention of putting her heart on the line with this man again.

"You agree that Mikhail needs me in his life."

"Yes."

"More than once or twice a year."

"Yes." It would mean moving and that would be really hard, but for Mickey's happiness, Emma would reshape her dreams again. "Do you still make your primary home in Seattle?"

"You do not follow news of me?" he asked again trying to tease.

He used to tease her all the time, but their relationship wasn't what it had been.

"Don't be an egoist. Just answer the question."

"I spend equal time in Mirrus and Seattle with business trips on behalf of Mirrus Global once or twice a month." He frowned, like something about that schedule bothered him.

"Okay. So, I'll relocate to Seattle," she said all in one breath, getting out the words that were so hard to say.

Her family still lived there even though they no longer acknowledged her. Maybe that could change. She could not imagine anyone being able to reject Mickey.

"You're willing to move?" he asked, surprise lacing his tone.

She did roll her eyes then. "You thought marriage was the solution to our situation. I assume that would have required me and Mickey to move."

"Well, yes, but…" His voice trailed off, the Prince seemingly without words.

"Will it be hard?" she asked. "Yes," she answered herself. "If you want the truth, it's going to be awful. I'm not just proud of the life I have built for me and Mickey, but I love it here. I fit in *The City Different* better than I have ever fit anywhere else."

"You will fit in our life in Seattle and Mirrus. I will make sure of it."

"I think that is something I have to make sure of, but thank you."

She sighed. "Look, I'm not so naive as to think you're going to change your base of operations just to be closer to your son, even if right now you're all gung-ho about the fatherhood thing." Konstantin was not that guy. "If I have the option, I want Mickey to have both of us in his life on a consistent basis."

Or as consistent as a prince could be in the life of his son. As yet, Emma didn't know what that was going to look like, but she did know that Mickey's dream of family had the best chance of coming true if she lived in the same city as his father.

That was the truth that had kept sleep so far from her the night before.

"You're a very special woman."

"No. I'm just a mom who wants what's best for her child." Emma didn't think that made her special, just committed.

"Mickey having both his parents is very important to you isn't it?"

"Do you really need me to answer that?"

"Enough for you to marry his father and give him a complete and stable home life?" Konstantin asked leadingly.

"He can have stability without us marrying."

"I can legally acknowledge him as my son, but the world is not as forward-thinking as we all might wish. There will be many who will not give him his due unless I am married to his mother."

"This isn't the Dark Ages." But she knew Konstantin was right.

"No, but we do not live in a perfect Utopia of understanding either."

She took a fortifying sip of her peppermint tea and wished it was a peppermint mocha, loaded with caffeine. "You don't want to marry me."

"That is one thing about which you are absolutely wrong."

"But why?" He had never loved her.

Permanent had never been in the cards for them, no matter what fantasies she'd woven around their relationship in the past.

"You are the mother of my child."

"I never thought you were such a throwback."

"Didn't you?"

Okay, maybe when he'd jettisoned his mistress to marry the woman chosen by his family, Emma had thought a Neanderthal playboy might be a step up from Konstantin, but this? Marriage? "You don't think I'm wife material."

"You have given birth to my child and raised him to the best of your ability, sacrificing in ways many women would not. You are eminently suitable to be my wife."

She shook her head. "You might even believe that right now, but spend a couple of hours talking to your family and your attitude is going to change fast enough."

"Not true. I told my brother I planned to marry you and he's all for it."

"Right."

"I will never lie to you, Emma, and I will keep reminding you of that until you believe me."

"Your brother the King is supportive of you marrying a bookkeeper?" she asked disbelievingly.

"Artist-slash-bookkeeper, but yes he is. His advice was to be willing to work for it."

"I find that hard to believe. You always said your brother was a stickler for propriety and you marrying your former mistress who gave birth to a child, even if it was *your* child, outside marriage isn't it."

"I have come to appreciate that my view of my brother was skewed by Tiana and my friendship with her."

Emma mulled that over. "I don't think Tiana was the friend to you that you believed her to be."

"Her wanting to buy my son and raise him as her own says you are right."

In a twisted way, the Queen might have thought she was protecting Konstantin. Emma found herself saying just that.

"No. With the TRO, maybe, but threatening you? Wanting to take our child? That was never about friendship."

"You knew her better than me. I only spoke to her once."

"And then you ran fast and far."

"Not intentionally. My parents had kicked me out. I needed a job right away but the TRO was making that impossible. I couch surfed with friends and started the proceedings to change my name. Once it came through, I started applying for nanny positions again. One of the positions was for a family that was relocating to New Mexico. I did some research and realized that the cost of living here would make raising Mickey on my own easier."

"So, you took the job."

"I did. Tiana died in her skiing accident the month after the move. I was already heavily pregnant and had no intention of moving back home. I couldn't be sure she was the only one in your family who felt the way she did about separating me from Mickey."

"She was. My father and brothers were all appalled when they learned what she threatened you with."

"That is good to know." She sighed and said what needed saying. "Five years ago, I would have married you without hesitation."

"Are you saying now you are hesitant?"

"I don't love you anymore, Konstantin." A twinge in her heart said she might be lying to herself and to him, but she ignored it. "I don't trust you. I cannot imagine marrying you."

"And I cannot imagine any other future for either of us."

"You're going to have to work on your imagination, then."

"We shall see."

He was so arrogant!

"I will compromise my dreams for Mickey's sake, but

I'm not marrying for anything but love. I won't compromise on that."

"Then I will just have to rekindle your love for me."

"As difficult as that would be, even more impossible would be convincing me that you feel the same way for me." Emotionally done, Emma stood up. "Look, when you're ready to discuss visitation with Mickey in a rational manner, give me a call."

He surged to his feet. "I was trying to do that."

"Throwing around the idea of marriage like it's a panacea is not being rational. Marriage is a lifetime commitment. At least for me."

"For me as well."

"So, just stating we're going to get married when we don't know if we can even spend a full day together in harmony is ridiculous."

Konstantin reached his hand out toward her. "You and Mickey have dinner with me tonight, please."

"You eat dinner too late for Mickey." Her voice sounded harsh to her own ears, but she was compensating for how that *please* made her feel.

His Royal Highness Prince Konstantin of Mirrus did not plead.

"I will eat whatever time is good for his schedule," Konstantin promised without hesitation.

She nodded, believing him. "We eat at five thirty." That was practically lunchtime for Konstantin.

"I'll be there at four to visit with him."

Konstantin brought a croquet set with him to visit his son and Emma. It was the first sport he'd learned as a child. A precursor to training for polo. His second had been skiing, a natural sport for an island country that had snow so many months out of the year.

"You do it like this?" Mikhail asked as he swung the mallet at the ball.

The croquet ball went careening across the small courtyard.

Konstantin smiled. "That was a good, strong hit, Mikhail. Well done."

Mikhail beamed and Emma smiled with approval. She was dressed in what he considered her bohemian Southwestern chic again. He was developing a real thing for turquoise and silver.

"Do you want to come to the park with us tomorrow?" Mikhail asked Konstantin. "It has water fountains. It's lots of fun, right, Mom?"

"I'm sure your dad is going to be busy tomorrow," Emma said gently. "He's here on business, Mickey."

What she did not seem to grasp yet was that no business could take precedence over Konstantin's newly discovered family.

"You don't live here now?" Mikhail asked, his face falling like an express elevator on its way to the ground floor. He turned to Emma. "Mom, he doesn't *live* here! He's going to go away, like Mr. Jensen."

"I am not leaving you, Mikhail," Konstantin promised, dropping to his knee beside his son. "I have just found you. You are my very precious son. We are family."

"Mr. Jensen went away from *his* family," Mikhail said accusingly.

"Who is Mr. Jensen?"

Mikhail didn't answer. He threw himself at Emma, wrapping his arms around her and burying his face in her stomach. She hugged their son, but looked up at Mikhail. "Mr. Jensen is my former employer. He traveled a lot for business and the year before Mickey and I moved out, he left the family to be with a woman he'd met on one of his trips."

Konstantin tapped Mikhail's shoulder. "*Moj mal'chik*, look at me…please." That word again. Pleading with his son and his former lover was becoming a habit. "I am going nowhere. I want no other woman but your own mama, Mishka. I promise you. Now that I have found you both, I will not leave you."

Mikhail turned around to face Konstantin, but held on to his mother. "What did you call me?"

Konstantin had to think, to remember what he'd said, his brain scrambling to keep up with the emotional upheaval. He had known his child for two days and it gutted him to see the little boy upset.

"I called you *my boy* in Russian." He ruffled Mikhail's hair. "And Mishka is like your mother calling you Mickey."

"Okay. I like Mishka better than Mickey, but Mikhail is best." The little boy gave Emma a significant look and she shrugged back.

Like they'd had this discussion before and she wasn't giving up *Mickey* anytime soon.

"But you don't live here," Mikhail said accusingly, showing he had not forgotten his worry in his curiosity. "We do."

Konstantin looked up at Emma, feeling helpless in a way he never did.

Emma's expression wasn't her usual confident, calm mom face. She looked just as lost as he felt.

Although she had said she was willing to relocate, they had made no firm plans. He had not even told her that he was scheduled to return to Mirrus the next day. Not that Konstantin planned to go, but he did not know realistically how long he could stay in Santa Fe.

Until Emma agreed to move, his heart insisted while his brain said that was not practical. He had business commitments.

But the little boy looking at him so warily trumped even Mirrus Global.

Emma dropped down so she was eye level with their son as well. "Listen to me, Mikhail Ansel Carmichael."

Mikhail nodded, then said in an aside to Konstantin, "She only uses my whole name when she's really serious."

Konstantin had a wholly inappropriate urge to smile, despite the emotional upheaval and gravity of the moment. He suppressed it. "So, we must believe what she says, then."

"I always believe my mom," Mikhail said with more loyalty than truthfulness.

Konstantin had seen in their brief time together that the boy's curious nature made him question nearly everything he was told about the world around him.

Emma gave their son a gentle smile. "Maybe not everything, but asking questions is not a bad thing. In this though, I need you to trust me."

"Okay, Mom."

"Konstantin is *your* dad and no matter where any of us lives, no one can take that from you."

"But I don't want him to live far away."

"I know you don't, sweetheart."

Their son grimaced at the endearment.

"I do not want to live far away from you either," Konstantin assured him.

"Are you going to move here?" Mikhail asked innocently, wholly unaware of how costly such a thing would be.

"I would if I could," Konstantin answered, meaning it.

Emma gave him a searching look, as if trying to read Konstantin's sincerity.

But he wasn't worried. He knew all she would see was honesty. If it meant being with his son, he *would* move anywhere. That did not change the truth that his active royal role as Prince and chief operating officer for Mirrus Global precluded him living just anywhere without letting down a lot of people.

Emma stood. "This conversation calls for lemonade."

"Homemade lemonade? The kind with mint leaves floating in it?" Mikhail asked his mother with enthusiasm. "It's the best," he assured Konstantin.

"Would I make it any other way? I have a pitcher I made last night. I was saving it for dinner, but I think we can all use a cool drink right now."

And something to put a smile on their son's face. Konstantin saw the motive to Emma's suggestion. It had worked, though Mikhail took both his mother's hand and Konstantin's, holding on tightly as they made their way into the brightly lit kitchen with its colorful tiles.

Emma was going to hate his home in Seattle, not to mention his apartment in the palace. The designer he'd hired had done both in elegant neutrals.

Apparently, the time had come for a change.

"Sit down at the table with your dad. I'll get the drinks," Emma instructed their son.

"I can help," Mikhail said, even as he obeyed, sitting down so that he would have Konstantin on one side and Emma on the other once she joined them.

"I've got it." Emma smiled reassuringly at the boy and gave a silent instruction to Konstantin to sit down with a nod of her head toward one of the chairs.

Konstantin found himself obeying as quickly as their son had done. Amused with himself, he chuckled softly.

"What's funny, Dad?"

"I don't usually get told what to do," he said with a smile.

"Cuz you're a prince?" Mikhail guessed.

"Yes."

"I think you better get used to it. Mom is bossy."

Emma's laughter said she hadn't taken offense at their son's pronouncement.

"Your mother has always had a way of getting me to do as she wanted," Konstantin told Mikhail conspiratorially.

"Not when it counted," Emma said under her breath.

But he heard her. Konstantin gave her a look that he hoped conveyed his regret for their past.

She just shook her head and carried a tray laden with a pitcher of lemonade and glasses to the table. Konstantin noticed that though his cup matched the two glasses, Mikhail's lemonade was served in a plastic cup that was sized for his smaller hands.

There were so many details in Emma's home that showed she took their son's needs into account in even the smallest of minutia.

Konstantin took a sip of his lemonade and was surprised at how perfect the flavor was. Not too sour. Not too sweet and the mint gave it a refreshing twist. "This is very good. You made it?" he asked Emma.

"Well, me and the lemonade juicer."

"She used to squeeze all the lemons by hand," Mikhail offered. "But it made her hand sore, so Mrs. Jensen bought her a juicer thing."

"I thought you were the nanny, not the housekeeper?" Mikhail asked.

"I had some light housekeeping duties."

"Like making juice?"

"And the beds. I used to help Mom make 'em. She said when I was a baby I helped too, keeping her company."

The idea of the mother of his child doing such menial tasks for another did not sit well with Konstantin.

"I know that look on your face, *Prince* Konstantin, but normal people make beds and juice and clean up after themselves and others all the time. Working for the Jensens allowed me to finish school and stay with my son until he was old enough for preschool day care. It was good for both of us."

"You have provided my son with a stable and good home life," Konstantin said, once again feeling the weight of guilt at the knowledge that she should never have had to do that alone.

"Our son, and it was my privilege to care in every way for Mickey. It always will be."

"Mom says being a mom is the most important and best-est job ever."

"Best," Emma corrected with a smile.

"Best," Mikhail parroted.

For just a moment, Konstantin had no words. This little family was his, through no great feat of his own, or even one good choice after the one to date Emma. This amazing woman had made a future he never thought to have possible.

Marriage to a woman he genuinely wanted and parenting a son who was already a wonderful little human.

Something of what he was thinking must have shown on his face because Emma's expression softened, but then she took a breath and her *no-nonsense* look came over her lovely features. "Mickey... *Mikhail*," she stressed. "Do you remember when you asked about your dad the first time, and I said that when you got to meet him, you might want to move to be near him?"

Konstantin knew that Emma had not planned for that day to happen anytime soon.

"You mean me and you move, right, Mom?"

"Yes, of course. You aren't going anywhere without me." And that was said with rock-solid certainty along with a warning look toward Konstantin.

As if he would ever try to take Mikhail away from Emma. "It is my hope, Mikhail, that your mother will agree to marry me and we can build a family together, but even if she does not," he said quickly when his son opened his mouth to speak and Emma looked ready to clobber Konstantin, "I am hopeful that you will both be willing to make your home in Seattle and Mirrus as I do."

"Two places?" Mikhail asked, sounding confused. "You can have two houses? Is that real?" he asked his mother.

Emma nodded. "Yes, some people have even more than two houses."

Konstantin was one of them, but he didn't mention that right now. His son had enough to process with the idea of living in two locations.

"Is Mirrus your country?" Mikhail asked. "Only Mom said it was an island and you're a prince there."

"I am a prince wherever I am, but it is my country."

"Oh. Mom only called you Prince when she was annoyed with you."

"You could tell that, huh?"

"Yep."

"Your mom doesn't have to call me Your Highness."

"Why?"

"Because you are my son and she is your mother."

"I do not believe that is protocol," Emma said drily.

"But it is the way it will always be between us."

"If Mom marries you, will she be a princess?" Mikhail wanted to know.

"She will, yes."

Mikhail's expression fell. "Oh."

"You do not want your mother to be a princess?" Konstantin asked, trying to understand.

"She doesn't want to be a princess," Mikhail said glumly.

"She told you this?"

Mikhail nodded, tears filling his eyes. "She won't marry you and we can't be a family." He jumped up and ran from the room.

Emma rushed after him and Konstantin followed. He found them in his son's room, Mikhail refusing the comfort of his mother's arms.

"You won't let us be a family!" the little boy cried.

"That is enough." Konstantin spoke firmly, needing to

stop their son's blaming his mother. "Your mother never said we could not be a family."

"But she did," Mikhail said to Konstantin tearfully. "When I asked her about my dad."

"I told him things hadn't worked out between us, but that was okay because I never wanted to be a princess."

"Give me a chance to convince her otherwise," Konstantin said to Mikhail.

"My mom is really stubborn. When I don't want to do something good for me, she tells me that she's more stubborn than me cuz she's been stubborn longer." Mikhail looked so forlorn.

"If that is how it works, then I must be more stubborn than she is because I am four years older than she is, so I have been stubborn longer. And I am a prince. That means I am used to getting my own way."

Mikhail's expression lightened, but Emma looked like a thundercloud.

"I love you more than anything in this world," Emma said to Mikhail. "But, sweetheart, I am not marrying your dad just to make you happy."

She sounded so sure, but suddenly Konstantin suspected that she probably would do that very thing. It was clear that nothing was more important to Emma than Mikhail.

It was Konstantin's job to show her that their becoming a family legally, because they were already a family in truth, would *not* be at the cost of her personal happiness.

He would show both her and Mikhail what kind of life they could have together.

CHAPTER FIVE

"YOU BOUGHT A HOUSE? Here?" Emma asked faintly, not sure she'd heard Konstantin right. "But why? I told you I would move to Seattle with Mickey."

"Eventually," Konstantin clarified. "And I think we will be returning to Santa Fe more than twice a year. It is a place that you love."

She ignored the way he talked like she and Mickey would travel with him and focused on her son.

They had spent the last week together more than she would have thought possible with Konstantin's schedule. It had become obvious to them both, from small outbursts to having trouble sleeping and disturbing dreams that sent Mickey into her bed for a cuddle, that their son needed time to adjust to all the changes in his life.

"But we discussed the move and you agreed Mickey needed time to adjust to having a dad before we uprooted him." She'd been relieved that Konstantin hadn't fought her on that.

Because Emma was self-aware enough to know that *she* needed time to come to terms with having Konstantin become part of Mickey's life as well.

Emma had gotten Mickey a counselor to help him with the transition but wondered if she shouldn't have gotten one for herself as well. She'd been almost as shocked when Konstantin had offered to attend any family sessions as she was right now.

"You can't do your job from Santa Fe." Could he?

"I will do it to the best of my ability, but naturally some adjustments will have to be made both in my palace schedule as well as my responsibilities as COO." Konstantin sounded way too calm about that, considering what a workaholic he was. "My father and brothers will be stepping into the gap and we are promoting someone to work directly under me in a managerial capacity."

"But...all that...so Mickey and I don't have to move right away?" He was putting his precious business second?

He was allowing others to fulfill his palace responsibilities?

Konstantin had never done that when they were dating. Though he'd been very respectful of her time, his had always been in short supply.

"You both have a life here. Mishka will be graduating from preschool in a matter of weeks. It would not be fair to take him away from the teacher he admires so much before the natural separation of him moving on from preschool."

"I agree." Only Emma's plan had been for her and Mickey to stay in Santa Fe until then, while she put her house up for sale.

The prospect of finding a home in Seattle to move to was daunting. She would have to find a job there as well. There was just so much to do.

Overwhelmed by what it all meant, Emma pushed her food away. Konstantin had asked to meet for lunch so they could talk without upsetting Mickey. She wished she didn't have to be part of this conversation either.

It was just all so much. She'd worked so hard to build her life here in Santa Fe and now she had to dismantle it.

Sometimes, she wished she could go back and deny, deny, deny. Only that was impossible now. She'd been the one to insist on having a paternity test done. She wasn't having anyone question Mickey's parentage.

Whom was she kidding? She would never have denied Mickey his chance at having his dad in his life. No matter how hard that change might be for her.

Konstantin looked at her with concern. "It is my hope

that you and Mikhail will move in with me, getting him used to having me around while staying in Santa Fe."

"What?" Move from her little house? The one *she'd* bought with no help from anyone else?

"Surely you can see this would be for the best. The counselor said that taking steps like this could help Mishka settle."

"I don't think she was talking about us moving in with you. We can help Mickey adjust to having you around without living with you." Couldn't they?

"Even if you refuse to marry me, surely you see that you and Mickey living with me would be the best course of action. Once he is introduced to the world as the new second in line to the throne of Mirrus, he will require a level of security that a place of similar size to your current home could not accommodate."

Emma couldn't deny it. Konstantin had already implemented security measures at her house that had required putting a portable bed in the living room for the night shift. That was not a tenable long-term solution.

"I can get a bigger house." But she'd looked at Seattle real estate. Even after selling her current home, she wouldn't have enough of a down payment to get anything bigger than a two-bedroom condominium. No yard for Mickey.

"I will buy you whatever size house you require, but I would prefer my son live with me."

"Which means me living with you." Nothing Konstantin had said implied he had any plans to try to take Mickey away from her, but she could not help worrying.

"Naturally. I would prefer as my wife, but yes, regardless. Whatever you feel about this truth, our son *is* a royal and he must be raised to his role. It will be better and easier for him if he lives that life 24/7."

Why hadn't she ever considered Mickey's role within the

royal family? Because after her confrontation with Queen Tiana, Emma had realized she was on her own with her son. Even before that, she never would have expected Konstantin to formally and publicly acknowledge him.

"Which means living with you."

"Yes."

While she had never expected him to take this step, part of her *had* been afraid Konstantin would try to take Mickey away from her. Emma had not trusted the Prince at all. Not after the restraining order and the Queen's threats.

So, this idea of living with him had *never* occurred to her and Konstantin talked like it was the most natural thing in the world.

Emma had become convinced that she'd never really known Konstantin. That the man she'd fallen in love with did not actually exist.

The jury was still out on that one, but his every action right now pointed toward a man who had no plans to try to steal her son away. Even so. "I know you are used to getting what you want, but can't you see you're asking me to change my whole life for you?"

"For Mikhail," Konstantin stressed. "After treating you as I did, I would never presume to ask you to change so much as your outfit for me."

"What's wrong with my outfit?" she demanded.

Her Prince blew out a frustrated breath. "Nothing is wrong with your clothes. They look fantastic on you as always."

Darn it. She'd thought of him as hers. She had to nip that in the bud right now.

Only did she? asked an insidious voice in her mind, or was it her heart? He wanted to marry her. Wouldn't that make him hers?

"Then why would you want me to change them?" she asked rather than let herself dwell on impossible thoughts.

If princes rolled their eyes, then Konstantin would have done so right then. She was sure of it.

His gorgeous lips twisted wryly. "I am *not* asking you to change them. Although, if I felt I had the right, I would point out that you might consider letting me buy you a designer wardrobe for public functions."

"Why would I be attending public functions with you? We aren't dating."

"That is going to change."

"What?" Why were they talking about dating now? Hadn't they been discussing her moving into his Santa Fe mansion?

"We are going to date."

"Not if I don't want to." Only she wasn't entirely sure she *didn't* want to.

No matter what Emma said, she could not ignore her son's happiness and desire to live as a "real" family. Nor was she in the habit of lying to herself, which meant she was fully aware of how attracted to Prince Konstantin of Mirrus she still was.

In the past week, her view of Konstantin had changed.

Although she was still very hurt by how he'd cut her so ruthlessly from his life, she no longer held him responsible for the restraining order that had caused her so much grief.

Konstantin had gone in the opposite direction, taking on a load of guilt that he freely acknowledged.

Both situations served to give her a less jaundiced view of her Prince. Oh, darn it, she'd done it again.

"Why are you frowning?" Konstantin asked.

"You are *not* my prince," she told him and herself.

His smile was sexy and devastating. "But I could be."

She just shook her head.

"I spoke to the counselor and she believes that having you and Mishka move in with me here in Santa Fe, letting us get used to being around each other as people who live in the same home while he still has the consistency of his preschool, would be good for our son."

"You spoke to the counselor about it? Before me?"

"Only to get her opinion. Naturally, it is your decision entirely."

Not really. Not anymore.

While Emma had no plans to give up majority custody of their son, so long as he continued to make Mickey's welfare a priority, she expected Konstantin to have a say in Mickey's present and future. While she would not allow him to dictate decisions about their son, she *would* take Konstantin's viewpoint into consideration.

Even if she didn't feel so strongly about allowing him to fulfill his role as father, so long as he did so with Mickey's best interests always at the forefront, the simple truth was Konstantin knew the intricacies of royal life in a way Emma did not.

Mickey needed his dad looking out for him and Konstantin was doing his best to do that very thing.

Emma needed to remember that.

"I don't want to move out of my home," she admitted baldly. "I know I have to, but I worked so hard for Mickey and me to have our own place."

"Would it be easier for you if I moved in there for a couple of weeks?" Konstantin offered.

Like that was practical, but she did appreciate his offering. "Where would you sleep? The kitchen?" she asked facetiously.

"We could put a travel bed in your bedroom with a standing divider between us."

It was a generous offer. They would be crowded beyond belief, but he was willing to do that so *she* had time to get used to moving from their home, not just Mickey. Only she wasn't a four-nearly-five-year-old. Emma was an adult and she could deal with the hard things in life.

She'd already proved that to herself many times over.

"I think it *would* be good if you stayed with us for a couple of days before we made the move to your mansion," she said, giving oblique acceptance to the move to his mansion and by extrapolation to a shared home in Seattle.

"I never said it was a mansion."

She gave him a look. "Is it?"

"Yes." His teasing smile invited her to share his amusement.

She returned it. "I know you better than you think."

"I don't mind that."

"Can we get an RV to park in my driveway for the security people?" Then she would have some semblance of having her home back again.

"That is an excellent idea. I should have thought of it already."

"You've been busy." She knew he had.

Konstantin worked late into the night most nights just so he had time every afternoon and evening to spend with Mickey. She joined them for most of that time because Mickey needed that sense of security.

However, Emma had continued to do her job and paint her commissions for the gallery as well.

Which meant as soon as Mickey went to bed both she and Konstantin began work on their computers. He'd surprised her by staying to work in her living room until she went to bed some nights. She wasn't sure why he did it, but Emma acknowledged, if only to herself, that she liked it.

Konstantin brought his things from the hotel and Emma made room in her closet for his suits.

The prince planned to sleep on the travel bed they'd brought in for the night security man.

She gave the single bed a considering look. "Have you ever slept on a single bed?"

"Not since being in the nursery." Konstantin shrugged. "The bed was good enough for my security man, it is good enough for me."

"I wouldn't expect that attitude from you."

"Why not? Because I am a prince?" he asked her with a slight frown. "Believe me, I have slept in much less comfortable surroundings."

That really surprised her. "You have?" He certainly hadn't while they were together.

"Indeed. I did my service in our military just as every Mirrussian must."

"You mean every Mirrussian male."

"No. Every citizen of Mirrus must serve at least two years in the military between the ages of eighteen and twenty-six."

"But what about pacifists?" she asked.

"There are many military roles that do not require combat readiness."

"Oh. And your citizens are allowed to choose?"

"If they swear a pacifist's oath, they are placed in a non-combat role."

"And you trust them not to take advantage?"

"It has worked for the two centuries of our country's existence."

"That's kind of wonderful."

"I am glad you think so. Mirrus is a very special place."

"You would think that," she teased.

She'd used to tease him about his absolute conviction there was no better country to live in than Mirrus.

"I hope you will agree." His smile said he was sure she would. "You and Mikhail will be living there for several months out of the year."

"If I say," she reminded him, but acknowledging in her own heart that he was right.

She hadn't come out and formally agreed that she and

Mickey would live with Konstantin, but she accepted that it was most likely inevitable.

Mickey *was* part of the royal family.

Which, even now, sort of blew her mind.

"If you say." The words agreed with her, but his expression said Konstantin knew what was what.

"You know, even back when I realized I was pregnant and tried to get a hold of you to tell you, it never occurred to me that you would want to recognize our child officially."

Konstantin frowned. "What did you think I would do?"

"Well, you'd made it pretty clear you *didn't* want to marry me," she pointed out. "So, I thought you'd help with his support and do visitation, I guess."

"It was never that I did not want to marry you. I never even allowed myself to consider the possibility. I believed I had no choice about marrying Nataliya."

"And yet you claim you would have married me if you knew. Saying stuff like that makes it harder for me to trust you now." Did he get that?

"Why? If it was true?" he asked, his brows drawn in confusion.

"But how *could* it be true? You put that contract ahead of our relationship from the beginning to the end. You want me to believe that me being pregnant would have made a difference, but I have very bad memories just trying to get a hold of you to tell you I *was*."

"And that was my fault. I acknowledge that. You tried every way you knew, I understand that now." The words were too stilted to be rehearsed.

He meant his belated apology and acknowledgment that Emma had done all that *she* could.

"Good."

"And then you spoke with Tiana and she scared you with her demands and threats. You should never have been subjected to that," Konstantin said like he was intent on getting it all out at once.

"On that we agree completely, but how is this supposed to convince me that if you knew I was pregnant, you would have walked away from that contract?"

"Because Mikhail is my son." He said it so simply, like that explained everything.

"So, shared DNA trumps family and business commitments?"

"That shared DNA means Mikhail is my family, and in my world, he's the most important member of that family."

"Your child is more important to you than your brothers, even the one that is King, or your father?" she asked, pushing for clarification, not sure she believed Konstantin about that claim.

However, if she was going to put her life in his hands, as it were, by agreeing to live in his space, she needed to know that Mickey came first and her own role as Mickey's mother would never be diminished.

"Yes."

Emma looked at Konstantin, trying to see into his soul for the truth. But she wasn't that gifted. "You did put everything on hold for him now," she acknowledged.

"I cannot stay here forever," Konstantin said, almost apologetically. "But I will make his transition into the world you think of as so foreign as easy as possible."

She frowned, but nodded. Konstantin's world was foreign to her and to Mickey. In so many ways.

"I think I want a contract with you," she mused, coming on a solution she would not have considered to be a benefit a week ago. "A shared custody agreement that guarantees my role as full-time mother to Mickey no matter what the future holds. And I want final say on all major decisions regarding him for at least the next year."

She needed to see Konstantin being the father he promised to be before she handed over any legal rights over Mickey.

Konstantin's brows drew together, his expression clearly unhappy. "You want a contract between us?"

"Yes."

"But our relationship is not business."

"Right now, it's not personal either." She should not have said *right now*. It implied she would be open to a personal relationship later.

And Emma just didn't know if she was. Even if she agreed to marry Konstantin, she wasn't sure how personal she was willing to be with him. Emma had never once considered a marriage of convenience as a possibility in her life. She'd grown up dreaming of marrying her soul mate, like her parents were to each other.

But then, she'd never really considered what it would mean if her son's father, who was a prince, showed up in their life either.

It had never occurred to her that they might just run into each other. She'd thought that when Mickey was older she'd have to help him get in touch with his father.

This situation? Had never even been on Emma's radar. So, she hadn't planned for it.

"You are the mother of my son. You are the only woman I have ever lived with. How much more personal can it get?"

"That was years ago. We don't live together anymore."

Konstantin looked around them significantly.

"Not like that. We aren't sleeping together."

"Not yet."

She glared at him. "Don't count your chickens, Your Highness. They're likely to fly the coop."

"What does that mean?" he asked, humor evident in his tone. "You are not a chicken."

"Neither am I a sure thing for you and you'd best re-

member that. You are *here* for Mickey's sake, not because
I want you sharing my space."

Later, as she tossed and turned in her empty bed, images of her ex-lover on his own narrow cot kept her from
sleeping.

Konstantin was the only man Emma had ever had full-
on sex with. Her parents had been overprotective, and
Emma had had a strict curfew when living at home.

After she and Konstantin had broken up, she'd been
too devastated to date. Then Emma had found out she was
pregnant. Her life since Mickey's birth had only recently
had *any* time that might be used for dating.

But Emma had been gun-shy. Her one relationship had
come at a high cost to her. She wasn't ready to trust someone else and she'd never been as attracted to another man
as she was to Konstantin.

She knew *he* hadn't been celibate. He was discreet, but
even discreet, there was gossip about his sex partners. Not
lovers, because like he said, Konstantin did not date. Nor
did he live with other women.

Even so, when Emma had seen the fashion articles about
Lady Nataliya's dates, Emma had been sure that they would
infuriate Konstantin.

Emma was probably one of a very few who had not
been surprised when Nataliya had ended up betrothed to
his brother the King. Konstantin could be a throwback and
she had no doubt he'd reacted poorly to Nataliya dating in
such a public way.

Emma admired the Princess of Mirrus and her refusal
to adhere to royal expectations, even though, if she were
completely honest, Emma would have to admit she had
also been jealous of the woman and her role as Konstantin's intended.

Now, Konstantin said he wanted to marry Emma. For
Mickey's sake.

Which was really nothing like his actually *wanting* to marry her.

She supposed it wasn't that much different for him than agreeing to marry Lady Nataliya as part of a business deal.

But Emma had always dreamed of marrying her soul mate. At one time, she'd thought Konstantin was that man.

Now, she didn't know what to think.

And it wasn't making sleep any easier to come by.

Mickey was over the moon to have his dad at the breakfast table, though Konstantin had been up for a few hours working already.

Emma knew that because she'd heard him get up a full two hours before her own alarm was set to go off.

She'd been so tired from her sleepless night, she'd just rolled over and gone back to sleep, waking to the smell of breakfast sausage, coffee and a distinct lack of an alarm. She'd found her phone missing from her bedside table, only to discover it on the kitchen counter when she arrived.

Konstantin and Mickey were both seated with plates of yummy-looking breakfast foods in front of them.

"Did you cook breakfast this morning?" she teased her son.

"No, Dad got some people to deliver it. It's good, Mom. You'll like it."

Emma picked up her phone and checked the time, frowning when she realized if she didn't hurry, she wouldn't make it to work on time. "I'm going to be late."

"I called and told them you had been unavoidably detained." Konstantin didn't look guilty about being so high-handed either.

"After you took my phone and made sure I didn't hear my alarm?" she asked with a grimace.

His own frown censured her. "You were sleeping soundly. You clearly needed your rest."

"That wasn't your decision to make."

"When do you plan to give notice at work?" he asked, ignoring her rebuke.

"I already put in my notice." And she'd started looking for a new job in Seattle, but she was beginning to wonder how that was going to work with them traveling to Mirrus every few months to stay for weeks at a time.

"Good." He dished up her plate. "Our son told me your favorites."

Emma took the plate of eggs ranchero and crispy hash browns with a polite thank-you. The food smelled so good, her mouth watered. And then her stomach rumbled.

Mickey laughed. "You're hungry, huh, Mom? It's good you don't have to wait to cook your food, right, Mom?"

"Yes, Mickey." She leaned down and kissed her son's head. "Very good, especially since we need to leave very soon to get you to school on time."

The first hour at Mickey's day care preschool was free time so children could be dropped off at different times before the morning preschool session started.

Mickey's mouth set in a mutinous frown that was becoming all too familiar. "I don't want to go to school. I want to stay with Dad."

"If it is all right with your mother, I can pick you up right after school so you don't have to go into day care," Konstantin offered, obviously intent on heading off a confrontation with their son. "But I too need to get some work done today."

Emma didn't know how she felt about the Prince's offer.

So far, all of Mickey's time with Konstantin had been under Emma's supervision. But a man didn't go to the trouble of setting up a mansion to live in if he planned to run off with her son, did he?

It all boiled down to whether, or not, she trusted Konstantin at his word that he would not try to take Mickey from her.

"Say yes, Mom, please!" Mickey pleaded.

Emma looked at Konstantin, and his chocolate brown gaze so like their son's snagged hers. His eyes asked her to trust him. "I…"

She didn't know what to say. Could she take Konstantin at his word?

He was right when he claimed he'd never verbally lied to her. Would he start now?

He had to know that if he tried to take Mickey she could make such an ugly scandal, his little country would be in all the wrong papers for months to come. Would he risk that?

She closed her eyes for a moment, centering herself, and sought the truth of her own emotions and beliefs.

"Don't worry, Dad. She does that sometimes. It helps her focus on what's real." Mickey sounded so grown-up repeating her words for Konstantin.

Emma opened her eyes and smiled at Mickey. "Okay, but you call me at work as soon as your dad picks you up." She looked at Konstantin. "If you want to take him to the park or something, you need to call and let me know you aren't going to be at home."

It would be only for a couple of hours, she reminded herself. He needed just the one to disappear with their son, but she wasn't going to think like that.

"Of course," Konstantin replied, his expression filled with a vulnerable gratitude she did her best to trust. "And thank you, Emma."

"For what?" But she knew. They both knew she was showing more trust than he probably deserved right now.

But she realized she was trusting her own judgment more than she implicitly trusted him.

"Trusting me with our son."

Emma just nodded.

CHAPTER SIX

KONSTANTIN PICKED UP Mikhail from his preschool, impressed by the security employed by the staff.

Despite traveling with an entourage and his obvious wealth, as well as being greeted by the bodyguard that had been watching over his son since Konstantin came into Mikhail's life, Konstantin was still required to show photo identification.

He also heard one of the staff calling Emma to tell her that Mikhail was being picked up. Though he knew that she'd taken time to go into Mikhail's preschool and arrange things so the Prince could pick up his son.

"You must be Mikhail's father. We've heard a lot about you in the last two weeks." The dark-haired man speaking looked to be a couple of years younger than Emma's age of twenty-five. He extended his hand. "I'm Jerome Leeds, Mikhail's teacher."

Now, Konstantin understood his son's insistence on being called by his given name. It's what the teacher he admired so much used.

Konstantin shook the younger man's hand. "It is a pleasure to meet you. I have heard a great deal about you as well."

Jerome Leeds smiled. "We aren't supposed to have favorites, but I have enjoyed teaching Mikhail very much."

"He likes Mom too. Lots," Mikhail said guilelessly.

Stiffening, Konstantin gave the teacher a look meant to intimidate and wasn't even a little ashamed to do it. "Is that right?"

"Yep. I think he wanted to date her, but Mom doesn't date." Mikhail frowned.

Konstantin didn't like the idea that his son might be disappointed Emma had refused to date the other man.

"I'm sure she had her reasons," Konstantin told his son. "Are you ready to go?"

Mikhail's sweet little-boy face lit up. "Yes! Where are we going?"

"Nowhere until you call your mother and check in with her."

"Oh, right." Mikhail turned back to his teacher. "See you tomorrow, Mr. Leeds."

The man, who was now showing every evidence of embarrassment, nodded. "See you tomorrow, Mikhail."

"I'll tell Mom *hi* for you like you always ask."

Mr. Leeds gave Konstantin a defiant stare and said, "You do that, Mikhail."

Konstantin took out his phone, dialed Emma's number and handed the instrument to his son.

He waited until Mikhail was engaged with his mother before saying to the teacher still standing there, "You are aware that the mother of my son is no longer available for dating." Though from what Mikhail said, she'd never made time for it.

Konstantin hadn't dated either, but he hadn't been celibate the last five years and suddenly, he regretted that. He didn't know why. He'd been single. He'd never regretted having casual sex on Nataliya's behalf.

Their contract had spelled out very clearly that until a formal betrothal announcement was made there were no personal obligations between Lady Nataliya and any of the Princes of the House of Merikov. Konstantin's father, King at the time, had signed on behalf of their house and the contract did not stipulate Konstantin personally.

Though both families had expected him and Nataliya to marry one day, it had been an unwritten obligation and one that did not carry with it the burden of fidelity to a relationship that did not exist.

Regardless, now he wished he'd handled a lot of things differently the past five years, not least of which was cutting himself off completely from Emma.

"Does she know that?" the preschool teacher asked. "Only a man who wasn't there for the first few years of his son's life isn't a great bet and I'm sure she knows that."

"That is none of your business." Konstantin knew he *was* a good bet and Emma would come to learn that as well.

That was all that mattered.

Jerome Leeds frowned. "I care about Mikhail."

"And I am glad to hear that. He deserves to have the people in his life care about him," Konstantin said honestly. "But he and Emma are *my* family. As long as you understand that, we will have no trouble between us."

The threat was there and Konstantin did nothing to soften it.

"Just don't hurt her again," the teacher had the temerity to instruct him. "She's a special person and I think you must be the reason she was so closed off to dating. She deserves to have the people in her life care about her too."

The younger man was speaking about things that he had no right to even mention, but Konstantin did not disagree with what he said. So, he chose not to take umbrage.

"She does." Konstantin smiled at his son as the young boy finished talking to his mother. "As I said, they are *both* my family and I will watch out for them now."

"That's good to know, Mr. Merikov."

Konstantin didn't correct the other man's address. He rarely felt the need to point out his royal status. He knew who he was. Random strangers, or even his son's teacher who would be in that capacity for only the next few weeks, did not need to.

"It's Prince Konstantin or Your Highness," Mikhail said, showing he was not so sanguine about the issue. "My dad is a prince."

The pride in Mikhail's voice touched Konstantin deeply. Unlike with Emma, apparently Konstantin's royal status was a check in the plus column for their son.

"Is that right?" Jerome Leeds asked indulgently.

"It is," Konstantin affirmed. "Now, if you will excuse us."

He put his hand out for his son to take and then led Mikhail out of the school without looking back to see how the news was received.

"Dad, how come Mr. Leeds didn't know you are a prince?"

"Perhaps because your mother did not think it was important to tell him."

"Oh. Because she doesn't want to be a princess?"

"I think because my role as Prince is less important to her than my role as your father. She told them about that, right?"

Mikhail brightened. "Yep. Where are we going?"

"Where would you like to go?"

"The park!"

Because he had accompanied Mikhail and Emma to the park twice now, Konstantin knew exactly where Mikhail wanted to go. Konstantin gave instructions to the driver and then called Emma to tell her where they were going.

The bodyguard riding with them engaged Mikhail in conversation while Konstantin was on the phone.

"I should have guessed that would be where you ended up. Given a choice, it's almost always the park." There was a smile in her voice.

"It would seem so."

"Mickey is really excited you picked him up today. He told me other kids had more than one person who picked them up and now he did too." She sounded a little sad and maybe wistful.

"You and Mishka will never be alone again," Konstantin vowed. "Not only will I always be there, but my father, brothers and sister-in-law are all very eager to meet my son and his mother."

"I don't know how I feel about meeting them. Queen Tiana told me that she had her husband's full support to take Mickey, and that of her father-in-law as well."

Konstantin didn't like the worry in Emma's tone.

He assured her, "She told you she had my support too, but we both know she lied about that."

Silence met that statement.

Konstantin waited, wondering if Emma would agree, ignore or deny his words.

"She did," Emma finally said with a sigh. "About a lot of things."

"Yes, about many things. My father and brothers learned about Mishka only after I met our son."

He couldn't wait for Mickey to meet Dima, his youngest brother. Both his brothers would be wonderful uncles, he was sure, but Dima was the youngest and had a special place in Konstantin's heart.

He looked to make sure Mikhail was otherwise engaged. His son was now playing a game on the bodyguard's phone with a set of headphones so he could hear his music without interrupting Konstantin. Konstantin nodded his thanks to the other man.

"I have not yet told you how grateful I am that you chose to continue your pregnancy and when you did that you did not choose to give Mishka up for adoption. Your strength inspires me."

"That's a nice thing to say, but my parents would have burned my name in effigy if I'd terminated my pregnancy," Emma said with dark humor. "Not that I ever considered doing so. I don't know. I just loved Mickey from the moment I knew I carried him. If I'd been able to give him up for adoption, Mom and Dad would not have disowned me. They thought I was being selfish toward them and him by keeping him."

Konstantin hated that this amazing, generous woman had lost her family just when she'd needed them most. "I never realized they were so unbending. I knew they were angry you'd moved in with me because you told me, but not that they would reject you for having a child without the benefit of marriage."

She sighed. "They were always strict, but I thought they loved me enough to forgive me for making choices they would not agree with."

"Perhaps it was a matter of believing *tough love* would bring you around to their way of thinking."

"Maybe." Emma didn't sound convinced though.

"Have you tried contacting them since having Mikhail?"

"I did when Mickey was a month old. I wanted them to meet their grandson."

"What happened?"

"My mom asked me if I'd kept the baby and I said yes. I started to tell her how beautiful he was, how amazing, but she hung up on me."

Konstantin had some very uncharitable thoughts about her parents. Whatever their reasoning, they had hurt her terribly with their rejection of Mikhail.

Not that he'd done any better on Emma's behalf, if unwittingly, but going forward that was going to change. Full stop. "I am truly sorry to hear that. Once we are married, they will no doubt accept you again. You will have to decide if that is something you want."

She gasped. "I never said I would marry you." Emma's tone was all sass.

And Konstantin loved it. Why when Nataliya read him

the riot act did he get nothing but annoyed, but when Emma took him to task, he found it more than a little attractive?

She was right, of course. Emma had in fact stated she would not marry him, but Konstantin wasn't giving up. Apprising her of the fact didn't feel like the next smart move, so he remained silent.

"I will be home in a couple of hours. Will you and Mickey be there?" Emma asked in an obvious effort to change the subject.

"We can be, or you can have an hour to yourself while I take him to the Children's Museum."

"You'll wear him out." Her tone was filled with warmth.

So, Konstantin didn't take the complaint seriously. "Mishka has an infinite source of energy."

Emma's laugh went straight to his libido. How had he gone so long without hearing that particular sound?

"I know it seems that way," she warned him. "But you'd better make sure he gets a snack, or you'll see how quickly that energy goes to the dark side."

"Noted."

"I've got to get back to work."

"Yes."

Neither hung up. It reminded him of the times they used to just sit on the phone and listen to each other breathe when he was out of town on a business trip. Their words would run out, but their desire to stay connected would not.

"This is... I..." Emma sounded lost. "I have to go." And she hung up.

But she'd felt it too. He knew she had.

Emma pressed End Call and dropped the phone like it was a snake.

That had been... That had been way too much like the way things used to be. For just a moment, she was living in the place where she still loved him, where she'd thought he'd actually cared about her, where her very being hung on the next word he said and knew his hung on hers.

She'd suffused with desire so intense, she'd lost sense of reality. For a moment, she had disconnected with her air-conditioned office with its perfectly uniform plants and cubicles for the other three bookkeepers.

It was the moan that she could feel making its way up her throat that brought Emma back to the present.

She'd told Kon she had to go and hung up before she did something crazy like ask him to come get her too.

Predictably, Mickey was too tired to do much playing outside after dinner.

He wanted a movie night on the sofa with Emma and Konstantin.

"I can sit with you, but I need to do some work on my computer," Konstantin told their son.

"Okay, Dad. Thanks for taking me to the park and the Children's Museum today. It was lots of fun." Mickey yawned.

"But now you want to relax. It is good you recognize what you need."

"Mom says that if I'm feeling cranky, I need to look inside and try to know why."

Smart mom, but everything Konstantin observed between Emma and Mikhail told him she was an exemplary mother. "Oh, were you feeling cranky?"

Mikhail shrugged. "Tired."

Konstantin nodded. "Sure. I'm a little tired myself," he admitted.

"But you still have to work?"

"I do." Konstantin swallowed his own yawn.

Emma came into the room carrying a big bowl filled with popcorn, which she placed on the coffee table. "You two get settled. I'll get the lemonade."

"What movie would your mom like?" Konstantin asked Mikhail conspiratorially.

Mikhail brought up their streaming service on the smart TV. He clicked on a family movie about a princess who saves herself. "She likes this one."

Naturally. "Your mom is a strong lady who can take care of herself just like this princess." However, it would be Konstantin's pleasure to care for Emma's needs going into the future.

"Only Mom isn't a princess."

"But she would make a good one, don't you think?"

"Like this princess?" Mikhail considered. "Yeah, maybe."

"I agree."

"What are you two agreeing about?"

"You're like this princess, Mom." Mikhail snuggled in next to Konstantin.

Emma sat on the other side of their son. "Am I?"

"Definitely," Konstantin answered as their son took a handful of popcorn and tried to shove all the kernels into his mouth at once.

He shook his head and smiled at Emma.

She grinned back and shrugged. "What can I say? He likes popcorn."

Mickey wasn't the only one who had been craving more family, Emma realized as she relaxed with her son and the man who had been her only lover.

She used to dream of simple evenings like this, her and Mickey cuddled on the couch for a relaxing evening in with the man in her life. That guy hadn't had a face in her dreams, but his body had been suspiciously like Konstantin's, his skin the same tone, his hands strong and capable.

She'd never dated, too burned by the double rejection of

the man she loved and the parents she adored to risk putting Mickey through anything similar.

But this? Felt right. Too right for a man who had ejected her from his life like dangerous waste.

Maybe she had been dangerous to him.

By his own admission, Konstantin had found it hard to stay away from her. However, he'd been determined to keep his commitment to that darn contract. He hadn't even tried to renegotiate it.

That was the sticking point that Emma found hardest to get past.

So, he *hadn't* taken out the TRO, or even known about it.

He *had* broken up with her and made it impossible for her to reach him to tell him about her pregnancy.

He *had* left her vulnerable to Queen Crazy.

But he *hadn't* broken his word where the contract was concerned. Maybe King Nikolai was right and she *could* trust Konstantin on some level. Oh, not as *her* family. Not even if she did eventually agree to marry him. But if he would sign a contract like the one she'd suggested, maybe she could trust he would be committed to sticking to its terms.

Konstantin had shown that when it came to putting his name on a document, her Prince took that seriously. When he made a legal commitment, he kept it.

Predictably, after his busy day, Mickey fell asleep halfway through the movie.

Emma stood to lift him, but Konstantin beat her to it. "Time for bed, I think."

"We'll both regret it if you don't take him to the bathroom first."

Konstantin did as she suggested, helping their sleepy son with a prosaic acceptance she would not have expected. They got him into his pajamas together and then tucked him into bed.

"What?" Konstantin asked as they came back into the living room.

She turned off the movie, wanting to talk without Mickey overhearing more than she wanted to finish a movie she loved, but had seen many times. "I just... You're really good at that."

"Am I? I worry that I'll do something wrong and hurt him without meaning to." Konstantin moved into her personal space.

Emma stepped back. "You're a really natural father."

"I had a good role model." Konstantin gave her a challenging look as he sat on the middle of the couch, leaving the only spot beside him.

The armchair had been moved to make room for the bed and wasn't ideal for sharing a conversation with someone on the sofa.

"Your father?" Emma bit the bullet and sat beside him, her body hugging the arm so their thighs did not touch.

Emma needed to focus for this conversation and she was fully aware that Konstantin in close proximity would not be conducive to that focus.

"Yes." Konstantin relaxed against the sofa, laying his arm across the back, mere inches from her shoulders. "He was a king first, I always knew that, but he was a good father, interested in my brothers and me, involved in our lives from infancy."

"How could you know that?"

"Dima is nearly eight years younger than me. I got to see my father with him as a baby. Nikolai has always been a hands-on older brother too. I let myself forget that when he became my sovereign," he said, his expression introspective. "Both of them modeled what being a good father-slash-caretaker looked like."

"I guess I thought you'd been raised mostly by nannies."

"We had nursery staff, but my parents were always the

last word in discipline and the first to give us the affection every child needs."

"That's why you're so comfortable hugging and playing with Mickey." Which had surprised Emma from the beginning.

As long as she'd known him, Konstantin had always kept a physical distance from others. It was like he walked around with an invisible barrier surrounding him.

When they were together, he'd invited her inside that barrier, touching her all the time. Which had been another reason she'd mistakenly thought she was special to him.

"The only people I have ever been comfortable touching are my family, and later you," he said as if inside her brain and responding to her thoughts. "As I got older, a natural distance developed between me and my family."

And he'd created a world's worth of distance between him and her when he broke up with Emma.

"Or maybe once you lost your mom, you all sort of pulled into yourselves instead of relying on each other for comfort," Emma mused, ignoring the obvious about their own lack of physical closeness.

Konstantin shrugged. "Perhaps. I was fifteen, and I wanted to accept her death like a man."

"But you weren't a man. You were still a kid." Her heart hurt for the teenager he'd been.

"Dima was the one who was still a child. He needed us all to be strong for him." Konstantin smiled indulgently at her. "Do not look as if I am sharing the great tragedy of our age with you. I never stopped hugging my little brother when he was a child, if that makes you feel better."

Dima was an adult now, finished with university and starting graduate school.

"It does." Taking a deep breath, she said, "Something else would make me feel even better."

"I have a feeling it is not the same thing that I am craving."

Suddenly the air around them was heavy with sexual energy.

Emma tried to concentrate on the flow of air in and out of her lungs, but it didn't stop her nipples beading to almost painful peaks and vaginal walls from contracting with a need she'd ignored since being thrust from his life.

"I'm pretty sure you are right," she acknowledged in a tone that was way too breathless for her liking. "Have you thought about signing a contract like I asked about last night?"

"Why?" he asked, sounding pained.

Forcing herself not to react emotionally to his obvious hurt, Emma drew on her own sense of certainty. "You never once even considered breaking that marriage-slash-business contract when we were together. You see your legal obligations as absolute."

"Not absolute. I broke the contract last year, when Nataliya humiliated me in the media." He didn't sound particularly proud of that fact.

"Did you?"

"I was feeling guilty and angry."

"That's never a good combination for you."

"No, it is not. It is how I ended up cutting you off so completely."

"What were you feeling guilty about then?"

"You were a naive nineteen-year-old when we met. A virgin. And I didn't care. I wanted you."

"So you've said. You were obsessed with my body."

"I was that. I wanted you all the time, but Emma, even more dangerous to my commitments was the truth that when I was with you, I was happy."

"So happy that you dumped me. Let's not rewrite history."

"I am not trying to rewrite anything." He blew out a clearly frustrated breath. "I am trying to be honest."

"Okay, so in all honesty, you dumped me because you had committed to marrying another woman in a contract."

"Yes."

"You want me to trust you with Mickey. You want to be his dad. You want us to move in with you."

"I want you to marry me."

"But I am not there. I may never be there. What *I* need is to know with as much certainty as I can have that I can trust you not to try to usurp me with my son. That even if I never marry you, you will not attempt to take Mickey from me."

"My word is not enough for you?"

"No." She swallowed, knowing she wasn't done, and he wasn't going to like her next request any more than the first. "I would prefer that your brother the King sign the contract as well."

"Why?"

"Because your former Queen took out a TRO against me on your behalf. I need to know that your current monarch will not do anything like that."

"He never would."

"You didn't think Queen Crazy would either."

"No, I did not. And the truth is I misjudged both my brother and my deceased sister-in-law. He cares for me far more than I thought, and she was no friend to me at all."

"I would agree, at least with the latter."

"You'll see that Nikolai is a good man."

"If he is, then he won't mind signing the custody agreement."

Konstantin frowned. "This is really important to you, isn't it?"

"I want to trust you, Kon. You don't know how much. I

see how important you already are to our son, how keenly he misses having an extended family, but I'm his mom."

"And no one will ever try to take that away from you," Konstantin promised fiercely.

"So, sign the contract. Get your brother to sign it. Give me something to trust."

"I am not enough."

"Stop saying that. Don't you see that you doing this shows me that you're as committed to Mickey's happiness and my safety as you claim to be? This would be *you* being enough. This would be *you* being trustworthy in the way that *I* need it."

The only question was would His Royal Highness's pride allow him to follow up all his verbal promises with action?

Konstantin grabbed his phone and dialed. "I have a task for you," he said into it rather than a greeting. "I need a custody agreement that guarantees Emma's role as primary custodian of our son, regardless of any other circumstances. In addition, you will include a proviso for financial support." He named a monthly sum that was ridiculously high. "The palace will take responsibility for security for both Emma and Mikhail."

The man, Emma thought it was probably the lawyer she'd met earlier, Albert Popov, squawked at the other end of the phone.

"That is not your decision to make," Konstantin replied.

The man said something else.

Konstantin's expression turned iceberg cold. "And why would I take *your* advice on matters of this nature after your colossal error in judgment regarding the TRO you took out on my behalf against the mother of my child?"

Emma could not hear what the lawyer said, but she now knew for sure it was Mr. Popov. Konstantin relaxed just a tiny bit, so whatever the man had said, it must have been conciliatory.

"There needs to be a place for me to sign, but also my father, my brothers and my sister-in-law." Konstantin frowned. "I am quite sure I know how my family will react to being asked to sign this agreement better than you do."

Mr. Popov said something else.

"*Da.* Have the paperwork officially recognizing Mikhail as my son ready to sign." Impatience lined every inch of Konstantin's face. "We have already done the DNA testing."

Emma had insisted on it that first week and now she was glad.

"Yes, it was Emma's idea. But there was never any question I am Mikhail's father." He said this to Emma, though she was sure the lawyer thought Konstantin was talking to him.

Konstantin gave the lawyer a couple of more directions that would put definitive protections for Emma's role in Mickey's life in place and then ended the call.

"Do you have a lawyer to look these papers over?" he asked her.

"I…no. I'll have to get one." She would use the rainy day fund she'd been saving for the house's repairs and remodel. "Thank you for that. You did more than I expected. Are you really going to get your whole family to sign the agreement?"

"Yes."

"But will they?"

"Yes."

"You're so sure."

"Mikhail is my son."

"You said he was next in line after you in the succession for the throne. I… Doesn't that mean King Nikolai wants a say?"

"I have just found out that Nataliya is pregnant."

"Which is really great for them, but doesn't change anything about Mickey's role in the monarchy until that child is born."

"Nikolai is a good man. He will understand your desire for the contract."

"Yeah, but he has to trust me in order to sign it," Emma said as that truth literally hit home with her. "How can he? He doesn't know me."

"He knows me. I trust you. He either trusts my judgment, or he does not."

"And if he doesn't?" she couldn't help pushing.

"Then Mikhail will stay with you in the States when I travel to Mirrus."

"Just like that? But that isn't what you want."

"I will do what I have to do to ensure you trust me to fulfill my role to Mikhail as his father without ever compromising your role as his mother. From the moment I learned of his existence, you and he became my priority."

"But that's not how it works, is it?"

"I lost you once to my responsibility to the crown. I will not lose you, or my son, again."

She was sure the nearly five years of life he'd lost with Mickey was the deciding factor for Konstantin, but even knowing how very much he regretted that helped Emma to trust Konstantin in Mickey's life.

If not her own.

CHAPTER SEVEN

DESPITE HIS ASSURANCE his brother and the rest of his family would sign the agreement promising not to interfere with Emma's parental rights and role as Mikhail's mother, Konstantin wasn't at all sure they would.

He and Nikolai had lost trust in each other since their mother's death. There had been a time they were best friends, despite their age difference, but they'd grown apart.

Now, Konstantin realized that they had both handled their grief at the loss by turning inward. Their father had done the same. The only person any of them had continued to show affection for had been Dima and even their youngest brother had eventually pulled himself into his own space and life, away from them all.

Nikolai's marrying Nataliya had brought a lot of warmth back to the palace and Konstantin realized that the same could not be said of his brother's first marriage.

Tiana had not been the friend Konstantin thought she was, but worse she had been a poor queen and an even worse wife. He'd been blinded to the truth, but he wasn't anymore.

He was learning to trust Nikolai's judgment again, but was his brother doing the same for Konstantin? He would soon find out.

Nikolai remained silent on the other end of the phone as Konstantin explained what he wanted his brother to sign and why.

"She said this would help her trust you with Mishka?" Nikolai inquired.

"Da."

His brother made a thoughtful sound. "Is she refusing to move to Seattle without it?"

"*Nyet*, but that is not the point."

"No." He could almost see Nikolai nodding to himself. "The point is you want her to trust you."

"*Da.*"

"Convincing a worthy woman to marry you is no easy task."

"It is not," Konstantin had to agree. "I am not at all sure I will convince her that marriage is the best solution for our future, even with Mishka on my side."

"I have confidence in you, brother. Even if you were not a prince, you would be a catch."

Konstantin was secretly pleased by his brother's words, but only said gruffly, "So you will sign the custody agreement."

"You are giving a great deal of power to her without any checks."

"It is the same power she would have had if I had not run into her and my son by accident in that bank."

"And some would deny the existence of miracles."

"I would not have thought you believed in them. You have always been so practical." A young king, Nikolai had not had room in his life for impracticality.

"Nataliya is my miracle," Nikolai said, all sincerity, no humor. "She could have married you and I would have been stuck pining for the rest of my life."

"So, I am forgiven for not fulfilling the contract earlier?"

"Forgiven? I will name my firstborn after you in gratitude."

"Nataliya will have something to say about that."

"Yes, she will." Nikolai sounded very satisfied by the knowledge his wife was no pushover.

"Nataliya will like Emma."

"Nataliya likes most people."

"That's a whopper of a lie. Your wife is charming and a

fantastic princess, but you and I both know she barely tolerates most of our country's nobility."

"That is true. However, she's an excellent judge of character, so I am sure she will like your Emma."

Konstantin only wished Emma *was* his. "You must think I am a good judge of character to say so." Since his brother had never met Emma.

"You were the one who recognized Nataliya carried a torch for me and that marrying her would be a travesty for both of you."

"But despite that, I never backed out of the contract."

"No, your sense of duty was too strong. And it cost you greatly. Don't think both Father and I aren't aware of that."

"I thought Tiana was the one who cared about my personal happiness, not you," Konstantin admitted.

"She was very good at pretending to be someone she was not."

"Emma isn't like that. What you see is what you get."

"Now that we know her name and whereabouts for the last five years, I've had her investigated." Nikolai spoke with an uncharacteristic caution.

"So, that is why you trust my opinion of her."

"No. I trust you because you are trustworthy, Konstantin."

"That is good to know."

"You must have been satisfied by what the report on her activities told you."

"You know she worked as a nanny for a family by the name of Jensen."

"Yes. She wanted to continue her education but stay with Mikhail until he was old enough for preschool and found a way to do it by becoming the nanny and sometimes housekeeper for the Jensens." Konstantin made no effort to stifle the pride he felt in Emma's resourcefulness in his voice.

"Mr. Jensen was a total womanizer, but she maintained

a distance from him when others did not. That marriage was not a happy one before he left."

"That is unfortunate, but Emma would never mess around with a married man."

"No, she would not. I think before she met you, no one would have thought she'd live with a man before marriage either." There was subtle censure in Nikolai's tone.

Konstantin did not take offense. "She was entirely innocent, but I ignored the treasure she was and pushed her out of my life."

"For the sake of a marriage contract you should not have been asked to sign. If Mother had been alive, you wouldn't have. She believed in the modern monarchy."

"Father still has some very old-world views."

"Yes, but he regrets the years he has lost with his grandson because of it." Nikolai paused and then said, "I'll sign the custody agreement, brother, and make sure Father, Dima and Nataliya do as well."

Relief washed over Konstantin. "Thank you."

Emma got advice from the director of Mickey's preschool day care for a good family law attorney.

She really liked the fiftyish woman who had a solid reputation in family law. The older woman told Emma that the contract was very generous in monetary terms—which Emma had already realized—and that while she was surprised, she was happy to see that it was heavily weighted in Emma's favor in regard to parental rights.

Again, it was as Emma had expected, but hearing there were no hidden caveats that might compromise her role in Mickey's life was reassuring.

Though provision for Konstantin's visitation with their son was one area that gave him more than usual access.

Emma didn't mind. She'd agreed to the terms he'd asked

for before the contract had been drawn up. She *wanted* him in Mickey's life.

However, the lawyer's last words stayed in Emma's head.

"He's still a prince. And you are still, as you have said, a normal person. A healthy dose of caution is in order. This isn't a fairy tale, but your life with your son."

The attorney's advice stayed in the back of Emma's mind even as she and Mickey prepared to move into Konstantin's Santa Fe mansion.

Mickey had only a few weeks left of school, during which she was hoping her empty house would sell quickly.

She and Konstantin had yet to talk about where they planned to live in Seattle. Partly because she was avoiding being alone with him.

It wasn't that she thought the discussion was unnecessary. In fact, it was starting to eat away at her sense of inner peace not to know where they would be living come summer.

It was just that her attraction to him was growing and Emma was finding it harder and harder to keep her hands to herself and her libido under control when she was around Konstantin.

"You want my room right next to yours?" Emma asked, her voice going high.

They'd come to Kon's mansion for a couple of hours every day to ease the transition of moving for Mickey, but today was her and her son's official move-in.

"You do not like the room?"

"Of course I like the room." It was more than twice the size of her old one, but whether the house had come this way or Kon had made it happen, her room had all the bright Southwestern patterns and colors that Emma liked so much.

But everything, right down to the towels in the en suite

bathroom, was high-end and luxurious. The bedding was new and had the discreet logo of a top designer. The furniture was the same.

No pieces found at a garage sale and refurbished for this mansion.

And yet the designer had managed to make the royal residence feel like a home and not just a showplace.

Emma sighed. "It's a gorgeous room. I just don't understand why I'm right next door to you. Won't that cramp your style?"

"Did you just ask me that?" Kon's tone was heavy with offense. "You know I am not seeing other women. My plan is for us to marry."

"I… That's not what I meant." She bit her lip, looked around and dredged up a smile for him. "I'm sorry, okay? I don't know what I mean." Just that being so close to him was going to play havoc on her efforts to keep her attraction for him under control.

But that was not his problem. It was hers.

Kon's intense brown gaze searched her face, his own expression giving nothing away. "Mikhail will feel more confident with both of us only across the hall from his own new bedroom."

Emma couldn't argue that. "You're right."

"So?"

"So, this is fine." She sighed internally, trying for gracious. "Better than fine."

"Good. Mikhail and I have a surprise for you." Kon's smile took Emma's breath and did some very interesting things to other parts of her body that she did her best to pretend were not happening.

Their son chose that moment to knock loudly and then come careening into the room. "Mom, Mom… Wait till you see what Dad and me did. You're gonna love it!"

Grateful for the timely interruption, Emma's smile for

her son was a lot more natural. She allowed him and Kon to lead her downstairs. She thought they were going to the outdoor pool, which Mickey was over the moon about, but they turned down the hall in the back and stopped at an open door, clearly waiting for her to go in first.

What she saw took her breath away. Floor-to-ceiling windows looked out over the beautifully landscaped grounds, the lush outdoor pool area off to the right.

The view and the size of the room were impressive enough, but it was what the room held that made it hard for Emma to even get out words of thanks; she was so overwhelmed. It had been outfitted as a painting studio, all of her things moved, but also added to.

Everything she could imagine needing to paint, not just her commissions, but multiple easels and a full set of watercolors, as well as acrylics and oils with the top-of-the-line brushes to go with each. A lot of artists stuck to one medium, but she'd always been happiest when she could flit back and forth between these three.

She looked at Kon. "You remembered."

"I remember everything about you," he promised her. "You said that your ideal studio would have the space for all your supplies and you would not have to pack up one medium to start a project with another."

It had been her dream, but one she'd never realized. She'd felt lucky to have room for any kind of studio in her and Mickey's little house. Being able to keep art in her life at all had been a luxury, but necessary for her sense of well-being. She'd stuck to watercolors for her commissions and had stifled every desire to create with something else.

"Look, Mom, see all the windows?" Mickey spread his arms expansively.

Emma grinned. "I do. They're wonderful." She opened her arms and got a big hug from her son. "You're wonderful. Thank you, Mickey."

"And Dad. It was his idea, but he wanted my help. He took me shopping."

That was some commitment to her happiness right there. Mickey was not the greatest shopper. He got bored when he wasn't moving.

Emma smiled at Kon. "Thank you. Really. This is amazing."

"Do I get a hug too?" he asked, a devilish glint in his eyes.

"You've gotta give Dad a hug too," Mickey demanded.

Emma gave her son a gently reproving look. "Hugs are always voluntary, you know that, Mickey."

"Right. Because we set our body boundaries," he parroted what she'd told him a hundred times and she was sure his preschool staff had as well. "But Mom, he tried real hard to make you happy."

Kon opened his arms, his expression quizzical and just a little bit challenging. It was the challenge that did it. Her back up, Emma found herself moving across the tile floor to him with determined movements.

She meant to give him a distance hug. Nothing too personal. Perfunctory. Only, her body leaned into his like it had been programmed to his touch. Maybe it had.

He had been her first and only real lover.

The last man she'd let into her personal space without limits. Somehow she let herself relax into his body, her arms going around him in anything but a *perfunctory* manner.

"Thank you," she whispered huskily into his chest.

Kon's arms wrapped tightly around her, pulling her even closer. "My pleasure."

That short, throwaway phrase held so much meaning beyond *you're welcome*. The way he held her, the unmistakable proof that this hug was having the same physical effect on him that it was her… It all said this moment really was *his* pleasure.

But it was hers too and that scared the life out of her. Even so, she stayed where she was.

Everything she'd told herself about getting over him was suddenly shown for the lies they had been.

Emma inhaled and his scent washed over her with all the sense memories it could invoke. Lazy Sunday mornings spent in bed, touching, laughing…talking. Nights of passion that left her replete and certain of her place in the world. Peaceful moments cuddling on the couch, watching his sports on the television, while she read a book.

For a moment she was back in that place, in love, certain she was cared for, the future nebulous but shiny.

"That's a good hug." Mickey's voice jarred, bringing Emma back to the present with a thump. "She can hug you like that cuz you're my dad. We're family."

Emma shoved against Kon, jumping back and nearly tripping over her own feet to put distance between them. Only then did she notice the pained look on his face. Her gaze skimmed his body and guilt assailed her. She quickly stepped between him and their son's line of sight.

The look of gratitude Kon shot her did a number on her heart.

"Right, Mom?" Mickey asked, his little face showing tension she hadn't noticed at first.

"Um…" Oh, man, what was she supposed to say?

I just hugged the stuffing out of your father because I forgot where I was, when I was and how much this man hurt me once upon a time.

Not. Going. To. Happen.

"*Da*, Mishka, I *am* your dad and we *are* a family." Kon, in his typical arrogant, I-know-what's-best fashion, had decided to answer.

The fact he stayed where he was, which showed he

wasn't able to get over his reaction to holding her that easily, gave her some satisfaction though.

"Mom?" Mickey wanted full-on assurance.

And Emma did what she was always did when her son needed anything it was in her power to provide. She gave it. "Yes, sweetheart, we are a family. I can hug your dad when I need to."

"And he can hug you, right, Mom?"

If Emma had a potty mouth it would have gotten a workout right then, if only inside her own mind. Wrapped neatly and tied with a bow by her own son.

"I'm sure he'd rather hug you than me," Emma said evasively.

"I don't think so, Mom." Mickey looked at Kon. "You like hugging Mom, huh? You looked really happy hugging her."

"I enjoy hugging you both very much," Kon said smoothly, making no effort to dissuade their son from his family-hugging agenda.

The rat.

"Because we're a family." Mickey's happiness with that truth was as obvious as a bright yellow swath down the middle of a desert watercolor.

Bright and out of place it might be in the desert of her life, Emma couldn't bring herself to dampen even the edges of her son's joy.

"Yes," Emma affirmed.

Mickey's smile let Emma know she'd made the right choice, but his father's smile worried her more than a little.

As the day wore on, it became clear that Mickey had appointed himself the role of matchmaker. Making sure that if they sat together, she and Kon were side by side. Talking about the future all bright and shiny as a family *all together*. Talking his dad up to Emma with a canny understanding that she was the one with reservations.

All of it so very clearly revealing Mickey's plans of seeing his parents reunited.

If Emma thought Kon had put him up to his shenanigans, she would be furious. But she didn't.

Mickey had been up-front and loud about his desire for a family that was more than just him and Emma since meeting his father. He adored Kon and thrived under his father's affection and presence.

Emma realized that her own need to protect her heart had taken a toll on her son's sense of security. He'd had only one adult in his life he knew he could absolutely rely on.

Her highly intelligent but equally sensitive son had felt the lack keenly.

That night as she and Kon tucked Mickey in, he said, "Now there's someone to take care of you, Mom." He smiled up at his father with trust she was used to seeing doled out only in *her* direction. "You'll always watch out for us, right, Dad?"

"*Da*. I promise you with all that I am." Kon's voice rang with the sincerity and permanence of a vow.

Hearing her son use that comfort-seeking phrase toward someone else went through Emma with a painful jolt.

It was hard to relinquish her spot as his only mainstay, but even more painful was the realization Mickey had needed to know she had backup. And she'd never given him that.

Fighting emotions she could not cope with right then, she kissed her son good-night and told him she loved him.

"Love you too, Mom. Love you, Dad."

"I love you too, Mishka," Kon promised as he tucked the blankets just a little tighter around him. Then he leaned down and kissed Mickey's forehead before standing. "See you in the morning."

"Or in the night if I have a bad dream, right?"

"Absolutely. Your mom and I are just across the hall." He

made it sound like they were sharing a room, which they were not, but it was part of that illusion they both seemed intent on building around her.

A full-on family with all the connections.

Mickey nodded sleepily and turned to his side, contentment coming off him in waves.

Emma stumbled from his room, headed for her own.

"Emma."

She stopped at Kon's voice, but did not turn around. "What?"

"I thought we could spend some time together."

"Not tonight." Her voice caught and she knew the tears she was fighting were too close to the surface.

"Emma, what is the matter? It was a good day, was it not?" Kon's hand landed on her shoulder.

Emma shuddered, that small connection more than her starving senses could handle.

He turned her, oh, so gently, his expression perplexed. "What is it, Emma *moi*?"

"You used to call me that all the time. But I'm not yours anymore, Kon."

"I think you have always been mine. And I have always been yours." He said it like he really believed his own words.

Only they could not be true.

She laughed, the sound too close to a sob for comfort. "Your legion of lovers would say otherwise."

"No legion and not one of them was a *lover*. I had sex partners and if could change that now, I would." His brown eyes were dark with some kind of intense emotion.

Maybe he did regret sleeping with other women, though she didn't know why he should. They hadn't been together. There had been no promises between them, not after Kon had evicted Emma from his life.

"Do you think it matters that you didn't give them your

heart?" He'd said that like it made *all* the difference, but it didn't make *any* difference. Not to her. "You never gave me that either."

The only thing that made her special in his life was that she'd given birth to his son. Emma needed to remember that, or she was going to get her heart shattered all over again.

"I think the only thing that matters is what happens now. We cannot change the past, no matter how much we may wish we could."

She had no trouble believing her Prince genuinely wished things had gone differently. He already loved Mickey and Kon had missed out on almost five years of his life.

"You would have loved being a dad from day one, even I can see that," Emma had no problem acknowledging.

"You and Mishka are the only ones who matter."

But Kon was wrong about that. "I should have given him more family."

"What?" he asked, sounding genuinely shocked. "Emma, you are an amazing mom."

"I let my own insecurities stop me from providing my son with what he needed," she admitted with shame. "That's not amazing. That's cowardly."

"No." Kon jerked his head in a negative motion, his expression filled with denial. "If there is a woman who is less a coward, I do not know her."

The tears fell then. Because Emma knew he was wrong. Unable to speak, she just shook her head.

Kon made a sound like his patient understanding had lost the fight with his need to act, and then he was picking her up.

She gasped her shock, but it came out choked with her tears.

His expression grim, Kon asked, "Your room, or mine?"

Even if she knew why he was asking, she couldn't have answered. Emma was too busy having a meltdown. She never cried. Never. She meditated. She did yoga. Emma did not lose it, emotionally, but right now? She was definitely losing it.

And instead of running in the other direction like a smart man would have, Kon was throwing himself into it like he could stand between her and her own emotional pain.

"Mine, then," he said, decisively. "It has been sound-proofed. Mishka will not hear you crying."

Emma didn't ask why the master bedroom was sound-proofed, only grateful that her son would not be woken by the sobs she didn't seem able to stifle.

Kon carried her into his room toward a butter yellow leather sofa near the tall windows. They overlooked the gorgeous pool area the three of them had spent time in after lunch. She'd been laughing and full of a sense of freedom, not being Mickey's only caretaker then, not the blubbering mess she was now.

Emma wouldn't have blamed him if he dumped her on the sofa and retreated, but Kon sat down without letting her go, settling Emma in his lap.

And she let him.

His arms were steady bands around her, his solid chest right there for her to rest her head against. "Tell me what is going through your mind to upset you so much," he insisted.

"Don't you see?" she implored him. "I was afraid to let anyone in and because of that, Mickey didn't have the people in his life he needed."

"I don't understand." Kon's brows drew together in a frown of confusion.

"He had no grandparents, no aunts and uncles."

Kon's gorgeous features were cast with guilt, showing

just who he thought was at fault. *Him*. "But that was not your fault."

But it wasn't entirely his either. Emma had her own burden of guilt she was just coming face-to-face with. "I could have built a family for him. Mrs. Jensen wanted to be my friend but I wouldn't even call her by her first name. It was Claire. I never used it. Not once. She needed a friend too."

But Emma had been too raw with loss to make friends with her employer. Later, she'd built walls around her heart she hadn't even realized were there.

"Because the people you had trusted with your heart crushed it." Kon's expression was as if light had dawned over the horizon to illuminate and turn dark, impenetrable shapes into something recognizable. "Your parents, me… We let you down so badly you didn't trust anyone else."

"And hurt my son in the process." She gulped in air, trying to control the tears. "I thought I'd got it together. That I hadn't let myself become that cynical, broken soul. But all the time I was so proud of my inner peace, I *was* that woman and I kept everyone who could have given Mickey a sense of security at a distance."

"Mishka had you. He was safe. He was loved."

"But he was worried!" She pressed her fist against Kon's chest. "I should have dated Mr. Leeds. Mickey adores him."

"No, he's not the right man for you," Kon slotted in with speed. "He's too young for you. You have nothing in common with him."

"He's closer in age to me than you are." She had no idea if she had anything in common with the preschool teacher, or not. Emma hadn't allowed him to get close enough to find out. Even as a friend.

"Mishka has grandparents, an aunt, two uncles. We will bring them all into his life. I promise you."

"But he should have had other people all along."

"Stop this. Emma, your tears…no." Kon sounded nearly

panicked. "You will stop crying and worrying about the past. Mishka is a well-adjusted, happy child. Stop beating yourself up."

She'd never heard him less than fully confident. Emma would have laughed at him instructing her to stop crying if she could have.

He was so arrogant and so very clearly out of his depth right then.

"But look how he is looking to you for reassurance now." It shamed her to admit, but that still hurt.

"Because you have allowed it. Your love for our son has enabled you to see beyond my monumental mistakes and allow me into his life. *You* gave him a father and now he has both of us to give him security, but only because your generous heart made that possible."

Konstantin did not know if he was saying the right things. He only knew he could not stand to see his Emma hurting like this.

He wasn't such an oblivious fool that he did not see how hard it was for her to share their son with him. Emma and Mikhail had been their own little family since his birth. Konstantin fully expected his son to go through some adjustments learning to share his mom's attention and affection as well.

But Konstantin was up to the task.

He was in regular contact with not only his family, but also Mikhail's counselor, seeking advice. Only no wise words could prepare him for this moment when the woman he wanted to be his wife cried in his arms because she thought she hadn't been a good enough single mom.

"You have been strong when Mishka needed strength. You gave him tenderness when he needed it. He lacked for nothing, do you hear me?" Konstantin willed her to believe him.

A watery laugh erupted from her and she gave him a wry look, no less effective for the tears standing in her beautiful blue eyes. "Just because you say it doesn't make it so."

"I am sure it does. I am a prince, if you did not know it."

Another choky laugh sounded. "I know it."

He considered those two moments of shaky laughter some of his best work.

Her fingers kneaded his chest in what he was sure was unconscious movement without any of the sexual intentions his body was reading into the action.

No thoughts of football stats or spreadsheet formulas could cool the ardor growing in Konstantin's body. He had craved this woman since the moment she walked out of his life. That it had been at his insistence did not matter.

No woman he had been with since had ever fulfilled that craving, or made him miss Emma any less.

She shifted in his lap and then stilled. "Kon?"

She could not know how much pleasure he derived by her calling him Kon like she used to. He wasn't about to point it out either.

Contrary woman that she was, she would probably make herself stop doing it.

"Ignore it. I cannot control my body's base reaction to you, but that does not mean I have to act on it." He was no hormonal adolescent.

Tension that had nothing to do with Emma's meltdown thrummed between them. Heated sexual desire charged the air around them so much he would not have been surprised to see actual sparks.

"That's not what you used to say." Her beautiful blue eyes were filled with feminine mystery.

Which only added to the ardent need growing in him to have her back in his bed, but even more important, she was no longer crying.

"I was an ass, pressing you into a physical relationship

you weren't ready for. I'm sorry." It was an apology long overdue.

"No apology needed. For that anyway. Make no mistake, I was ready for it." She pressed her fingertip to his lips when he went to interrupt. "Listen, Kon, I may not have been ready for what came after, but I wanted you every bit as much as you wanted me."

"I knew what was coming, but you did not."

"The breakup, you mean?"

"Yes. You were right, I should have reminded you that what we had was not permanent." He'd convinced himself that telling her that one time was enough.

It had not been. Full. Stop.

"Maybe part of you wished it could be."

"Maybe. I did not allow myself to entertain thoughts in that direction, but nor did I dwell on the inevitable end."

She pushed against his chest and as much as he hated to, Konstantin had to let her get up. He was pleasantly surprised when she moved only as far as the seat beside him on the sofa.

"You said that you finally reneged on the contract when Princess Nataliya embarrassed you in the media."

This was not something Konstantin wanted to talk about, but with Emma, he found himself willing to do what was not comfortable for him. In many ways.

"Yes, I did." His brother had spun it for the media like Nikolai had swooped in and stolen Nataliya from under Konstantin's nose.

But the truth was that Konstantin had played right into his sister-in-law's hands and rejected her as a potential wife in front of their two families, all but negating the contract.

"It's hard to accept that you were willing to break the contract you held as sacrosanct for the sake of your pride, but hadn't been willing to do it so we could stay together."

"I did not see it that way." And would never have suspected she did.

Her mind was still a big mystery to him in so many ways and yet he felt like he knew her better than anyone else in his life and that she knew him more deeply than even his own family.

"How else could you see it?" she asked, like she really wanted him to answer. Like Emma, the amazing woman she was, was *willing* to listen.

"When we were together, I never even let myself consider breaking the contract and trying to build a future with you."

"I'm not exactly princess material."

"Technically as my wife, you would have the title of duchess until Nikolai decreed otherwise, but Emma, it had nothing to do with that."

"What, then?"

"I'd made a promise. I had to keep it."

"You broke it later."

"I had changed, my perception of what I owed my family had changed."

"What changed it?" Emma's blue gaze demanded full honesty.

Konstantin could not deny her that, even if telling her things he'd never shared with anyone else left him feeling exposed. "At first, I thought it was losing my friend. Tiana was so young when she died, and her death made me reexamine my own life."

"You said you went looking for me then," Emma said, sounding thoughtful.

"I did, but you were gone and I was still stuck in the groove of believing that contract dictated my ultimate future."

"But something changed."

"Time changed me. Having sex with women that were

not you changed me." This was the hardest thing to admit. It showed her how much he needed her, and Konstantin did not like needing anyone. "It was empty and one day I had the lowering realization that was what marriage to Nataliya was going to be like. I'd had perfection and knew what it felt like to share something more than empty, fleeting pleasure with a woman."

Emma gasped as if his words had shocked her to the core. "You didn't see our time together that way."

"I assure you, I did."

"So, you're trying to tell me that having sex with other women made you realize that what we'd had was special."

Konstantin felt heat climb his neck. "Yes."

"But while we were together you didn't think it was so special." She left unsaid that if he had, he would not have broken up with her.

"Please try to understand. I was not raised to consider my *feelings*, my *emotions* as any kind of valid basis for making choices. Our parents were loving toward us, but if they loved each other, I never knew it. They loved Mirrus and its people. Their actions were driven by that love and duty."

"Duty they taught you to revere."

"Yes." Could she understand?

A woman raised to honor her parents, but without the weight of royal duty he had known from his first memory.

"I can't say that makes the past okay, but I think I'm starting to understand what drove your actions then and now."

That was something. "Thank you."

"For what?"

"For listening. For trying to understand a perspective very different from your own. We should all aspire to be so open to those we don't understand."

"That's a great attitude even if you are kind of over-blowing my virtues."

She was so humble, maybe too humble. "Not at all. I have it on the best authority, our son's if you are wondering, that you are *the best*."

"And I thought it was only your praises he was singing to me."

"Oh, no. That child has plans and I'm not sure either of us is going to be able to stand against them."

"According to you, you don't want to."

"True." And maybe she didn't want to so much either any longer.

Emma's smile went straight to his groin.

He offered a promise that he thought she might need, and even if she didn't, he needed to give.

"I don't know if you will ever forgive me those other women, but I promise you that if you marry me, there will never be another." Even if Emma never agreed to marry him, Konstantin doubted he could ever settle for empty sex again.

"You think I need to forgive you for sleeping around *after* we broke up?" she asked.

"Yes." Emma might not realize it, but Konstantin was sure of it.

She was his. He was hers. Even if they had not been together. He had betrayed that in an attempt to prove that he *didn't* need her and had only succeeded in proving to himself that no other woman could ever replace her in his life.

Even if he'd followed through on that damn contract.

"If Nataliya and I had actually made it to the wedding, I would have left her waiting at the altar. And I'm not proud of that," he admitted.

But even now, even after everything, he could tell Emma things he would never admit to another living soul.

"You wouldn't have," Emma said, sounding very sure.

"I would. I could never have spoken the vows to her. They would have been a lie."

"That sounds an awful lot like you loved me."

Konstantin felt those words like an ice pick to his soul. "Love? No. Emma, I know you think you need me to love you to marry me, but consider, I am offering a companionship that few ever experience, sexual compatibility that is *very* special and fidelity in both body and mind."

"But not love?" she sounded more musing than upset by that.

"I don't think I'm capable of romantic love. I'm just not wired that way," he admitted, hoping his honesty wasn't scuppering his efforts at courtship.

Courtship. Konstantin let out a humorless laugh. He now understood what that word meant. And it wasn't just sending a bunch of meaningless gifts to a woman.

It was *working* to show her that their lives would be better joined than apart.

"What is funny?" she asked, her voice gentle, her lovely features open in a way they had not been since he ran into her in that bank.

"I finally realized what it means to court a woman."

"Oh, and what does it mean?"

"You are going to find out," he promised.

His brother wasn't the only son of the Royal House of Merikov that knew how to court a woman.

"If my new art studio and the effort you make with our son is any indication, I'm going to enjoy it very much."

Konstantin suddenly realized that this woman deserved every bit of the courtship he had not given her before. When he hadn't been able to see her as anything but a temporary lover.

It would be no platonic courtship though. He would be a fool to give up the one area he'd always gotten right with her.

And Konstantin's father hadn't raised any fools.

* * *

Emma wasn't sure what that expression on Kon's face meant, but it intrigued her and sent a frisson of feminine awareness through her.

His gaze locked with hers, Kon pulled her hand to his lips and kissed her palm, flicking his tongue out to tease.

Need kindled by Emma's first sight of him at the bank whooshed into a flash fire. An all-over body shudder sent that heat spiking through her every capillary. Emma's nipples peaked into aching rigidity just that fast, her sex contracted with need, her lips parted ready for his kiss, her eyes slid shut as decadent anticipation rolled over her.

All from that single sensual caress of his tongue against her palm.

Memories of him turning her hands into erogenous zones, of tasting her entire body with that clever tongue, inundated her so that it was hard to separate the past from the present. Her body was starved for his touch, but she hadn't known it.

She knew it now.

Could not miss how everything in her strained for his touch.

His big body moved, Emma's heightened awareness telling her he was closer than he had been. Warm air puffed over her lips as he asked, "May I kiss you?"

"Yes." Her brain screamed caution; her body wasn't listening.

The kiss, when it came, was electrifying, everything she remembered and more somehow. His lips moved gently over hers at first, like he was relearning the taste and texture of her lips.

She responded in kind, molding her mouth to his. Emotions she thought long buried if not obliterated entirely erupted inside her, causing a maelstrom of feelings she no longer had a compass to navigate.

She hadn't been kissed like this in more than five years, but it *had* been years and what had once been oh, so natural between them was now something different.

Something intense and dangerous.

She no longer trusted this man with her heart, but her body craved him so badly she felt she'd fly apart if they didn't keep kissing.

Sensation poured through Emma, strong and urgent, setting every single nerve ending alight with anticipation.

With need.

With longing.

A longing that was familiar from a very different setting.

How many nights had she lain awake, aching for *this man* after he dumped her?

Pregnancy had sent her hormones into overdrive, intensifying every single unrequited emotion and unfulfilled desire.

Those memories filled her with a kind of dread even as her body strained toward his.

Emma pulled away from the kiss, panting.

CHAPTER EIGHT

"WHAT?" KON ASKED, his pupils blown with pleasure. "What is it? I locked the door. So Mickey wouldn't just walk in on you crying," he hurriedly clarified.

Emma's brain wasn't working at its normal speed. It took her a moment to realize he thought she might believe he'd planned this.

The kiss. A seduction.

Honestly? Maybe he had. Maybe he hadn't.

Right now it wasn't his plans that had her in knots. It was her memories. Her fears.

She gulped in a breath. "Give me a second. I need…"

"What do you need?" he asked when she didn't finish her thought.

Distance. Control. A steel case for her heart.

Something to protect her emotions.

When they'd been together before, Emma had dived head-long into the sensual tsunami that was their lovemaking.

She'd let her heart rule her head. Her libido had fed her heart's desires, but that had led to an emotional devastation and loss she never wanted to experience again.

She couldn't afford to let herself drown in sensation like this.

"What?" Kon repeated. "What is it?"

"I just need to catch my breath." Emma pulled in air and released it, trying to bring her desire under some kind of control.

"Let's both get breathless," he invited, his dark eyes glowing with masculine need. "I want to give you more pleasure than you've ever known."

Emma's thighs pressed together convulsively, her entire body quivering with anticipation at that promise.

She had no doubt he would keep it.

But her brain, the atavistic part that warned her of dangerous driving conditions and questionable surroundings, sent out a warning claxon.

"What happens after the pleasure?" she asked, baldly.

"Whatever you want to."

"But…" Her wants had played no role in what happened the last time.

"Emma, this *is* a courtship. Make no mistake, my end game is marriage, but I need you as I have never needed another woman. I believe you need me too."

"Sexually," she clarified, knowing he did not need her heart like she'd needed his at one time.

"To start," he said and then kissed her softly, almost tentatively. "Yes?"

In a moment of perfect clarity, Emma realized this was the direction they'd been headed ever since his first clumsy, unromantic proposal.

He was looking at a long-term future for them. Something that had never been on the table before.

It was now.

It was not love. It was not even romance.

It was mutual need. Mutual desire. It was an acknowledgment that she was special in his life and her admitting, if only to herself, that he was still someone she wanted in hers.

"Yes," she whispered against his lips and then Emma deepened the kiss on her own.

He tasted so good, his lips moved so perfectly against her own, his tongue teasing hers into responding.

But she didn't want only to respond. She wanted to make him as hot for her as she was for him.

If she was going to do this, Emma was going to get maximum pleasure from it.

She climbed into Kon's lap, his hard thighs under hers

driving her ardor higher. They both started shedding clothes, breaking their kiss only to get her top off, and then his shirt.

Buttons popped, scattering with little tings across the floor, and neither of them cared.

They touched and squirmed and managed to divest themselves and each other of every stitch of clothing, all the while caressing each other like two desperate teenagers.

Kon's usual finesse was entirely missing, but then Emma wasn't any better. She wanted to feel every change five years had wrought on his body. The way his fingertips mapped her stomach, her thighs, her shoulders, everything in between said Kon wanted the same thing.

Emma rubbed the apex of her thighs against his erection, pleasuring them both.

Kon's big body shuddered, his mouth breaking from hers to trail biting kisses down her neck. "Yes, Emma, that's right, *solnyshko.*"

The familiar endearment was like another touch right to the core of her. He used to call her his *little sunshine* because he said she brought light into his life.

Had he missed that light all this time?

He clasped her hips, but let her set the pace and ferocity of their bodies' movement together.

Emma remembered *this.*

Kon might be a prince and a totally take-charge kind of guy, but he'd never needed to completely control their lovemaking. He always encouraged Emma to seek her own pleasure and seemed to derive his own from it. In a very big way.

He thrust up, meeting her body with his own, increasing the pressure of his sex against her clitoris and sending ecstasy arcing through her.

"Touch me," Emma demanded, thrusting her breasts against his hard chest.

Kon muttered something in Russian against her ear, the puffs of air sending shivers rolling through her. It must not have been a denial because his big hands shifted to cup her curves, thumbs brushing over already stiff and sensitive peaks.

The caresses went straight to her core and Emma moaned, pleasure building inside her along with a need to be filled that would not be denied.

They kissed again, Emma matching Kon touch for touch, their bodies moving in an increasingly frantic rhythm.

One of Kon's hands moved down over her backside, sliding down until his fingertip dipped inside her most intimate flesh. She was wet and swollen and he moved easily inside her despite the years since she had been this close to another person.

He added another finger almost immediately, pressing in and out of her body, making love to her with his hand even as she craved the ultimate connection.

Her climax hit her out of nowhere, rolling over her body with so much intensity she screamed against his lips and then tried to hold back further cries.

"Give me all your sounds."

"But Mickey—"

"Can hear nothing."

Emma rubbed herself against Kon, enjoying the aftershocks of pleasure and making no further effort to stifle her cries.

Despite the powerful orgasm and its aftershocks, Emma never went limp in satiation.

"The soundproofing. That's why," she gasped against him, shuddering with prolonged pleasure.

"Yes." He arched up against her and groaned. "Also because I believe there should always be a safe room to discuss things that small ears cannot accidentally overhear."

"You were very sure of yourself."

"I had hope, Emma. Hope and need that only you can meet." The way he moved against her so frantically gave credence to his claim.

"Is this part of the courtship?" she asked breathlessly.

He went very still and very serious, his chocolate gaze locking on hers. "Between us how can it not be?"

Emma had no answer as Kon claimed her mouth again. His lips were so very familiar and yet not.

Her body just craved more after such a long drought of this type of pleasure. Emma shifted and Kon seemed to know what she wanted because he slid his fingers out of her to grab his own sex and hold it in position for her.

She slid down, taking his sex into her waiting channel, reveling in every millimeter of stretch to tender tissues. Emma had always loved the feel of Kon inside her and that had not diminished in the years apart.

She rocked her hips until he filled her completely, pressing against her cervix and sending shards of sharp pleasure through her.

Kon's hand pressed on her backside, encouraging her to move.

Emma was only too happy to oblige, lifting her hips and then lowering them down, pleasuring them both.

Kon broke their kiss, gasping. "Birth control." His jaw was so taut, he looked in pain. "I need a condom," he gritted out.

Emma stilled, need and common sense at war in her body.

It could be too late already, they both knew that. She was not on any form of birth control. There had been no call for it since their breakup.

Using every nanometer of her self-control, Emma remained motionless and met Kon's eyes.

His expression was intense and filled with heated desire. "I want more children with you, *solnyshko*, but that will be a decision we make together, and not when we need each other so badly we are both shaking with it."

She nodded, unutterably touched by his care for her. He'd never taken risks with her body. She'd gotten pregnant with Mickey when her birth control failed, not because either of them had dismissed the need for it.

Still so turned on she felt on the verge of a second climax, Emma went to move off Konstantin.

However, he stood up before she could do so, one arm firmly under her bottom and the other wrapped around her back, keeping their bodies connected in the most intimate way.

He carried her to the bed and laid her down, withdrawing from her body only then, and eliciting a whimper of need from her.

"You are so beautiful, Emma." Kon's expression was filled with something she could not read, but the admiration was genuine and easy to see. *"Krasavitsa."*

She felt a purely feminine smile come over her features. "I'm glad you still find me attractive. Giving birth to Mickey changed my body."

"You are everything that turns me on," he said in a guttural tone, all smooth prince charm in abeyance. "All the more so because of those changes that testify to you giving birth to my child."

Those words fell like sweet water on the parched recesses of her heart. Kon wasn't, and had never been, looking for plastic perfection.

He wanted a real woman. He wanted *her*.

"You're physically it for me too, Kon." The only man who had ever been worth lowering her defenses for.

The first time had ended in heartache, but this time she wasn't trusting blindly and he was offering permanence even when she said she didn't want it.

He leaned down to grab a condom from his bedside

table. He fumbled and swore when it slipped from his hand and went sailing when he tried to tear it open.

This sign that he was as lost to need as she was only sent Emma's desire skyrocketing even as she smiled at him. "Having trouble there, stud?"

He growled. Like some big jungle cat. He grabbed another one, tearing it open with his teeth this time and then rolling it on with a look of pained ecstasy that sent pleasure jolting through her.

Kon came down over her, but even as he kissed her, he rolled them so she was on top again.

She leaned up, sitting on top of him, sliding her body so they were once again angled for perfect penetration. There was no buildup this time; she took him inside her in one downward thrust.

They both groaned and she started moving, riding him with absolute intent.

There would be no more interruptions. For this moment he was entirely hers and she held nothing back as she brought them closer and closer to orgasm.

He praised her, his hands running over her body in knowing caresses, giving pleasure and driving them both higher and higher.

He came first this time, his shout loud and all primal male.

She grabbed one of his hands, pressing it against her mound and he touched her just like she needed, bringing her over the precipice. Her entire body convulsed, her inner walls contracting around him, the pleasure exploding through her like a hurricane wave crashing over the shore.

She collapsed down on top of him and he hugged her to him like he couldn't let her go.

Emma patted his chest with a desultory movement. "That's every bit as good as it ever was."

"Better." Kon hugged her tighter. "Better."

It had been amazing, but better? "Why better?"

"Because for the first time I made love to you without knowing in the back of my mind there was a time coming when I had to let you go."

Sometimes…he said stuff that made her think he *did* love her. Like the way he'd described how he felt about her earlier. And now, talking like his worry that he was going to lose her eventually had always colored their time before.

In a bad way, not an inevitable-change way.

Emma wanted to believe that Kon just didn't understand his own feelings, but she'd made the mistake of believing his unstated feelings were something they were not before.

She would never allow herself such naive optimism again.

He'd hurt her too badly. Her son had been hurt too badly for her to delude herself.

Even so, there could be no denying that Kon wanted a future with her.

Emma just didn't know if she could trust that future.

And she wasn't taking his word for it that his royal family supported his marrying her without meeting them first.

Emma went to shift, but Kon's arms tightened around her.

"Let me go, stud. You've got to take care of the condom," she reminded him.

They'd already taken a big enough risk.

He grunted agreement and let her move off him then, before rolling off the bed to do what he had to. He was back moments later, pulling her into his arms.

"I'm not sleeping here, Kon."

"Why not?" he asked, sounding *hurt*?

Emma steeled herself against giving in. "Mickey doesn't need to find us in the same bed."

"He wants us to be a family."

"We are a family. You said it before, whether we marry

or don't marry, we will always be connected through Mickey."

"I love my son, but he is not the only connection I want to have with you, Emma."

"I believe you."

"You do?"

"Yes, but…"

"But? How did I know there had to be a *but*?"

Emma couldn't help smiling. "Because you know me."

Kon's smile was sensual as well as amused. "I do know you, so tell me about this *but*."

"I want to go to Mirrus." His family had all signed the custody agreement. Even so, it was a huge step of trust for her to take, but Emma couldn't figure out how to find out what she needed to without meeting a bunch of royals.

"I thought we were going to Seattle from here?" he asked, his dark brows drawn together in question.

"I want to go to Mirrus first."

"Why?" Kon didn't sound worried, just curious.

"I want to meet your family."

"You want to know they support us being together like I told you."

"I never said you were stupid," she commented, tongue in cheek.

But Kon frowned. "I bet you did, after I dumped you and you were pregnant with Mishka and could not contact me to tell me about our son. I bet you thought I was stupid then."

"I thought you were lots of things, but most of them were wrong, so let's not dwell on that time."

"So, Mirrus?"

"Yes. I want to see how your family reacts to Mickey." How they reacted to her as Mickey's mother.

"My father will be thrilled. He's threatened to come to New Mexico more than once. He wants to meet his grandson badly."

"Threatened?" She latched onto that word quickly.

"For me having him show up while I am doing my best to court you and build a relationship with my son is a threat."

"I see."

"He wants to meet you as well. He wants to apologize."

"For what?"

"For pushing me into breaking up with you."

"He did?" That did not sound good.

"He didn't know he was doing it. He was upset I had not fulfilled the contract yet and put me on some pretty spectacular guilt trips until I agreed to start things in motion with Nataliya."

"Only you had to break up with me first."

Which spoke well of Kon's personal integrity.

"Yes."

"You didn't get together with Nataliya though."

"I needed time to get over us."

"I bet that didn't make your dad happy."

"Considering he had no idea why I was dragging my feet? No. He was very angry with me."

"And then Queen Tiana died."

"And I was off the hook." At least during the period of formal mourning.

Even an announcement of engagement would have been considered in poor taste during that time. Not to mention, it would have been unkind to flaunt the idea of marriage in front of his brother who had just lost a wife.

That his father had not continued to push the issue after that time was up was something he'd always been grateful for and hadn't questioned too closely.

"But not entirely."

"No." Kon shrugged. "Though I put off fulfilling the contract as long as I could."

"Why?" Emma didn't believe Kon had been holding out for getting back together with her.

"Nataliya had a thing for my brother. She always felt more like my sister than my potential bride."

"But you did court her."

It was Kon's turn to grimace. "I had my staff send her gifts and flowers. I never even called her."

"Not much of a courtship."

"It was a business deal." He shrugged. "Not a romance."

"Are we a romance?" He had said he wanted to court her.

"We belong to each other. I am the best man for you. You are the ideal woman for me. Courting you is only natural."

Typical Kon, avoid a *yes or no* answer if it wasn't what he thought she wanted to hear. But his answer wasn't a bad one regardless.

"Hmm…" Emma didn't quite know what to say to that.

He was talking like his feelings for her were something deeper again, but Kon had been pretty clear that he didn't consider himself capable of romantic love.

"When do you want to go to Mirrus?" Kon asked her.

"Mickey graduates from preschool in two weeks. We can plan to fly out any time after that, but do you have business in Seattle you have to attend to?"

"I can work from Mirrus as well as Seattle, if not as efficiently."

"Okay."

"We will fly out the day after Mishka's graduation. Is he really going to wear a graduation gown?"

"Yes. I ordered it months ago. It's pretty adorable. We went to last year's graduation so he could watch his friends. I've rarely seen anything as cute."

"Do many preschools do this?"

"All the ones I know of do it now." All the ones she'd researched for both her charges when she'd been a nanny and those schools she'd looked into for Mickey.

"That is sweet."

"Mickey's really excited about it."

"I know."

Emma smiled. They'd both heard how excited their son was about the ceremony. Even the prospect of leaving his beloved teacher behind wasn't dimming his enthusiasm.

But then he had a father now, someone who took precedence over Mr. Leeds.

"I need to get to my own bed. Thank you for letting me cry all over you."

"Thank you for showing me the honor of trusting me with your tears."

Emma wasn't sure if she'd trusted him so much as hit her limit and he'd been there for the fallout. She didn't disillusion him, however. Kon seemed too happy to think she'd cried on him on purpose.

She went to slide from the bed, but Kon was there.

He kissed her lips until she was panting and then moved down to that spot behind her ear. "We're not done, I don't think."

And they weren't. They made love again, and this time he set the pace, seemingly determined to wring every last ounce of pleasure from Emma's body.

It was all she could do not to fall into a comatose sleep after, but Emma made it back to her own room and her own bed, only to immediately miss Kon and his warmth.

But their son didn't need to get any more ideas than he already had about them, she reminded herself.

Sleep was a long time coming.

The next two weeks flew by, Kon working a little more than he had when he'd stayed at her house, Emma finishing up her notice and then overseeing the movers Kon had hired to pack her and Mickey's things to ship to Seattle.

They kept some favorite toys and books, and, of course, clothes for the remainder of their time in Santa Fe and for use on their trip to Mirrus.

Not as many clothes as she'd planned because Kon insisted on buying both her and Mickey wardrobes more appropriate for the colder climate of Mirrus. It might be summer, but he informed them both they would need warmer clothes.

Kon even ordered Mickey two suits tailored to fit their son perfectly even though he would probably grow out of them in a matter of months.

"Why does Mickey need suits?" Emma asked in bemusement as her son showed as much excitement over the formalwear as he had the new game system Kon had purchased.

"He'll wear one to graduation."

"Yes, and?"

"I'll be like Dad!" Mickey said excitedly. "I'll look so fly for my graduation and to meet the King."

"Fly?" Emma asked.

"Another word we can probably thank Mr. Leeds for."

"Oh." Her son was growing so fast and changing even faster. "Mickey, you *want* to wear suits?"

"I'm an earl, Mom. I need to look like Dad."

Emma held back her grimace at the noble title. Mickey said it the same way he announced he was four years and three-quarters. With pride and practicality.

It just was.

Something else that just was? The incredible sexual intimacy between Kon and Emma. He might be working more now, but he'd still managed to take advantage of time alone in the house without Mickey while their son was at preschool on several occasions.

And every night, Kon invited her into his bed after they put their son in his own.

Sometimes those invitations took the form of words. Sometimes, Kon just picked Emma up and carried her into the giant master bedroom.

He always asked before the first kiss. He always wore a condom and she always climaxed at least twice.

The pleasure should have just been physical, but every time they made love, Emma's emotions came closer and closer to the surface.

CHAPTER NINE

IF EMMA HAD thought that tailored suits for their son, and the other myriad clothes Kon had insisted on buying for Mickey, were over the top, her Prince's plans for expanding Emma's wardrobe blew her away.

He had representatives from three top designers bring a selection of casual to formalwear in the colors she'd learned to love.

Turquoise. Melon. Sand.

There were geometric shapes redolent of the Southwest in some of the prints and used as chic, subtle accents.

The clothes being modeled for her by beautiful, willowy creatures Emma would never look like were definitely in the style she'd developed for herself since moving to New Mexico, but high-end.

Sophisticated in a way she wouldn't have thought that particular style choice could be.

Emma gave Kon a considering look. "You do realize none of this is going to fit me the same as these models, right?"

For one thing, they were all size two with almost no busts, definitely no tummies and very little in the way of any behinds.

Emma's post-pregnancy body was a size twelve with a C-cup bust, a no longer flat tummy and hips that filled out her capris.

Kon let a heated gaze travel over Emma. "I'm counting on it. On you, they will look so much better."

One of the models got a little pickled look on her face, the one who had been trying to flirt with His Highness since her arrival. Another gave Emma an envious look, but one just smiled and sent Emma a discreet thumbs-up.

Emma couldn't help smiling back.

"Young love is so inspiring," one of the designer reps said, his expression filled with approval.

Lust more like, but Emma didn't correct the man.

"If you see something you like, we have everything in your size, available for you to try on or buy without trying, if that is your preference."

"Why would I buy clothes without trying them on?" Emma asked. "What if I don't like the way they look on me?"

"Anything you do not like will be returned or disposed of," Kon assured her.

"I don't even know how much these clothes cost." But nothing had price tags and that was a red flag toward *expensive* in Emma's book. "But *get rid of*? How spoiled are you?"

"In some ways, very," Kon admitted without hesitation or embarrassment. "I would feel even more spoiled if you were willing to try the clothes on for me in a private setting."

"You want me to give you a private fashion show?" she asked, blushing.

She couldn't help it. Here were professional models showing off the clothes for him and he was asking her to follow that?

"I would enjoy that very much, yes." The sensual timbre of his voice said he wasn't just planning to *watch*.

"Isn't that a little kinky?" she asked in a teasing tone, still embarrassed, but pleased too.

Because she could not doubt that the only woman in this room who interested Kon was Emma. Not some willowy model with perfect makeup and hair.

Someone coughed. Someone else made a strangled sound and one of the models just laughed right out loud. It was the one who had given Emma the thumbs-up.

And Emma realized she probably should not have said that about being kinky, even in a tease.

Kon just smiled though, his chocolate gaze filled with humor. "I'm pretty sure it takes more than wanting to see my lover try on her new clothes to make me kinky."

"You should be careful what you say," the oldest designer rep admonished Emma repressively. "Comments like that could give rise to all sorts of speculation in the media."

Kon turned a frown on the older woman. "But everyone in this room has signed nondisclosure agreements, have they not? Any leak will be dealt with punitively and quickly, I assure you," he said in freezing tones.

Then Kon leveled his gaze on each designer rep and model in turn. To a one, they all gave nods of assent.

Kon nodded his own head, like he was satisfied, and turned his attention back on Emma with a charming smile. "You have no need to censor yourself with me."

While the sentiment was lovely, Emma didn't agree. She didn't apologize for her words, instinctively knowing that would have invited Kon's wrath on the woman who had corrected Emma. However, she *did* think about what the older woman had said and determined to be more circumspect in her speech around others.

NDA signed, or not, things had a way of getting out. It was why Emma had been so careful in her wording of emails and messages when trying to get a hold of Kon to tell him about Mickey's imminent birth.

While she was sure both she and her Prince would always regret that he had not been part of Mickey's life from the beginning, she could not regret protecting Kon and his family from the media circus that knowledge of her pregnancy at that time would have created.

So far, they'd been left alone, but it suddenly struck Emma that once Mickey's existence was announced to the world in relation to him being Kon's son, that media circus would be inevitable.

"What?" Kon asked her, his expression concerned.

"I don't... What do you mean, *what*?"

"What were you just thinking that made your lovely face grow so pensive and not in a happy-contemplation way?" he asked, showing a perspicacity she wished he had not developed sometimes.

Emma looked around at everyone and then back at Kon. "Later."

He jerked his head in acknowledgment and then the fashion show recommenced.

Emma was judicious in her selections, but Kon was not. For every item she picked out, he added two to her growing closet.

Finally, Emma just said, "Stop. That's enough for three women who *like* to dress up and change at least once a day."

"But you may not keep them all," he reminded her.

Like Emma had *any* intention of keeping even half of the clothes. "I can pretty much guarantee it." She rolled her eyes. "We could fund free lunches for at-risk children for two years with what you want to spend on clothes for me, I'm certain of it."

Even if she didn't know exactly how much each article cost, Emma knew the clothes they'd set aside already would cover more than her wages for the year. Or two.

"I'll make a deal with you."

"A deal?" Emma asked warily.

"Whatever I spend on your new wardrobe I will match as a donation to any charity of your choice."

Emma heard a couple of gasps, but her eyes were only for Kon. "You want me to spend more money?"

"We haven't gotten to the lingerie yet," he said with that look.

The one that turned her knees to water and sent sensations spiking through her core.

"And if I want to split the donations up?"

"Anything you like."

"Bring on the lingerie," Emma said with renewed enthusiasm.

Kon's laughter had her gaze sliding back to him.

"What?" she asked.

"You weren't particularly thrilled about the new designer clothes, but you are giddy with excitement at the thought of being able to donate to causes that you care about. You make me happy, Emma, *solnyshko*."

"I'm pretty happy right now too, Kon," she told him, her mind whirling with ideas about whom she would donate the money to.

But moments later, she was blushing to beat the band, because Kon wanted to see Emma in every single piece of lingerie and made no bones about it.

Knowing that each item bought added to her fund for donations, Emma didn't want to say no, but it was getting ridiculous.

And embarrassing.

"I'm never going to wear something like that," she muttered as he instructed the designer rep to add a lacy corselette with garters for stockings to Emma's order.

"Why not?" Kon asked, sounding genuinely surprised.

"For one thing, I don't wear stockings or pantyhose."

"But on more formal occasions, you might find that you do."

"Attached to *that* corselette? I don't think so."

"Only you and I will know you're wearing something so sexy under your dress," he promised her.

"And that's supposed to make it better? I'll spend the whole time excited or embarrassed, or embarrassed because I'm excited."

Kon's expression said he saw no downside.

Emma shook her head. "No, Kon. I already said yes to those ridiculously tiny nightgowns that in no way are intended for sleeping comfortably."

"I'll give up one of the nighties if you get the corselette," he bargained.

"Seriously?" she asked, a little flummoxed that he was so keen for her to wear something like that.

She'd never worn any kind of sexy lingerie before.

"I'm very serious, I promise you." The expression on his handsome face was enough to make Emma wish the entire entourage of designer reps and models to the moon.

Anywhere but here.

She swallowed. "Okay, I'll get the corselette." And she would wear it.

Because that look? That was worth stepping outside her comfort zone.

Konstantin walked into his room after his international conference call negotiating the rights for a new mineral source and nearly swallowed his tongue.

Emma lay on his bed reading a book, wearing one of his shirts. It was not a scene of over-the-top seduction, but the very domesticity of it got to him in ways nothing else would have. She was not even wearing one of the super-sexy nightgowns he'd talked her into buying, but his instant erection said his body did not care.

Konstantin cleared his throat and Emma looked up from her book, her gaze unfocused and dreamy.

"Good book?" he asked.

"Yes." But she set it aside without hesitation, shifting to reveal that she wore a turquoise thong underneath his shirt.

Konstantin made no effort to stifle his groan of appreciation. "I thought you might go straight to bed."

He'd planned to join her in her room if she had, but

didn't mention that. They'd had sex every night since their first physical reconnection and he had no desire to break that streak.

However, he'd been unable to get out of tonight's call.

Finding Emma waiting for him turned him on, no question, but it touched something deep inside him as well.

"You would have just come looking for me." She smiled guilelessly up at him. "I thought this would be easier."

"You know me so well."

She slipped one button undone and smiled. "Oh, yes, I do."

"You look incredibly sexy in my shirt." If his voice had an underlying tone of surprise, he could be forgiven.

He'd talked her into the lingerie because he'd had plenty of fantasies about her wearing something like those pieces and yet, he could not imagine being more turned on than he was right at that moment.

Because Emma in *his* shirt felt right. And it was so damn sexy, his erection was pressing painfully against his slacks.

Her hands stilled in the efforts to unbutton the shirt. "Maybe I should leave it on." She gave him a flirty look.

And just like that, he was all in.

"Don't you dare." He stripped in record time, giving no care for his clothes falling in a wrinkled heap on the floor.

Emma undid the last button, her expression coy, her body sinuous against the bedding. Then she opened the shirt, revealing her gorgeous breasts, their peaks like ripe berries. His mouth watered to taste her.

The bright bit of silk that was her thong barely covered the apex of her thighs, but even that covering was too much.

Konstantin dived for her, his hands busy divesting her of the remaining clothing.

Her laughter cut off as he kissed her and what followed was intense and amazing and so incredibly satisfying.

But still, Emma went back to her own bed afterward like she always did.

Konstantin did not like it, but he did not know how to convince her that he would never let her down again like he had when he'd broken up with her.

And until he did, she wasn't risking Mickey's believing they were back together in a romantic capacity.

He respected her need to protect their son from potential heartbreak, but that didn't make it any easier for Konstantin to accept.

His brother had warned Konstantin he would have to work hard to rebuild his relationship with Emma.

The King had been frustratingly right.

Sitting on matching loungers, Emma and Kon took advantage of their last afternoon by the pool.

They watched their son swim and do tricks interspersed with the occasional, "Watch me, Mom. Look at this, Dad."

"He's amazing," Kon said, his voice heavy with love for their son.

"You know, when I was pregnant, I thought you'd be a great dad and then everything happened with not being able to reach you…"

"And having Tiana threaten you." His tone still carried guilt over that.

"Yes," Emma acknowledged, not sure how to alleviate Kon's guilt over a past that could not be changed. "I convinced myself then you wouldn't add anything good to Mickey's life."

"And now?"

She turned so their eyes met, his fixed on her with intense regard. Her answer mattered.

"Now, I think I was right when I thought you'd be a good dad. You really are, Kon." He was way more hands-on than she would have ever expected a workaholic like her Prince to be.

The fact he'd delegated responsibilities on both the company and palace front to free up time to get to know Mickey and help him acclimate to the changes in their lives said a great deal about Kon's dedication to fatherhood.

"I'm very glad you think so." Kon gave her one of his devastating smiles. "You know I believe you are the best mother our son could possibly have."

Emma wanted to believe that, but there was this tiny part of her that doubted. The part that could not forget she hadn't been enough before.

She was doing her best to let those feelings go, but they persisted and reared their ugly little heads at the worst times.

"He's really excited about the trip to Mirrus." Went unspoken was Emma's desperate hope Mickey's enthusiasm would not be dashed by the royal family's reaction to him, or to her.

"What about you? Are you looking forward to it?" Kon asked.

"Yes." She might have her trepidations, but she really was. Emma had craved access to Kon's life five years ago, now she was getting it. "I want to see where you grew up. I want to see the environment that helped define who you are, the place that will be so important to Mickey as he grows older. I want to know and understand Mirrus and its people."

And thereby maybe understand Kon a little better. She'd thought she'd known him before. She'd been wrong. Emma had been blind to both his acute sense of duty before all else and his ruthlessness when faced with making something happen.

Whether those traits were personal, cultural or fostered within his family, Emma wanted to know.

"You're such a special woman."

"Am I?"

"I think so, yes. You see the world from your own unique perspective and in that perspective my being a prince is only part of who I am, not the definition of who I am."

"Well, of course not. No single role can define any of us." Wouldn't life be boring if it did? "Even mine as Mickey's mom does not define me entirely."

Emma was also an artist, a bookkeeper, a friend…and a daughter, if estranged from her family. She was also Kon's lover. All those roles played some part in making her who she was and defining the parameters of her life.

"But it is the most important role to you at the present." He sounded very sure of that.

And, of course, he was right, only there was another role that was growing in importance to Emma. That of his lover and, possibly, one day his wife.

Not that she was saying so.

He had enough confidence without her giving any free boosts.

And because of Kon's generosity, Emma's art was consuming more of her time and talents in a good way, rejuvenating her and giving her an outlet for emotions she was in no way ready to acknowledge, much less express.

"Mickey is going to love having a grandfather, uncles and an aunt." Emma still felt guilty she'd done so little to build a family of adults for him to trust in and rely on.

Her son should never have had to pay for her introverted nature and fear of rejection.

Kon nodded, his expression showing full agreement. "And a cousin in a few months' time."

Emma smiled, remembering Mickey's reaction to that news. "He's over the moon about that one."

"He wants siblings." Kon said it like a warning.

As if Emma wouldn't know. "He told me." That had been

an interesting conversation. Not least of which had been because of Mickey's final sally in that direction.

But what if Dad married someone else to give me a brother or sister? He wants more kids too, Mom.

Apparently Kon and Mickey had discussed it too. Which did not surprise her. Mickey could be very determined when his mind got set on something. What did surprise Emma was the shard of pain that sliced through her heart at the thought of Kon having children with someone else.

She'd thought she'd accepted that possibility long ago when he'd broken up with her so he could marry Nataliya. The marriage had never taken place, but Emma had prepared herself for the eventuality of it and what it would entail.

Or so she'd thought.

Her heart said, *Don't bet on it*, no matter what her brain wanted to believe about Emma's emotional distance gained.

"Nataliya's mother is all set to play grandmother to him as well," Kon said, for once clearly oblivious to the direction Emma's thoughts had taken. "I think she and my father have something going on."

That piqued Emma's curiosity. "Really?" The former King, now Prince—Kon had explained that was the title his father had chosen upon abdication in favor of his eldest son—and the Countess?

"Well, Lady Solomia moved into our palace within a month of the marriage. And she seems very happy to be there."

"Her daughter is there… Isn't that reason enough?"

"The Countess and my dad spend a lot of time together." Kon sounded disgruntled and a little confused by that.

"Do you mind?"

"No." He grimaced. "Maybe a little, but I know I shouldn't. It's strange though." For once he did not look like a prince, but an adult man trying to come to terms with changes in his family he hadn't seen coming. "I don't know how either Nataliya or Nikolai feel about it."

Emma hid an indulgent smile. These moments when Kon showed his own imperfections made him feel more relatable and *touchable* in her life.

"I'm just glad Mickey is going to have some extended family, surrogate grandmother included." There would always be a part of Emma that wished her own parents could be in Mickey's life too. And her own.

She missed them.

"Would you want to renew your relationship with your parents, if you could?" Kon asked, once again firmly on her wavelength.

"I think so. If I wasn't afraid of their rejection, I probably would have reached out to them again already," she admitted. "But that last phone call, it devastated me."

And she'd been absolutely unwilling to open Mickey's life to their potential rejection.

"They've had five years to miss you, to wonder about their grandchild."

"If they miss me at all." It was that *if* that made it impossible for Emma to contact them.

She'd missed them so badly after only the months of her pregnancy, she'd been sure their hearts would have softened. Emma had been wrong and hurt so very badly because of it.

"I'm sure they do." Kon sounded so convinced of his own belief.

Emma wished she could share it. "You never met them."

"But you talked about them. They love you."

"You couldn't tell that by the way they pushed me from their lives."

"Is that why you're hesitating about marrying me?" he asked. "Even though I'm asking for a future with you, you can't bring yourself to trust me. But it's not just what I did to you that you have to overcome," he said like he was discovering something new. "Your parents, the rest of your family…and me. We all did the same thing to you and all that emotion is still tangled."

He was right about the rest of her family. Emma had never been close to her cousins as they were so much older, but her aunts and uncles had always been wonderful to her. Until they all agreed to close ranks with her parents and shun her for keeping a baby without the benefit of marriage.

Kon was also right that all that pain and rejection were mixed up inside her.

Emma looked off into the distance, but the view of the mountains offered little solace and no answers. "You're pretty insightful for a prince."

"I'm also a COO, and believe me, both roles require insight into how the human psyche works."

"I suppose they do." She sighed. "I miss my parents. Still," she admitted. "They were good parents. I know they loved me, even if that love wasn't unconditional like mine is for Mickey." Emma could not imagine anything her son could do that would cause her to reject him.

"Maybe they saw themselves as loving you when they rejected you. Tough love."

She shrugged, wishing she could believe that. "All I know is that they rejected me and my son. And that still hurts."

Maybe her continued estrangement from her parents did play a significant role in Emma's refusal to commit to a lifetime with Kon.

Parents made a lifetime commitment when they had children, adopted or otherwise. Her parents had broken that commitment to Emma, and she didn't know if she could trust Kon to keep his promises in the future.

After all, they'd loved Emma and he did not.

* * *

Mickey's preschool graduation went off without a hitch. He absolutely glowed under all the compliments he got on his little suit and he told everyone it made him look like his dad.

When they arrived and everyone was getting settled before the ceremony began, Emma got teary eyed, watching her son take his place at the front of the banquet room.

She swiped at her eyes. "He's growing up so fast."

"Our little man," Kon agreed, his voice ringing with pride.

Emma smiled up at her Prince through the tears. "He's more excited about this than turning five."

Kon reflected her smile, reaching down to squeeze Emma's hand. "Naturally. That milestone is two months off. The immediate is always more exciting than something in the future."

A rush of emotion washed over Emma, making her tears spill over.

"Are you all right, *solnyshko*?" Kon asked with concern.

Swallowing, trying to get control of her wayward emotions, Emma nodded.

"Then why these tears?"

"That you know they are different than only a moment ago is kind of scary," she said on a hiccup.

"Good. Not scary."

She smiled. Her arrogant prince, so sure he knew what was best for her, but in this case, maybe he was right.

Maybe his knowing her so well *was* good.

"I've never had anyone to share his milestones with," she said in explanation. "I'm happy for Mickey." She gulped back more emotion. "And for me too."

"This is a very strange way to show happiness, *krasavitsa*."

"I'm hardly beautiful right now, with my mascara running." Her nose was probably pink too.

Kon handed her a handkerchief to mop herself up. "You are always beautiful to me, Emma."

"Why don't you say stuff like that to me?" a woman behind them asked her husband.

Emma recognized the voice as belonging to the mother of one of Mickey's friends he'd had playdates with. A woman with a wry sense of humor, Emma wasn't surprised she'd teased her husband that way.

"Because the last time I did you told me to get my eyes examined. Doesn't mean I'm not thinking it," her husband answered gamely.

Emma grinned at the exchange and shared a moment of rapport with Kon as humor shone in his eyes as well.

"I will always be there for the milestones, for both of you, from now on," Kon promised her, all serious again.

Emma choked up again, so all she could do was nod.

"These tears of yours are killing me," Kon told her.

She tried to blink them away. "I'm sorry."

Kon groaned and then kissed her. Right there in the middle of all the chatting parents waiting for the ceremony to start.

"That's my mom and dad," Mickey yelled.

Laughter erupted and Kon pulled back, his expression holding none of the humor from before. "I vow it."

Emma didn't know how to respond to that, so she ducked her head and then looked toward their son, who was giving her a thumbs-up. If she didn't watch out, Mickey would be planning their wedding before they ever got to Mirrus.

And would that be such a terrible thing? a small voice in her head asked.

Mickey was an absolute gem on the trip to his father's homeland. Of course, the fact that Kon had made sure he had plenty to entertain him *and* a nap en route helped loads.

Emma was instructed to simply relax and she tried, even

taking her own nap, but the closer they got to their destination, the more anxious she grew.

Kon took her hand and brought it to his mouth to kiss it. He'd been a lot more publicly affectionate since the kiss in front of Mickey's school the previous evening.

Their son knew they were *dating* and Kon saw no reason to pretend they were not as close as they were. Or so he said when she'd questioned him about the good-morning kiss he'd given her at breakfast.

Emma had still insisted on sleeping in her own bed the night before though.

Actually sleeping with Kon, allowing their son to find them in the same bed in the morning, would signify a level of commitment from her she was still hesitant to make.

"Is it going to be a media circus at the airport?" she asked him, drumming a tattoo with her fingers against the armrest.

Kon reached out and stilled her fingers with his hand over hers. "Relax, *solnyshko*. No media circus. My family will be waiting at the palace for us. Not because they do not want to meet our plane but because we can land unremarked this way."

She nodded, like that made sense, only really? Emma had never been exposed to the public side of Kon's life. And her own life had never had that component.

So, honestly, she had no idea.

"We will make the announcement about Mickey at the end of our first week on Mirrus. I want you to get to know my family in relative privacy before the media catch wind of our son's existence and start asking intrusive questions."

"It would be easier on all of you if you could announce our marriage at the same time, wouldn't it?" she asked, trying not to feel guilty.

She had to do what was best for her *and* Mickey, she told herself.

"I am not interested in what is easy for me," Kon assured her. "I am only concerned with what makes you comfortable. When you agree to marry me, it will be because that is what *you* want, not because it is an expedient public relations move."

"You know I really appreciate you haven't tried to guilt me into agreement." She acknowledged to herself it would probably work at this point.

It wouldn't have before. Not when they'd first reconnected, but her heart had softened and so much of the resentment she'd carried toward Kon was gone now.

"I would not."

"Thank you. I believe you."

"I've spoken to my father, but even so I cannot promise he will not attempt it," Kon admitted with a rueful twist of his lips and no small amount of frustration. The man liked to be in control. "He's very good at guilt trips."

"He must be." Prince Evengi had used them to coerce Kon into not only signing that blighted marriage contract but also breaking up with Emma to follow through on it.

"Remember, he is as susceptible to them as his sons. If he gets too pushy, just remind my father that if it were not for his insistence I follow through on that contract, you and I would have been married long ago."

"You say that now."

"I say it because it is true," Kon said forcefully, like it really bothered him she still doubted on that score. "Seeing how I am with our son, can you doubt I would have moved heaven and earth to be his father from the moment I learned of his existence?"

Emma was saved answering that emotionally charged question by the captain coming over the loudspeaker of the private royal jet to instruct them on preparing for landing.

CHAPTER TEN

WHILE THERE WERE no other royals or dignitaries in evidence when Kon, Emma and Mickey disembarked from the plane, there was an entire second security detail and three imposing SUVs with a limousine slotted in between the first and third ones.

"Wow! Do we get to ride in the limo?" Mickey asked excitedly.

"Yes. It has been fitted with a child safety seat for Mikhail," Kon told Emma before she could even ask.

"I have no doubt." Emma was wearing one of the designer outfits Kon had bought her and Mickey was all decked out in one of his tailored suits.

He'd changed after his nap on the plane.

Emma was tense on the ride to the palace, though her attention was fixed keenly on the view out the window, as she got her first view of Kon's homeland.

There were similarities to where she'd grown up outside Seattle. The same towering evergreens and lush deciduous summer vegetation. The mountains in the distance were snow-capped and she knew that there were glaciers on the island.

Kon had been right to warn her that the temperatures were not what they were in New Mexico. Although it was summer, there was a chilly wind that the evening sun could not make up for. Emma shivered, wishing she'd put a jacket on.

Then warm fabric fell around her shoulders and she looked up to find Kon smiling at her. "Better?"

He stood there in his shirtsleeves, which she was sure went against protocol, but didn't even shiver.

She nodded. "Thank you."

Emma tried to give him back his suit jacket when they got settled inside the limo, but Kon shook his head. "Keep it on. You still look chilled."

"Did my blue lips give me away?" she teased. It wasn't *that* cold, but it was by no means warm either.

At least outside. The limo was comfortable, but Emma found herself too willing to keep Kon's jacket, like a security blanket, around her. His delicious scent reminded her that she was here at his invitation and *for* him and their son.

She might not be a princess, but she belonged here because she *was* Mickey's mom and maybe even because she was the woman Kon wanted to marry.

Even if it was for the sake of their son.

"It's not that cold, Mom. My suit keeps me warm anyway," Mickey informed her. "Like Dad."

"A good-quality suit has many uses," Kon said, like imparting great wisdom.

Emma bit back a smile as their son nodded sagely.

These two.

"They're going to like me, right, Dad? I'm going to have a grandpa now, right, Mom?"

Emma was surprised it had taken this long for Mickey's nerves to show up. And a little impressed. His mother had been a nervous wreck for hours. Nevertheless, she gave him her most reassuring smile. "Yes, a grandfather, two uncles and an aunt."

"They are going to love you just as I do," Kon assured their worried son.

"They have to, don't they? I'm their family."

Emma did not mention that family did not always love as they should. She just nodded.

Their first view of the palace left Emma speechless. She'd seen it in pictures, but up close? It was awe-inspiring.

"Wow, it's so big!" Mickey was not similarly afflicted.

"Did you get lost lots when you were a little boy?" he asked his father.

Kon shook his head. "No. Nikolai took me exploring from my earliest memory, making sure I knew where I could go and shouldn't go and how to get back to the nursery. He and I did the same for our younger brother, Dima."

"Don't only babies live in nurseries?" Mickey asked.

"Not in the palace. The nursery is the room with toys and room for a train set on the floor. I lived in it until I was a teenager and then I got my own suite. I was given an apartment in the palace when I graduated from university."

"Will I have my own apartment in the palace some day?"

"I do not know. It depends on how much of the year you live in Mirrus. Palace apartments are reserved for adult family that live here year-round."

"But you don't. Do you still have an apartment?"

"I do." Kon didn't offer to explain why.

Emma was glad. Mickey might not act like it, but he was already on information overload. The way his gaze flitted everywhere and landed nowhere indicated nerves her son wasn't giving voice to.

"Will I stay in the nursery?" Mickey asked, sounding like he wasn't sure he liked that idea.

"I had a room in my apartment prepared for you to stay in, but if you would rather stay in the nursery, you can."

"I want to stay with you." Mickey frowned. "What about Mom?"

"Your mother has a suite across the hall from us." It was Kon's turn to sound slightly disgruntled by *that* reality. "You can stay with her if you would rather. A bed can be put in her sitting room for you."

"Why isn't she staying with us? We're a family!" Mickey's volume was startling and unexpected.

Emma and Kon reached out at the same time to touch

him in comfort. She took Mickey's little hand in her own and Kon laid his big hand on Mickey's shoulder.

"I had my own room at the house in Santa Fe, Mickey."

"But that was different. That house was *ours*. The King owns the palace, only the apartment is Dad's. You should be in it with us. I'll sleep on the couch. You can have my room."

"And this is important to you, that we are all in a space that is *ours*?" Kon asked, like he was trying to understand what prompted Mickey's outburst.

"Yes!" Mickey was adamant.

Kon looked to Emma. If she was reading him correctly, he would follow her lead.

She looked around the limo just a little wildly, worried that the door was going to open any moment and there would be no more privacy for this conversation.

"I will not give the signal to open the door until we are settled on this matter," Kon said, proving that once again, they were very much in tune.

Emma let out a little sigh of relief. "Let's get you unbuckled," she said to Mickey.

Like she expected him to, her son insisted on undoing the five-point harness on his own. The act of doing something so familiar should help him calm down a little while Emma's brain scrambled for a solution to his clear upset.

"Why don't you sit here, between your dad and me, so we can all figure out our feelings right now." Undoing her own seat belt, Emma scooted over to make room for him between her and Kon.

Mickey moved into the opening rapidly, showing he was in need of both physical and emotional reassurance. "Mom, I don't want you to stay in a suite. Someone might think you aren't part of our family."

Emma did not tell him that was a silly thought. She'd discovered that children's minds had their own brand of logic.

He drew his conclusions based on how he understood the world. She would try to help him with that understanding, but she would not dismiss his worries, even if they did not make sense to her.

"Mikhail Ansel Carmichael, I need you to hear me. No one is going to question that I am your mom, your family."

Mickey chewed on his lip. "Why does Dad have a different name from me and you?"

Emma opened her mouth and then closed it, wishing she always had just the right answer for her son. Only she didn't. "Your dad and I aren't married, but even if we were, I might choose to keep my own last name."

"Really?"

"Really."

"Why?"

Emma shrugged. "Because it's mine. Because I want to. It's my choice."

"Do I get to choose my last name?" Mickey asked.

Emma cast a quick glance at Kon, who looked pained. "You are in the royal succession. Your name will have to legally be changed to Merikov," Kon answered.

"Oh. That's okay."

"It is?"

"Yes, then everyone will know you are my dad."

"You are not worried they will not know Emma is your mom?" Kon asked, like the words were drawn from him.

"No. She's always been my mom. She tells everybody." Mickey frowned. "But some people won't know she's yours too. She has to stay with us, Dad, in *our* place."

Emma knew it! Mickey already had her married, even if the wedding hadn't taken place yet, much less her agreement to it.

"I do not belong to your dad," Emma told her son, but the words felt like a lie.

Instead of getting upset that she'd disagreed, Mickey rolled his eyes. "You're my mom."

"Yes."

"He's my dad."

"Yes."

"You belong to each other because of me."

"Mickey, you know some parents are not together." He'd known the Jensens, seen the parents separate and divorce. More than that, he'd had friends in his preschool that came from unconventional families where the mom and dad had never even been a couple.

Mickey shrugged. "You and Dad are together. You kissed. Everybody saw you."

She knew that would come back to bite her. Only she couldn't regret that Kon had shown her affection in that moment. It had felt so spontaneous, so right.

"Yes, we kissed, but we aren't engaged, or anything."

"Mom, I think you need to figure out your feels."

Oh, man. He was so right. Emma needed to figure out her feelings for sure, but right now she still had to deal with Mickey's need for her to stay in Kon's apartment with him and his father.

Kon's stifled snicker said he agreed with their son.

She gave her Prince a pointed glare. "I agree, Mickey. I do need to figure out my emotions and having my own space will help me do that."

"You can have my bedroom in Dad's apartment."

"Why give up your bedroom when I have a perfectly good suite across the hall?"

"Because we're a family," Mickey replied stubbornly.

"I hear you, Mickey, and I care very much that you feel secure in our new environment—"

"She talks like this when she's going to say *no*," Mickey told his father, interrupting her. "Don't say *no*, Mom. I don't wanna be scared."

"Scared, why scared?" Kon asked.

"I don't know." Mickey's eyes filled with tears. "I just know I want you and Mom both safe in *our* place."

"The whole palace is safe, I promise you," Kon said, his tone filled with reassuring calm.

"Please, Mom. Please," Mickey said, clearly unable to express why he needed this so badly.

Emma hugged her son tight. "Listen, Mickey, I don't understand why this is so important to you. I don't think you understand it either, but what I do know is that you've had a lot of changes in a short amount of time. And maybe that has you feeling insecure. I'll sleep on Kon's couch if that will make you feel better."

She wasn't a prima donna who needed her own suite of rooms.

"I will have an extra bed brought into my room, there is plenty of space," Kon said, all autocratic prince.

Before Emma could even reply, Mickey was jerking from Emma's arms to hug his dad. "That would be so great, Dad. Thank you! I know Mom will be safe if she's in your room."

Emma wanted to laugh at the gallows humor of that one because one thing she knew, her heart would *not* be safe with her staying in Kon's bedroom.

The interior of the palace was everything Emma could have expected it to be. Marble floors in the grand foyer, twin curved staircases up to the next floor and gold accents everywhere.

Her artist's eye told her that that gold was genuine leaf and not just paint.

But it was the people waiting to meet her and Mickey that drew her attention. She recognized Prince Evengi, King Nikolai and the Princess of Mirrus, Nataliya, from pictures, as well as Prince Dimitri, whom the family called Dima and looked more like Nikolai than Konstantin.

Nataliya's mother, the Countess, was the only other person present who was not security. No dignitaries. No staff. This was a meeting between family and only family.

Emma found a great deal of comfort in the fact even a royal family understood the need for this kind of intimate gathering.

"It is such a pleasure to finally meet you." Nataliya took Emma's hands in both of hers and pressed a kiss to each of Emma's cheeks. "Konstantin is so different since finding you again."

"He seems very much the same to me," Emma admitted.

Which was both worrying and comforting at the same time.

The King took his wife's place in front of Emma. "I need you to know that my deceased wife did not have my support in her plans for your child. She would never have gotten my approval to threaten you the way she did."

"Thank you for saying that." Emma had no idea how much she'd needed to hear those words from the King's own lips. "Mickey is my life."

"And now you are both my brother's."

Emma did not reply to that, but looked where her son was interacting with his grandfather for the first time. Prince Evengi had seemed very stiff and formal when introductions had been made, but he knelt on the floor with his grandson now, intent on whatever Mickey was saying.

Emotion swelled inside Emma.

Kon had made this possible. He had given Mickey a family and he'd done it without ever once threatening Emma's place in Mickey's life.

She wasn't stupid. She knew that he could have gone for custody of their son. He might not have won. It would have been an ugly battle, but never once had Kon ever even implied he wanted Mickey without Emma.

And there could be no question that Kon wanted his child in his life. He was such a devoted father.

Kon's own unwillingness to bend, the threats of Queen Crazy and Emma's own fears had cost them five years apart.

In that moment of clarity, Emma realized it wasn't enough to say she didn't want to act out of fear any longer. She had to actually do things differently to honor that desire.

There would be no more time apart. No more waffling on building a family together, not just building individual relationships between Mickey and his father.

"Konstantin was moved beyond words that you named Mikhail for him."

"It felt right at the time," Emma said, repeating something she'd told Kon once.

"Thank you for being such a good mother to my nephew and for giving my brother a chance to be in his life."

Emma finally turned her gaze back to the King. "You do not have to thank me for being a decent person."

"I think I do. I was married to the woman who threatened you. I know we are not all motivated by what is best for our family and those we are supposed to care about."

Emma's eyes widened. If she was not mistaken, the King was telling her that his marriage to Queen Crazy had not been all sunshine and roses. "Do you know why she wanted my baby so badly?"

"She never wanted to be pregnant. I think she saw your baby as her easy way out of something she did not want."

Emma nodded. That made sense. "Kon always thought she was too young to take on the role of queen."

"He talked to you about her?"

"Yes. Before, when we were living together."

"Before he dumped you," Nataliya said from near Emma's shoulder. "To marry me." The Princess of Mirrus rolled her eyes. "Like that was ever going to work."

A laugh was startled out of Emma. "Some people obviously thought it would."

"Some people were wrong." Nataliya didn't sound the least apologetic about making that pronouncement. "I owe Konstantin an apology though."

"Why?" Emma and the King asked at the same time.

Nataliya looked up at her husband, the love she held for him so clear to see and that it was reciprocated could not be doubted. The King looked besotted. "I judged your brother as a playboy when all the time he was nursing a broken heart from giving up his *One True Thing.*"

"I'm not that," Emma denied immediately. "Kon doesn't love me."

"If you say so." But Nataliya sounded like she did not agree.

"He told me so." But did it matter?

That was the question Emma really had to answer. Did it matter if Kon loved her, or if he did love her, if he was ever able to recognize that?

She loved him. She always had. Always would. And that was why she had not dated. It had not just been fear of rejection. Or being too busy raising and providing for their son.

But because Emma *had* found her *One True Thing* and had always known that anything less in a relationship would not be enough.

"Nik told me that he didn't love me either. Before we married." Nataliya gave the King a look of indulgence that made him grimace.

"You, of course, were fully aware of your own feelings."

Color washed into Nataliya's cheeks. "That is not the point."

Emma smiled at the royal couple, so much less intimidated than she'd expected to be by them. "No, the point is that when you love someone, you take risks with your heart even when you're scared."

Nataliya's eyes widened. "Um, yes? Sure, that was the point I was trying to make."

Emma smiled at the other woman, suddenly sure that she and this person who had always stood in her own mind between Emma and her happiness would be a great friend.

"If it helps you at all, I am certain my brother will never let you down again," Nikolai said, like a sibling who cared and with just a smidgen of the arrogance of a king.

Emma nodded. "You know? I think you may be right."

That night Emma and Kon tucked Mickey into bed together as they'd done every night since that fateful morning in the bank.

"You're staying on the couch, right, Mom?" Mickey asked drowsily.

"I'm staying here, in the apartment with you and your dad. We'll all have breakfast together when you wake up."

"Mmm, 'kay…" Mickey snuggled down into his blankets and fell asleep just like that.

"He is exhausted."

"It was an eventful and emotional-filled day. He got an adoring grandfather, surrogate grandmother, two uncles and an aunt all in one fell swoop." Emma turned off the bedside lamp, noting that Kon had already turned on Mickey's night-light.

They stood at the same time and headed out of the dim room.

"My father is like a child himself in his excitement over getting to know Mikhail." Kon sounded both pleased by that and indulgent toward his father.

"He calls him Mishka too." They all did.

Kon made an *mmm* sound. "It is a sign of affection to use the diminutive."

"I think that's why I've pushed back against calling him Mikhail. Every time I say Mickey, it's like I'm saying I love him."

"He may not realize that in his head, but his little-boy heart hears the words, *solnyshko*."

Emma walked into Kon's bedroom and then turned to face him. "Am I still your sunshine?"

"Can you doubt it?" Kon asked, his dark gaze serious and intense. "You have brought the light back into my life."

"Mickey shines pretty brightly too."

Kon pulled Emma to him, their bodies touching, and kissed her gently before smiling. "I adore our son, *krasavitsa*, but it is *you* who brings light into all the dark places in my soul."

For once, Emma did no mental gymnastics to dismiss how loving his words sounded. She simply soaked them in and accepted them as they were.

"You sound so Russian right now," she told him with a small smile.

"Mirrussian."

"Mirrussian," she corrected herself and reached up to kiss him. "My Mirrussian prince."

"Solnyshko moi."

No more words followed. Only kissing and touching. Emma felt cherished as Kon divested her of her clothing. She returned the favor, caressing his gorgeous body with a sense of possessiveness she'd not allowed herself before now.

He *was* hers. And she *was* his. And that truth had not changed in their five years apart.

"I forgive you," she said against his skin as she mapped his sculpted torso with her lips.

* * *

Konstantin stilled, instant comprehension thrumming through his body. She *forgave* him.

Suddenly their slow loving was not enough. He needed all of Emma. Now.

He flipped them and leaned down to kiss her passionately. "Thank you." He kissed her all over her beautiful face, thanking her over and over again between each press of his lips against her silky skin.

Emma grabbed his cheeks and held his head so their eyes met. "I mean it, Kon. I forgive you for breaking up with me. I forgive you for the other women. You're right that we belonged to each other, but I was right too. We *weren't* together and you did not owe me fidelity. You do now though," she said with a look that would have intimidated better men than him.

"You are it for me. For the rest of our lives."

Her smile was blinding. "For the rest of our lives." She rubbed her thumbs over his face and he moaned. She was still naked under him, after all. "Breaking up with me is what hurt me. Not letting me contact you afterward. That cost all of us, but believe me when I say that I forgive you for all of it. No more crushing guilt. No more letting the past get in the way of our future."

Was she saying what it sounded like? "You're going to marry me?"

"Is that a proposal?"

"You know it is." Konstantin felt like kicking himself. "I know it's not a romantic moment in Central Park, damn it." Konstantin was *not* his damn brother. His patience had a hell of a lot more limits. "I should do better. But I need to know now."

Another blinding and beautiful smile sent his already stiff erection to rock-hard status. "Yes, Kon, I will marry you. You and Mickey aren't the only ones who want to give him a younger sibling."

What happened after that would not live in his moments of pride for his vaunted control, because Konstantin had none. No control left, he made love to his sunshine like a starving man feasting on her every gasp and moan of pleasure.

He drove them both to the height of pleasure and then over, only to do it all again.

His hunger refused to be sated with a single bout of lovemaking. Or even two. He and Emma finally fell into an exhausted sleep after their third time joining their bodies and their souls in a union he had never known with another woman.

Mickey's squeal brought Emma out of sleep better than any alarm clock.

She sat straight up and realized with instant relief that someone had put a nightgown on her. It wasn't her usual boring T-shirt-style garment, but it covered the important bits and made this morning greeting with her son relaxed rather than awkward.

Gratitude for Kon's thoughtfulness filled her even as she grinned at her son. "Got something to say, Mickey?"

"You're in Dad's bed! I knew it would work," Mickey crowed.

"What would work?" Kon asked from the other side of the bed.

"If Mom stayed here with us, she'd see."

"See what?" Emma asked her precocious son.

"That me and Dad, we're both your family. You're supposed to be together."

"You think so, huh?" Emma teased, not at all bothered that her son had been matchmaking again.

His distress the day before had been genuine and maybe

it had been sparked by fear of her separating herself from Kon, or just plain old insecurity. Emma didn't care. She loved her son. She loved his father. She wanted a life together as a *real family*, as Mickey called it, more than just about anything.

"He looks like he wants to kiss you all the time," Mickey said with a roll of his eyes.

"You're very insightful, Mishka. How does your mom look at me?" Kon asked in a humor-laden tone.

"Like she wants to trust you. Like after I do something bad and I'm really sorry, but she has to make me go to my room and think about it anyway."

Their son *was* insightful. Emma put her arms out and Mickey joined them on the bed without hesitation, snuggling between her and Kon. "From now on, I'm going to look at your dad like I want to kiss him all the time too. What do you think about that?"

"That's kinda gross, but you're grown-ups so it's okay, I guess."

Kon and Emma shared laughter.

"It is more than okay," Kon assured him. "It is everything good."

The rest of that week was filled with family bonding and Emma learning what her life as part of the royal family would be like.

She would have to take classes in etiquette and get coaching on public relations, politics and a bunch of other stuff that frankly didn't sound very fun.

She would do it though, just like she'd gotten her degree in bookkeeping.

Emma hadn't particularly enjoyed those courses either, but she'd learned what she needed to be the best mom she could be for Mickey. So she could provide for him.

This was much the same. Only she had both Mickey and Konstantin's welfare to think about.

Nataliya, who had insisted that Emma drop the honorific unless they were in a formal setting, took a personal role in helping Emma slide into her role as future Princess.

As Kon had told her, it was up to the King whether to confer that title to Emma upon her marriage to his brother and King Nikolai had made it clear he intended to do so.

Mickey had been in alt.

Emma not so much. But, princess or duchess, she had to learn the role and she was committed to doing so.

The royal family planned to introduce her and Mickey to the rest of the world at a banquet for the country's most elite dignitaries, nobility and business associates. The wedding would take place in only a month's time.

Emma hadn't balked at the rapidity of it all, hoping that less time to prepare would equate to a smaller event.

Nataliya, who was fast becoming a very dear friend, had told Emma not to bet on it. Her mom had gotten all the practice she'd needed on Nataliya's speedy wedding and had stepped in to plan this one with an almost frightening glee.

Emma ached a little, wishing her own mom were there to put her own two cents in, but tried to quash thoughts like that.

Her life was so blessed, Emma didn't want to dim the joy she could have by grieving what she could not change.

CHAPTER ELEVEN

"ARE YOU SURE you shouldn't have warned Emma about this?" Nikolai asked after Kon told his brother he needed him to cover a meeting so he could go to the airport and greet the arrival of Emma's estranged parents.

"I didn't tell her I planned to contact them in case they were no more interested in renewing their relationship with their daughter than they were five years ago."

Nikolai snorted. "She's marrying a prince. I'm pretty sure that changes things for them."

"I didn't tell them about the upcoming wedding. It would hurt Emma to find out they only agreed to see her and Mickey because she was going to be *respectable* again." Konstantin hadn't told the elderly couple that he was a prince either.

Just a friend of Emma's who hoped to see the estrangement ended.

"And they still agreed to come?"

"They jumped at it. They miss their daughter so much. Her mother cried and begged me to promise I wasn't tricking them."

"If they missed her so much, why let the separation go on so long?"

"They couldn't find her." Apparently her parents had run into the same difficulty Konstantin had when they'd finally decided to look for their daughter.

They didn't know the name of their grandson. Didn't know she'd changed her last name. Didn't know she'd moved out of state.

"How did you explain them needing to come to Mirrus to see her?" Nikolai asked.

"I told her that this is where she and Mikhail were living right now."

"Technically, that is true."

"If not the entire truth, yes. Mirrus will always be home for my family."

"You just love saying that, don't you?"

"What?" Konstantin asked, but he knew.

"*Your family.* I am truly sorry that five years ago you did not feel you could come to me and tell me that this woman was your family."

"I didn't recognize it then. I wouldn't let myself. That is not on you, or our father. That is on me, but she's forgiven me and the past is no longer a weight around my neck, choking me."

"I know you. You still feel guilty."

"I am trying not to."

"Because she wants you to."

Konstantin didn't bother responding. His brother knew him well enough to know that was exactly it. For Emma's sake, Konstantin was doing his best to let go of the guilt that his own ruthlessness had caused.

And maybe one day, when she loved him again and wasn't just prepared to become a family for their son's sake, he would.

Emma was enjoying a rare moment alone in their apartment in the palace.

Mickey was visiting with his grandfather and Lady Solomia. Kon was at work and for this moment, Emma had no classes on etiquette or meetings with wedding purveyors. How they were managing to keep a lid on her and Mickey's existence while going forward with wedding plans was mind-boggling to Emma.

The loyalty of the palace staff had to be amazingly deep.

Or their NDAs were truly punitive in a way no one wanted to risk invoking.

Either way, Emma needed a moment to catch her breath.

So, when a knock sounded on her door, she grimaced, not really wanting to talk to anybody. Not even Nataliya.

Sighing, Emma got up to go to the door, only to have it open before she reached it.

Konstantin stood on the other side, two people behind him.

"Why did you knock?" she asked before registering the identity of the people with him.

Her parents? Her parents were *here*. In Mirrus.

"Mom?" she asked, her voice barely above a whisper. "Dad?"

And then her mother rushed around Kon and ran to Emma, pulling her into a hug so tight Emma could barely breathe. "My baby. My daughter. I'm sorry. I'm so sorry." The litany of apologies did not end when her dad joined them, only intensified as he added his voice to her mother's.

Emma pushed out of her parents' arms and took a step back. "You're here."

Her mother's eyes shone brightly with tears. "Yes. Your friend called us and told us this is where you are living now."

"I started looking for flights right away," her dad said, clearing his throat. "But he said he could get us on a private jet sooner than a commercial flight could get us here."

Emma looked at Kon and mouthed the word *friend*?

Kon nodded, but what did that mean?

"Why are you here?" she asked her parents, still trying to understand what was happening.

"You're here. We missed you so much," her mother said.

Her father got that look he did when he was feeling emotional and didn't want to show it. "We made a mistake when we pushed you away. We should never have done that.

You're our daughter and you should *always* have been able to rely on our support."

"Did Kon tell you that?"

"You mean Mr. Merikov?" her mother asked, making no effort to hide the tears tracking down her face. "No, though I'm sure he's thought it if he's your friend. We missed you and we couldn't find you."

"You looked?" Emma asked, shocked.

"Oh, yes, but we couldn't find you. We thought maybe you'd gotten married and changed your name, but there was no marriage record in Washington or the surrounding states. We even had our private investigator check into Nevada marriages. So many people get married in Las Vegas."

Disappointment filled Emma. "So, that's why you're here. You found out I'm getting married and now I'm acceptable to you."

Her mom gasped, her hand fisting over her heart. "You're getting married? To who?"

"You do not need to be married to be acceptable to us," her father said forcefully at the same time. "You are our daughter and we will always love you."

"Then why reject me?" Emma asked, the pain inside her lacing her voice.

"We thought if we stayed strong you would see we were right. You were so young, not even done with college yet. You had your whole life ahead of you and we thought being a single mom would make it so much harder than it had to be," her mom tried to explain.

"I was a fool," her father said, sounding tired and sad. "I thought you refusing to give your baby up for adoption was your way of saying that being adopted wasn't the best thing for you. I felt like you were rejecting me as your father. I was so darn selfish and I have no excuse."

Emma stared at her father, incomprehension holding her

immobile. He'd believed she didn't like that she was adopted and that's why she wanted to keep her baby?

"I kept Mikhail because I already loved him, because I could not imagine giving him up and I knew that even if it was hard, I would and could give him a good life. I could give him what you'd always given me. Love."

Her mother started crying in earnest then. Emma found herself back in her mother's arms, her own tears coming to the surface. Her dad held them both.

But as the storm of healing weeping ended, Emma sought out the one person she needed more than her parents right then. Kon.

He was there, waiting patiently.

After extricating herself from her parents' arms again, this time with words of love and promises they would work things out, she went to her fiancé and let him draw her into his embrace.

"Thank you," she said against his chest, finding immeasurable comfort in Kon's hold.

"Oh, you are going to marry Mr. Merikov?" her mother asked in a water-clogged voice.

Emma looked up, giving her mother a smile that was not strained at all. "Yes. Mom, Dad... I want you to meet my fiancé, His Royal Highness Prince Konstantin of the House of Merikov."

She peeked up at Kon. "Did I get that right?"

"Perfect," he said with a warm smile. "Now you tell me their names."

"Even though you already know them?"

He shrugged. "Etiquette."

Emma nodded. Okay, then. "Kon, may I present my parents? Ansel and Belinda Sloan."

Her mother was staring at Emma like a landed fish, her mouth opening and closing with nothing coming out.

Her dad's eyes widened. "Well, I'll be damned. And he

doesn't mind about Mikhail?" he then said pointedly to Kon. "You will accept my grandson as your own?"

"Even if he were not mine, yes, I would."

"You're the man that…" Oh, her dad's eyes could still glitter with pure disapproval and it was all directed at Kon. "You seduced our innocent daughter and then abandoned her?"

"I did," Kon said unequivocally. "That is my mistake to bear, but believe me when I promise you that I will never let her down that way again."

"I should hope not," her mother said, sounding discombobulated. "A prince." She shook her head. "And you managed to keep his identity private?"

The discussion that followed was filled with explanations and updates. Her parents were hurt to learn Emma had changed her name to her birth surname, but had understood the need after learning about the restraining order.

"You just make me so proud," her mom said. "You're such a good mom."

Emma thought her heart would burst at those longed-for words coming from her parent.

"You make us both proud. We don't deserve your forgiveness, but I hope we can earn it over time."

"Your daughter excels at extending grace," Kon said before Emma could assure her parents she would forgive them.

There was a moment Emma found humorous, even if the others did not. Kon demanded promises never to hurt her again from her parents while her father assured Kon that *he* would be watching the younger man to make sure he never let their beloved daughter down again.

Emma rolled her eyes. "All this posturing is lovely, I'm sure, but please, all of you, remember that I did an excellent job looking out for myself and my son for five years."

Her mother's expression turned hungry. "I understand

you're hesitant to allow it right away. We'll have to prove ourselves… But when do you think we might meet our grandson?"

"You want to meet Mickey?"

"Oh, yes. He's part of you. He's part of *us*. It's my own fault, but I've grieved knowing I had a grandchild out there I did not know for the past five years."

Emma didn't remind her mom about the phone call after Mickey's birth. The older woman was already filled with repentance. She did not need another load of guilt.

"You don't have to prove yourselves. You've said you're sorry and I believe you. I can still remember all the years of my childhood and how loved I felt. I know who you two are and it's not people who want to hurt others."

She might never fully understand what drove them to be the way they were five years ago, but she had some inkling after the watershed talking they'd done.

Her parents meeting with Mickey was emotional in all the best ways. They had relaxed some of their strict attitudes in the five years since Emma disappeared from their lives.

They wanted nothing more than to get to know their grandson and reacquaint themselves with their daughter.

No question, they were a little overwhelmed by the whole royal thing.

However, Emma's mom readily participated in the wedding preparations with Lady Solomia. Emma overheard the countess tell her mom that parents sometimes made grievous mistakes with their children, but the lucky ones had daughters who understood that they were loved and gave that love back, despite their parents' failings.

Emma thought there was a story there, but she didn't go digging for it. She had enough to keep her occupied keeping up with her own life.

Mickey thrived as his family expanded in the days leading up to the royal wedding.

Kon and his family did an excellent job of shielding not only Mickey but also Emma from the media interest the announcement of their existence sparked.

Her wedding was over the top with way more guests than she'd anticipated, but Emma didn't mind.

Because the only two people who really registered with her were Kon and Mickey. Looking so proud he could bust his buttons, Mickey stood as Kon's best *man*. They both waited, their attention fixed entirely on her, as Emma walked forward to join them and the priest.

She spoke her vows with conviction and a lot of emotion she wasn't surprised to feel. Emma loved this man to the very depth of her soul and adored her son. Kon spoke his vows with an intense emotion that Emma had a very difficult time *not* calling love.

This moment wasn't just about Kon and Emma and their commitment to each other, but it was about Mickey too. Their commitment to him and any future children they might have together.

And the little boy knew it. He'd insisted on making his own promises as part of the ceremony, to the obvious delight of the attendees.

Kon and Emma surprised Mickey with vows of their own to him and including each other.

It was a really special moment and the number of guests, the camera crews... None of it mattered as Emma gave and received vows that would govern the rest of her life and that of her little family.

Konstantin did not know what was wrong with him, but throughout his wedding and the reception that followed, he kept getting overwhelmed by emotion.

He would go to speak to someone and have to pause,

take a breath and get his feelings under control. It was unlike anything he'd ever experienced, but his relief...his utter joy that Emma had not only agreed to be his wife, but had genuinely forgiven him knew no bounds.

She had promised everything that mattered during their wedding vows, looking him right in the eye when she said she would *love* and honor and cherish him for the rest of their lives.

He needed to get her alone, to ask if that meant what he thought. Even more important, he needed to tell her that he loved her.

It had struck him as she approached him and Mishka at the church. She'd looked so beautiful, but it was the light shining from inside her that completely took his breath away.

In that moment, he'd accepted that he *needed* her, that she sat as firmly in his soul as any member of his family, including their son, but that she was the one person he craved above all others as part of his life.

He loved Mishka and would be the best dad he could be, but it was Emma who gave their little family heart.

Coming up behind her, Konstantin slid his arm around her waist in a very uncool show of affection.

Emma gasped, like his action surprised her. And it should. This did not fall under proper protocols for public behavior.

And for once, he did not care.

He needed to be close to her.

"Hello, *solnyshko moi*. Are you enjoying yourself?"

Emma had been talking to Nataliya and Belinda Sloan. The Princess of Mirrus gave Konstantin a shocked look while Emma's mother blushed, like his small PDA embarrassed her.

But Emma? Tilted her head back and smiled up at him. "I'm having a wonderful time. Everyone is so kind."

"Of course they are kind. You are so sweet, to be unkind to you would be anathema."

"You might be exaggerating, but that's okay. I like it."

"You said you loved me," he blurted out with a complete lack of aplomb.

The sound of his younger brother groaning behind him told Konstantin that Dima had heard too. "Way to sound desperate, Konstantin."

Emma just smiled. "I did."

"Did you mean it?"

Emma turned in his arms, so their gazes met and no one else could intrude on this moment. "Yes, Kon. I meant it. I love you. With everything in me."

"That is why you forgave me."

"It is part of it."

"What is the other part?"

"I realized you loved me too and breaking up with me tore your heart into pieces just like it did mine."

"I'm not sure this is the best venue for this discussion," Nataliya tried to interject.

But Konstantin was enthralled by the expression in his wife's beautiful blue eyes. They were filled with understanding and yes, love.

"I do love you," he told her, needing to give her the words.

"I told you they loved each other," Mickey piped up, having come up with both his grandfathers in tow.

Everyone laughed except Emma and Konstantin.

He was too choked up to laugh or speak. She dropped her head against his chest. "I pictured you saying those words so many times, but maybe not in front of a bazillion people for the first time."

"I am not ashamed of my feelings," he assured her.

"That's a given," someone said, followed by more laughter.

"I think he should kiss her," Mickey opined.

Konstantin thought his son's idea was brilliant and proceeded to do just that.

Emma's wedding night was everything she could have ever dreamed it would be and then some. Saying "I love you" turned out to be a huge erotic trigger for her husband and they got very little sleep and a surfeit of pleasure.

Because neither of them seemed capable of stopping saying it.

And that was all right.

Emma would rather drown in the sentiment than ever live another day without it.

Kon made it clear he felt the same. She didn't think they were ever going to have a typical royal marriage, but they sure would have an adventurous one filled with love.

* * * * *

COMING SOON!

We really hope you enjoyed reading this book.
If you're looking for more romance, be sure to
head to the shops when new books are
available on

Thursday 11th November

To see which titles are coming soon, please visit

millsandboon.co.uk/nextmonth

MILLS & BOON

THE HEART OF ROMANCE

A ROMANCE FOR EVERY READER

MODERN

Prepare to be swept off your feet by sophisticated, sexy and seductive heroes, in some of the world's most glamourous and romantic locations, where power and passion collide.

HISTORICAL

Escape with historical heroes from time gone by. Whether your passion is for wicked Regency Rakes, muscled Vikings or rugged Highlanders, awake the romance of the past.

MEDICAL

Set your pulse racing with dedicated, delectable doctors in the high-pressure world of medicine, where emotions run high and passion, comfort and love are the best medicine.

True Love

Celebrate true love with tender stories of heartfelt romance, from the rush of falling in love to the joy a new baby can bring, and a focus on the emotional heart of a relationship.

Desire

Indulge in secrets and scandal, intense drama and plenty of sizzling hot action with powerful and passionate heroes who have it all: wealth, status, good looks…everything but the right woman.

HEROES

Experience all the excitement of a gripping thriller, with an intense romance at its heart. Resourceful, true-to-life women and strong, fearless men face danger and desire - a killer combination!

To see which titles are coming soon, please visit

millsandboon.co.uk/nextmonth

MILLS & BOON

Coming next month

A CONTRACT FOR HIS RUNAWAY BRIDE
Melanie Milburne

'Could you give me an update on when Mr Smith will be available?'

The receptionist's answering smile was polite but formal. 'I apologise for the delay. He'll be with you shortly.'

'Look, my appointment was -'

'I understand, Ms Campbell. But he's a very busy man. He's made a special gap in his diary for you. He's not usually so accommodating. You must've made a big impression on him.'

'I haven't even met him. All I know is, I was instructed to be here close to thirty minutes ago for a meeting with a Mr Smith to discuss finance. I've been given no other details.'

The receptionist glanced at the intercom console where a small green light was flashing. She looked up again at Elodie with the same polite smile. 'Thank you for being so patient. Mr...erm... Smith will see you now. Please go through. It's the third door on the right. The corner office.'

The corner office boded well- that meant he was the head honcho. The big bucks began and stopped with him. Elodie came to the door and took a deep calming breath but it did nothing to settle the frenzy of flick-knives in her stomach. She gave the door a quick rap with her knuckles. Please, please, please let me be successful this time.

'Come.'

Her hand paused on the doorknob, her mind whirling in ice cold panic. Something about the deep timbre of that voice sent a shiver scuttling over her scalp like a small claw-footed creature. How could this Mr Smith sound so like her ex-fiancé? Scarily alike. She turned the doorknob and pushed the door open, her gaze immediately fixing on the tall dark-haired man behind the large desk.

'You?' Elodie gasped, heat flooding into her cheeks and other places in her body she didn't want to think about right now.

Lincoln Lancaster rose from his chair with leonine grace, his expression set in its customary cynical lines- the arch of one ink-black brow over his intelligent bluey-green gaze, the tilt of his sensual mouth that was not quite a smile. His black hair was brushed back from his high forehead in loose waves that looked like they had last been combed by his fingers. He was dressed in a three-piece suit that hugged his athletic frame, emphasising the broadness of his shoulders, the taut trimness of his chest, flat abdomen and lean hips. He was the epitome of a successful man in his prime. Potent, powerful, persuasive. He got what he wanted, when he wanted, how he wanted.

'You're looking good, Elodie.' His voice rolled over her as smoothly and lazily as his gaze, the deep sexy rumble so familiar it triggered a host of memories she had fought for seven years to erase. Memories in her flesh that were triggered by being in his presence. Erotic memories that made her hyper aware of his every breath, his every glance, his every movement.

Continue reading
A CONTRACT FOR HIS RUNAWAY BRIDE
Melanie Milburne

Available next month
www.millsandboon.co.uk

LET'S TALK
Romance

For exclusive extracts, competitions
and special offers, find us online: